Five of Knights

Five of Knights

K.W. Santoro

Page of Swords Publishing

CONTENTS

CONTENTS

To Kate
Thank you for your effortless inspiration of Ashleen

1

The Transfer

"You can trust me, Ashleen. Everything you say in this room is confidential and off the record."

"I told you. I don't remember what happened." Ashleen pressed her fingers against her eyelids and struggled to lose her headache in the swirls of blue and green. "It's been six months, I don't even know why we're still doing this."

"Your mother believes––"

"I don't care! It doesn't matter what she believes. I'm never getting out of here."

"If you don't remember what happened, why did you plead guilty?"

"There were witnesses."

"Most of whom were drunk, and the few of which came forward all claimed it was self-defense."

"So?"

The woman across from Ashleen sighed, a frown deepening the fine creases on her face. "Ashleen, no one ever claimed the body. There was no case against you except the one you built."

"Ugh. Stop!"

"Ashleen––"

"I screwed up, alright?! I'm tired of hearing everyone make excuses for me. Just––leave me alone."

The woman pressed her lips into a firm line and tapped her notes against the table to straighten them. "We'll talk again in a week."

"Sure. Whatever," Ashleen said, watching the lawyer leave. She thought she spotted a grey strand or two in the lawyer's short black hair. They were probably her fault.

A jangle of keys announced O'Reilly as she rounded the corner into the room. She beamed amicably. "Well, how'd it go?"

"She wants to see me again next week."

A tiny wrinkle appeared between the stout woman's brows, "I see."

Ashleen tugged against the cuffs that anchored her wrists to the table. "Are you gonna unlock me or not?"

O'Reilly heaved an exasperated sigh and fished the keys from their place at her belt. "Miss Gallagher," she began, "you ought to show more gratitude. I'm sure Miss Albrecht is doing her best to help."

Ashleen grunted with disinterest. This was the third lawyer her mother had sent in as many months. She doubted this one would have anything to say that she hadn't already heard.

"You're absolutely hopeless," O'Reilly chastised her as she released Ashleen's cuffs from the table.

"That's what I keep telling everyone," she grumbled.

"Come on, let's get you back to your cell. You obviously need a nap."

On another day, Ashleen might've laughed. She and O'Reilly got along most of the time. Right now, everyone was getting on her nerves.

When the cell locked behind her and O'Reilly relieved her of her cuffs, Ashleen retreated to the uncomfortably small cot in the corner. She watched dust dance in the meager shafts of sunlight as they slipped through the grating on the grimy window and waited to fall asleep.

There wasn't much to do these days besides sleep, though O'Reilly occasionally brought in books for her to read. The latest was the fifth installment in the Harry Potter series, *The Order of the Phoenix*. She'd read the series as a child, and when O'Reilly had brought her the first book, Ashleen had hoped to find some of her wide eyed innocence still caught in its pages.

She'd completed her third read through of *The Order of the Phoenix* yesterday, but she'd given up on finding her childhood. Instead, she heard echoes of herself in Harry's growing frustration at not being heard.

She didn't regret her decision to plead guilty, confinement was still her best option. That didn't mean she enjoyed it. Ashleen did her best to avoid the other inmates, though they mostly left her alone when they realized she was stronger than they were.

She could have used that to her advantage and reigned over the prison yard, but Ashleen didn't care about power. Her life behind bars had been dreary at best, but she preferred that over the constant fear of accidentally hurting someone she cared about.

Ashleen missed coffee the most. She didn't mind it black, but everything they gave her in prison was watered down, scorched from sitting on the burner plate too long, and lukewarm. She'd almost made up her mind to switch to tea, but they'd find a way to mess that up too.

There was little entertainment, the prison was in the middle of nowhere and only three channels came through clearly on the television in the rec room. When she was little, she hadn't believed anything could be more boring than the small town she'd grown up in. Now she knew better.

The only respite from it all was sleep, though she wasn't sure if the nightmares she had could be considered respite. Ashleen had always struggled with bad dreams, but they'd grown more intense lately. The counselors kept saying they were a byproduct of the trauma, but Ashleen didn't see how she had any right to be traumatized, since she'd been the aggressor rather than the victim.

Ashleen awoke to the clank of keys against the bars of her cell. O'Reilly had reappeared, whistling absently to herself as Ashleen sat up on the cot.

"Back for me so soon?"

"Your mom's here!" O'Reilly chirped.

"Is it Friday already?" Ashleen didn't want to see her mother today, but guilt denied her the option to say no.

Alice Gallagher was all alone now. Ashleen was an only child and her father, Connor, had been lost to them before she'd been much older than four. Alice never remarried, but it wasn't common for people who'd lost their counterweight to do so without a blessing from the gods.

Ashleen blew a huff of air past her lips, displacing the brassy ginger wisps that had fallen into her eyes. She rocked up to her feet and dragged herself to the bars, passing her arms between them for the cuffs.

O'Reilly waved at her dismissively, "I can trust you, right? I don't want your mother to curse at me again."

Ashleen chuckled and pulled her hands back through. Alice could be quite vocal about how much she hated seeing her daughter in shackles.

As soon as Ashleen spotted her mother among the other visitors, she realized exactly what day it was. Silently, she thanked herself for coming, even though she hadn't wanted to.

Alice's eyes were puffy, any attempts at mascara or eyeliner she'd made earlier in the day were now hopelessly smeared. She had Connor's covenant ring pressed against her lips.

"It's your anniversary isn't it?" Ashleen asked. "You didn't have to come."

Alice's gaze jerked to her daughter as she snapped out of her reverie. The tears welled anew in her eyes. "You look so much like him," she said weeping, her words catching in her throat. She stood and bustled around the edge of the table to cradle her daughter's face in her hands, thumbs brushing over the freckles that crowded Ashleen's skin.

Ashleen freed herself from her mother's grasp to pull her into a hug. She rested her chin on Alice's head. "You took the day off work at least, right?"

"Not quite, I was hoping it wouldn't be so bad if I stayed busy."

It would do no good to chastise her mother, Alice had been through enough as it was. She'd raised Ashleen on her own after her husband's death.

Alice rarely spoke of Connor. When Ashleen was sixteen, she'd gone through her mother's things hoping to find old photographs. Instead, she'd come across a letter. She could still feel the worn paper threatening to come apart in her fingers as she reread it in her mind's eye.

Mrs. Alice Gallagher

I wish I were writing to you with better news. Just two weeks past, my garrison was brought low by a coup. We suffered many losses in the chaos, among them some of my best huntsmen.

While I'm sure you were kept in the dark as to the details of your husband's work, I assure you he was one of our proudest hunters. He saved countless lives during his career and was respected by those who followed him. I am certain more than a few attribute their success to his guidance.

It is with an aching heart that I must inform you he was killed in the attack. I have my people working tirelessly to patch up the leaks in our security. Rest assured as soon as order is restored, I will put together an elite team to track down Connor Gallagher's killers.

I am sorry to say that I can't offer you the more direct vengeance you deserve, but in life Connor insisted that you did not have the skills needed to thrive within our ranks. Instead, I would offer you the option to send your daughter, Ashleen Gallagher, to be tested for eligibility to join us.

My people have reported that she takes after her father and bears potential to rise to the top of her class in a matter of months. With enough dedication, Ashleen could be present to deliver the justice Connor deserves.

I understand you will need time to recover, but please consider my offer carefully. Your daughter would be welcome among us. We could offer her methods for controlling her anger and she would have the opportunity to form meaningful relationships with others just like her.

My deepest sympathies:
Amaris Faustian, Archwarden of Alexandria

The letter had resulted in a fight that put Ashleen and her mother at odds for several months. She couldn't understand why Alice wouldn't send her to the Archwarden. Undoubtedly it was too late for her to help avenge her father, but if Ashleen could use her abilities to save lives, she wanted to go.

Alice had never given so much as an inch, and eventually Ashleen had come to accept the finality of her mother's answer.

"I'm sorry." Alice worked her way free of Ashleen's arms. "I didn't mean to project my grief onto you."

"Mom--"

"How are things going with the new lawyer?"

Ashleen heaved a sigh. "Mom..."

"You could at least give her a chance. It won't hurt you to work with her."

"I told you to stop sending lawyers a month ago!" Ashleen snapped with a bit more venom than she'd intended.

"And I told you I wouldn't. We're getting a retrial one way or another." Alice planted her hands on her hips, and Ashleen swallowed a grin. Her mother had never been afraid of her. Alice often stood toe to toe with her daughter, never mind that Ashleen had almost a foot on her in height and was strong enough to snap her like a twig.

"I made my choice."

"You shouldn't be in here over self-defense!"

"It wasn't self-defense. He was feeling up Prue, not me."

"So?"

"You weren't there," Ashleen swallowed a wave of nausea at the images that flashed through her mind. "You didn't see what I did to him."

"I don't see how it matters. Some asshole tried to assault your girlfriend, I think retaliation is completely justified."

"Yeah with intervention, not murder!"

"I've been doing some research. Technically you were provoked, and your condition could make this an automatism case. It was a party, it's possible you could have been inebriated--"

"I wasn't drunk Mom!" Ashleen barked, "Besides, you know as well as I do that it's safer for everyone if I just stay here. They let me have books, the food is edible, I'm fine."

"You're not fine!" Alice's tears welled up all over again and spilled fresh mascara stains down her cheeks.

Ashleen fought to keep her tone soothing, "I am fine. And we don't actually have any other options, since you won't even let me try Alexandria." As soon as the words were out of her mouth, she regretted them.

It was the wrong day to bring this up, but bitterness had pushed the statement past her lips before she could stop it.

"Don't you dare," Alice began, her voice wobbling in time with the tears caught in her lashes. "That Raven-cursed pit of zealots took your father from me. I am not going to hand over my daughter on a silver platter."

Ashleen felt imaginary hackles bristle along her neck and shoulders. "They're not zealots! They could help me. If they have a way to stop the rages, then I could live a normal life. If you'd sent me there in the first place I wouldn't be here!"

The sting of her mother's palm across her face took Ashleen's breath away. Alice had never hit her before, not even to spank her as a child. It was an unspoken agreement that likely protected Alice more than Ashleen.

She saw her own shock reflected in her mother's eyes. The physical pain was almost nonexistent, but the sense of betrayal cut deep.

"Honey, I'm sorry. I didn't mean––"

Several of the guards started toward Ashleen, even though it was her mother who'd struck.

Ashleen pressed her lips into a line and sank to her knees, presenting her wrists for cuffs. These guards were afraid of her, she knew they'd jump to force if they saw even the barest reason to.

"Ash! Sweetie--"

O'Reilly shouldered past the skittish guards and waved them off once she had Ashleen cuffed.

"We're done, take me back to my cell."

Ashleen waited until she was sure O'Reilly had gone before she let the dam break. She sank into her cot and sobbed for the better part of an hour. It was unfair. All of this was unfair. She hadn't asked for any of it and she was sick of having to stifle herself to protect everyone else.

She'd spent her life trying everything from meditation to therapy to deal with the burning rage that lingered, barely constrained beneath her skin. Even medication hadn't worked. Her metabolism burned through it too quickly for it to do anything.

It all had to mean something. The gods she'd grown up praying to had to have a plan, she just couldn't see it yet. They couldn't mean for her to languish here, stagnating with no hope of a future.

She'd been raised Ravenite, worshipping Muginn, the raven deity of death and balance. According to scripture, Muginn wasn't directly opposed to murder in certain circumstances. Still, Ashleen couldn't help but feel as if the gods were displeased with her.

She didn't have access to the incense she normally would have burned to draw the Raven's attention as she prayed. There'd been a recent bust on a band of inmates that had been sneaking in contraband disguised as religious items.

Her mother had always told her that Muginn did as she pleased, and was unlikely to make alterations to her grand designs without fair compensation. Usually where Muginn was concerned, that meant blood tithing.

Ashleen had tithed once or twice when things were dire, but she certainly wasn't allowed any sharp objects now. Short of biting herself, there wasn't much she could do, and she hadn't reached that level of desperation quite yet.

Still, she closed her eyes and asked the Raven for a sign, something to indicate whether she was on the right path or not.

She fidgeted with the covenant ring on her pinkie, rolling its silver bands over and over each other. Muginn sent most people a unique band by the time they turned thirteen, which according to the scripts would eventually lead them to their soulmate. Not everyone believed in the rings, but Ashleen had always kept faith in hers.

She'd grown up isolated, fabricating numerous fantasies over the years of how her counterweight might have the ability to soothe her rage with a mere word. She'd thrived on the belief that they would compensate for her shortcomings, just as she would compensate for theirs.

She'd projected those fantasies onto Prue, her girlfriend before all this had happened. Even though her ring fit Prue's tiny finger, it didn't heat up like Ashleen's mother said it would. Even if it had, the ring Prue carried didn't even fit onto Ashleen's smallest finger.

Ashleen tried not to think too hard about her hands. They were masculine to match her blocky, broad-shouldered build. Prue liked it, but Ashleen could barely stand to look at her reflection in the mirror. Coming in at five foot ten with almost no curves to speak of, her body had done nothing to help mask her threatening demeanor.

Prue had saved Ashleen, which only emphasized the sting of her silence since the events of her twenty-first birthday party. If Prue had shown up to testify, Ashleen might not have pleaded guilty. Perhaps if Prue had forgiven her, Ashleen could have forgiven herself.

There hadn't been so much as a word from Prue since that night. Ashleen tried to write her letters for the first couple of months. Some begged for forgiveness, others irately accused her of cowardice, then more to apologize for the previous letters.

Even Ashleen's mother hadn't heard from Prue. It was as if the petite girl had dropped off the face of the planet. Perhaps she had. Ashleen wasn't sure she would blame Prue anymore if it turned out she had cut and run.

The first thing Ashleen remembered after coming out of her haze was the blood spatter across Prue's face. She'd looked as if she were about to throw up. The second thing Ashleen had noticed was the blood all over her hands, and the third was the misshapen remnant of a man's head where he'd collapsed on the floor between them.

All at once it became clear that she'd expected too much of Prue. Still, Ashleen had hoped that Prue could one day forgive her, that she hadn't driven away her first and only love.

When she drifted off that night, Ashleen dreamed of Prue. Faded memories of what it had felt like to kiss her in the dappled sunlight danced tantalizingly out of reach. Dream Prue threw coy glances over her shoulder as Ashleen chased her through the woods behind the house.

She laughed as they tumbled through the underbrush, stars in her eyes when Ashleen finally pinned her to the forest floor.

"Gotcha," Ashleen chuckled and nuzzled her face into the crook of Prue's neck affectionately. Prue giggled.

Something sticky clung to Ashleen's cheek, but it didn't smell like the lavender lotion Prue liked. She leaned back to ask about it. Ice stabbed outward from her stomach.

Prue's throat was ripped open, her arterial blood soaking into the mossy ground. The expression on her face remained placid as she spoke, voice unchanged by the gaping wound.

"Don't you realize, if I had stayed, you would have killed me too?"

Beneath her, Prue's body began to rapidly decay, maggots hatching out and chewing away the edges of the gash in her throat. Her eyes went white and her cheeks hollowed as the corpse desiccated between Ashleen's arms.

Ashleen jolted awake and rolled out of bed, barely making it across her cell to the toilet in time to heave into it. The imagined taste of Prue's blood lingered in her mouth. She spat several times in an attempt to clear it, but it coated her throat in a pungent film.

Her head pounded, and she sat back against the wall to catch her breath.

"You alright in there?"

Ashleen whipped around so fast she saw stars. It was too early for visitors, but it wasn't O'Reilly's voice outside the bars.

She rubbed at her eyes, struggling to focus. Irritation sparked inside her when she recognized the new lawyer.

"Go away. I don't want to see you anymore."

"Bit too late for that, unfortunately." The lawyer spoke with a slight German accent. Ashleen wasn't sure why she hadn't noticed it until now. "You're being transferred."

Ashleen pinched a pressure point in her wrist, struggling to quell another wave of nausea, "Transferred? Where?"

"Alexandria."

Ashleen peered at her through the grey light of dawn. "Birdshit. How do you even know that name?" Nobody she asked had any idea what she was talking about when she mentioned Alexandria, except her mother.

"I'm not sure we've been properly introduced. Hello, Ashleen. My name is Neele Albrecht. The Archwarden sent me to collect you."

2

Voices From the Past

Ashleen's heart paused in her chest every time she and Neele passed a prison guard on their way out. This couldn't be happening. It was too good to be true. They'd stop her any minute now, drag her back to her cell, never let her see the light of day again.

No one so much as cast them a second glance. They met O'Reilly at the gate, and she smiled as she glanced over the papers Neele offered her. "I'd ask you to come visit, but it's probably better if I don't see you again, eh?" She snorted a laugh and slapped Ashleen lightly on the arm.

Ashleen managed a smile, but she was still waiting for all this to come crashing down about her ears.

The ride out to the general parking lot was uneventful and quiet despite the questions buzzing inside Ashleen's chest. She didn't know where to start and she was half afraid that if she spoke, she'd wake up back in her cot, tormented by more cruel dreams.

When they'd disembarked the shuttle and it drove off back down the dirt road behind them, Ashleen broke the silence. "Did you know my father?"

"Connor?" Neele replied, "A long time ago. Yes."

"What was he like?"

Neele led the way towards an unassuming beige car and fished a set of keys out of her pocket. "Stubborn. Charismatic. Wise. He had a way of guiding people through tough situations. You could lose both arms and Connor would convince you to write."

Ashleen waited for Neele to unlock the door and then swung herself into the passenger seat.

Before the car had a chance to start, more questions tumbled past her lips. "So what is Alexandria, actually? Where is it? What do you do there?"

Neele chuckled, "It's a city, somewhere over the North Pacific, and I'm the head medic."

"Did you say over the Pacific?"

"Yes, Alexandria orbits the planet in the upper stratosphere."

"What? How has nobody seen it?"

"How well do you know your mythology?"

"Pretty well, I think."

"So you know about ichor?"

Ashleen scoffed, "Everyone knows about ichor." The mythical substance was said to be the blood of the gods shed during the first great conflict, when the new trinity had gone up against the old deities.

"It's real. The Archwarden is a leading pioneer in harnessing it with modern technology. It's fused with all the materials used to build the city. It allows Alexandria to float and keeps it hidden from the rest of the world."

"You know, that's a lot to take on just your word." With every detail Neele shared, Ashleen felt more as if she'd been tossed into one of the books she'd read as a child. Ichor was spoken of as if it had been real in scripture, but Ashleen hadn't seen any substantial evidence of it still existing within the last two hundred years.

These days it was about as believable as Bigfoot or the Loch Ness Monster. People on the fringes of society frequently reported sightings, but no one could provide any real evidence. Ashleen had often watched documentaries and reality shows on the topic from the edge of her seat, but they all ended the same way. The self declared scientists would say something like, 'the search continues', or 'the truth remains a mystery', and no new information would surface.

Neele shrugged, pulled out of the parking lot, and started towards the freeway. "It doesn't matter if you don't believe me. You'll see for yourself soon enough."

She drove onto the on ramp before she spoke again, "Your team is eager to meet you."

"My team?"

"Izzy requested you by name. Team leaders get the final say on the members of each group, but most of them trade amongst themselves. It's unusual for someone to pick from the watchlist."

"There's a watchlist?" Ashleen had no idea who Izzy was, or why he might have any interest in her. Perhaps this was the sign she'd asked Muginn for. It seemed too unlikely to be a coincidence.

"Of course. Did you think you were the only one out there with unique abilities? You ought to consider yourself lucky. Izzy is one of our best, his team is well regarded."

Ashleen wondered if it might be more accurate to compare these events to a comic book than a novel. It was true that growing up she had tried to reconcile her strength by comparing herself to superheroes, but nobody sane actually ran around fighting crime in a cape these days.

"Who else will I be working with?"

"Demetrius and Dahei. The latter is a firecracker, but they're both experienced huntsmen. The vesper is somewhat new, though. Morpheus. Keep an eye on him, he's got a reputation." Neele cast her a sidelong glance, and Ashleen didn't have to ask what she meant.

"What's a vesper?"

"There are five classes of huntsmen. You're a tranq, they're the heavy hitters. Dahei will accompany you on the front lines, he's a scofflaw. They're fast, masters of bladed weapons. Izzy is a deadeye, marksmanship and demolitions are his specialty.

Demetrius is a beckoner. They're a higher class of the Apostles of Muginn. He has a direct link to the Raven, and can summon a variety of creatures under Muginn's sway. Vespers are similar, but they're a higher class of Ikaluscan Adherents. Most of their abilities are vocal. Generally they're against using their hymns on humans without consent, but their abilities are fueled by physical intimacy. Hence the warning."

Ashleen pursed her lips. She'd heard of the Adherents, but she'd never met one. The apostles in her hometown had always described them as over indulgent anarchists. She'd been taught to keep her distance from such people.

It was a lot to take in. The Archwarden's letter had mentioned huntsmen, so she wasn't unfamiliar with the term, and Neele's explanation of the classes made sense. Parties of five were fairly common in the games Ashleen had played. Tranqs and tanks aligned, deadeyes, scofflaws, and beckoners were all good examples of damage per second classes. Ranged, melee, and casters, respectively. That left vespers as either another caster type or a support class. Perhaps both. From what Neele was saying, they sounded a lot like stereotypical bards.

"You called them huntsmen. What do they hunt?"

"Everything from the myths is real."

"Everything?" Her mind raced with the implications of that statement.

"Everything. We've brought down the population over the years and there hasn't been a large-scale attack since 2011, but they're still out there."

"What happened in 2011?"

"Remember that earthquake that hit Japan?"

"The Fukushima disaster?"

"It wasn't an earthquake."

Ashleen had seen footage of the aftermath. No one said anything about a monster, but it seemed unlikely that they'd just keep quiet about it. She wondered how they'd managed to cover up such a large event.

The silence stretched on between them. Roughly a half hour later, Neele pulled off the highway. They exited towards an airstrip Ashleen would have thought nothing of had they been passing it under any other circumstances.

"What are we doing here?" Ashleen asked as they got out of the car.

"You didn't think I was going to drive to the middle of the Pacific, did you?"

"I guess not," She tugged a lock of hair sheepishly. Stupid, of course they'd be flying. She'd never been on a plane before; her mother always thought it was a bad idea.

Ashleen struggled to ignore the way her nerves itched at the thought. She had never liked heights much to begin with, and now it was starting to hit home that she was about to be confined to a floating city for the foreseeable future.

"What are you dawdling for?" Neele called from somewhere ahead of her.

Ashleen jogged a few paces to catch up and forced her anxiety to the back of her mind. She didn't have much of a choice at this point.

Neele reached up and the air blurred at her fingertips. As Ashleen watched, a ship unlike any she'd seen before flickered into existence.

It wasn't nearly as big as a commercial jet, but it dwarfed the tiny crop duster planes that occasionally passed over her hometown.

The craft was shaped like a manta ray, and reminded her more of an alien spaceship than anything of human design.

"Is that made of ichor too?" she asked, too in awe of its appearance to remember her fear.

"Yes," Neele answered. "Don't worry. It's safe. The Archwarden's designs are remarkably stable."

Ashleen wasn't sure if the reassurance made her feel better or worse, since Neele seemed to think reassurance was justified.

"Come on!" Neele pressed a hand to the side again and a door opened along the belly of the craft. She led the way up a ramp Ashleen hadn't even seen descend.

Ashleen hesitated a split second before she followed. The interior of the craft was surprisingly plain. There were two seats on each side, and one in the front. Neele slipped into this one and started the ship.

"Strap in! It's a short trip, but we can't have you just flying around the cabin, can we?"

Ashleen settled into one of the seats in the back and took a moment to figure out the crisscrossing belts.

When the mantacraft lifted off, she felt her stomach drop out of her body as they accelerated with speed to rival a fighter jet.

"She really moves, doesn't she?" Ashleen commented breathlessly, trying to swallow her anxiety.

"Oh, this is nothing. Wait til you fly with Izzy! He likes hairpin turns and rolls!"

"Mother Raven."

"Good luck!"

The flight to Alexandria didn't even last as long as the drive from the prison to the airstrip. Ashleen couldn't see much of anything from where she was sitting, but she felt when the craft landed.

Neele was up and on her way out before Ashleen could even finish figuring out how to unbuckle herself. When she finally made it out into the hangar bay, she saw scores of other craft shaped just like this one. Two rows of them ran parallel to each other in both directions as far as she could see. Each one had a unique paint job that put the one she and Neele had arrived in to shame.

As she looked, she realized she couldn't see any sort of engine or system of propulsion. Nor could she see any place where the craft actually touched the ceiling or floor. She'd felt it settle when they arrived, but all the ships were hovering, suspended by a means she couldn't understand.

A high-pitched chime echoed back to them off the walls. Ashleen was startled.

Neele retrieved her phone from her pocket and frowned at the screen. "I'm sorry, I wanted to show you around, but I have to go. A team got back a little ahead of us, they need medical attention."

Before Ashleen could ask, Neele was gone, crossing the hangar to a door she hadn't noticed yet. She tossed her hands upwards in exasperation and turned on her heel. Great. Where was she supposed to go?

She spun around again and squeaked as she came face to face with a man she hadn't seen in the vicinity before. His reddish blond hair fell into his eyes, which couldn't seem to decide what color they were. His face was warmed by a sprinkle of freckles and the beginnings of crow's feet. They deepened as he smiled at her.

"Sorry, I didn't mean to startle you."

"You didn't."

The man's smile widened, "Of course not." He extended a hand for her to shake. When she took it, he introduced himself, "Romulus. But I prefer Rome. I'm one of the wardens here."

Ashleen glanced at his outfit. It was simple, a windbreaker and pants with streamlined patterns in black, grey, and burgundy.

"Wardens?"

"We recruit a lot of convicts. Some are innocent, like yourself. Others need help staying in line. That's our job. Since Neele has her hands full, I thought I would walk you to your dorm."

"I was starting to think I'd have to figure it out myself."

"This way!" Rome turned and led the way towards the door Neele had disappeared through.

His hand pressed to the wall prompted the door to slide open. When Ashleen saw what was on the other side, she balked.

A short hallway connected the hangar to the rest of the city. The floor was covered in coarse carpeting, but the walls and ceiling were transparent. Through them, she could see puffy white clouds spread out below her feet.

Rome was halfway across before he realized she wasn't following. He turned to face her. "What's wrong?"

"Don't like heights," she managed, backing further into the hangar.

Rome squinted at her, "Just because you can't see it now doesn't mean it's not there. You're still in the sky."

"That's true. But I feel much safer here."

"You can't just stay in there."

"Watch me," Ashleen quipped, fear shortening her temper.

"You're here now. There's nowhere to go but forward." Rome crossed the last few steps to the other side. "Close your eyes if you have to. But one way or another you have to cross."

She groaned a protest, but he was right. Ashleen screwed her eyes shut and rushed across the hall. Rome opened the next set of doors and steered her through them.

"See, that wasn't so bad."

The air was noticeably warmer in this part of the city. Growing up in the Pacific Northwest, Ashleen was used to a chill, but the change was welcome. She opened one eye. They were in another hall. This one ran parallel to the hangar, but the ceilings were lower and the hall itself was narrower. It was also dimmer, lit as far as she could see in either direction with glowing strips running along the walls.

"These are the dorms. Odd numbers are the inner wall," he said, gesturing at hatches lining the hall. "Even are outer. You're in number eighteen, that's this way."

They didn't need to go far before he stopped again, pointing out one of the hatches on the right.

"This is where you'll stay while you're with us. It's also where I'll leave you. Your team ought to have further instruction." He turned the latch and shoved the door inward with an audible pop that reminded Ashleen of an airlock.

She warily craned her neck to see through the opening. Inside was a warmly lit living area. The floor was solid and from where she stood she couldn't see any windows.

When she turned her head, Rome had already disappeared back the way they'd come.

"Well bye, I guess," she said to the empty space he'd once occupied.

She stepped over the threshold and pulled the door closed behind her. It slid into place with a satisfying thud.

The room's centerpiece was a cheap-looking coffee table, surrounded by three battered couches. Against the far wall an ancient television sat on a rickety dresser. To one side of the television, there lurked an angry mini fridge, which whirred a reluctant greeting at her. It definitely looked like a bachelor's flat, but Ashleen supposed the space was far more welcoming than the cramped cell she spent the last few months in.

There were two offshoots from the main space. Down one, she counted two doors. Down the other, three. One of the three doors had a note taped to it. There didn't seem to be anyone home, so Ashleen assumed the note was hers.

The handwriting was barely legible. Its letters were a jagged mess of varying sizes, as if written by a child.

Hey Ashleen,

Sorry I wasn't here to greet you. Things came up. There's a map and some clothes on the nightstand. Look for Cyrus in the cafeteria, he said he knows you. His team will keep you company until we get back.

-Izzy

The room that greeted her was plain, dingy, and had no windows, but the bed in the corner had a real mattress and comforter. A part of her wanted to climb in and take a nap right now.

Just like the note had said, a change of clothes sat on the nightstand. The only other furniture in the room was an old, scuffed dresser.

She closed the door behind her, felt along the wall for a lightswitch, and bathed the room in yellow light. She inspected the outfit. It appeared to be standard issue. The same windbreaker and pants Rome had worn with a plain white T-shirt. The only difference was that the accents on hers replaced burgundy with orange.

Ashleen had never liked orange, but at least there was less of it than the prison jumpsuit she'd been wearing. She stripped down to her plain undergarments and grimaced. She hadn't had a chance to shower before Neele came to collect her. She felt sticky. She made a mental note to ask the next person she bumped into where the showers were.

She didn't know what to do with the hideous jumpsuit, so she folded it and stuffed it in one of the dresser drawers. The map looked less like a map and more like a blueprint, but it didn't take long for her to decipher it.

The city was made up of concentric rings, the largest one ran perpendicular to the rest and was labelled 'Gardens'. Inward from the gardens was the hangar, then dorms, sim rooms, cafeteria, infirmary, and an unlabeled central node.

Ashleen struggled to ignore the little pulse of panic she felt at the realization she'd have to cross two more of those horrible hallways. She didn't have a choice, but that didn't mean she had to like it.

When she approached the first one she closed her eyes before the door was even open. She rushed across and felt along the wall, listening for the hiss of the door. She all but jumped into the next ring. She couldn't get her eyes to open until the door slid shut behind her.

When she did, she offered a silent prayer of gratitude that no one had been present to witness the display.

The only difference between the sim rooms and dorm rooms was that the hatches were bigger and ran along the ceiling instead of the walls. Since it was the only door on the wall, it didn't take Ashleen long to find the pass she needed.

She crossed as slow as she could. When she emerged into the new ring, a flood of daylight welcomed her. Blessedly, it didn't come from the walls. Instead, only the ceiling was transparent, continuous sunlight streamed in from above. In here, Ashleen could pretend they were on the ground.

"Hey, fledgling!"

Ashleen tore her eyes from the skylight to seek the source of the exclamation. Two men were making their way toward her.

Both were shorter than she was. The smallest addressed her first. "Ashleen! It's me, Cyrus!"

His face was framed by a mess of blonde curls and he had large, child-like eyes. He wore the standard jacket with yellow accents. Ashleen didn't recognize him.

"You are Ashleen Gallagher, from Dheering, right?"

"Yes." She drew out the word, stalling for time.

"Come on!" he said, stomping his foot. "I can't believe you don't recognize me!"

"Calm down Cyrus," the larger man rumbled, "She's been through a lot." He held out a hand for her to shake. "I'm Leo."

Leo dwarfed Cyrus, but most of his size came from the width of his shoulders. His skin had a bronze hue, and his hair was cropped so close to his skull Ashleen couldn't tell if it was brown or black. The jacket he had slung over one shoulder was identical to hers.

"You must be the new tranq. Let me know if you need any pointers," he turned towards Cyrus, "I'm gonna go check in with Janice and the others."

"Okay!" Cyrus barely hesitated long enough for Leo to walk away before he babbled on. "Kindergarten! We used to go to school together."

That narrowed the window considerably. Ashleen had only gone to school for a total of six months. Her mother had pulled her out of public school after an incident where she'd broken another child's arm.

"Oh! You were––I'm so sorry!"

Cyrus waved a hand dismissively, "Don't be. It's in the past! Besides, it was partly my fault."

"Please. Hair pulling didn't warrant that much retaliation."

"Perhaps not, but we were kids. Anyway, welcome to Alexandria! City of losers," he spread his arms, presenting the cafeteria.

Ashleen chuckled.

"I heard you were hand-picked by Izzy. You've got a great team. You're lucky, some of the newbies spend years drifting between teams before they catch the interest of one that's any good."

Ashleen shrugged, "He'll be disappointed." Still, she couldn't help but be curious. So far, everyone only had praise for Izzy. On the one hand, he seemed nice. On the other, Ashleen worried he'd made a mistake picking her. He seemed highly skilled, and she had no combat training whatsoever.

Cyrus waved a hand at her, "Psh, nah. He picked you for a reason. And if you're anywhere near as strong as I remember you, you'll do fine." He inclined his head the direction Leo had wandered off to. "You wanna meet my team?"

"Sure!" She followed him through the crowd to the table. Three people were already there: Leo, and two women. Both were gorgeous in completely different ways. The one sitting closest to Leo had rectangular glasses and brown hair cropped in an asymmetrical bob. Her posture suggested she would be more comfortable in a pencil skirt than the standard issue tracksuit.

The other woman had tawny skin, a gold hoop through her left nostril, and a long black braid. She wore plum lipstick that coordinated beautifully with the magenta on her jacket. She beamed and reached for Ashleen's hand. "I'm Sushila. How do you like Alexandria so far?"

"It's a lot to get used to," Ashleen took her hand, then jerked away when her skin prickled at the touch.

Sushila flashed her a cheeky grin, "Just a nibble, love. I didn't mean to startle you."

Ashleen pressed her lips together in a hollow semblance of a smile. Sushila must be one of the vespers she'd been warned about. "Maybe you could ask, next time?"

Before Sushila could answer, a plate clattered to the floor behind them. Ashleen turned to investigate. Her heart slammed into her ribcage and slid up into her throat. How many hours had she spent staring into those doe eyes?

The woman's ash blonde hair was shorter than she remembered it, but still worn in a half-up crown. Her delicate hand was twisted in the fabric of her jacket, lips half parted as she grasped for words.

Cyrus beat either of them to it, startling both as his glass clanked against the table. "Hey, Prue. You alright?"

3

Meet the Crew

Ashleen didn't remember running, but she wasn't in the cafeteria anymore. Her thoughts clamored over each other and rose to a crescendo. They tumbled through her mind so quickly that each new thought interrupted the one before it and only noise was left. Ashleen couldn't tell if she was going to choke on her heart or throw it up. Steel bands tightened around her ribs. Glass prickled in her lungs. She sucked in air, but it didn't calm her down. There wasn't enough oxygen. The atmosphere was too warm and stagnant.

Prue couldn't be here. Prue was gone. She knew that conclusion didn't make sense, but she couldn't force logic in this situation. She checked her hands for blood. Her vision wavered and she couldn't tell if there was any or not. Her fingers ached.

Ashleen pressed her trembling hands over her ears. The silence deafened her. Perhaps it was just the sound of her own blood screaming in her skull. The lights flickered and Ashleen shut her eyes to block out whatever tricks her mind wanted to play.

Someone touched her arm and she lashed out. The heel of her hand impacted someone's body and felt their breath gust over her shoulder.

She couldn't draw enough air to say anything, but her vision started to clear. Someone slid down the wall opposite her, a hand pressed against their ribs. She watched them struggle to draw breath and rocked forward into a crouch. The edges of her panic burned with the onset of a rage.

Before she could draw any closer, whale song drowned out her panic and supplanted her fury. In place of the aggression she'd grown up used to fighting, she felt someone else's will press in against her mind. The sensation was remarkably similar, her head filled with cotton, her limbs moving against her will.

Ashleen blinked the bleariness from her eyes and focused on the man before her. At least, she was fairly certain he was male, his fairy-like build could have fooled her. His lips weren't moving, but she knew he was the source of the unearthly song.

The hair on one side of his head was buzzed short, the rest fell in fantastical red curls to his jaw. It was the kind of red Ashleen had grown up wishing she had. The kind of red that clashed spectacularly with the magenta accents on his coat.

Her stomach twisted. He was a vesper, like Sushila. She tried to stand but a swell in the whale song pressed her back. Ashleen knew what it felt like to be a puppet. Whenever she slipped into a rage it was like watching someone else in her body. This felt almost the same. She hated it, but she could fight this. Fighting another person was much easier than fighting herself.

Ashleen began to inch forward on her hands and knees. A tiny crease appeared between the man's eyebrows. A low bellow pushed on her, but now that the panic had gone, it was easy to shoulder through.

She gradually made it across the hall until she was close enough to plant one hand on the wall next to his head. He shrank before her, uncertain what she planned to do.

"Please stop."

He dropped the whale song and her head cleared. He didn't say a word, tensed as if he expected her to snap his neck.

"Are you alright?"

A tiny puff of air ghosted past his lips, and for a split second Ashleen caught a glimpse of relief on his face before he hid it under a smirk. "I should have kept my distance." His tone was reedy, as if he couldn't get enough air for full bodied words.

"Did I break anything?"

"Bruised rib, maybe, I've had worse."

If he made a habit of touching women without asking, Ashleen wasn't surprised.

"Help me up?"

Ashleen straightened and pulled him up by a handful of his jacket, careful to avoid skin contact. He hissed.

"I don't think I've seen you before. I'm Morpheus. What's your name?"

She didn't answer, too busy kicking herself for the grand impression she'd made on a member of her team. She hadn't even been here an hour and she was already on her way to getting kicked out. She should walk him to the infirmary. She owed him that much.

"Come on," she said, leading the way back to the cafeteria.

The glimpse of the clouds as they crossed the connecting hall made her heart race, but Ashleen refused to show him any more weakness than he'd already seen. Who knew what he would do with it?

She tugged Morpheus forward to stand beside her and used his taller frame to hide herself from Prue and the team she'd run out on earlier. She'd face them eventually, but not now.

They burst into the infirmary, startling several medics. A round woman with brown hair was the first to react. She strode forward, reaching for Morpheus and leading him to an empty station. Neele emerged from behind a counter, tugging off and throwing away a pair of rubber gloves.

"What did you break this time?" she barked at Morpheus. She looked different than Ashleen remembered, less 'government-employed paper pusher' and a lot more 'manic laboratory pixie'. Ashleen decided she liked the change.

"Nothing! I promise!" Morpheus swore.

Neele scoffed, "Birdshit. It's been two months since you broke anything, you're overdue." She shooed away her assistant and pried Morpheus' arm away from his side. Her movements softened as she felt along the ribs he'd been hiding. "You hit him, didn't you?"

"No, I just--He--" Ashleen gestured to herself, then to Morpheus, put off by Neele's accusation. "I mean, yes, but he just--I was..." She scratched the back of her head and tried to organize her thoughts to explain what had happened without incriminating herself.

Neele turned, her expression soft. "I never gave you your prescription, did I?"

"What prescription?"

Neele crossed to a cabinet at the back of the room and returned with an orange pill bottle. She tossed it to Ashleen, "Take one every eight hours, they'll stop your rages."

Ashleen eyed the small blue pills incredulously. It wasn't that she didn't believe Neele, but she'd expected more fanfare.

"I have something else for you." She jerked her chin towards an empty station, "Rosie, if you will."

The brown-haired woman Neele had shooed away from Morpheus reappeared and met Ashleen at the station. She began to prep a syringe and Ashleen flinched away from her. She wasn't afraid of needles. The substance inside, however, was another matter.

"What's that?"

"Just birth control," Neele assured her from where she was still checking Morpheus' ribs. "I pulled your records, you're up to date on everything else."

Ashleen's face burned. She wished she hadn't asked; it wasn't really a topic she wanted to discuss with men in the room, let alone Morpheus. "Actually, I don't need it."

"Mandatory," Neele countered. "Several hundred young people in mixed quarters with no supervision?" She squinted accusatorily at Morpheus. "A sizable portion of which are vespers? This is a top-secret military operation. Not a nursery."

Ashleen couldn't argue with that logic, but the situation still made her cringe. She waited barely long enough for the shot to be administered and pushed away from the station on her way to the door. "We're done now, right?"

"Yes. Ashleen?" Neele called after her.

"Yeah?" She turned and caught a glimmer of recognition on Morpheus' features.

"Try not to break any more of your team members."

"No promises." Her face warmed another degree, and she slipped back through the doors to the cafeteria.

Morpheus hissed as Neele gave his ribs a harsher poke. "Quit while you're ahead, she's too much for you."

"Maybe. Maybe not." He tore his eyes away from the door and glanced at Neele. "How are my ribs?"

"Bruised."

"Isn't that what I said?"

Neele rolled her eyes, "You broke them a few months ago, I had to be sure. I'll get you something for the inflammation."

Ashleen reflexively searched the cafeteria for Prue. She wasn't ready to face her ex-girlfriend, but she couldn't help the way hope nagged at her that maybe they could try again. There had to be an explanation at the very least.

The more logical voice in her head told her to drop it. The relationship was over. Prue hadn't been her counterweight anyway. If Ashleen chased her, she'd be wasting her time and her tears. She spotted Prue's table. Though she'd left, the rest of the team was still there. Cyrus waved her over.

When she reached them, Sushila offered her a concerned expression. "Prue explained the situation. Are you alright?"

Ashleen took a steadying breath and nodded. "Yeah, it's in the past, actually. I'm sorry."

Cyrus reached up to pat her on the back. "Don't sweat it. Happens to the best of us."

"Did you get your tranquilizers? Have you taken one yet?" Leo pressed urgently.

Ashleen fished the bottle from her pocket, "They're here."

"Take one. They'll kick you out if you're not on them."

Cyrus slid his water glass across the table. Ashleen knocked back one of the pills.

"Your team is probably back by now," Sushila started, "You could meet them if you want."

"I could also introduce you to some of the other tranqs," Leo suggested.

Ashleen wasn't ready to face her team so soon after her encounter with Morpheus, but she'd have to eventually either way. On the other hand, the longer she lingered with Leo's team, the more likely she was to run into Prue.

"Actually, I'd better meet the rest of my team. Thanks though."

"You'll hang out with us later, right?" Cyrus pleaded, "I know things are a bit weird with Prue, but I don't think she'd want you to avoid her."

Ashleen hid her grimace. Avoiding Prue was sort of the whole plan. "Okay, I'll see you later."

Cyrus beamed.

She managed a tight-lipped grin that didn't reach her eyes and gave a timid wave before she headed back towards the dorms.

Ashleen dragged her feet once she'd made it out of sight. She didn't want to be around people. Surely she didn't have to meet her team this instant. She could investigate the gardens instead, but that would mean crossing two more of those horrible hallways.

She wasn't sure how much more anxiety she could handle today, so instead she planted her back against the wall between two dorms and slid down to the floor. She'd take a minute to collect herself.

The hatch to her right popped open and she startled. A young man stepped through it. He was nearly as pale as Morpheus had been, with black hair and dark eyes that picked her apart. The predatory way his gaze swept over her head to toe set Ashleen's teeth on edge.

She tried to return his scrutiny, but her eyes caught on the magenta highlights of his jacket. Another vesper. They were everywhere, pigeons strutting about city sidewalks. She fought the urge to shudder.

"You're far from home. You lost?" he drawled.

"No."

He lifted his chin and gazed down his too straight nose at her, "You here for me then?"

She narrowed her eyes at him, "No." He might've been attractive if he weren't staring at her like a piece of meat.

"Do you know any other words?"

He was baiting her. She chose not to answer. If she ignored him, maybe he'd get bored.

"There are English classes, I could show you the way."

"Leave me alone." She turned her head and refused to look at him.

"Ah, so she does speak. Is she interested in a good time?"

"No."

Something about him soured. His expression and posture hadn't shifted a millimeter, but the feel of the space around them had gone bad, like rotten milk. Her heartbeat picked up, her anger building--she could send him flying, if she wanted. Then again, perhaps she couldn't. If Morpheus could sway her, who knew what he could do? Or make her do?

He straightened even further and inhaled steadily through his nose, a carefree smirk still plastered to his face. Ashleen shrank back.

"Pavane." A stern baritone cut through the tension between them.

Pavane froze and the sour aura dissipated. A hand appeared on his shoulder and Ashleen followed it up to a man of similar height and African descent. The upper half of his face was concealed behind a mossy green blindfold and his black dreadlocks were caught half up in its knot.

The hall was dim, but Ashleen thought she could see decorative scarring down the bridge of his nose and on his chin. His jacket had green accents. She hadn't noticed that color on anyone else yet.

"You know," a new voice interjected, "somewhere out there, there's a tree working hard to replace all the oxygen you waste. You ought to apologize to it."

Pavane glowered and slowly raised his hands. "Dahei. Is that a knife, or are you just happy to see me?"

Dahei rested his chin on Pavane's other shoulder, "You wanna find out?"

"Not today." He took a step towards Ashleen, then to the side, and ducked away from them to vanish down the hall.

Ashleen curled her lip after him, "What a skeezy troglodyte."

"'Skeezy troglodyte'. That's very good, may I use that?" Where Pavane had been standing a moment ago was an Asian man who couldn't be more than five foot four. He deftly concealed a knife in his sleeve. His mussed-up hair had been bleached all the way to white. His ears and eyebrow were pierced, but it was the snake bite piercings that held her attention.

"Sure, I guess."

The man in the blindfold offered her a hand. When she took it, he pulled her to her feet. "Are you Ashleen? I am Demetrius."

Dahei's eyebrows shot up. "Sou desu ka? For a tranq you're pretty docile. Most of the ones I know would have put Pavane through a wall."

"Trying to turn over a new leaf."

Dahei chuckled, "Good luck with that. I've been trying for six years."

"Be nice," Demetrius chastised. "We are on our way back. You are welcome to join us." He tossed his hands in a gesture Ashleen couldn't follow. A cloud of cerulean butterflies tumbled out of his dreadlocks and fluttered about the space.

Demetrius tossed his head left and right, orientating himself, then led the way in the direction of dorm room eighteen.

Dahei unlatched the door and threw his full weight into opening it when they arrived.

"You're late! What sort of birdshit did you start this time?" The accent that welcomed them was unmistakably Australian, and preceded a third man. Everything about him was sunkissed, from his even tan to the darker roots of his sandy blond hair. The right side of his body was furrowed with extensive scars, one of which tugged the corner of his mouth down.

When he caught sight of her, his face split into a grin that could dim the sun and he pushed the tinted goggles he wore up into his hair. "Ashleen!"

"Me!" She tried to match his enthusiasm, but her brain was starting to stretch with the exhaustion of memorizing so many new faces.

"I'm Izzy, glad Demetrius found you. I was starting to worry. Morpheus was supposed to get you from Cyrus. Probably got distracted canoodling with his girlfriend though, didn't he?"

Ashleen wondered if he meant Sushila or the girl who belonged in a pencil skirt. She laughed nervously. She didn't want to lead by telling them she'd almost broken his ribs. "Why me?"

Izzy laughed, "What?"

"I mean, why did you pick me?" The question had been nagging at her since Neele had first mentioned Izzy. She didn't know him, she doubted he knew her. How had he looked at a list of names and differentiated her from the masses?

"Ah." He shrugged, turning back to whatever he'd been tinkering with before they arrived. "Why not? Could use some change around here, throw a monkey wrench in Anshathane's plans."

His answer was not encouraging. Ashleen didn't follow, Anshathane, the wolf god, but she wasn't sure how much she wanted to be a monkey wrench in the plans of any deity.

Demetrius ran a thumb along the edge of his blindfold. "I cannot support interfering with the will of the gods."

At least someone in this room was sane. Morpheus, Dahei, and Izzy all seemed to be individual brands of chaotic. It was good to know at least one of the boys she'd been thrown in with had a sense of self preservation.

"I can," Izzy countered, his voice muffled by a pair of wires tucked between his lips. "I'll kick the arse of anyone who messes with innocent bystanders, god or no."

Demetrius made a noise halfway between displeasure and pain.

Ashleen cast about for a way to change the subject. She agreed with Demetrius, but she wasn't about to argue with the person who'd just freed her from prison and offered her an opportunity to start over.

"What's that?" Ashleen asked, leaning over the back of the couch to take in the assortment of mechanical components spread across the coffee table.

"Bomb," Izzy answered simply.

Her voice skipped up two octaves. "What?!"

Dahei pushed past her to investigate the coffee table. "You're starting a new project? I told you I needed more stun grenades."

"Non-lethals are no fun."

"Excuse me?" Ashleen glanced at Demetrius for a que. Was it normal for Izzy to assemble explosives in the living room? Demetrius seemed unphased. Perhaps it was. That would take some getting used to.

"Nothing to worry about," Izzy assured her, "It's just the casing."

"Oh." Of course it was. She felt stupid now. Why would Alexandria supply ex-cons like herself with live explosives?

Izzy saved her from the silence. "Have you eaten?"

"Not exactly." She'd meant to, but her encounter with Prue had sort of thrown things off. "What time is it?"

"Threeish."

Ashleen sighed. It was still too early to sleep.

"Tired?" Demetrius asked.

"A little." It was the understatement of the twenty-first century. Ashleen's tolerance for excitement must have diminished during her months in prison. She hadn't felt this drained in a long time.

"I'll have Morpheus bring us some dinner," Izzy stated. "In the meantime, maybe you should get some rest."

4

Bitter Words and Healing Tears

Ashleen woke early and stumbled her way to the showers. They weren't as private as she would have liked, but they were an improvement over the open space she had to put up with in prison. She didn't have a fresh change of clothes, so she put the uniform she'd been given on and made her way back.

She opened and shut the hatch as quietly as she could. Izzy was already up. He sat cross-legged in the corner of one of the couches. A pen hung from the corner of his mouth as he focused intently on a planner open in his lap. The goggles he'd been wearing yesterday were pulled down around his neck.

If he noticed her entry, he gave no sign of it. When she took a step closer, he snapped out of his trance and raised his head to look at her.

"Morning," he said, his trademark smile spreading across his face. "Sleep well?"

"Better than I have in months, actually." She sat in the corner opposite him.

"The others should be up soon. We'll get breakfast first, but we're due for rankings."

"Rankings?"

"Alexandria is based on a point system. Each person has a point value, add them all up and you get a team's value. Higher the rank the better the privilege. Take a guess at our team's rank."

"Eighteen?"

"You catch on quick. Like that. But you don't have a rank yet. So we'll need to get you one."

"How's it work?"

"Supervised duels within classes. There are six ranks, but the last two are for a single person. Got the bottom-feeders, they're just scrappers. Up from that you get centurion, gladiator, and knight. After that there's one knight-captain for each class and one archknight for each class."

"What rank do you think I am?"

"Counting on you to make at least gladiator. Any lower and you'll drag the team down a whole rank."

Ashleen swallowed, but before she could say anything more, a door opened. Morpheus emerged from the room across from hers, already alert and fully dressed. Ashleen schooled her features to non-chalance. She'd been the first to bed––had he told the others what had happened?

"Morning," Izzy raised a hand to greet him. "This is Ashleen. She's our new tranq."

Apparently he hadn't. But he was about to. She held her breath, but Morpheus only smirked.

"Nice to meet you." He gave no indication that he'd ever seen her before.

"Yeah..." Ashleen scrutinized him, trying to get a grasp on his motives.

Izzy's eyes flicked back and forth between them, as if he was already deducing what happened without either of them having told him.

The next person to join them was Demetrius, blindfold still in place. A few butterflies accompanied him, taking perches in places out of harm's way.

Dahei's awakening was announced by an ungodly, blaring alarm and a clatter that Ashleen could only assume meant he'd thrown the clock. He stumbled out of his room with an impressive bedhead for someone whose hair was so short.

Izzy opened his mouth to greet him and Dahei flipped him a three-toed raven gesture, "Coffee first."

Dahei growled at anyone who tried to speak, so they made their way to breakfast in relative silence. Ashleen took the time to analyze her teammates. They were all required to wear the color-coded uniforms, so she focused on their covenant bands.

She'd spent countless hours combing through articles on them in her youth, so she knew that each band was unique to its owner. The rings usually appeared unexpectedly when a person reached puberty, but there were exceptions.

Ashleen had found hers between the couch cushions. They had a tricky sort of magic that prevented them from being lost. Even a discarded ring would return to its owner, unless the owner's counterweight was holding it.

Izzy's caught her eye first. The flat band of hammered copper had begun to turn his finger green. Copper was a powerful conductor; articles that analyzed band materials claimed it was indicative of a sharp wit and agile mind. People with copper rings were commonly tactical geniuses, with a knack for engineering, mechanics, or other sciences.

She'd only known Izzy for part of a day, but from what she'd seen, she'd guess that this one had been given to him. He already had a counterweight.

Dahei wore two rings. The realization hit her like a truck. Assuming neither was for decoration, people with more than one ring belonged to one of two groups. The bearer could have more than one counterweight. This was rare, but not unheard of. More commonly, a person wearing more than one ring had lost a counterweight. Ashleen's mother wore two rings.

She wasn't sure she would have fared as well as her mother if she'd lost her counterweight in the same manner. Ashleen had often used the fact that her counterweight was still out there waiting for her to motivate herself through life. Sometimes she wondered how her mother was able to drag herself out of bed in the morning.

Assuming Dahei had been through the same experience, she'd see him in a new light now. The first of his rings was ferrous, a warrior's metal. It was wrought in the shape of a crown and set with small black stones. Without closer examination, Ashleen wouldn't know if they were onyx or tourmaline.

The other band wasn't metal at all. She'd heard of rings like this, but she'd never seen one. It was a solid piece of pale stone with a distinctive pattern Ashleen recognized as fossilized coral. The stone was rare in covenant bands, she would have had to look it up to be sure of its meaning.

Neither Demetrius nor Morpheus had any decoration on their hands. Since Demetrius appeared to be as devout as she was, Ashleen wasn't sure why he would hide his band. Where Morpheus was concerned, she had a guess.

Some people thought the idea of the gods deciding one's fate to be outdated and restrictive. The vespers all seemed promiscuous in nature. It wasn't a stretch for Ashleen to imagine they fell within that group.

Upon their arrival at the cafeteria Dahei broke away from them, undoubtedly seeking the coffee he'd mentioned earlier. Demetrius followed, quick on his heels.

Morpheus slipped away in another direction, the wisp of his form swallowed by the crowds and the dim twilight of dawn as the sun breached the horizon somewhere far below them.

Izzy led her to one end of a buffet set up on the far side of the cafeteria. The spread was mostly fruit, with options from apples and oranges to peaches and berries. In between fruit baskets there were platters full of either eggs or oatmeal.

Ashleen filled her plate with a little bit of everything until she came to the coffee. She didn't know what she'd expected, but she was rather surprised to find packets of instant coffee. The idea of it both fascinated and disgusted her. Perhaps the addition of one of the flavored creamers would make it palatable. She tucked a few packets under her arm and made her way back into the crowd with her plate and mug.

She spotted Cyrus and Izzy waving at her from one of the larger tables. She wound her way toward them and set down her food next to Izzy. He and Cyrus were like two peas in a pod, blond hair and chipper attitudes lighting up the room while they bickered about guns and bows.

Across the table Dahei sipped at his coffee and slumped against Demetrius. Demetrius didn't seem to mind. He waited for his tea to steep, periodically testing the temperature with the tip of a finger.

The woman with the asymmetrical bob--Ashleen had learned her name was Janice--kept to herself. She poured over a spiral-bound notebook, her body tucked neatly into the arm Leo had draped about her shoulders.

Ashleen crunched a ripe grape, scowling at Sushila and Morpheus as the two playfully flirted with each other. The more she saw of vespers, the more they seemed to live up to the reputation Neele had warned her of.

A familiar giggle had her heart tripping over itself. Prue skirted the table and set down a plate. She twined her arms around Morpheus' neck and planted a kiss on the corner of his mouth. Sushila's only reaction was to warmly greet her in an equally flirty tone.

Ashleen's gaze snagged on the oversized lavender flannel Prue wore. Ashleen knew that shirt; it was hers. She'd lent it to her a few days before Prue's birthday. A few days before she'd murdered someone. Ashleen was half convinced that if she stared hard enough, she'd be able to spot blood stains. Why did Prue still have the damn thing?

Prue had somehow squeezed herself onto the seat next to Morpheus. She clung to him to maintain her balance and not slip into a heap on the scuffed linoleum floor. He winced when she jostled his ribs, but he still didn't say anything about having been injured at all. What game was he playing?

"Ashleen," Prue stared at her wide-eyed, as if she'd forgotten all about their meeting yesterday.

Panic surged up in Ashleen's chest, and she forced it to stop there, a frantic sparrow trapped in her ribcage. She wouldn't run. Not this time. She took a large sip of her coffee and grimaced. It was little more than bitter water. She let her disgust distract her from the anxiety.

"Prue."

"You two know each other?" Izzy gestured between them with his fork.

When neither of them answered, Demetrius broke the silence. "They are, how do you say–– split up." Ashleen would ask later how he figured that out.

Prue untangled herself from Morpheus and sat down in her own chair. "So... How have you been?"

"I went to jail, Prue." Ashleen sharpened each word with cold brutality.

Prue shrank in her chair, guilt casting shadows in her eyes. "Can we talk about that later?"

"Why? I want to know why you abandoned me."

"I didn't abandon you."

"You didn't? I suppose I just called the wrong number and made all my letters out to the wrong address."

Prue recoiled. "It's a bit more complicated than that."

Ashleen shoveled a bite of food into her mouth and swallowed it quickly to push down the lump in her throat. All this and Prue was still pushing her away. She'd known this would happen, but she'd never been able to leave well enough alone. Prue had been Ashleen's whole world. She'd messed up, epically, but it still stung that Prue could walk away from her so easily.

"I've waited six months. Isn't that enough?"

Morpheus put an arm around Prue, and Ashleen's temper simmered. She was making a monster of herself, handing him the opportunity to swoop in as Prue's dashing rescuer. She hated it, but she deserved an explanation.

"Everyone here knows the story, Prue," Demetrius interjected, "None of us are judging you."

Ashleen resisted the urge to snort. She might be. Maybe Prue couldn't have saved her from the cell, but she might have saved Ashleen from herself, and the countless nights contemplating how to tie a noose out of her bedsheet. All it would have taken was a few words.

"April twenty-seventh," Prue said finally.

"What about it?" Ashleen shot back. She couldn't forget the date even if she wanted to. It was Prue's birthday, the day they'd hosted the party. They day she'd killed someone.

"Do you remember what happened to me?"

Without the pills Neele had given her, Ashleen might've jumped the table to shake Prue. "I threw away everything for you. I killed someone for you! And you couldn't even be bothered to write a letter!"

"I didn't have a choice!" Prue's frustration boiled over.

No one else at the table seemed phased by the words flying between them. Did they all know her story already? Damn it. So much for turning over a new leaf. "Birdshit."

"I was possessed!" Prue shook with the statement, as if she hadn't come to terms with it yet and saying so hurt her. "I'm a beckoner. I didn't know it at the time, and without guidance a lot can go wrong. Right, Demetrius?"

He nodded. "Prue's story is common with others of the class."

"Cyrus says a lot of popular horror movies on the surface are probably based on the experiences of newly awakened beckoners," Dahei added.

Prue took a shaky breath. "I didn't even have a chance to breathe when he hit the floor. He was on me again that fast."

Ashleen scowled into her disgusting coffee and tried to hide behind the veil of her jaw length hair. Her face burned. Shame simmered in her veins.

"It was so much worse. I would rather have just let him have his way and be done with me. At least then he wouldn't have been inside my head."

Ashleen wanted to apologize, but a mix of pride and shock caught the words in her throat and trapped them there.

"You couldn't have known," Prue assured her, as if reading her mind. "I'm sorry I couldn't help you."

Ashleen knocked back the rest of her coffee in an attempt to dislodge the lump in her throat. She wouldn't cry. Not in front of all these people. Not in front of Morpheus. "I'm full," she muttered. She picked up her half-eaten food and left the table.

As soon as she'd tracked down a bus tub and escaped into the empty sim room hall, sobs bubbled up from her chest. Everything had been her fault. Somehow the truth burned, even though she'd been blaming herself the whole time anyway. Compared to what Prue had been through, she'd had it easy. She had no right to say what she'd said, and no right now to be this upset.

The sheer magnitude of how much she missed Prue was like a slap across the face. She wished someone would hold her, but no one could be allowed to see her like this.

The door next to her hissed open. Ashleen sucked in a breath and swiped at her eyes. She put a valiant but futile effort into affecting a façade of indifference. A soft hum filled the space, not unlike the ringing sound one could make with a wine glass.

A calming warmth coated the shame in Ashleen's chest, but she could still feel it lurking there, like an old color showing through a patchy paint job.

Sushila leaned against the wall next to her. For a few moments she didn't say anything, just continued her strange hum. When she stopped to breathe, she spoke. "Are you alright?"

"I'm fine."

"If you ever want to talk, I'm here. But you don't have to." She let the silence hang for a few seconds before she continued. "The others have already gone ahead to the sim room. Walk with me?"

"How bad is it?" Ashleen asked after a while, gesturing to her face.

Sushila gave her a sympathetic smile. "Still pretty bad, but it won't show up once you're in the sim."

5

Simulation Theory

Sushila stopped under sim room number ten. She reached up for the hatch, and it opened without her having to touch it. A ladder slid down into her hand. Ashleen followed her up and glanced around the stark white space.

There were about twenty people, but no one noticed their entrance even though they all sat in a circle around the door in the floor. There were two gaps in the circle. Sushila crossed to the one between Cyrus and Janice.

Ashleen's spot was between Izzy and Dahei, and when she reached it she glanced at Sushila, unsure of what to do next. Sushila smiled at her from across the circle, rested her hands on her knees, and closed her eyes.

Ashleen mimicked her. For a moment, nothing happened. Then a draft stirred her hair and she opened her eyes to see where it was coming from.

A roar of applause drifted down from the stands of the Roman colosseum. Easily ten times as many people milled around her than when she'd closed her eyes. All of them wore varying colors of the huntsman jacket.

Ashleen stood up and marveled at how real everything seemed. The sun warmed her hair, and the breeze carried faint scents from the concession stands down to them. Dust from the ground clung to her pants and came off in clouds when she brushed at it.

A sharp whistle drew her attention. At the center of the gathered huntsman, there stood an older woman. Her jacket was accented burgundy, which marked her as a warden. Her face was creased with "no nonsense" frown lines, and her salt and pepper hair was pulled back in a low ponytail.

To the woman's left, Ashleen recognized Rome. He surveyed the huntsmen with mild interest, his focus drawn towards the orange accented tranqs.

"I don't have all day! Scofflaws, let's get this show on the road!" the woman barked.

Everyone in a purple jacket split from their groups and crowded towards the center. The rest of the huntsmen drew back to give them room.

"Damn it, Ivanoff," Dahei grumbled as he passed Ashleen. "It's too early for this."

Izzy bumped her shoulder, "Hey, glad you made it. Let me know if you have questions."

The woman called Ivanoff drew a claymore from the air and planted the tip of it in the dusty ground. "Would anyone like to challenge for the title?"

Janice stepped into the center of the circle and made a show of drawing a rapier. She flourished her weapon and settled into a perfect fencer's stance.

Ashleen nudged Izzy, "Is Janice the knight-captain?"

"Of the scofflaws, yes."

No one stepped forward to challenge Janice, not even Dahei, whom Ashleen had assumed enjoyed a fight. After a few more breaths, Janice left the ring.

A quivering girl with frizzy blonde hair stepped in. She broke the silence with the clatter of a gauntlet she materialized and hurled at the ground. "I want to challenge for centurion."

"Recent events have dropped Misty's point value into the scrapper range," Ivanoff explained. "According to the laws of our society, if she cannot raise her rank soon, she will be excommunicated."

Ivanoff turned to face the girl. "As it stands you have two options. You may fight and defeat all other scofflaws with a scrapper rank, or you may challenge one gladiator."

It didn't seem fair to Ashleen. Misty either had to win a war of resilience, fighting several people back to back with no rest, or she had to defeat someone two ranks better than her. She hoped she never found herself in the same position.

"Gladiator," Misty's voice caught on the word. It was probably all she could get out around the nerves.

"Gladiators!" Ivanoff's voice boomed across the arena. "You've been issued a challenge. Would anyone like to accept Ms. Marshall's gauntlet?"

Dahei stepped into the circle and stooped to retrieve the gauntlet. When he straightened, it dissolved and slipped through his fingers like sand.

"Excellent." Ivanoff backed up to the edge of the circle. "On my whistle." She blew a sharp blast that hurt Ashleen's ears.

Dahei lunged forward so fast, Ashleen thought he'd teleported. Misty barely managed to duck as one of his blades passed through the air where she'd just been. She danced skittishly backward and pulled a pair of daggers into her hands.

Dahei hesitated a moment, bouncing on the balls of his feet and swinging twin gladiuses in skillful loops. Misty stared at him, the look in her eyes reminding Ashleen of prey begging a hunter for its life.

Dahei pursued her in leaps and bounds. Misty squeaked and turned her back to run. The other scofflaws, Ivanoff included, winced. It was a clear mistake. It left her wide open for Dahei to strike. He didn't. Instead, he flipped one of his swords backward in his hand and grabbed a chunk of her hair with his remaining fingers. He yanked. Hard. Misty yelped and stumbled off balance.

Ivanoff blew her whistle. "Foul! Mr. Kaibara that is your one and only warning!"

Ashleen leaned over to whisper to Izzy, "If it's actually a simulation, why is that a foul? It won't hurt her, will it?"

"Ichor tech is just as volatile as ichor itself. Sometimes it blurs the line between illusion and reality. We're supposed to avoid head blows and fatal strikes just in case."

Ashleen's chest tightened, "Does that happen often?"

Izzy shrugged, "It's fairly rare."

His answer did not reassure her.

Dahei fell back a few steps to give Misty a chance to recover. She whirled on him with her daggers, then realized he was too far away from her for the attack to land. Instead of pursuing him, she scrambled a little farther away.

"Ms. Marshall," Ivanoff barked, "if you refuse to fight, you will forfeit the duel."

Misty tensed, her whole body projecting her attack, and charged at Dahei. She raised her right dagger to strike at him. Dahei blocked with his left sword. Misty drove her left dagger towards his torso.

Instead of blocking, Dahei tossed his right sword into the air, caught her by the wrist to pull her off balance, and drove his knee into her stomach. When he let go Misty hit the dirt, gasping for air. Dahei raised his hand to catch his gladius as it spun back down.

Before he could strike a finishing blow, Misty rolled out of reach and jumped back to her feet. Her eyes watered and Ashleen could hear the desperation fraying her gasps for air. She lunged again and Dahei side stepped. As she passed him, she crumpled to the ground and dropped both her daggers.

Ivanoff's whistle pierced the air. Ashleen's breath caught in her throat as she realized Dahei had struck Misty full force in the side of the head with the pommel of his sword. The whole room held its breath, waiting for her to move.

Dahei dismissed his swords and crouched at Misty's side. He gingerly rolled her onto her back and brushed the hair out of her face.

"Misty."

When he said her name, Misty groaned and grimaced. She blinked and pressed a hand to the side of her head, "I'm okay."

The whole room exhaled collectively. "Dahei," Ivanoff spoke, an exhaustion in her voice that hadn't been there a moment ago, "You're disqualified. Misty, you gain a hazard rank. Until further notice you're a centurion."

It took Misty a second to react, then she burst into disbelieving laughter. She sat up and threw her arms around Dahei's neck. "Thank you," she said through sobs. "Thank you so much."

He extricated himself from her grasp awkwardly, "Don't mention it."

"That's enough from the scofflaws today," Ivanoff said, waving them off.

As Dahei approached them, Demetrius' lips thinned with worry. "Is she alright?"

"She'll have a headache for the rest of the day. If she's smart, she'll spend her recovery time training and in a few weeks she'll actually be able to hold her own as a centurion."

Demetrius' frown deepened, "You could have seriously hurt her."

"But I didn't, and she doesn't have to return to whatever hell she escaped by coming here."

Ivanoff interrupted further bickering before it could begin. She made a quick gesture and the simulation began to change in bits and pieces every time Ashleen blinked.

In a matter of seconds, the colosseum had vanished. In its place was a forest that seemed to function like an elaborate obstacle course. Targets of various sizes hung from the branches. Some were towards the ends of the branches, swaying in the pine-scented breeze. Larger, more stable targets hung closer to the trunks.

"Deadeyes!" Ivanoff called the next class forward.

The group shifted like a human kaleidoscope as purple jackets traded places with yellow. Izzy pulled his goggles down over his eyes and stepped into the center. He pressed his palms together and as he drew them apart, a modified rifle formed between them. The gun looked like it had been pulled from the pages of a steampunk novel. Ashleen had never seen anything like it.

"How is everyone doing that?"

"Ichor is, I have heard others say, 'psycho-reactive'?" Demetrius explained. "It copies people's personalities and the pictures in their minds."

"Challengers for the title?" Ivanoff asked.

"Izzy's the knight captain?"

Demetrius nodded. "He works very hard to stay there."

"Nerd," Dahei scoffed.

Cyrus hopped out of line and hurled a gauntlet at Izzy's feet. Izzy grinned and bent to retrieve it.

Ivanoff chuckled, "Again, Mr. Dunnam?"

"I'm getting that title. Maybe not today. Maybe not tomorrow. But soon," Cyrus assured them.

"They do this every week," Dahei supplied, "He always loses."

Demetrius smothered a grin, "I think it's cute."

Dahei made a displeased noise and dug an elbow into Demetrius' ribs.

Ivanoff blew her whistle and Cyrus spun on his heel, pulling a compound bow and quiver from the air as he took off into the woods.

Izzy turned in the opposite direction, but instead of running into the trees, he picked one with low hanging branches and took his time climbing as high as he could manage.

He braced himself against the trunk and brought up his gun to peer through the scope. He fired shots one after another, pausing only long enough between each one to adjust his aim by incremental degrees.

Ashleen didn't know much about guns, but she was pretty sure he should have had to stop to reload by now. She said as much.

"He's showing off, imagining bullets directly into the gun," Dahei snorted.

"He knows his weapon well," Demetrius agreed.

"Well? His knowledge of that rifle probably competes with his knowledge of his girlfriend." Dahei teased, then gestured at Ashleen. "Do not tell him I said that."

Demetrius laughed out loud.

Cyrus exploded back into the clearing, doubling over and resting his hands on his knees to catch his breath. Izzy began to make his way down from the tree.

Ivanoff made a gesture like she was pulling something towards her, and a score of targets flew out of the trees to land on the ground at her feet. She took a few seconds to arrange them in two groups.

One group of them had arrows sticking out of them, and the others had splashes of color. Had Izzy been using paintballs? His gun didn't look like any of the paintball guns Ashleen had seen, but what did she know?

The arrow targets were all semi-accurate hits, but only one was actually a bullseye. The paint targets, on the other hand, were the opposite. All of them were dead on perfect hits, except one.

Izzy cursed when he noticed it.

Ivanoff shot him a quizzical look.

"My arm seized up on me. I need to learn how to compensate for that better."

"Give it a rest!" Cyrus pleaded, "That target is still dead, isn't that one from the five hundred yards group?"

Ivanoff flipped it over and read something off the back, "Six-sixty."

Cyrus choked. "Raven eat your eyes! How much more practice could you possibly need? That shot is impossible!"

"There's no such thing as too much practice," Izzy insisted.

"You're a damn perfectionist."

"Yes, and?"

A few more competitions took place between the remaining deadeyes, and someone managed to gain a rank before Ivanoff finally dismissed them. Ashleen spent the whole time trying to focus, but her thoughts kept interrupting her. She couldn't help but compare herself to Morpheus.

She didn't know what Prue saw in him that she didn't have. He seemed to be her complete opposite, and Ashleen couldn't help but wonder if that was a measure of how badly she'd messed up.

She wished she knew what to say. An apology didn't seem like enough. Prue had forgiven her, but Ashleen didn't feel any better. Prue had moved on, but she couldn't. The realization that perhaps Prue had never been as invested in their relationship as Ashleen had been hurt more than she cared to admit to herself.

Instead of shifting gradually like it had between the colosseum and the forest, the sim went completely black when Ivanoff called the beckoners.

Ashleen heard her surroundings before she saw them. Thunder rolled overhead, bringing a drum beat she remembered hearing at funerals and celebrations for the deceased. She skipped forward several steps as fire exploded to life in a large circle surrounding the huntsmen.

In the illumination, she saw Demetrius pull a small black blade from his pocket. He stepped into the center of the ring in perfect synchronicity with the other beckoners. Ashleen had to wonder how many times he'd done it before, since it seemed effortless despite his apparent blindness.

Ashleen unconsciously sought out Prue. The constant uncertainty she'd grown used to seeing in Prue's eyes was gone now. Inside the simulation, Prue wore the suffering she'd experienced like a crown. Come to think of it, all the beckoners had a similar aura to them. A 'wise beyond their years' and 'seen things you could never imagine' attitude that hung from their shoulders like a cloak.

In unison with the other beckoners, she slid her blade lightly along the pad of her thumb. Though each beckoner only spilled a few drops, elaborate runes and spell circles formed from the blood, spiraling ever inward. They stopped at the feet of a middle-aged Native American woman.

As Ashleen watched, the woman began to gesture, throwing her whole body into the movements until they became a dance. She created her own music and Ashleen could see something glimmering just beneath her skin. A huge golden eagle surged through her and burst forth with a deafening cry. On the downstroke of its enormous wings, a gust blew back the hair of everyone present.

Dahei thumbed his lower lip and leaned toward Ashleen, "Demetrius has been trying to figure out that technique for months."

"What is it?" She asked, only half listening.

"Winona's spirit guide. Demetrius says everyone has one, but most people can't sense theirs, let alone command them like that."

Winona and the eagle spoke at the same time. "Any who would seek to test their mettle are invited to do so now." When no one moved, she absorbed the eagle and left the circle.

A young Asian boy entered the ring and tossed a gauntlet at Demetrius' feet. "Rematch?"

Demetrius accepted the challenge, summoning his butterflies with a graceful roll of his wrist and shoulder. None of the beckoners seemed to mind being perched upon, and a few of them even smiled adoringly at the small blue creatures.

"Demetrius is the last person standing between Jin and a knight ranking. They've been at it for weeks," Dahei told Ashleen, a glimmer of pride in his voice.

On Ivanoff's whistle, both men dropped to a seat on the ground cross-legged in one fluid motion.

Demetrius drew his hands inward in a circular motion. He curled his last two fingers into his palms, and let his index and middle fingers remain extended. One hand drew a line straight towards the sky. The other continued the line down into the earth. He drew his hands quickly back past each other, palms brushing, until the tips of both extended pairs of fingers met end to end. An eerie whinny echoed through the woods.

"Tch," Jin exclaimed with a scowl. He clasped his hands together perpendicular to each other. He curled his middle and ring fingers over the backs of his hands, leaving his thumbs, pinkie, and index fingers extended. He slid his palms past each other, uncurling his middle and ring fingers and interlocking them. He twisted his hands so his index and pinkie fingers pointed outwards. Then broke the link, touched his thumbs to his pinkie, ring, and middle fingers in turn. He flipped his palms skyward with a flourish. The noise that came from somewhere behind him sounded unnervingly like the cackling of hyenas.

A smile played at the corners of Demetrius' mouth. "You've been practicing."

Jin inclined his head. "Think you can take them?"

"We will see."

"Hellhounds and a dullahan. This will be good." Dahei wasn't even trying to hide the idiotic grin on his face.

Before Ashleen could ask, several shapes crossed the flames, coalescing as they drew closer to their respective beckoners.

Demetrius and Jin brought their hands up and burst into a flurry of gestures. Three hellhounds pounced into the ring, passing through the gathered beckoners as if they weren't even there. They paced around Jin, sniffing his shoulders curiously. A couple of them bared their teeth at Demetrius.

They were built like hyenas and glowed like the sooty embers of a fire on the edge of being extinguished. One of them barked, its mouth opening far wider than should have been possible. The sound came out as if it had been played backward. The hollow sockets of their eyes looked far darker than darkness had any right to be and when they growled, molten blisters glowed along their rib cages.

Ashleen dug her fingernails into her palms. She wasn't sure how anyone could sleep after seeing this. She'd heard the legends of course; some of Muginn's most devout apostles were accompanied and guarded by cackling hounds. When a soul escaped limbo, it was said to be swallowed by black dogs. Even so, seeing the myths manifest right in front of her had her mind buffering like a bad streaming connection.

The hellhounds cackled and shrank back as a mounted horseman galloped into the clearing, leaping over the bystanders. The horse's skin clung to its bones, its eyes were dark pits.

The man on the horse's back held a wicked spear in one hand and his head in the other. He hoisted his head by the hair and swept it before him, as if he were getting a good look at the enemy he'd been summoned to fight.

The head also had empty eyes. At some point his lower jaw had fallen off and the upper lip was frozen into a curl, exposing pearly teeth. The dullahan swung his head around to look at Demetrius and hoisted his spear.

Demetrius gave an almost imperceptible nod and the horse reared back. The dullahan jabbed its spear at one of the hellhounds, which skipped backward, snarling and snapping.

Jin made a quick gesture, and the three hellhounds began to circle the horse. The horseman jabbed at another hound with his spear. He moved fluidly with his horse as the beast bucked and kicked a hellhound, sending it flying from the ring. The hound vanished in an arcing spray of ash.

Jin cursed and made another gesture. His two remaining hounds peeled off and attacked the horseman from both sides. They leaped at him with teeth bared, their strange, backwards barking echoing through the clearing.

The dullahan seemed unphased when one of them sunk its teeth into his spear arm. He twisted, and drove the tip of his weapon into the hindquarter of the other hound. As the hound fell back, the dullahan took his spear in his free arm and flipped it to bring it down on the head of the first hound.

The hound yipped, dropped to the ground, and fell back. The second hound snarled but seemed to have trouble moving with its injured leg. Magma dribbled from the tear in its skin as it strained and snapped at the horseman's head, missing by mere inches.

The dullahan twisted in his saddle, swinging his spear low and wedging one end of it under the hound's belly. With surprising ease, he leveled the spear across his horse's shoulders, and catapulted the hound from the ring. As it cleared the ring of fire, the hound disappeared in a cloud of smoke.

Jin grumbled. At this point, he didn't stand much of a chance. He spread his hands, palms down, and made a pushing motion towards the ground. His last hellhound vanished into the soil, "I concede."

The dullahan swung its head over to face Demetrius, inquiring about further orders. Demetrius waved a hand dismissively. The dullahan turned his steed and trotted back into the forest, his form fading with each step.

The ring of beckoners parted for him. Those closest passed their pricked fingers through his incorporeal form, offering their blood both to Muginn and the victor of the battle.

Jin and Demetrius stood, offered each other respectful bows, and returned to the edge of the ring. As with the deadeyes, there were a few more beckoner battles. When Prue pushed her rank from centurion to gladiator, her team cheered for her. Morpheus worked his way around the circle to join them and Ashleen's chest hurt when he kissed Prue. It didn't seem so long ago that she would have done the same.

It wasn't until Izzy leaned in and asked if she was alright that she realized she was clenching her fists. Ashleen struggled to release the tension she held in her shoulders and made a noncommittal noise.

This wasn't time for another meltdown, especially with this many witnesses.

When the beckoners had dispersed, Ivanoff called the vespers into the center. Morpheus reluctantly abandoned his congratulatory kissing of Prue to join the rest of his class in the center of what was now a vibrant garden. The air hung heavy with the scent of jasmine. Ashleen followed the rest of her team to the edges of the clearing to sit on mosaiced benches.

Rather than circling up quickly like the previous classes had, the vespers mingled. They exchanged light touches and the occasional kiss as if it were nothing more than saying hello. Ashleen decided she hated it.

She glanced at Ivanoff and Rome, but neither warden seemed fazed by the display. Rome hadn't said a word this whole time, but Ashleen had seen him tending to Misty and the others that had suffered defeats.

By the time the vespers fell into the loose semblance of a circle the air hummed with energy. Ashleen's heart fell clean out of her body when the knight captain stepped into the center. Pavane's jaded gaze scorched Ashleen's skin as it raked over her.

When no one challenged for the title, he slunk back to his place in the loop with a smug smirk.

There was a long pause before Sushila lifted her chin and stepped into the center. She threw down a gauntlet.

At first, Ashleen thought no one would accept. Then Pavane reentered to scoop it up. Dread flashed across Sushila's face. A few vespers cast distasteful glances at the captain behind his back.

Even Ivanoff seemed displeased, "That's unnecessary. One of the other knights can answer."

"I didn't see anyone else offering."

Ivanoff huffed out a sigh. "Fine. But if she beats you, I'm giving her the title."

Pavane snorted, "I'd like to see her try."

Sushila kept a stiff upper lip, but Ashleen could see the trepidation in her eyes. She cleared her throat, and began to recite clear verses with perfect enunciation.

Pavane met her word for word in the lilting cadence of a language Ashleen couldn't identify.

Dahei muttered something in Japanese, and Demetrius answered haltingly. She raised an eyebrow at them.

"He is toying with her," Demetrius supplied before she could ask. "That is a divine dialect."

"It's how he keeps his rank," Dahei interjected. "That language is spoken by sidhe, and presumably by the gods. He's the only human who can speak it. Nobody even knows how he learned."

Sushila began to suck rapid breaths between her teeth as she rushed to keep up with him. Pavane's mouth curled into a savage smirk. Ashleen wanted to see him spit blood.

Morpheus seemed bored by the display. He exaggerated the roll of one shoulder, and the jacket he wore slipped off it.

"Is he honestly always like this?" Ashleen whispered to her team.

Izzy followed her gaze and raised his eyebrows. "Well done Morpheus," he murmured, "Watch Pavane."

Pavane continued his hymn, but his attention had drifted from Sushila to Morpheus. He stumbled over a word and Sushila took her chance. She drove a wedge through his focus with a rapid verse in a completely new language.

Pavane fought to save face, but it was too late. Ivanoff blew a blast on her whistle.

"That was cheating," he snarled.

If Ivanoff had seen anything, she gave no sign of it. "What was cheating? Everything I heard was completely legal."

Sushila lifted her chin. "He can keep his title, Mrs. Ivanoff. Knight is all I want for now."

Pavane ignored her. He threw a gauntlet at the ground so hard it bounced off. "Morpheus."

Morpheus held up his hands, "I'm just a gladiator, I don't stand a chance."

"Damn straight you don't," Pavane hissed and spun on his heel, striding back to his place in the circle.

Morpheus maintained a serene smile, but curled his hands into fists and stuffed them into his pockets. When Ivanoff finally dismissed the vespers, they de-escalated via another bout of mingling.

Ashleen would have expected Morpheus to join his peers, but he broke away immediately and headed straight to them.

"Nice play, with the shoulder," Dahei told him, "I wouldn't have guessed it would work so well."

Morpheus' voice was thin. "He's sort of predictable when you get to know him."

"Heads up," Ashleen warned. Pavane escaped the fray and strode toward them with purpose.

He raised a hand in greeting and Morpheus stepped back into her space with a noticeable flinch.

"Hey--" she started to protest, but stopped when Dahei, Izzy, and Demetrius closed ranks around them.

"Tsk, tsk, Pavane," Dahei started, drawing out the syllables of his name mockingly. "I thought you were a professional. But here you are getting distracted by shoulders like a horny high schooler."

Pavane ignored Dahei's jab, his focus on Morpheus unwavering. He rubbed a thumb across his lower lip. "You got something you wanna say to me?"

"People like you don't deserve titles," Morpheus spat.

"Oh?" he purred, "I was expecting something more along the lines of an apology, but if you're so bent out of shape over my title, why don't you... take it from me?"

"You know I can't."

"You know," Pavane mocked Morpheus' tone, "I think you're lying."

Morpheus pressed his lips into a line and didn't answer.

Pavane chuckled mirthlessly. "You always cower behind others. I can't be the only one wondering what you really sound like when you don't hold back."

"Pavane," Izzy's tone took a dangerous edge that made the hair on the back of Ashleen's neck stand up. "Quick reminder: I can kill a man from a mile away. If you threaten Morpheus again, you won't see me before your body hits the ground."

Pavane laughed like he'd been joking the whole time. "Your friends are so serious. You must be bored out of your mind. When you finally snap, you know where to find me." He swept one more scathing glance over Ashleen, and sauntered away from them.

6

The Wolf in the Shadows

Ashleen hated the way Pavane looked at her, as if he could see straight through her clothes. Like he was cataloging her flaws, or calculating her measurements. What had he done that had Morpheus flinching like that? How much longer before he tried it on her? Or Prue?

"Are you okay?" Izzy mouthed at her.

Ashleen blinked rapidly and nodded. He jerked his thumb over his shoulder towards the center of the room.

Before she could catch his meaning, Ivanoff barked her name. "Ms. Gallagher. Were you planning on joining us or is the ranking system beneath you?"

"No ma'am. I'm sorry," She took her place with the others on the large padded floor mat.

"You get points for not wasting my time with excuses. Try to keep them by not delaying this session again."

The tranq knight captain prowled into the middle. She was short––Ashleen wasn't sure she even cleared five feet––but her body rippled with muscle. Her auburn hair was caught in a rushed loop that barely qualified as a bun. Every move she made was an open challenge to underestimate her and pay the price. Unsurprisingly, no one took up the challenge.

When she left the floor, Ivanoff waved Ashleen forward. "Let's get you ranked then. Centurions?"

"Hiya!" A chubby girl with bobbed mousy hair jogged to join Ashleen and assumed a loose boxer's stance. "Name's Gwen. You ready, fledgling?"

Ashleen had spotted Pavane in the spectators. He was whispering something to an Asian tranq who seemed to hate her just as much.

"I said, are you ready?" Gwen said, raising her voice.

Ashleen bared her teeth. "What are you waiting for?"

Gwen took a swing at her. She could have dodged the blow, but instead Ashleen took it, hoping the pain would clear her head. All at once she knew she'd made a mistake. A headache stabbed at her temples as the beast in her veins roared, fighting the chains she'd bound it with.

She should withdraw. They could do this another time, when she was safe to be around. When she tried to call off the fight, she gagged on the words. The jaws of her monster closed around her throat.

When she could breathe again, she had Gwen pinned to the mat in a rough submission hold.

"Let go! Let go! I've had enough! I'm done!" Tears rolled freely down Gwen's round cheeks.

Ashleen released her as if she'd been burned and rolled several yards away. She pressed the heels of her hands into her eye sockets and tried to scoop the anger out of her head. "Sorry," she managed.

Ivanoff barked a warning, but when she uncovered her face, Rome was the one leaning over her.

"Can you hear me?" he asked.

"Is Gwen okay?" She blinked and Rome had moved.

Ivanoff answered, "She'll live. You might not. Gladiators! Are you just going to take that or are you going to put this fledging in her place?"

Something was wrong. She couldn't remember anything after Gwen had hit her. She'd blacked out before, but after what had happened on Prue's birthday, the occurrence made her nervous. She opened her mouth to call for a break but couldn't get the words out.

Ivanoff didn't seem like the pitying type and Ashleen was already a hair's breadth from her bad side. She had the feeling any explanation she tried to give would be received like an excuse.

She could do this. Ashleen hadn't spent all her life with anger management specialists just to start giving in now. She took a deep breath, counted to ten, and forced herself back to her feet.

Izzy scrutinized Ashleen's sway as she stood. Something was off. The fight had lasted seconds, but she shook and her breaths were uneven. He could see sweat beginning to glisten on her upper lip.

"Did Ashleen take her pills?"

Dahei frowned, "How should I know? I'm not her babysitter. Morpheus?"

"You think I am?" Morpheus countered. "She was up before me."

Ashleen clapped her hands over her ears when Ivanoff blew her whistle. The piercing sound made the edges of her vision pulse red. Vaguely, she was aware that Leo had joined her on the mat.

The beast she'd locked away gnawed on the bars of its cage. Ashleen tried to ignore the shriek of metal in her head. Her opponent circled her, unaware of the savage wolf that hung in his shadow, breathing down his neck.

Her heart stopped. She'd seen this shape before, on the man that hurt Prue. It growled her name. She cast an imploring look about the room and settled on Rome, but if he noticed the creature, he didn't show it.

The wolf loomed outward, and the same voice she'd heard in her dream about Prue's death addressed her. "How long do you think they will pretend to accept you? Your friends will always abandon you when they learn the truth. But I won't. I'll always be here. All you have to do... is listen."

"What's she looking at?" Izzy asked. Nobody had an answer for him. "Demetrius, do you sense anything?"

"Nothing unusual."

"Something's wrong." Izzy took a few steps along the edge of the crowd, trying to catch a better look at Ashleen's face.

"Like what?" Dahei asked, falling in step beside him.

"I don't know, she keeps twitching. It's like she's hearing or seeing something we can't." Izzy watched her eerily imitate Leo's movements without looking at him, "This looks like possession, but Demetrius doesn't sense anything."

"Maybe we should call off the fight?" Morpheus suggested, clearly unsettled.

Before any of them could, a bellowing roar that didn't seem human ripped itself from Ashleen's throat. Her fingers curled around Leo's neck and she lifted him off his feet.

Ivanoff was the first one to react, but she wasn't fast enough. Ashleen slammed Leo into the floor. His skull hit the mat so hard even Izzy saw stars.

Ivanoff put herself between Leo and Ashleen, her claymore materializing at her fingertips. "Leo, you still alive back there?"

"I'm fine." He didn't sound fine, but Izzy let out a breath he didn't realize he'd been holding when Leo rolled up to his hands and knees.

Ashleen snarled when he tried to move further away. Izzy pulled a tranquilizer gun from the air and shouldered through the ring of tranqs for a clear shot.

He settled behind and slightly to Leo's right. "Ivanoff, keep the close range fighters back."

Ivanoff made a disapproving noise but backed away. Ashleen ignored her as if she hadn't even noticed her approach in the first place.

"Morpheus and Sushila, leave the sim. See if you can get her back under control." Izzy ordered. He didn't check to see if they complied.

Leo tried to distance himself from Ashleen and she lunged for him, stopping herself mere inches from his throat.

Izzy raised an eyebrow. She was fighting the rage that had overtaken her. He'd never seen a tranq succeed or even try to do the same at this stage. "Leo, don't move."

"Yeah, I got it," Leo answered through grit teeth.

Izzy leaned between Leo and Ashleen, hoping to block her view. "Ashleen, can you hear me?"

She stared at him with unblinking eyes, her pupils blown wide, blinded by rage and adrenaline. She continued to tremble and Izzy couldn't tell if that meant she was gearing up to attack or fighting for control. Perhaps it was both.

Izzy was no vesper, but he fought to keep his tone low and even. "You have to get a grip on this or I will put you out." In truth, he didn't know how effective tranquilizers would be. He didn't want to shoot her, but if she didn't believe the darts would work, they might not. The only other way to put her out would be to convince her she was dead. He hoped it wouldn't go that far.

"Your new fledgling giving you trouble, Izzy?" Izzy narrowed his eyes and Pavane laughed.

"Now isn't a great time, Jun."

"No? I thought it was perfect." A tall man with dark hair and slanted eyes accompanied Pavane into the circle.

"You should stay back."

Jun scoffed, "Worried I'll break your new toy?"

"Worried she'll break yours." Izzy kept his eyes on Ashleen, but gestured at Pavane.

Even as he made the gesture, Ashleen seemed to realize Pavane's presence. She leaned towards him, and for a split second, Izzy wondered if he would pull the trigger, or if he'd let her rip Pavane apart.

"Leo, move."

This time, when Leo began to slip away, Ashleen ignored him. She took a step towards Pavane, and Jun growled at her.

Izzy cursed and traded his tranquilizer gun for something more lethal. "As much as I'd like to watch her tear you two apart, I don't think she'd forgive me. Take your vesper and go."

Jun narrowed his eyes at them, but he was smart enough to know Izzy was right. "For the record, you wouldn't be having this problem if you hadn't kicked me off your team." He grabbed Pavane's upper arm and turned to lead him away.

Ashleen lunged. Izzy took his shot and breathed a quick prayer that Anshathane wasn't ready to surrender her to Muginn just yet as the bullet tore through her chest.

Ashleen violently broke from the sim and lashed out at the blurred shapes of people she couldn't quite see. A startled noise halfway between human and whale shoved her back under as Morpheus struggled to subdue her.

Ashleen gasped for air and fluid filled her lungs as she fought the feeling of drowning and clawed her way towards clarity. The addition of Sushila's thrumming wine glass froze over the lake she'd been thrust into and trapped her in its depths.

When Ashleen woke a second time, it was with a head full of cotton and a dull ache in her chest that she had to struggle to breathe through. She couldn't decide whether or not she was glad that she could remember what had transpired. On the one hand, she hadn't repeated the events of Prue's birthday. On the other, she couldn't shake the words she'd heard in her head. What if the wolf was right? How could her peers trust her if she attacked them at the drop of a hat?

She forced her eyes open and recognized her surroundings as Neele's infirmary. When she worked her way into a sitting position, Izzy heaved a sigh of relief.

"Thank the Raven. You scared us all half to death." He said, leaning forward in the seat he'd borrowed from one of the other stations.

Ashleen flinched. She didn't deserve his relief. He should be mad at her. Any normal person would be.

"For a while there, I thought we'd lost you."

"How's Leo?" Ashleen rubbed at her face, hiding in her hands while she cleared her head.

"Sore, but I think his ego is bruised worse than he is."

"Ash!" Prue came around the corner. She ran the last three steps to Ashleen's bedside.

Ashleen avoided looking at her, suddenly finding the wrinkles in her sheets fascinating.

"Izzy told me you missed a dose."

"I guess so." She mentally kicked her herself. She'd only been here two days and they were already going to throw her out. She couldn't do anything right.

"It doesn't happen often," Izzy stated. "But I've heard high ranked tranqs can react violently to skipped doses."

Ashleen supposed she should thank him for his attempt to soften the blow of what she'd done, even if it didn't help.

"How did you manage to get me out?" She'd never had anyone manage to break her free of a rage before it had run its course before.

Izzy scratched the back of his head. "Made a gamble."

Ashleen peered at him, "What sort of gamble?"

"The sort where you bet the will of the gods against two vespers and hope for the best." he replied, shrugging.

"He means he killed you and crossed his fingers," Prue translated, shooting a glare at Izzy.

"What?!"

"It was a sim! Morpheus and Sushila had it under control. Besides, it was that or let you kill everyone else. Would you have wanted that?"

Ashleen sighed. He was right. "Thank you."

The thud of Neele's combat boots announced her arrival. "Good, you're awake. You had me worried."

"I'm sorry." Ashleen wasn't sure if she was apologizing for making Neele worry, or for what she'd done. Neele deserved apologies for both.

"How are you feeling? Look here," Neele demanded, shining a bright light at each of Ashleen's eyes in turn.

"Sore, but I'll live." Ashleen replied, blinking the colored spots from her vision.

"I'm glad. I hate to cut the festivities short, but the Archwarden asked to see you as soon as you are able."

Ashleen's heart skipped a beat. This was it, she was being thrown out. Though her experience with prison hadn't been that bad, after a taste of Alexandria she wasn't sure she could go back to her old life. Even if they sent her home instead of to prison, she would only languish about the house.

She loved her mother, but Alice often struggled to understand how detrimental her hovering could be. Ashleen had grown up coddled, confined to the property like it was an ivory tower. She'd never rebelled against the rules because she understood they were to protect her as much as they were to protect everyone else.

If she'd screwed up this colossally at home, her mother would have cut all ties and moved them to a new state. Ashleen wouldn't have been surprised if Alice had changed their names and made her dye her hair.

No one on her team was even mad at her. Of course they didn't have the final say, but Ashleen promised herself that if the Archwarden gave her a second chance, she'd never let something like this happen again.

She drew in a steadying breath. Time to rip the bandaid off. "Where can I find her?"

The hall she crossed to reach the city center was at least three times as long as any she'd crossed so far. Ashleen had to resist dropping to her hands and knees and crawling the whole way. Somehow she managed, but by the time she could reach the activation panel on the door frame, her heart was in her throat.

The inside of the Archwarden's office was unlike anything Ashleen had seen elsewhere in Alexandria. The circular room boasted a palette of warm beiges and creams with expensive antique furnishings Ashleen imagined her grandmother would have collected. A hidden radio played a classical piano piece Ashleen could almost place. The Archwarden's cat watched from atop one of several full bookshelves.

She resisted the urge to inspect the collected titles and focused on the magnificent desk at the center of the room. The Archwarden sat behind it in a red velvet armchair. She wore a fluffy sweater and kept her silver hair knotted low on the back of her neck.

When she noticed Ashleen, she slipped off her glasses and dropped them to dangle on a chain about her neck. She waved Ashleen over. Ashleen took a seat in the plush chair opposite the desk and fidgeted with the doily draped over the armrest.

"Tea? Cookies?"

"Ma'am?"

The Archwarden chuckled, "Amaris is fine. Do you like honey?"

Ashleen hesitated, then nodded. She wasn't about to be impolite.

Amaris stirred a spoonful of honey into Ashleen's teacup and gestured to a plate of cookies. "Please help yourself."

Ashleen cradled the teacup in her hands, hoping to bolster herself with its warmth. "How much trouble am I in?"

"Trouble? My dear you're not in any trouble at all." Amaris looked offended that the thought had even occurred to Ashleen. "You must think me a terrible host, if you assume I would throw you out over a mistake. All the tranqs miss a dose once in a while. Busy on a hunt, overslept, just plain forgot.

Admittedly most of them don't react quite as strongly as you do, but it would be rather judgemental of me to punish you over an offense so small just because of a difference in biology, don't you think?"

"I suppose," Ashleen mulled over Amaris' statement. Leo had made it sound as if missing a dose was a highly punishable offence. Perhaps he had been mistaken. Maybe it had been so long since anyone reacted like she did that most cases flew under the radar and exaggerated stories were all that was left.

As if she'd read Ashleen's mind, Amaris continued, "It is true that if you continue to miss doses, or intentionally stop taking the tranquilizers, I will have to respond more firmly. An unfettered tranq can do a lot of damage in a setting like this, I'm sure you understand."

Ashleen nodded enthusiastically, "Of course. I'm relieved no one was hurt."

"I'm glad we agree." Amaris nudged the cookie plate closer to Ashleen, "Please, I shouldn't finish them all by myself."

Ashleen resisted the urge to laugh and took a cookie. They were still warm, and the chocolate melted in her mouth when she nibbled it.

"I meant to meet you the day you arrived, unfortunately, Alexandria has kept me quite busy of late. I had hoped that you would join us sooner, but perhaps it was not meant to be."

"I found the letter you sent my mother. To be fair, I doubt it would have been a good idea for her to send me here when I was four."

Amaris chuckled, "I suppose you're right. But I wanted her to know she had options, if raising you became... too much for her to handle alone."

"Because I'm a tranq?" Ashleen asked, thumbing the lip of her teacup. She was well aware she hadn't been the easiest to raise, but her mother had always disagreed with her when she'd said as much. It stung to hear her concerns confirmed.

Amaris inclined her head. "Yes, most huntsmen can be rather trying on their parents, with the exception of deadeyes and scofflaws. I anticipated more strain on your mother, since she did not share in your abilities. But she surprised me. Of course she had quite a few questions."

Ashleen's brow furrowed. She hadn't been aware of further correspondence between Amaris and her mother. "What do you mean?"

"She never showed you the other letters?"

Ashleen shook her head.

"That's odd," Amaris stated. "I would've thought she'd want you to know the details of what happened to your father."

"I didn't think she knew." Her chest felt tight. Ashleen and her mother occasionally had disagreements, sure, but she'd never suspected that she'd been lied to. She'd always assumed her mother's silence with regards to her father was due to pain, not secrets.

"Your father approached me a bit before the incident. He told me he had seen something, that the tranqs, we called them berserkers back then, were beginning to behave strangely. He suspected the issue traced all the way back to Anshathane himself."

"The god?" Even after she'd found out about her class and how it connected to the wolf deity, it hadn't occurred to Ashleen that her rages were anything more than a fluke of genetics.

"Yes," Amaris said as she stirred another spoonful of honey into her tea. "I didn't believe him at the time. It wasn't much later that all my berserkers turned on me. He was killed in the resulting chaos. It has taken us years to rebuild, but the development of tranquilizers greatly stabilized the tranqs as a class."

Ashleen hadn't given Anshathane much thought before this point. She knew he was Muginn's mate, and Ikalusca's father, but the one church her hometown had in his honor was dilapidated and empty. She knew he was a god of war, healing, and protection. He'd also been associated with agriculture and sovereignty.

She'd mostly seen him described as a benevolent deity, less prone to meddling than Ikalusca and Muginn both. She'd heard tales of his battle frenzies, most often triggered when those under his protection were harmed.

"I wanted to talk about what you saw." Amaris interrupted Ashleen's train of thought.

"What I saw?"

"Your father said he could see Anshathane more clearly when he raged. I was hoping you might have seen something similar." Amaris explained, sipping her tea thoughtfully.

Ashleen remembered the dark shadow she'd seen stalking Leo. She'd seen it before, the night Prue had been attacked. It had spoken this time, with the same voice she'd heard in her dreams. Up until this point, she'd thought the voice was Prue's. Now, she wasn't so sure. "Maybe... what does he look like?"

"You'd know better than I."

"I saw... something," Ashleen paused to gather her thoughts. "There's this... dark shape that talks to me sometimes when I lose control."

"How long has this occurred?" Amaris pulled a pen and notepad from her desk and began to jot things down.

"I've only seen it twice. First the night I was arrested. Then again earlier today. It's sort of like a wolf, but much bigger, and wrong somehow. It feels evil."

"Interesting," Amaris mused. She finished her notes and set aside her pen, "I'd like to put you on the fast track towards an archknight ranking."

Ashleen gaped at her. "What? I've only been here two days!"

Amaris held up a placating hand, "I know it's sudden, but I have confidence in your abilities. For now you will continue your regular activities. Do you have any questions?"

Ashleen had enough questions she could have filled a book. "Why me? Don't you already have someone more experienced?"

"Unfortunately, no. Connor was the last person to hold the position of Vanquisher. Tranqs have only recently stabilized since his death. I'm hoping your ability to sense Anshathane can guide us to him."

"You want to find Anshathane?" Ashleen stared at her incredulously, "He's a god, if he doesn't want to be found there's nothing I can do about it."

"What if he was already in the city? All I'm asking is that if you sense anything strange, or if you have more visions like this, you report them to me."

"Let's assume for a minute that I succeed in locating him. What then?"

Amaris steepled her fingers and frowned. "I'm still working on that. Before the incident, berserkers were able to control their rages. Now that all of you can feel Anshathane's battle cry in your bones, your will belongs to him. Tranquilizers will only work for so long."

"Great, so not only do you want me to move against a god, you want me to move against one that already has partial control of me? How am I supposed to fight that?"

"Traditionally the only way to fight a god is with another god. But Muginn has been silent for decades, and Ikalusca is too weakened by the injuries he suffered in the first conflict to fight his father directly."

Ashleen gestured emphatically, her voice slipping up an octave. "So we're just screwed?"

"Maybe not. Your father believed a complete archknight team might be able to compete with a weakened Anshathane."

Ashleen doubted that. She didn't see how a human, even an extraordinary one, could compete against a god. "How?"

"With this." Amaris reached into her desk and held up a strange vial for Ashleen to examine.

Black oil sloshed about inside the glass, creeping up the sides as if it wanted to escape.

She'd read descriptions of ichor, but it had been scarce long before cameras were invented. All she had to go on any more were artists' sketches. Even the most detailed work couldn't hold a candle to the real thing.

There was something distinctly unearthly about the fluid in the vial. It was easy to believe it had come from a god. The ichor moved as if the laws of physics didn't apply. If she watched closely, it almost seemed to have intent, like it was just intelligent enough to realize it was contained and seek an exit.

"That's not--"

"Ichor? I assure you it is. All of my archknights are given this much, with it they can do things no human could achieve. However, the procedure isn't without risk. Ichor has a will all its own, and until I am sure yours is stronger, I cannot give this to you."

The wary part of Ashleen argued that this wasn't a good idea, but her father had done it. While he'd been gone long enough that she didn't feel the need to avenge his death, defeating Anshathane offered more than that.

If she could find him, perhaps they wouldn't need to fight at all. Perhaps he could be reasoned with. If she could negotiate the release of the tranqs from the rages, it might be worth the risk to accept Amaris offer.

She'd decided to sleep on it. There was so much to think about and she was still exhausted from her experience in the sim. Once her head had hit the pillow, her eyes fluttered shut and she'd gone out like a light.

Whale song played at the edges of her subconscious, and someone's fingers weaving through her hair drove her upright in bed. Nobody was there; she must have caught the edge of a dream.

She swung her legs out over the edge of the mattress and rubbed at her face, yawning. She shook one of her pills out into her hand and took it dry. By now whatever Neele had given her would be wearing off and Ashleen definitely didn't need a repeat of this morning.

She eyed the bedroom door and chewed her lip. Izzy hadn't seemed upset with her, but that didn't account for the others. Her team and Leo's seemed to be close. If they considered her attack a betrayal, she wasn't sure she would blame them.

Ashleen forced herself to stand and padded over to the door. She turned the knob as quietly as she could and slipped through, hesitating in the shadows to listen.

"She just ignored the hypnosis," Morpheus was saying, "She pushed me away like swatting a fly."

"She was still raging," Izzy countered.

"I've dealt with raging tranqs. Besides, she's resisted me before without raging."

If Izzy found that detail to be of any interest, he didn't show it. "Look, I know where your head is. I need you to keep it in the game."

Morpheus sighed, "I know, but you don't know what it's like to care about someone and watch their eyes cloud over when they look at you. Even Prue has started doing it now."

Ashleen didn't need to hear any more. She silently opened her bedroom door and closed it again with an audible click to reinforce the illusion that she'd just gotten up.

When she stepped out into the main area, Izzy and Morpheus were on one of the couches with their backs to her. Morpheus hummed something to himself while he kneaded at Izzy's scarred shoulder.

"Hey you," Izzy greeted her as she came around the couch to face them. "How you doin'?"

Ashleen folded her arms across her stomach, "Actually, I feel pretty horrible."

"Sorry," Morpheus paused his humming to speak, "Sometimes hypnosis has side effects."

"It's not that," Ashleen countered, pushing the cobwebs of her dream from her mind. "I know you said Leo was okay but..."

Izzy smiled. "You're worried we're mad at you."

Ashleen nodded and dug her fingernails into her arms.

"No one is holding a grudge, Ashleen."

She wasn't convinced, but it didn't seem like a good time to argue.

Izzy patted the couch in front of him. "Come, sit. Dahei and Demetrius will be back soon with dinner."

Ashleen shyly sat on the couch across from them. From this angle, she had a clear view of Morpheus' hands while he worked. His thin, elegant fingers reminded her of Prue's, with the exception of his lack of ring. She scowled, but couldn't work up the courage to ask about it.

Dahei's arrival saved her from continued silence. He deposited a pizza tray on the coffee table and flopped onto the other couch. Demetrius took a seat next to him with far more grace and dismissed his butterflies.

"Perfect timing," Izzy said, pulling himself away from Morpheus and leaning forward to retrieve a slice.

Ashleen grabbed her own piece and inspected it. It seemed homemade and the vegetables looked fresh, presumably from the gardens. She wondered if there was livestock in Alexandria, or if the city had connections somewhere on the ground.

Dahei passed a slice of pizza to Demetrius, then addressed Ashleen. "The guy you killed, was he your first?"

"What?" Ashleen sputtered.

"Do not be so rude!" Demetrius scolded him.

Dahei rolled his eyes.

"And do not roll your eyes at me."

"We're criminals!" Dahei scoffed, "They recruit us out of prison. The overwhelming majority of us are murderers."

Morpheus shot Dahei a reproachful look, "I'm not."

Dahei gestured at Morpheus with his slice of pizza. "Hey, you don't remember."

"We need to have a talk about your manners." Demetrius frowned in the direction of Dahei's voice.

Dahei curled his lip, "You're the one that told me talking about things makes people feel better. I was trying to make friends."

His question had caught Ashleen off guard, but she understood what he was trying to do. In encouraging them to share their stories, Dahei was putting them on even footing. He knew she felt guilty, and he was trying to help in his own way.

"I'll share if everyone else does," she started, "but I'm not going first."

For a moment, no one spoke, surprised that she'd agreed. Izzy broke the silence, "Alright, I was born in the Australian prison colonies."

Ashleen had heard of them. They'd been established centuries ago by Britain, but their original purpose had long since been forgotten. Though no country had publicly laid a claim to them in over a century, they remained one of the most secure institutions on the planet.

"My father was born there too," Izzy went on. "We used to guess whose crime first got us in. Are we descendants of serial killers? Freedom fighters? Government spies?" He laughed mirthlessly. "Nobody knows."

"That's horrible!" Ashleen said.

Izzy shrugged, "It's a different culture. I grew up in a gang, surrounded by guns we stole from the guards. Never thought much about what it meant to pull a trigger 'til I got here. Probably killed more people than I remember."

"How do you manage the guilt?" Ashleen asked, her stomach twisted just thinking about it.

"Don't have any," Izzy answered. "Like I said, it's a different culture. Kill or be killed. Why do you have guilt?"

Ashleen wasn't sure how to answer. She'd grown up used to people whispering when she entered a room. She'd fought hard to prove they had nothing to fear from her. All of it had come crashing down in one night.

"I don't care that he's dead," she began. "I care that it proved people right about me. And I care that it didn't save Prue."

"She doesn't blame you," Morpheus tried to reassure her, but Ashleen bristled.

"I know that! Maybe I blame myself."

"Don't you think that's a little selfish? You clearly want her forgiveness, but when she offers it you won't take it. It's like you're having too much fun punishing yourself."

"Our relationship is none of your business!"

Morpheus opened his mouth to argue, but Dahei interrupted. "From what I've heard, the guy deserved it. Maybe worse."

When no one spoke, he went on, "Izzy and I have similar stories. I come from a large family. I have two younger brothers, and my grandmother lives with us. My mother does most of the housework, so my father was the only one providing income."

"As I got older I wanted to help bring in a little extra money, but I fell in with a bad crowd. It started with petty theft, but then I stole from the wrong person and ended up on the bad side of the local yakuza boss."

Ashleen pushed her hot embarrassment at Morpheus' accusation aside and focused on Dahei's story, biting down on the inside of her cheek.

Dahei spun his coral ring around his finger. "If his son, Hideo, hadn't taken a liking to me, I'd probably be dead. Hideo suggested I should work off my debts by collecting them from others. For a while everything ran smoothly, but things got complicated."

Demetrius shifted, his leg pressing up against Dahei's in a subtle show of support.

"The boss didn't like me much when he discovered our relationship. I lost Hideo in the 2011 tsunami, but his father blamed me when the body washed up. He sent people after me. I killed some of them, but I was running out of places to go when the Archwarden picked me up."

Ashleen wanted to say something comforting, but she didn't have the words. Dahei didn't seem like he was in a place to hear them anyways.

Demetrius started his story, saving them from the settling silence. "The village I'm from burned down."

Ashleen pressed her lips together. Clearly the mood wasn't about to lighten. While she knew Dahei's intentions had been kind, she was beginning to have regrets.

"My people have a rite of passage when we are seventeen. Around that time, I began to see the ghosts of my ancestors. I thought it was a blessing, but they became angry. It frightened me, so I told them to return where they came from.

I thought they had gone, but when my rites were complete, our dead rose from their graves. They attacked us; we did not have a way to fight them. Most of the women among my people are beckoners, but none of them were strong enough to break the command I had given."

"When my parents died, I turned to the gods for help. The Raven answered me. They said they would correct my mistake, for a price. The dead stopped rising. But it cost me my eyes, and the souls of everyone who had been affected by my curse. Only my newborn twin sisters and I were left.

The divine activity drew attention. The Archwarden found me. She arranged for my sisters to be adopted by a couple in the Americas. They are ten now."

"I'm glad they're safe," Ashleen murmured, pleased that the end turned out somewhat happy.

"Me too. Eventually I hope to rebuild." Unlike Dahei, Demetrius' mood remained even. As dismal as his story was, it didn't seem to weigh on him.

"So, you don't blame yourself either?" Ashleen asked. She couldn't imagine what it would be like to have the blood of half her family and an entire village of innocents on her hands. She'd never sleep again.

"I did not say that, but..." Demetrius gestured to his blindfold, "I have no tears to shed. And dwelling in the past will not change the future."

"You're such a fortune cookie." Dahei commented. In spite of his grief, the corners of his mouth twitched upward.

Demetrius grinned, "Are you ever going to tell me what that is?"

"Never," Dahei stabbed a finger at Ashleen, "And don't you tell him either."

Ashleen held up her hands in surrender, "I won't."

Her attention drifted to the only one who hadn't shared yet. Morpheus was folded into a ball in the corner of the couch as if he wanted everyone to forget he was there.

Ashleen wouldn't allow it, "What about you?"

He winced like she'd slapped him. "I actually uh... can't remember," he admitted.

"Really?" Ashleen pressed incredulously. "Nothing at all?"

Morpheus shook his head. "I woke up in the infirmary and Neele told me my name was Morpheus. Beyond that, there's nothing."

He worried his lower lip between his teeth. He'd lied. Or was withholding details. Ashleen was sure of it, but he still hadn't told them about her hitting him. She owed him her silence.

"What time is it?" Ashleen asked instead.

"Just after ten," Izzy answered. "You should all get some rest. It's been a long day and tomorrow won't be any easier."

7

Aberwich

A quiet knock drew Ashleen away from her blanket sanctuary before she was ready to leave. She opened the door a crack and peered through groggily. Morpheus was standing on the other side. Ashleen remembered her dream and felt his fingers creep through her hair. She shut the door again without a word.

"I brought coffee," Morpheus said, his voice muffled by the door.

She sighed and composed herself, then opened the door again.

He held out the mug to her wordlessly, she took it and swirled the contents, remembering how nasty the stuff had been.

"What do you want?"

Ashleen saw a flirty quip die in his eyes as he thought better of it. Good. "Prue wanted to talk to you this morning. And I wanted to apologize for what I said last night."

She stepped out into the hall and shut the door. It took her a few seconds to recall what he was apologizing for. "Is that all?"

He stepped back and nodded. "You were right, your relationship with Prue isn't my business. I didn't mean to impose."

Part of her didn't want to accept his apology, but resenting him for his relationship with her ex was childish. She heaved a sigh, "I'm sorry for reacting as harshly as I did."

Her mind began to clear as she inhaled the scent wafting from the coffee mug. She narrowed her eyes at Morpheus. Something was different about him, but she couldn't put her finger on it.

Morpheus glanced down at himself, confusion etched in his features. "What? Do I have lipstick on my face?"

"You were taller than me yesterday. Now you're not."

"Oh," Morpheus chuckled, "Shoes."

Ashleen glanced at his bare feet. "Shoes?"

At her perplexed expression, he crossed the hall to his room and returned holding up a boot with a four-inch wedge heel.

"What?"

"Dahei makes fun of me too, but I like them."

Ashleen wasn't the type to judge, but imagining Dahei's jokes had her suppressing a giggle in a sip of coffee. She stared into the mug in surprise. It tasted good.

Morpheus awaited her reaction apprehensively, "Did I get it right?"

"Yeah," Ashleen admitted, taking another sip. "I didn't think it was possible."

"I'd like to take all the credit, but Prue told me how you used to like it."

Ashleen narrowed her eyes at him. Bringing her coffee as part of an apology didn't seem so strange, but collecting information about her from her ex was. "Are you using Prue to hit on me?"

"It was her suggestion!" Morpheus stammered. "It's a peace offering."

Ashleen pressed her lips together and gave him a disapproving scowl. "She's your girlfriend, you know. You ought to treat her with more respect."

He opened and closed his mouth, grasping for an answer. She didn't wait for him to find one. She downed the rest of her coffee and took one of her tranquilizers. Prue wanted to talk, fine. They would talk. Ashleen would make sure she knew all about her preferred partner's questionable behavior.

She stormed through the common area and slammed the hatch closed behind her. Dahei looked up from the gory action flick he'd been watching and raised an eyebrow. He glanced at Morpheus, standing stunned in the hall.

"Dude what did you say?"

Ashleen dumped the empty mug in a bus tub and gritted her teeth. The idea of speaking to Prue again set her nerves on edge. Their last exchange hadn't gone well, and no matter how she tried, she couldn't shake her lingering bitterness over Prue and Morpheus' relationship.

She supposed she should get something to eat, but none of the food available could satisfy her nervous urge to break things. She settled on toast, which could at least be torn into tiny pieces.

Out the corner of her eye, she saw Prue waving excitedly at her. Ashleen grumbled, stalked over to the table, and aggressively pulled up a chair. Its legs scraped loudly over the floor. "Your boyfriend is a pigeon."

"Sure you aren't just jealous?"

The way Prue's eyes crinkled at the corners when she smiled made Ashleen's heart ache. Of course she was jealous, but she wasn't about to admit it. "Of who?"

"Maybe him. Maybe me. Pretty sure both of us are your type," Prue shrugged.

Ashleen snorted and changed the subject. "What do you want?"

Prue pushed another mug of coffee towards Ashleen with the tip of her finger. "You've been avoiding me since you got here. I was hoping we could talk about things."

"Why?" Ashleen wrapped her hands around the warm mug and stared into it.

"What do you mean, why?" Prue demanded, her brow furrowing.

"We're not getting back together, so why bother making reparations?"

"Because we were friends first! We didn't work out, but it doesn't mean I don't like you." Prue exclaimed. She sat up so emphatically that her coffee sloshed in her mug.

The animated way Prue expressed her feelings brought on a wave of nostalgia and Ashleen blinked back tears. Prue reached across the table and tapped her knuckle. She jerked away from the touch and relaxed her grip on her mug, pretending not to see the hairline cracks she'd sent splitting across the ceramic.

"I know you're upset, but I can't fix it if you won't talk to me."

Ashleen bit the inside of her cheek. It hurt that Prue still knew her so well after all this time, that she could still read feelings Ashleen didn't even know she had.

"I told you what happened to me," Prue continued when she didn't speak. "Why don't you tell me what happened to you?"

"Nothing happened. I was in prison." She didn't want to talk about it. Prue obviously wanted to reconnect, but Ashleen wasn't sure she was ready.

Prue pouted, "That's not what I meant, and I think you know it."

Ashleen took a sip of coffee and didn't respond. Prue wanted her to talk about her feelings, but Ashleen wasn't sure she could dredge them up without drowning in them.

"Why did you tell Morpheus how I liked my coffee?" she asked finally.

Prue perked up, but confusion was evident on her features. "Why wouldn't I? Is your coffee recipe a secret?"

"No," Ashleen scoffed, "but don't you think it's weird that he's asking you about me?"

Prue smiled. "Not really. He has an odd way of going about such things, but I think Morpheus wants to be your friend."

"How did you two meet?" Ashleen wasn't sure she wanted to hear the answer, but the question was already out.

"Morpheus and Demetrius helped with my exorcism," Prue murmured. "He saved my life."

He'd saved Prue's life, but she knew that Prue wouldn't have even been in danger if it weren't for her. Ashleen forged ahead to distract herself from her downward spiral into guilt. "Doesn't it bother you that he flirts with everyone?"

Prue shrugged, "Not really, that's how vespers are."

"Do you ever worry that you're not enough for him? That he's just toying with you until he gets bored?"

Prue wilted. She'd hit a nerve.

"I'm sorry."

"Don't be," she said, blinking away tears, "I think I've shared enough about myself. Your turn, I can't be the only thing that's bothering you."

"My mother lied to me," Ashleen admitted after a pause. It seemed like a safe topic since it had nothing to do with Prue or Morpheus.

"About what?"

"My father, Alexandria, all of it. She knew and she didn't say a thing."

"I'm sorry, that must hurt."

Ashleen bit down on her lip. "A little." She tried to wash down the lump in her throat with another sip of coffee. "The Archwarden invited me to Alexandria when I was still a child. I guess I can understand why my mother might've wanted to wait then, but what about when I was fifteen? Or eighteen? I'm twenty-two now and she still wasn't going to say anything. Why did I have to spend so many years alone, thinking I was some sort of mistake?"

"You've never been a mistake," Prue insisted, "I was there, at least for part of it."

"Yeah, but you've always had other friends. Do you know how much it hurt when you didn't even write? All I had left was my mother, who's been lying to me since the beginning."

"I don't have to be your only friend anymore. Izzy is probably the friendliest person in the whole city. Morpheus will befriend you if you let him. Dahei and Demetrius are sort of a closed unit, but if Demetrius likes you, Dahei will too. My team already likes you."

Ashleen shot her an incredulous look. "Honestly?"

"Okay, you're gonna have to work on Janice. She's standoffish and you hurt her counterweight."

Ashleen flinched. She hadn't realized Janice and Leo were that close.

"But she's a rational person, and Leo already forgave you. She'll come around." Prue checked her watch, "Speaking of which, I'm sorry to cut this short, but my team has a hunt this morning. I have to go."

"I'll see you later then?"

"Of course! I'm glad we could talk."

She watched Prue leave, thumbing the lip of her coffee mug. Maybe this could work. Prue had a point. She didn't have to be Ashleen's only friend, and it was unfair of her to expect Prue to always be there.

It would take time, of course. Ashleen had never been one to shift gears so quickly, but they could work on it. Things would never be the same between them, and maybe that was okay.

Ashleen had a good feeling about the hangar bay, so she let her feet carry her that direction. Izzy hadn't been in the dorm when she woke, nor did she see him in the cafeteria. He'd suggested they had a full day today, so she wondered if her team, like Prue's, would be going somewhere.

Seconds after she stepped into the hangar, a deafening bang startled her. Several huntsmen cast accusatory glances down the hall to Ashleen's right.

She heard Izzy yell, "Sorry!"

Ashleen approached the disturbance, inspecting the mantacraft as she passed them. One was decorated with vibrant Mesoamerican patterns. Another blatantly drew its inspiration from the United States flag. A third seemed to be influenced by old fighter planes.

When she drew up on it, Izzy called her from somewhere to her right. "Hey, Ashleen!"

She turned and spotted him leaning out a door on the side of his ship. Smoke billowed out around him. His goggles were pulled down over his eyes, and he had dark oil stains all the way to his elbows.

Ashleen inspected the ship. It was painted in sleek orange and black patterns. The orange that cut a swath over the wide wings was accented with stylized wolves in a darker shade.

None of the mantacraft were very subtle. "Thank the Raven for stealth tech, huh?" Ashleen said, gesturing at one of them.

Izzy looked up at his ship, "Something like that, but we're probably still to blame for some UFO sightings."

"Wouldn't somebody notice if a lot of the same kind of craft were being reported?"

"Not if they think it's just a hoax."

After a pause, Ashleen continued. "If only some of it is us, what are the other sightings?"

Izzy gestured at her, "That's the question, isn't it?" He wiped his hands on a rag. "Speaking of questions, what brings you out here? Something happen I should know about?"

"No, I was just exploring. Hey, is there a way we can contact family on the surface?"

"Just a sec," Izzy disappeared inside the mantacraft.

When he returned, he handed her a pen-shaped recorder, "You can just write people, but I think it's nice to hear a voice, since we're not allowed to visit."

"How does it work?"

"There are envelopes and a drop box, but watch what you say. The wardens listen to it all before they ship them."

Ashleen grimaced. "That's a violation of privacy."

"Yeah, but they don't have much choice. Top secret military force with no loyalty to any one government? Can't have us discovered by the simple folks."

She didn't like it, but she supposed he was right. Besides, it wasn't like she was going to say anything that would get her in trouble.

"It's not all bad. You'll see more of it when you have a rank. The better you are, the more privileges you get. Reach at least gladiator and Alexandria will send monthly support checks to your family if you want."

Ashleen blinked. She'd heard her mother mention she'd started getting the support checks again, but didn't know who they came from. Her father had been dead for over a decade. "Do they continue the checks if you die in the field?"

"No," Izzy said, shaking his head. "It's a high risk job, that much spending wouldn't be manageable."

"Then who--"

"I did."

Ashleen was silent for a few beats, "Wait, what? Why?"

"Call it a donation in good faith. My father doesn't need money. Once you make gladiator, you can take over, if you like."

As grateful as she was, the payments belonged to her father. They should pass on to her. "I will. Thank you, but you're a bit young to step into my father's shoes."

Izzy snorted, "What? Your mother's not into twenty-six year olds?"

Ashleen laughed, "She doesn't get to be into twenty-six year olds."

"Aw, junior, you're breakin' my heart."

She scrunched up her face around a grin. "Don't do that."

"Alright, you win." He gestured to the recorder in her hand, "You should save that for later. We're gonna run a sim in about half an hour. I'd like to see how you handle pressure and work with everyone before I drop you into the field."

Ashleen's chest tightened, "Do you think I can handle it?"

"We'll see in half an hour, won't we?"

"No pressure or anything." She raised the recorder he'd given her, "Thanks again."

True to his word, Izzy arrived at the dorm half an hour later. The rest of the team trickled into the common area from various places around Alexandria. Once they'd all arrived, Izzy led them to a nearby sim room.

"Would it kill them to invest in some cushions?" Ashleen asked as she sat down on the chilly floor.

No one replied, but she thought she saw Izzy smile, "Run the Aberwich sim."

Dahei flinched. "Hontō ni?"

Demetrius rested a hand on Dahei's shoulder, "Izzy would not run this one unless he was sure."

The exchange made Ashleen uneasy, but it was too late to ask questions or protest. Together they blinked a grassy hillside into existence. A chill breeze stirred Ashleen's hair about her ears, and the dull lavender sky whispered of either early morning or just after sunset. At a glance nothing was wrong, but the acrid tang of smoke hung in the air.

"Come on. We've got work to do." Izzy led the way to the top of the hill. The others followed him, a grim resolve lingering about them that Ashleen didn't understand until she too made it over the rise.

The town that spread out before them burned. Choking black smoke spiraled from the square and carried with it the scent of charred wood and bodies.

Ashleen stared, completely at a loss for words.

"Sometimes, plans fail," Izzy explained. "All you can do is save as many as you can."

"Then what are we doing still standing here!?" Ashleen took off towards the city, covering the distance easily in leaps and bounds.

"I like her," Dahei stated.

"She's doing well so far," Izzy agreed, "Demetrius, if you don't mind."

Demetrius made a complex gesture and four nightmares rose from the ground. The team vaulted onto the fiery horse-like creatures and galloped down the hill after Ashleen.

Ashleen crashed into a building, struggling to catch her breath and make sense of the scene before her. People screamed and ran as fire caught on their hair and clothes. Others tried to smother or douse the blaze, but only caught fire themselves as the tenacious flames consumed all.

"So?" Dahei crept up beside her. "What's your plan?"

"Find the source," Ashleen answered. Luckily the houses were small, and she had no trouble jumping high enough to pull herself up onto the nearest roof.

Izzy stopped next to Dahei, dismounted from his nightmare, and materialized a gun. "Is she keeping her head?"

"I think so," he replied. "But you're pushing it. Throwing the no-win scenario at her on the third day is a bit harsh."

"It's difficult for all of us, but I need to know how she'll handle it."

Morpheus and Demetrius arrived and dismounted. Demetrius dismissed the nightmares. Izzy waved them over. "Ashleen takes point. Follow her directions unless they put your life in danger."

Ashleen stared at the scene before her in abject horror. Three figures stood in the town square. They were perched in the midst of a great pyre, flames flickered over their bodies and escaped from their mouths when they spoke or breathed. They had extra sets of arms sculpted from the blaze and everything they touched was set alight.

She could feel the heat radiating off of them from where she stood several yards away. They were making a gesture over and over. It was the same one she'd seen Jin making, but they had three sets of arms each to do it with. Scores of hellhounds rose from the depths. Each waited only a second to receive fire from its summoner and took off through the streets, baying joyfully as the blaze spread.

"What are they?" Ashleen called down to the group at large as they gathered beside her perch.

"Ifrit," Demetrius replied. "The Raven sends the souls of their beckoners to deliver justice when deals with them are broken."

"I can't get close to them." It didn't matter how strong she was if her flesh was melting off her bones.

"No. You can't," Izzy concurred.

Ashleen tangled her fingers in her hair, thinking. "Okay, so if Dahei and I can't get near them, can you shoot them?"

Izzy fired off several shots in rapid succession. Nothing happened. The ifrit didn't even glance in his direction. The bullets melted in the heat before they reached their targets. Izzy would be of no use either.

"Demetrius?" Ashleen pleaded, desperation creeping into her voice.

"Against that many there's not much even I can do by myself." When Ashleen sighed, he continued. "I might be able to confuse the hellhounds. Slow the spread of the flames."

"Yes. That. Do that," Ashleen commanded. "Morpheus?"

"I can shield you or Dahei from their auras, but not both, and only for a few minutes. You'd have to move quickly."

"Shield me," Ashleen demanded, "Anyone without a job, get as many people out as you can."

Izzy glanced at Dahei and spoke quietly. "She's losing a point for not sending you, but I like her initiative."

"She's cautious," Dahei replied in kind, "Give her time to learn our strengths."

"She's self-sacrificing. If she can't temper her need to play the hero, she could get us all killed."

"Izzy--" his tone carried a note of warning.

"Let's go," he interrupted, and took off back the way they'd come.

Demetrius raised his hands, his shoulders pulling the rest of his body in a series of fluid gestures impossible for Ashleen to track.

Morpheus drew in a breath as he began to mutter something she couldn't hear over the roar of the flames. When the air around her cooled, she wasted no time.

Ashleen leapt from the roof and threw herself into the fray. She grabbed the nearest ifrit's wrist and crushed its bones in her grasp.

The ifrit whirled on her and spat flames, its face crumpling in both pain and rage. It grabbed at her with its fiery arms and cradled the broken human limb to its chest.

The other two ifrit turned. They protected their vulnerable limbs close to their chests and continued to gesture. Six pairs of fiery limbs clawed at Ashleen. She struggled, but though she could grab a burning limb, it didn't have bones for her to break and she only had two hands.

The screams of the townspeople urged her on and she forced her way through to break another wrist. It wasn't enough. The arms she had managed to grasp evaporated between her fingers and reformed out of reach. The only uninjured ifrit fell back and returned to gesturing with all its hands.

The soles of Ashleen's shoes were starting to stick to the cobblestone, and heat blasted her as if she were standing before an open oven. Morpheus' shield began to fade.

"Ashleen! Time's up!"

It wasn't clear who'd yelled the warning, but she didn't care. A heartrending wail split the air and from the corner of her eye, Ashleen saw a young mother go up in flames as she cradled her squalling newborn to her chest.

She lunged for the nearest ifrit's throat and stretched towards the rage she knew she should feel. The rage that she could use to crush a man's skull. The emotions surged in her blood, but the mind-numbing power lay just out of reach.

"Ashleen!"

She tuned out her teammates and her fingers closed around an ifrit's throat. She raised it off its feet and the flames it spat raised blisters on her wrist almost instantly. The air burned her nose and dried her mouth, but there wasn't time to care.

She hurled the ifrit into its allies and sent them all sprawling across the superheated stone. Her hair billowed on the currents of heat, threatening to catch fire.

Morpheus drew a breath to restart the shielding as it fell. Izzy interrupted him. "Don't. Let her burn."

"You can't be serious," Morpheus stared at him, appalled.

Izzy's frigid glare was almost potent enough to rival the ifrits' flames. "It's a sim. She'll be fine."

Ashleen could feel the air starting to peel her skin, could smell her own flesh as it burned, but she couldn't, or wouldn't stop. One of the ifrit sat up enough to begin gesturing again, and the hellhounds wheeled like a flock of birds. They circled her three-deep, blowing puffs of their acrid breath into her face.

"Izzy," Demetrius gestured emphatically, but the hounds were no longer interested in his commands. "That's enough."

The first pair of jaws clamped down on Ashleen's forearm, and she felt each bone crunch. She swallowed her cry of pain, even as more sets of teeth sank in. Struggling only seemed to egg them on. More hellhounds poured in from the alleyways and forced their way into the fray.

"Izzy!" Dahei shouted over their frantic baying.

Ashleen felt something tear. Nausea twisted inside her as she watched one of the dogs gleefully chomp on a chunk of flesh that it had ripped off. The rage she'd grasped at slipped a little farther out of reach as terror crept up her spine.

Something snapped. She wasn't sure if it was her temper or one of her bones, but she gave up on stoic silence. She swore and shouted at the dogs, at the ifrit, at anyone who could hear her. Her curses devolved into wordless screams.

"This is sick," Morpheus broke ranks and started forward.

"Morpheus," Izzy warned, but Morpheus ignored him.

A lilting hymn broke through the baying of the hounds and for a moment, Ashleen wondered if she was dead. Then the dogs calmed, parted, and allowed someone to pass between them. Ashleen struggled to recognize who it was, but she couldn't see through the pain and stinging of her eyes.

The haunting lullaby drew to a halt and the air cooled. Ashleen's anger evaporated as the agony sank into her bones. She wanted to roll over and curl inward on herself, but she couldn't move without making it worse. So she simply lay there and pretended no one could hear the whimpers that slipped out against her will.

"Begone," her rescuer murmured a command and the hellhounds vanished.

"End simulation," Izzy quipped coldly from somewhere at the edge of the square.

The pain dulled to a throb as Ashleen blinked away the burning town, but still she ached like she'd been hit by a train. She glanced at Morpheus. The ethereal voice she'd heard from him seconds earlier had hit notes she doubted were human. He'd touched the ceiling of what she'd heard sopranos reach and then punched through it. Pavane's comments from the day before echoed in her mind.

"What are you?"

Morpheus avoided her gaze and busied himself with stretching. "I don't know what you're talking about."

"Don't you dare risk yourself like that again," Izzy interrupted, standing to yell down at her.

"Isn't that our job?" Ashleen twisted toward him, "We save people, don't we?"

"You can't save people when you're dead, Ashleen! What if the simulation had killed you? Huh? Then where would we be? You would have died before you could even save a single person!"

"What was I supposed to do then?! Run away?"

"Yes!" Izzy said emphatically. "You can't win every fight! You need to consider the consequences of your actions. If you die, think of how many people you leave behind! Think of all the people you condemn to death that you could've saved if you had lived."

"If I don't try to save everyone every time, how many do I condemn then?" Ashleen got to her feet so he had to look up at her. "You can't ask me to choose who lives and who dies!"

"You made that choice anyway, by choosing to sacrifice yourself. How many people do you think your little stunt actually saved?" Izzy was unfazed by her height. "If you're not strong enough to make that choice, if you can't walk that line, you have no place on our team. Or in this city."

"Fine. Find yourself another tranq, cause I refuse to turn a blind eye on suffering." Ashleen strode away and dropped through the hatch before he could stop her.

Izzy's gaze fell on Morpheus. "You. I'll deal with you later." He stormed across the room, shoved open the hatch Ashleen had left ajar, and slammed it behind him.

Ashleen stalked back to the dorm and barricaded herself in her room. Hopefully the others would give her space, for their sake. She screamed into her pillow. When she emptied her lungs of air, she threw the pillow as hard as she could at the opposing wall. The soft thump it made on impact was nowhere near satisfying enough. She resisted the urge to seek out something that might do real damage.

The tranquilizers did their job a bit too well. Ashleen was fairly certain she could have taken the ifrit if she'd been able to confront them without her proverbial muzzle.

In spite of that, she couldn't bring herself to be anything but grateful for the pills. She'd have to adjust to their effects, but she didn't have to worry that she'd black out and murder someone anymore.

She curled up on her bed and retrieved Izzy's recorder from her pocket. Homesickness crawled into the vacant space in her chest as she rolled the device over and over in her fingers.

Her mother deserved an apology, if nothing else. Before Alexandria, Alice would have been the first person she turned to. Now she couldn't tell her mother the truth. If she wanted to talk about what happened, she'd have to twist the story. When she'd settled on an acceptable version, she rehearsed it in her head and pressed record.

"Hey, Mom. I'm okay, but I'm not sure that my situation has improved. I've been transferred to Alexandria. They've saddled me with a group of absolute goosehats. The leader just yelled at me, so I hate him right now. Prue's been here the whole time, one of them's dating her. I hate both of them too. Dahei and Demetrius aren't so bad but..."

She trailed off and sighed, "Playing hero isn't all it's cracked up to be. I'm sorry for what I said when we last spoke, but I think I deserve an explanation. Amaris says you knew a lot more than you ever told me. I've tried to understand why you would lie to me like that, but I keep coming up empty."

A knock on her door interrupted her train of thought and she stopped the recording. "Who is it?"

"Dahei."

Ashleen slid out of bed and opened the door. Dahei gestured for her to follow him and led the way to the common area. He collapsed haphazardly on a couch in such a way that he completely filled it, despite his small frame. Ashleen took a seat on one of the other couches and for a moment, neither of them spoke.

Dahei broke the silence, "Look, Izzy's a grown man and he can apologize for his own damn self. But I've been a part of this team almost as long as he has and there's something you should know."

"I'm listening."

"Before Demetrius was transferred to our team, we had a different beckoner. Her name was Alexis and she was a hothead to rival even you. She never knew when to quit. On one of our missions, she went back for a straggler instead of regrouping.

Since she separated herself from the team, none of us could get to her in time and a pack of lycans tore her apart. She was Izzy's counterweight." Dahei took a breath. "That's why he blew up at you. He's never been the same."

What was left of Ashleen's lingering resentment disintegrated. "I had no idea."

"Of course you didn't," Dahei laced his fingers behind his head, "I like to tease him about the amount of time he spends working on the ship, but they modified it together. It's all he has left of her. He's probably in the hangar right now, ranting to it like a raven-cursed loon."

Ashleen had paced back and forth before the door leading to the hangar for nearly half an hour, trying to work up the courage to confront Izzy. Just as she had almost convinced herself, the door hissed open and Cyrus stepped through it.

He almost ran into her. "Ashleen!"

Sushila followed him through. Her brow furrowed as she gave Ashleen a quick once over, "Oh honey. You look horrible."

Leo threw her a knowing glance. "Aberwich?"

"How did you know?"

"Izzy runs all his new recruits through it," Janice answered, her icy glare melting away. "I think Morpheus cried for a week."

Considering what Ashleen had seen him do this time, she had difficulty picturing that.

"I know just the thing," Sushila nodded sagely and beckoned for the rest of them to follow her.

To Ashleen's relief, Prue didn't linger with them for very long after they'd reached Leo's dorm. However, the fact that she was undoubtedly leaving them to seek out Morpheus gave Ashleen's relief a bitter aftertaste.

"I'm sorry about earlier," she said, apologizing to Leo lamely.

"I'm fine," Leo grumbled. "Hurt my pride more than me."

"Why?" Ashleen asked, "Cause I'm a girl?"

Leo shot her a quizzical look, "No. My team is mostly female. Women are badass. I'm just mad that I couldn't even put up a fight." When Ashleen remained silent, Leo cracked a smile, "They say the female tranqs are the more vicious ones anyway."

She laughed half-heartedly, and Sushila passed her a drink. Ashleen sniffed it and reeled back. "What is that?"

"Just try it!" Sushila giggled, "It's part of the privilege I was awarded for my rank up. You'll like it, I have good taste."

Ashleen returned to the dorm that night far more sober than she'd been hoping to be. The first taste of Sushila's potent concoction had brought memories of Prue's party rushing back, and along with them, a wave of nausea. She'd set the drink aside and opted to just enjoy the company.

She closed the door behind her as quietly as she could. Several shapes broke up the familiar outline of the couches as her eyes adjusted to the darkness. One of them revealed itself to be Dahei and Demetrius. The two had fallen asleep so entangled that their silhouette looked like a many-armed monster from the pits of oblivion.

The other shape stood up as she drew closer, and Ashleen recognized Izzy.

"I wasn't sure you were coming back." He spoke softly, so as not to wake the conglomerate being on the other couch.

"Dahei told me," Ashleen whispered, "About Alexis."

Izzy flinched at the name, "I'm sorry I lashed out at you like that. You didn't deserve it."

"I deserved it a little," Ashleen admitted under her breath. "You're right. It was a sim and maybe I took it more seriously than I needed to."

"Try not to get yourself killed?" Izzy teased. "Would be embarrassing for both of us if you died your first week."

"No promises," Ashleen joked. "Good night."

8

Castle Nope

Morpheus had opened and closed his mouth six times in the last twenty minutes, not that Ashleen was counting. Every time he looked like he was about to break the silence, he would glance at Izzy and stop himself.

And that was seven. "Will you just spit it out?" Ashleen demanded.

Amusement spread across Izzy's face, but he kept his gaze on the day planner in his lap and pretended not to care.

Morpheus glanced at Izzy again.

"Stop that. If you have something to say, say it!"

"Fine," Morpheus managed finally. "I wanna know how you resist hypnosis so easily."

"What?"

"The whale song sound I make. You shouldn't be able to resist it as well as you do."

"Why not?"

"Because I'm––" He caught himself and glanced at Izzy again.

Izzy met his gaze and shrugged. Morpheus gestured at Ashleen and shot him a pointed look. Izzy raised his eyebrows.

"Stop not-talking about me as if I weren't in the room!" she snapped.

Before either of them could reply, Dahei's door banged open, and he stumbled out groggily. He hurled an empty drink can and it bounced harmlessly off of Ashleen.

"Some of us are still sleeping," he slurred.

Izzy retrieved the can and inspected it. "Dahei, are you drunk?"

"No," he scoffed.

Demetrius emerged from the open doorway and a few scattered butterflies alighted on Dahei's slightly swaying form. He didn't say anything, but he mouthed the word 'birthday' over Dahei's head.

Izzy's brow furrowed with concern, "We should cancel the hunt."

"Don't you dare," Dahei snapped.

"I do not think that is wise," Demetrius said at the same time.

Izzy's frown deepened, "Are you sure? It might be better if..."

Demetrius shook his head silently.

"Alright," Izzy conceded. "Dahei, do yourself a favor and get a painkiller from Neele."

When they'd left the room, Ashleen raised an eyebrow at Izzy. "Birthday?"

"It's Hideo's birthday," Morpheus answered before Izzy had the chance.

"We should get ready to go; Dahei doesn't handle grief well. Demetrius is right. It's better to keep him busy." Izzy's gaze slid to Ashleen. "I hope you're ready for the real thing."

"I guess we'll see," Ashleen replied, smiling through her nerves.

Ashleen and the others had already been in the hangar bay for several minutes when Dahei finally rounded the corner. He still looked like Ikalusca had swallowed him and spat him back out, but at least he wasn't swaying anymore. Demetrius' hands kept skipping up to hover just centimeters from Dahei's shoulders, but each time he would think better of it and lower them again.

Izzy pressed a hand to the side of the mantacraft and strode up the ramp when the door opened for him. The interior of the craft was plain, and looked no different from the inside of the craft Ashleen had arrived in with Neele.

"Buckle up!" Izzy chirped. "I'd direct you to our emergency exits and safety devices except... there aren't any! So try not to die."

Ashleen couldn't tell whether he was joking or not, but either way it didn't help her anxiety. She tightened her grip on the bottle of tranquilizers in her pocket like they could save her.

The mantacraft lurched and they fell through empty space. Ashleen felt her insides floating, and bit back the squeal that leapt into her throat. Her heart slammed against her ribcage. The ship banked hard and whipped into a hairpin turn. Neele hadn't been exaggerating about Izzy's piloting habits.

"What's our briefing?" Morpheus called to Izzy from beside her.

"Suspected haunting in an abandoned castle. Thought it'd be a good starter for Ashleen. Low threat, out in the country so no risk of civilian losses and collateral damage isn't a big deal."

"Seriously?" Ashleen squeaked. Her insides, which had just righted themselves, were all wrong again. She'd never liked ghosts. "That's just great! How am I supposed to punch something that isn't even solid?"

"I have something for that," Izzy said over his shoulder, "But don't worry too much, this one's more Morpheus' and Demetrius' area. The rest of us just have to watch their backs."

Ashleen wished that knowledge made her feel better. It didn't. "Any other helpful advice?"

"It's probably a geist," Izzy explained, "Which means it will try to possess us. Morpheus will do his best to prevent that, so if you have to pick someone to protect, pick him. That said, shit happens. So I hope you're good at shutting things out of your head."

Ashleen swallowed. She was the least experienced in the group and she'd never had to worry about being possessed before. She chewed her lip and spent the rest of the flight trying to clear her mind.

Dahei and Izzy gathered the weapons they needed from compartments in the ship's floor when they arrived. Cold air blasted Ashleen when the door opened and she emitted a short whine of protest.

Fresh snow covered the ground and her breath clouded the air with little puffs. "Couldn't they give us anything a little thicker to wear?"

Morpheus pushed ahead, unfazed despite being skin and bones. Ashleen grumbled and stomped after him, hoping if she moved enough she would warm up.

They made their way up a winding, cobblestone road. Ashleen slipped and skidded along the icy stone, fighting to keep her footing. Before long, a walled fortress came into view. The abandoned building rose out of the surrounding mountainside like a snarling gargoyle.

Ashleen felt like a trespasser. Snow crested the parapets and the ancient banners were frozen to their flagstaffs. Even Demetrius' butterflies seemed fatigued by the cold, pausing every few wingbeats to rest on various team members' heads and shoulders.

The heavy doors had been torn from their hinges, leaving a gaping maw ready to swallow them. Ashleen slowed her steps and let the others pass in front of her. There was no reason to take the lead as inexperienced as she was. It was smart to hang back for the time being, not cowardly. At least, that's what she told herself.

Demetrius reached the doors first and brought up his hands, readying himself for any gesture he might need. Dahei followed quickly after him, then Morpheus. Izzy paused at the entrance, waiting for her to catch up.

When she did, he held something out: "A solution to your problem." Ashleen cupped her hands and he dropped a pair of iron rings into them.

"What are these?"

"Raven-consecrated rings. I borrowed them from Leo. We'll get you your own soon. They won't destroy a geist, but they'll make your strikes sting. Thought you might like an edge."

"Thanks," she was still afraid, but the weight of the iron in her hands did make her feel a bit better.

Izzy squeezed her shoulder. "You're welcome. Now come on, we've got a job to do." With that, he disappeared into the shadows. Ashleen hung back another few seconds, trying to mentally fortify herself one more time, then crossed the threshold.

Complete darkness swallowed her and left her blind. "You guys?" she hissed, "Where'd you go?"

An ominous rattle sounded from somewhere behind her. Ashleen spun to face the sound and stumbled backward. She collided with someone. Or something. A yelp of fright escaped her and someone pressed a hand over her mouth.

"Shh!" Dahei hushed her from somewhere further up the hall.

Ashleen heard the familiar cant of Gaelic against her ear. The space around them filled with shimmering lights as all of Demetrius' butterflies began to emit a soft blue glow. Morpheus withdrew his hand from her mouth and Ashleen hurriedly stepped away from him. She resisted the urge to shove him, if only to prevent further noise and draw the geist down on their heads.

The group split off as if they each knew exactly what the plan was. Ashleen, not wanting to break the silence again and ask, chose to stick close to Izzy.

As they made their way deeper into the castle, the air grew impossibly stiller. The chill bit at her bones and an unseen gaze made the hair on the back of her neck prickle. Izzy opened each door as they passed, scanning it for any sign of the geist before moving to the next room.

Ashleen wanted to be grateful they hadn't found anything. She wanted to believe that maybe the castle wasn't haunted and it was just a false alarm. The absence of anything, however, was beginning to fray her nerves.

"Do you hear that?" Izzy asked, his eyes darting back and forth.

"Hear what?" Even as she said it, Ashleen thought she heard someone call her name.

"This way," Izzy sprinted around the corner into a majestic hall.

Massive, decrepit chandeliers hung from the ceiling. Frigid wind whistled through the shattered glass of elegant windows. Blue lights danced along the walls, bouncing off of nonexistent water.

The end of the hall was barricaded by an imposing set of double doors. Izzy drew up before them and threw his shoulder against the rotting wood. They didn't give. He took a few steps back and slammed into them again.

"Wait a minute," Ashleen started, "What are you--"

Izzy ignored her and ran into the door a third time, to no effect.

"Izzy--"

He snarled a curse at the doors, reached into his coat, and produced a grenade.

"Izzy!" Ashleen grabbed his arm and wrestled the explosive from his hands. Izzy struggled to snatch it back. She kept him at arm's length. "What are you doing? You'll bring down the whole castle!"

"Can't you hear her?" His tone was edged with desperation as he fought futilely against her grip.

Ashleen had thought the rest of the team might be calling for help, but there were no other women in their group. "Hear who?"

As soon as the words left her lips, her father's voice rang through the hall. Ashleen released Izzy and spun towards the door, stunned.

Izzy snatched the grenade back from Ashleen. Before he had a chance to prime it, Ashleen slammed into the door. The rotten wood exploded around her and she was standing in her living room. Her father stood by the hearth.

Ashleen's heart skipped a beat. It was as if he'd stepped right out of the photograph her mother kept on the mantelpiece.

He smiled and extended his arms towards her, "Ash. Look at you. You've grown," he said, greeting her.

Ashleen hesitated. "You're... dead."

Connor frowned and checked his pulse, "Not last I checked. You must have had a bad dream." He extended his arms again. "Come give me a hug. We'll make it all go away."

The hair stood up on the back of her neck. Something didn't feel right. She was missing time. What had she been doing five minutes ago? She had to fill in the blank. If she had killed someone, she doubted she'd be forgiven this time.

Ashleen startled. Someone was touching her, but there was no one there. "Come on. I know you can hear me." The whisper was barely audible.

"What's wrong?" Connor didn't move, but he seemed to loom towards her. "Won't you give your old dad a hug?"

Ashleen took a step back. "Give me a minute."

"Ashleen, we haven't seen each other in eighteen years. All I want is a hug." His smile widened.

"Then we can definitely wait a few more seconds. Please."

"Ashleen, please." There was that voice again. Someone touched her face. "Please, please, please,"

She squeezed her eyes shut. When she opened them again, she was kneeling on the dusty floor of the decrepit castle. Morpheus had her face cupped in his hands, his forehead pressed against hers.

Ashleen jerked away from him. "You just can't help yourself, can you?"

Morpheus clapped his hands over his mouth. For a second, Ashleen thought he was going to cry. "I could kiss you!"

She bristled and shoved him. "Don't you dare."

He held up his hands to placate her. "I won't."

"What happened?" Ashleen cast about the spacious dining hall.

The others were slumped against half-rotten benches and tables. Dahei and Izzy's eyes were open, but they appeared to be unresponsive. Izzy was muttering rapidly to someone Ashleen couldn't see. Demetrius rocked back and forth, his hands over his ears. Dahei was just staring at them. Eerily.

"I don't know," Morpheus answered. "Dahei took off, Demetrius followed him. When they got here, they just shut down. I was trying to wake them up when you and Izzy broke down the door."

Ashleen remembered that much. "I saw my father."

"People you've lost, that makes sense."

"How?"

"You all lost someone, the geist is using that. But I can't remember my past. Even if I had lost someone, I wouldn't know who."

"What do we do?"

"I can force the geist out, but it won't go peacefully. While I'm focused on them, I'll be vulnerable. I need your help. Unfortunately you'll be on your own until I can snap one of them out of it."

Ashleen grimaced. "Work fast."

Morpheus nodded firmly. He turned toward Demetrius, Latin already rolling off his tongue. Ashleen touched the rings on her fingers and backed a few steps closer to the group.

Each doorway, and there were far too many of them, darkened ominously in her peripheral vision. Shadows flickered, but no matter how she searched, she couldn't spot whatever had created them.

Something just out of sight was gnawing on the abundant decaying wood. She could hear it. From another direction, she heard labored breathing. Something skittered through the walls.

Ashleen took another step back and brushed against Morpheus. She hoped he was too engrossed in what he was doing to notice. She promised herself she would never admit that his presence made her feel safer.

Demetrius gasped for air, breaking through his trance as if breaking the surface of water. "Muginn have mercy," he spluttered, "They are everywhere."

"They? When did 'it' become 'they'?" Ashleen demanded. The room looked empty except for the five of them.

Demetrius whipped his head back and forth. "This is the center of the nest. We should not be here."

"Nest?" Ashleen willed her voice to remain steady.

"Morpheus, hurry. They grow restless."

Morpheus had already turned towards Izzy, the notes of his hymn shifting their resonance.

"What are they?" Ashleen asked, still straining to see whatever it was that Demetrius could sense.

"Shadow people," Demetrius told her. "Which means, somewhere..." he spun around, searching the room. "There is a queen."

Izzy exploded out of his illusion with even more violence than Demetrius. The yell that tore from him startled a squawk out of

Ashleen. He was on his feet, with his gun raised, before she even had time to turn around.

"Where is she?" Demetrius muttered, still sweeping the room.

"Shadow people?" Izzy asked, panting.

"Yes."

Izzy swore.

"I cannot sense the queen," Demetrius informed him, growing more agitated by the minute. "What are they waiting for?"

"Guys..." Morpheus interjected.

A menacing chuckle echoed from behind them. Izzy closed his eyes, "Damn."

Demetrius turned, "That is not possible. He has my talisman."

Morpheus passed Demetrius a bird's foot amulet. "This one?"

Demetrius ran his thumb over the claws and grimaced. "Yes."

Izzy rounded on Dahei and raised his rifle.

Dahei narrowed his eyes incredulously. "Try it, boy," he challenged in a voice far too feminine to be his own.

"Demetrius," Izzy began, "How many are there?"

"Dozens. They have us surrounded."

"That's unfortunate," Morpheus murmured, searching the room.

"We've been outplayed," Izzy told them, "Morpheus, tell me you've got something."

Morpheus drew a sharp breath and unleashed a shrill scream that pierced Ashleen's ears. The windows exploded outward, shards of glass rained down the cliff face dissonantly. The air quivered, resonating with the pitch he'd conjured.

"Raven, warn me next time," Izzy chastised him, digging at one of his ears.

Morpheus didn't pause long enough to answer, instead breaking into a wordy ballad that combined a mess of Slavic, Gaelic, and Germanic tongues.

Ashleen fought against the sudden urge to sink to her knees and cry. She couldn't explain it, but the song sounded like home; if home could have a sound.

Cerulean light bloomed through the space as dozens of human-like bodies began to glow, giving away their positions. An iridescent lavender bubble descended over them. As it neared the ground, Dahei snarled. He lunged for the gap and attempted to escape.

Demetrius gestured sharply with one hand, and Dahei slid backward as if pulled by invisible strings. Demetrius brandished the bird's claw in his other hand, and the thing possessing Dahei hissed. The temperature dropped a few more degrees.

"You will not have him," Demetrius spoke through his teeth.

The glowing shapes surged forward at their queen's call. The bubble stretched and flexed as they strove to claw through it. With them came a foul odor akin to the remains of a corpse several weeks old. Ashleen gagged.

Demetrius pulled at the air, and the cry of agony that tore from Dahei was in his own voice this time.

Demetrius' hands stilled and he swore. "She is in deep. He cannot differentiate his soul from hers. If I force her out, she will take him with her. He will die. I need Morpheus' help."

A new verse found its way into Morpheus' song, and he sank to his knees. His already pale skin took on a greyish quality.

The shadow people sensed his exhaustion and surged against the barrier, their chittering voices gleeful. One of them got an arm through and wrapped a frigid hand around Ashleen's wrist. Something crawled through her hair. Ashleen squealed and slapped the shadow person. Her iron ring singed the being, and it released her, hissing.

"Keep it together, Gallagher," Izzy commanded her.

"Why did it have to be ghosts?" Ashleen protested shrilly. Anything else she might've handled better, but restless souls were unnatural. The apostles in her hometown had said that a soul left to wander amongst the living was a bad omen.

There were stories in Muginn's scripture of ghost towns. All the people in an area would mysteriously die, their souls left to wander as their houses fell to ruin. The stories were vague, but most Ravenites agreed that Muginn had placed a curse upon the region for one reason or another. What had happened in this castle to earn the Raven's ire?

The shield Morpheus had been maintaining burst. Dahei skittered out of range and the mass of shadow people plunged towards them. Ashleen didn't have time to consider her plan of action, so she fell back on the only order she could remember. Protect Morpheus.

Even as she folded herself around him, she could feel him pulling vampirically at her energy. "Stop that."

"I can't. If you don't like it stop touching me."

Demetrius brought up his hands in Raven talon warding gestures. The shadow people crawled backwards, and the glow that had outlined them ceased as they faded into the corners of the room.

"If you two are quite finished," Izzy teased from somewhere to Ashleen's left.

Ashleen glowered at Morpheus and shoved him away from her, hoping the dim lighting hid the blush she could feel burning her cheeks.

"What's your problem?" Morpheus grumbled at her.

"You are. Where did Dahei go?"

Demetrius pointed, and when Ashleen looked, she shuddered. Dahei had crab-walked backwards up the wall and was now skulking near the ceiling.

"How you doin' Morpheus?" Izzy asked.

"Not great."

"Let's get this over with then." Izzy produced a small pouch and opened it. With a flick of his wrist he scattered its contents into the air. Blackened salt and raven feathers fell heavily to the ground in a perfect triangle around the group.

Dahei cackled. "You've put up quite a fight, haven't you? But not much time left, is there? Why don't you just leave this one with me and go?"

"What do we do?" Ashleen hated the feeling of uselessness that nagged at the back of her mind.

"You're gonna go get him."

"Me?"

Demetrius offered her the bird's foot charm. "You will be fine."

"I'll cover you," Izzy assured her.

"What am I supposed to do?" Ashleen asked.

"Distract her. If she's busy trying to get away from you, she won't be focused on resisting Demetrius."

"Ooo," the eerie voice crooned, "So scary. Come on then, I'm eager to see you try. It's been ever so long since anyone sent me a real challenge."

Ashleen curled her lip. She wouldn't be mocked by this affront to nature. She took Demetrius' talisman and hung it about her neck. "Since you asked so nicely."

She stepped over the salt line and rushed the wall. The shadow people lit up again as Morpheus restarted his aria.

Ashleen tried not to startle when they exploded. Izzy shot them as they drew near to her. She told herself he wouldn't miss and prayed that she was right. When she reached the wall, she pulled herself up, stepping between footholds in the crumbling structure.

As she drew closer to Dahei, he scuttled away. Two ethereal ravens swooped over her shoulders and dove at him cawing raucously. Undoubtedly they were Demetrius' doing. Dahei hissed and chittered at them, crawling backward onto the ceiling as he tried to swat them away.

Ashleen swore and tried not to think about how high up she was. She peered at Dahei, estimating distances in her head. Morpheus' song changed again, Latin creeping back into his hymn. Echoes filled the space and bounced off the broken walls as if the acoustics were perfect.

Dahei curled inward on himself and the shadow possessing him made a horrible, agonized sound. Darkness seeped out of the cracks on the ceiling around him and dripped past Ashleen with an ominous sizzle. The inky substance exploded into swarms of flies as it hit the ground.

The queen screeched incessantly as it tried to drown out Morpheus' words. Morpheus slid from Latin to Slavic verses as if they were his native tongue. The flies froze, hovering in the air. Demetrius' ravens squawked excitedly and pulled something free from Dahei's chest. They shredded and devoured it between themselves.

The flies fizzled out of existence, and Dahei stilled. Ashleen braced herself and launched off the wall just as he began to plummet towards the floor. She caught him out of the air and landed heavily across the room. She lowered him to the ground and checked for a pulse. She could feel one, but he wasn't conscious.

"He's alive," she assured Demetrius as he hurried towards her.

"I could sense that much for myself, thanks," Demetrius quipped.

Ashleen frowned at him. "You're welcome." Her heart continued to pound against her ribs. She tried desperately to relax now that she was back on the ground, but apparently the adrenaline had other ideas.

She picked Dahei up again and draped him over her shoulder. "Can we get out of here?"

Morpheus nodded. "Please."

"Do you sense any more?" Izzy asked, putting a hand on Demetrius' shoulder

Demetrius gave the room a quick scan and shook his head, "No. If there are any left, they have retreated."

"Good. Let's get out of here before anyone else passes out."

9

Echoes of Hideo

Ashleen analyzed the specks of color on the linoleum floor of the infirmary. She felt like an intruder, but she couldn't think of anywhere else she ought to be. Morpheus was also new, and he hadn't run off in search of Prue. If he could be comfortable here, she could be too.

"I should not have argued," Demetrius said, his fingers tracing delicate lines over Dahei's face, a tremor obvious in his movements. "We should not have gone."

Izzy raised his gaze and reached across Dahei's prone form to squeeze Demetrius' arm. "Dahei wouldn't have taken no for an answer, we both know that. How is he?"

Demetrius took a shuddering breath to steady himself, "I can barely feel him at all. I cannot tell how bad the damage is from outside, but if he was fine, he would be awake by now."

"Damn, if I'd known we were dealing with shadow people and not a typical geist..."

"I cannot do this with only one beckoner, minds are too delicate. I need Winona."

"I'll go find her," Izzy straightened and left the infirmary.

Neele had hovered at the edges of the group since their arrival. She kept fussing over their minor injuries as if they wouldn't just heal on their own. Ashleen suspected Neele hated the feeling of being helpless just as much as she did.

Izzy's return and Winona's arrival saved Ashleen from another bout of Neele's prodding. Winona bustled forward, stealing a chair from one of the other medical stations.

"What can you tell me?" she demanded, her low voice rolling over them like a morning fog.

"I made a mistake," Demetrius admitted.

"You can't take all the blame," Morpheus interjected, "I underestimated how much shielding he would need."

"And I wasn't expecting an entire hive of shadow people," Izzy added. "He had a run in with the queen. We were able to exorcise her, but we're not sure how much damage she did."

"Let's have a look." Winona reached for Dahei and rested her thumbs against his temples. In the same breath she snatched her hands back as if he had burned her. "Oh dear. She sank her roots in deep. I'd feel safer sending two of you."

Izzy held up a hand, "I'll go. Known him almost six years."

"That should suffice," Winona beckoned him closer. "I'll act as a guide and anchor. Have either of you done this before?"

Izzy shook his head. "Never."

"I have dabbled a little," Demetrius admitted. "Nothing to this degree."

Winona pressed her lips together. "It isn't ideal. But it will have to do. I trust both of you know how important it is that you be extremely careful?" They nodded. "Good. Let's save your friend."

Winona formed an eye with her fingers and fluidly slid through the gesture to place her palms on Demetrius' and Izzy's foreheads.

Demetrius listened to his surroundings. He'd manifested on the outskirts of a city. Dissonant sirens and honking horns shattered the stillness, but they were far off. In the opposite direction, distant foghorns bellowed. Much closer by, he could hear water lapping against a shore. The air hung heavy with humidity and carried the scent of salt.

A metallic crash and the yowl of a cat announced Izzy's arrival. "Demetrius?"

"Yes?"

"Can you..." he gestured toward his face, "See?"

Demetrius blinked rapidly and realized as a matter of fact, he could. He hadn't thought to register visual information, since he hadn't summoned any of his wisps yet. Scaffolding and graffiti littered the walls of warehouses and stacks of abandoned boxcars. It was nighttime, but an abundance of light pollution made the darkness of the sky irrelevant.

"What made you ask?"

"You have eyes," Izzy said, still looking at him quizzically.

A massive golden eagle swooped down from the sky and alighted on a nearby crate. It spoke with Winona's voice. "We are in Dahei's subconscious. There will be..." She cocked her head at Demetrius, "Differences..."

"He must have given me Hideo's eyes," Demetrius guessed. He touched his face, searching for burn scars that were no longer apparent.

"We should find Dahei quickly. Where would he seek sanctuary?" Winona asked.

"With his family?" Izzy suggested.

"Not today," Demetrius countered. "Today, he is in the cemetery."

"When you said you dabbled," Winona started, "Was it with him?"

"Yes."

"I apologize."

Demetrius frowned. "For what?"

"Misinterpreting the nature of your relationship," Winona replied. "I meant no offense."

"We have more pressing matters to attend," Demetrius said, waving a hand dismissively.

"You said he was in the cemetery," Izzy interjected. "How do we get there?"

"I'm not sure, usually Dahei leads the way."

"What is that?" Winona drew their attention to a small blue butterfly flickering in and out of existence at the entrance to a decrepit warehouse.

"One of yours?" Izzy asked.

Demetrius shook his head. "I have not summoned any."

"Maybe it's a hint?"

"It could be a trap," Winona warned.

"I do not think so," Demetrius disagreed. "Dahei has always used butterflies as guides in his subconscious."

Izzy made his way towards the butterfly, and it stuttered into the warehouse. Demetrius followed. The cement flooring was stained with old blood. A simple metal chair sat in the center of the empty space, and a lone incandescent bulb hung from the ceiling.

The butterfly lingered to one side of the chair. As they watched, it jittered in place and for a split second it wasn't a butterfly, but a young man. He was Japanese, like Dahei, but his features were softer and he was several inches taller.

"What was that?" Izzy asked.

"Hideo," Demetrius explained. "I have been trying to extract him, but pieces of him linger here, trapped by Dahei's grief."

Winona's feathers puffed out. "Muginn does not condone such practices."

"It is not intentional," Demetrius countered calmly.

"Do you think he wants to help?" Izzy suggested.

"Probably," Demetrius approached the tiny insect and cupped his hands together. Hideo allowed himself to be captured and spoke in a voice only Demetrius could hear.

Demetrius released the butterfly and led the way towards a door on the other side of the warehouse. "This way."

Behind the warehouse, a stormy ocean churned as far as the eye could see. The waves broke with heaving sobs, and the thunder rolled as angry screams.

"A sea of unshed tears," Winona clucked thoughtfully. "I've never actually seen one."

"What now?" Izzy asked.

"I'm not sure." Demetrius strode forward until he stood at the edge of a massive sea wall, leaning over the guardrail as he looked for clues.

Hideo reappeared standing on the rail. He paced to and fro like a cat, watching them with mild interest. Izzy watched right back, unfazed by Hideo's patient eye contact.

"How did Hideo die?"

"What?" Demetrius asked, only half listening. "In the twenty-eleven attack, you know that."

"How, exactly?" Izzy pressed.

"Washed out to sea by the tsunami, I suppose. Dahei says he drowned."

Izzy watched as Hideo's hair began to stream water down his face. He spread his arms in invitation.

"Right," Izzy said as he jogged forward and stepped up onto the bottom rung of the guardrail. "That's what I thought."

Hideo offered no protest when Izzy planted a hand in the center of his chest and shoved him backward over the edge.

"What are you doing?!" Demetrius exclaimed.

"Breaking the cycle. Get ready to drown."

The water rapidly receded with a flash of lightning as Hideo broke its surface.

"Are you serious?" Demetrius watched as the tempestuous waves came rushing back with a vengeance. "I never learned to swim."

"Good, this will be easy for you."

"You are an ass."

"Where would you be if I wasn't?" Izzy climbed over the guardrail and let himself fall backward just as the tsunami hit. Demetrius lost sight of him as he was sucked off his feet by the tide.

The waters tore at him as he sank deeper, beaten by the undertow, slammed against the barnacle encrusted concrete of the seawall. His lungs burned. The seconds stretched into minutes, each more agonizing than the last. Without oxygen, even struggling against the current became impossible.

Demetrius tried not to think of Hideo, tried not to imagine what would happen if he never tasted air again. Sea water burned at his eyes and the fresh scrapes he'd acquired. He scrabbled for something to hold on to, anything to anchor himself.

His head cracked against something and Demetrius surrendered. He could hear Ikalusca whispering to him through the water. The ocean would be his grave, there was no use in holding his breath any longer. He could try again in his next lifetime. Demetrius let his lips part and invited the sea into his lungs.

As soon as he tasted the salty water, something yanked him upward. The currents surged past him and his ears popped. When he broke through the surface, he was completely dry and standing in an ankle-deep puddle. He fell to his hands and knees in the marshy grass and gasped for air until he choked on it.

Izzy slapped him on the back. "Fought it, didn't you? Coulda told you that was a dumb idea."

If Demetrius had remembered a few of Dahei's favorite curses, he would have used them, but right now he was just grateful to be back on solid ground.

The irritable grey sky spat rain at them, but none of the droplets made contact. They were surrounded by rows upon uniform rows of simple white gravestones.

"Where's Winona?" Izzy asked as Demetrius pushed himself upright.

"Not invited," Demetrius answered, "The cemetery is off limits to strangers. We will have to convince Dahei to open the way for her when we are ready to return."

"Okay, what now? You're more likely to know how he thinks."

"By now he knows we are here. This is where it gets complicated, if Dahei doesn't want to be found, we may not be able to find him."

"Fantastic."

"Sorry," Demetrius said with a shrug. "Look for butterflies?"

Izzy sighed and scanned the cemetery. The name on one of the gravestones caught his eye. "Wait a minute. What's this?"

Demetrius glanced at it. "What do you mean?"

"This name shouldn't be here. I killed this man back in Australia."

"Minds are strange, ours may interact with his in odd ways."

Izzy started off down the row and read the names on each tombstone. "None of these names are Japanese."

"Are they African?"

"Yeah, I think so."

"They must be my kin. Everyone I lost to my mistakes."

Izzy searched the cemetery again. There were no mausoleums or any other indicators of a place Dahei might hide. "Do you know where the center is?"

"This way, I think," Demetrius started in a seemingly random direction.

Izzy jogged to catch up with him. They made it a few rows inward and a set of graves ahead of them began to glow ominously. Two ghostly figures rose from the ground and hovered above their markers. They drifted closer until they stopped a few feet away, a perfect reflection of Izzy and Demetrius.

Demetrius shook his head. "I should have known."

"What?" Izzy eyed the figures warily.

"Dahei is at war with himself. We will not get any closer to him without a tranquility that surpasses his," Demetrius explained. He raised his hand in an inviting gesture towards his reflection. "What would you like to say?"

"You wiped your entire culture from history," his reflection accused.

"I have preserved what I knew and with my sisters, I will rebuild."

"You could have saved her," Izzy's reflection stated.

"I--" Izzy started, but he couldn't finish the argument. Not when he agreed.

"You killed all those people," Demetrius' spirit continued.

"There was no path that could have been taken to avoid it," Demetrius told himself, "I did not have any of the knowledge I would have needed to prevent that outcome."

Izzy's reflection didn't give him a chance to try his answer again. "You led her killers straight to her. If you had stayed away, she would have lived."

"I couldn't have known--" Except that Izzy could have. If he had just stopped a moment to think, he would have foreseen what had happened. He'd known the risks and turned a blind eye on them.

It was Demetrius' turn again. "You abandoned your sisters. They have no one."

Demetrius didn't take the bait. "They have their adoptive parents, I send them messages frequently. I will reunite with them when the time is right."

"All of this is your fault," Izzy's reflection accused.

"It isn't!" Izzy protested, finally presented with a statement he could counter. "My hand was forced. It's always been forced."

Both the reflections fell silent for a moment, as if weighing the answers given to them. Demetrius' reflection stepped aside and gestured for him to pass. Izzy's did not.

Demetrius offered him an apologetic look, "It seems that you have your own knots to unwind. You cannot expect others to follow examples you do not set."

Izzy avoided his gaze, "I know."

"You know which tombstone you have to find. She will guide you back to Winona."

"Thanks," Izzy lifted his eyes to watch as Demetrius disappeared through a bank of fog that hadn't been there a moment earlier.

Demetrius stopped. The cemetery had vanished. All that was left before him was a single grave. The rain that had been steadily pouring down froze. Droplets hovered in the air and orbited about the clearing. They parted for Demetrius as he strode forward, feet squishing in the marshlike grass. He sensed the jagged cadence of Dahei's soul before he saw him.

Dahei was lying on his back, arms flung wide. He stared unblinking into the sky. The rain around him continued to fall. His drenched hair and clothes clung to his skin. Blood stained the ground around him as it steamed from slits in each wrist.

He didn't respond as Demetrius approached and leaned into Dahei's field of view, redirecting the rain with his presence. "Dahei."

Dahei stirred, "Hideo?" He stared through Demetrius as if he weren't even there.

"Not quite."

Dahei sank back into the swampy ground, and became despondent again.

"You cannot stay here."

Dahei closed his eyes. "There's nothing left out there."

Demetrius scowled at him. "You are behaving like a child. I have been through much to get here."

"That's your mistake."

Demetrius knelt down, unconcerned by the blood and water soaking into his clothes. "Maybe. But do you not think this is an insult to his memory?"

Dahei jerked. He opened his eyes and looked at Demetrius for the first time.

"He is never coming back. Yet you keep him from peace while you squander the life he was denied."

Dahei glared up at him. "How dare you."

"How dare you. Wallow here in your self pity if you like. But do not pretend it is for him. You have not even noticed him watching you yet."

Dahei sat up to yell at him and finally remembered that Demetrius wore a blindfold. His retort died on his lips as he gazed into the eyes Demetrius shouldn't have.

He raised his hands to rest against Demetrius' face. "Hideo." The name came out small, edged with shame.

Demetrius gestured the Raven's invitation. The next words he spoke were in perfect Japanese, "What are you doing?"

"I... I'm--" Dahei stammered, unsure of how to continue.

"Breaking your promise?" Hideo replied, "You do remember, don't you? The dreams we had? You promised me we would travel the world. You've been somewhere I never could have dreamed of. For six years. You go to a different country each week. And look at you now."

Dahei opened and closed his mouth like a fish, at a loss for words.

"You're a shadow of your former self," Hideo continued, "You should be living for two. But you can't even live for one."

The raindrops reversed direction, rising steadily into the sky, pink with Dahei's blood. "Do you even remember what you asked me?" Hideo asked, voice softening.

"Where should we go first?"

"What was my answer?"

"You said it didn't matter. We could chase butterflies for all you cared."

The ascending raindrops burst, each one transforming into a shimmering blue butterfly. They eddied about the two men, blocking out the sky and all their surroundings.

When Hideo spoke again, his voice was fainter. "So go then. Chase butterflies." He left Demetrius and vanished into the cloud of fluttering cerulean wings.

Demetrius broke his gesture. He couldn't see anymore. Hideo was gone.

Dahei was before him, stable now, his attention fixed on their surroundings. Demetrius felt around for Dahei's hand, turning it over in his and running his thumb along Dahei's now healed wrist. "Did you hear what you needed to hear?" he asked.

"Yes." After a pause, he refocused on Demetrius and continued, "Thank you."

The corners of Demetrius' mouth twitched. "For what?"

"For being a voice of reason."

"All I did was speak, it was up to you whether or not to find reason in my words."

Dahei snorted. "Good to know you're still a fortune cookie."

Demetrius laughed. "One way or another I will figure out what that is."

"No you won't," said Dahei with a grin. "Did you plan a way out? I didn't exactly come here with an exit strategy."

"Winona is waiting for you to open the door."

"Then I guess I should let her in."

Demetrius grinned and stood, "Let's go home." He pulled Dahei to his feet and wrapped an arm tightly about him. With his free hand gestured rapidly towards the sky.

The cloud of butterflies scattered as Winona's eagle form dove through them with a screech. She wrapped her talons around Demetrius' extended arm, and with a great flap of her wings, ascended with both of them into the sky.

10

The Turn

For the hundredth time that morning, Ashleen drew up the memory of taking her tranquilizer and checking it off in the day planner Izzy had given her. She couldn't help but fuss over it. Today she'd have a second attempt at her placement test, and she was convinced she'd mess it up somehow.

It had taken the better part of a week for Neele to clear Dahei for duty, and Ashleen had skipped one of the placement tests in favor of spending a few days training with the other tranqs. She needed to know that the pills would keep her sane even in real combat situations.

Last weekend, Izzy had explained how she could use her points to accessorize and her rank to unlock weightier privileges. She'd sent out her recorder, and if today went well, she'd be able to take over Izzy's donations to her mother.

She glanced at Morpheus and quickly averted her gaze when his eyes slid toward her. She'd accumulated a list of pressing questions for him, chief among them what he'd meant to say when he'd confronted her about her ability to resist his hypnosis. That tied into what she'd seen him do in the Aberwich sim, and the implications of things Pavane had said even earlier.

Her cheeks heated up. She'd had a few more dreams since, and even though she never saw a face in them, it wasn't difficult to fill in the blank when the whale song was omnipresent. Besides that, there was the issue of Prue. Prue and Morpheus were stuck in their own mire of drama; something she'd prefer to keep away from.

Ashleen tore off a chunk of her biscuit and chewed it thoughtfully. She wished the rings everyone wore could make things simple. Unfortunately, nothing involving love was ever simple. As if people weren't complicated enough, the rings behaved mysteriously.

When Dahei woke up, Hideo's ring was gone. No one had seen it fall off or disappear, but the fact of the matter was, it no longer seemed to exist.

Izzy cleared his throat to draw the team's attention, "We should get going."

When they synced up, the sim had already been set to the boring, foam mats of the tranq setting. A few of the other huntsmen cast wary looks at Ashleen, but no one said anything. Some of the tranqs had circled up on the floor, but most of them continued to mingle about the room.

Leo had planted himself in the dead center of the mat and was staring Ashleen down with an intimidating intensity. Rome lingered at the edges of the crowd. He eyed her with casual interest.

When Ivanoff finally called the circle together, Leo hurled a gauntlet on the ground and barked a challenge before she had a chance to say anything else.

Ashleen retrieved it and Ivanoff stepped between them. "I don't want to see another episode like that ever again," she said as she surveyed the gathered tranqs. "From any of you."

There were a few nods and murmurs of agreement. She fixed Ashleen with a harsh gaze. "Am I understood?"

Ashleen ducked her head, ashamed. "Yes ma'am."

Ivanoff stared at her a few seconds longer to drive her point home, then she huffed and stepped aside, retreating to a spot somewhere near Rome.

Leo sank into a low stance, muscles bunched like a cat ready to spring. "You think you're ready for me?"

Ashleen bared her teeth to grin at him, "Give it your best shot."

"Oh, I intend to."

The sharp blast of Ivanoff's whistle interrupted their banter. Leo slammed into her with the full weight of his body. She stumbled backward, but it wasn't enough to knock her off her feet. She threw a quick jab at his side, aiming high for his armpit.

Leo twisted, and the blow glanced. He pinned her wrist between his ribs and his arm and stepped back to pull her off balance. As she fell forward, he sank into his defensive stance.

Ashleen rolled into her fall and was back on her feet before Leo could strike again. If she wanted to do anything she'd have to break that stance. She dropped back to the floor and kicked at his feet. He jumped her kick with practiced ease.

He backed away from her and Ashleen dropped low to counter another charge. That was a mistake. Leo leaped into the air at the last second and aimed to come down on her with the full force of his bodyweight.

Ashleen's body moved before her mind could process it. She stepped to the side and caught his arm as he came down. Before he could hit the ground, she pulled him off balance and let his momentum send him spinning out across the mat.

She could have gone for the pin right then and ended the fight, but he deserved at least one free pass after what she'd done to him last time.

A split second after he got his feet under him, he was sprinting toward her. "You want my arm? Here, have it!" He swung his arm directly at her head.

Ashleen blocked and twisted to drop the elbow of her other arm onto his thigh. She missed and her blow slid to one side.

Leo's fist struck her exposed ribs. She winced. She needed to pay attention. Her bruised side protested as she aimed a kick at Leo's head. He ducked.

Ashleen wasn't sure she could beat Leo in a fair fight. He was more experienced, and took her blows like they were child's play. She'd have to try another angle. An angle he wouldn't expect from a tranq.

As he lunged for her again, she stepped to the side and adapted a technique she'd seen Dahei use. Just as Leo's momentum carried him past her, she slammed into him. When he went down, Ashleen followed, going for a pin.

She caught his arm before he hit the ground and dug a knee into his back immediately upon impact. She pulled the arm she'd captured up behind him and hoped his weight and the awkward angle would keep his other arm pinned beneath him.

To her surprise, he pushed against his pinned arm anyway. His body shifted as he began to force her off balance. Ashleen jerked the arm she held up and bent his little finger at an odd angle, threatening to crush it in her grip. Leo hissed and fell back to the mat.

He chuckled. "That's a clever trick, but it won't work next time. I yield."

Ashleen let go of him and stood up, then turned and pulled him to his feet. She grinned, "What makes you think there'll be a next time?"

"Oh, there'll be a next time." He returned her grin and took his place on the sidelines.

Rome padded out onto the mat. "You're doing well. A word of advice? Your next opponent will not be a tranq."

Before she could ask what he meant, Rome turned on his heel and strode back to his place as Ivanoff took the floor.

"Alright, who's next?" She surveyed the assembled tranqs.

Nobody moved. Ashleen tried not to let it get to her. Instead she focused on Rome. He shook his head. She didn't know what he'd meant. Perhaps he had arranged something. She hoped he hadn't. She wanted to earn her rank fair and square, not have it handed to her by someone else.

Her thoughts were interrupted by the rattle of a gauntlet hitting the mat. "I will put the fledging in her place," the knight captain growled as she stalked into the center.

"Very well, Tatyana." As Ivanoff left the ring and raised the whistle to her lips, the other tranqs took a wary step or two back. Whispers broke out among the spectators.

"When was the last time Tatyana fought?" someone murmured.

"No one's challenged her for years," another voice added.

Ivanoff's whistle silenced any further gossiping. Ashleen fought against the nerves prickling under her skin. Tatyana rippled with muscle. She certainly looked the part of tranq knight captain. Ashleen didn't see how she could be anything else.

They circled each other, and Tatyana sized her up. Ashleen sank into a defensive stance. Tatyana smirked at her and remained relaxed as if Ashleen wasn't worth the effort. The tension grated on Ashleen's last nerve.

Tatyana seemed impressed that Ashleen had lasted this long. Perhaps this was how Tatyana had held her reign. Patience was a quality mastered only by a few, and never by a tranq. Tatyana sank into a stance and beckoned for Ashleen to attack.

Ashleen clenched her jaw and held her ground. She knew this game, the first one to strike would lose. She'd force Tatyana to throw the first punch even if she had to wait all day.

Tatyana recognized the resolve in Ashleen's eyes, and inclined her head respectfully. Then the small girl launched herself into the air, coming down towards Ashleen with all four limbs extended. Ashleen darted out of the way, and Tatyana hit the mat with an intimidating crack.

Tatyana closed the gap between them rapidly, coming at Ashleen from a low angle. She used her smaller stature to her advantage. If Tatyana got any foothold in close, Ashleen didn't think she stood a chance against the vicious young woman.

She had longer arms, but that was all she had. Still, Ashleen could use that. She extended a hand to grab Tatyana's arm. Tatyana caught her wrist and locked it, turned her body, and heaved Ashleen over her shoulder.

Ashleen sailed through the air. She hit the mat and the breath whooshed from her lungs. She rolled out of the way of Tatyana's ruthless follow up kick. Tatyana gave chase, attempting to drop a knee onto Ashleen's chest. She rolled to the side again and clambered to her feet as Tatyana struck the mat.

If Leo fought like a tranq, Tatyana fought like a beast evolved over millennia specifically to hunt tranqs. Maybe that was what Rome had meant. At least Ashleen's fear that she would be handed the title was unnecessary.

Ashleen threw three punches in quick succession. They passed through empty air. Tatyana didn't give an inch of ground. She feigned dipping to the right and changed direction as if momentum was a forgotten relic of a bygone era. Her boney knee slammed into Ashleen's left side. Ashleen yelped as pain bloomed across her ribs.

Anger flickered at the edges of her consciousness. She shoved it down and aimed a punch at Tatyana's stomach. Tatyana slapped her arm as if to push it away, then recalculated and twisted to avoid the strike. The fabric of her shirt fluttered against Ashleen's hand. She'd almost landed the hit. Tatyana wasn't blocking. Her slap hadn't even moved Ashleen's arm.

Ashleen narrowed her eyes and swallowed her frustration. She couldn't let it cloud her vision now. She threw a kick at Tatyana's side. Tatyana ducked low to avoid the blow. Leo would have blocked it.

As her foot passed over Tatyana's head, Tatyana slid to one side. She threw her weight against the back of Ashleen's thigh and Ashleen stumbled, ankle twisting as the momentum carried her further than she'd been expecting.

Even as she struggled to right herself, Tatyana was up again, her kick flying at Ashleen from the opposite direction. Her heel sank deep into Ashleen's stomach and countered her momentum.

Ashleen hit the ground on all fours. She tried to sweep Tatyana's feet from under her. Tatyana jumped to evade the attack. As her legs came back down, Ashleen reversed her kick, bringing her heel back against Tatyana's ankle. Hard. If she let Tatyana regain her balance, she'd miss her chance.

Ashleen lashed out at Tatyana's knee, and as she stumbled, came in from the other side with a strike at the meat of her thigh. Ashleen repeated the strike, realizing her mistake a second too late as Tatyana regained enough footing to drive a knee up into Ashleen's jaw. Ashleen's head snapped back, and she bit her tongue. She tasted blood.

As Ashleen reeled, Tatyana stumbled away from her. Ivanoff hadn't called the foul, but head blows were against the rules. Ashleen glanced at her and frowned pointedly. Ivanoff didn't react.

Ashleen shot a look at Rome to back her up. He had to have seen that. Rome lifted his chin and mouthed the word: "Revenge."

Ashleen felt anger seethe under her skin as every fiber of her being agreed with him. She jumped to her feet just as Tatyana aimed another kick at her. This time, she caught Tatyana's foot and stepped forward to shove the woman off balance. She dug her fingernails into Tatyana's ankle.

Tatyana cried out. Startled out of her momentary rage, Ashleen let go, and immediately cursed herself for doing so. She was unlikely to get an opportunity like that again. Tatyana growled in the back of her throat and closed distance. She broke into a storm of relentless strikes, all aimed at the left side of Ashleen's body.

Ashleen recoiled and wobbled in her attempt not to fall. If she hit the mat, the fight was as good as over. Tatyana would go for the pin. She wasn't playing anymore. There was a new desperation in her eyes. Somehow, when Ashleen hadn't been looking, the tide had shifted. She regained her footing.

Immediately, Tatyana dropped to the floor and kicked, sweeping Ashleen's feet from under her. She went down, but Tatyana was down too. Ashleen made a grab for her. A panicked huff escaped Tatyana, and she struck, fist impacting solidly with Ashleen's nose. Ashleen yelped and brought her hands to her face. Her fingers came away bloody.

Again, Ivanoff hadn't called the foul. Ashleen was about to say something when she realized Tatyana hadn't gone for the pin.

"Is that it?" she taunted. "I was just getting warmed up!"

Ashleen's grip on her temper started to slip. Frustration frayed her patience, and she fought to control it. She forced herself back to her feet and threw a kick at Tatyana's stomach.

She switched her focus from strength to speed. Hitting hard didn't mean anything if she couldn't make contact. Her shin slammed into Tatyana's stomach.

Tatyana hit the ground and instantly bounced off of it, her upper body strength and light frame allowing her to counter the fall and land on her feet effortlessly. Ashleen aimed another kick at her. Tatyana caught her foot and pinned it under her arm. Her features didn't betray a thing, but Ashleen could feel her struggling to draw air back into her lungs.

Tatyana kicked Ashleen's remaining leg out from under her. Ashleen hit the mat flat on her back, huffing to catch her breath and shaking sweaty hair out of her eyes as she rolled onto her knees and stood up. She wasn't done yet. Not when she could taste victory.

She feigned a punch at Tatyana's head, and when Tatyana moved to dodge it, drove a knee into her solar plexus. Tatyana stumbled backward. She was still avoiding blocking.

This had to end soon. They were both exhausted. Sim or not, everything felt real, down to the tremor in Ashleen's muscles as they threatened to give up. She willed her limbs steady.

Tatyana threw a kick and Ashleen braced herself. She took the full force of the blow and countered by knocking Tatyana's leg from under her. She followed Tatyana to the floor, determined to stick the pin.

Tatyana squirmed, slippery like a weasel. She grabbed Ashleen's arm and locked her shoulder, but Ashleen still had a hold of her leg. It was a stalemate.

Or was it? Ashleen bit down on her lip. Rome's words still nagged at the back of her mind. She had to wonder if the reason Tatyana wasn't blocking was because she couldn't block. It was a gamble, but Ashleen could get her free arm around Tatyana's neck and go for a grapple. To do so, she would have to dislocate her shoulder.

If Tatyana was stronger than Ashleen, she could then break the grapple and Ashleen would be down an arm. Tatyana would win. But if she wasn't stronger... It was worth the risk. There wasn't any shame in losing to a knight captain, especially in the first fight.

She twisted and yelled as her shoulder wrenched free of its socket. Tatyana's eyes widened. Astonishment slowed her reaction, and Ashleen trapped her in a headlock.

Tatyana struggled and clawed at Ashleen's arm, digging angry red furrows into her skin. Ashleen tightened her grip, waiting for Tatyana's inevitable escape. It never came. Tatyana's breaths became brief pants, unable to inhale fully as Ashleen's arm restricted her airway.

The other huntsmen looked on in stunned silence as finally, when she couldn't draw in a breath and was blue in the face, Tatyana feebly slapped Ashleen's forearm to surrender.

Ashleen relaxed her grip and Tatyana fell forward onto her hands and knees, coughing violently. Ashleen cradled her injured arm against her chest and rocked up onto her feet.

When Tatyana caught her breath, her expression crumpled into a fearsome snarl as she spat out the word "congratulations" with enough venom that it sounded more like an insult than good sportsmanship.

Ashleen gazed down at her unfazed, "I'd offer you a hand up, but I only have the one."

Tatyana pushed herself up and curled her lip. "I don't need your help." She stormed off the mat and flickered out of existence as she left the sim.

Ashleen glanced around the room for cues. For a long minute, it was silent. Even her team didn't say anything as she rejoined them.

She began to worry she'd done something wrong. Uncertain, she turned to Izzy.

"Was I supposed to throw the fight?"

Izzy shook his head, "No. No, it's just... Tatyana has been knight captain for longer than any of us have, except maybe Winona. We all expected you to lose in the first thirty seconds."

"Well thanks for the vote of confidence."

Izzy scrunched up his face. "Honestly, I'm a little put out. I spent years training nonstop to get the title. You've only been here for, what? Two weeks? I'm trying to figure out if there's any way you could have cheated."

"Hey!" Ashleen shoved him and winced as her dislocated shoulder protested. "It's not like I resorted to head blows. Unlike somebody." She grumbled and rubbed her jaw.

"Here, there's a way to reset by--" Morpheus' fingers crept into Ashleen's hair and brushed the back of her neck. Images from the previous night's dreams flickered through her mind's eye and she jerked away from him, stumbling into Demetrius.

"Please don't."

"I'm just trying to help," Morpheus cast her a look somewhere between perplexity and reproach, and backed off.

Izzy was glancing back and forth between them again. Ashleen didn't know the conclusion he was drawing, but she already didn't like it.

Instead she brought her focus back to Morpheus. "Why are you always so touchy? It wouldn't hurt you to ask permission once in a while."

The look on Morpheus' face said nobody had ever told him something like that before, but she heard Dahei smother a laugh.

Izzy struggled to mask his amusement as well and stretched a hand toward Ashleen's neck. He hesitated long enough for her to stop him if she wanted. When she didn't, his fingers pressed into a pressure point near the base of her skull.

Her arm went static with pins and needles, and she didn't even feel it when her shoulder relocated. A second later she realized the throbbing in her nose had stopped, and she couldn't taste blood anymore.

"Better?"

She nodded.

After the rankings had concluded and they'd left the sim, Leo approached them. He slapped Ashleen's arm. She flinched. It wasn't dislocated anymore, but the memory of the pain was still fresh.

"Congratulations. I'm having trouble believing what I just saw, but a celebration is in order."

"One hour?" Izzy suggested.

Leo nodded. "My dorm?"

"See you then."

Ashleen glanced back and forth between them. "Wait a minute, I didn't agree to a party."

"Come on!" Cyrus wheedled. "That was amazing! It's been years since there was a new knight captain. Can't we be excited for our friend?"

Ashleen held her breath. She'd rather have a rematch with Tatyana right now than go to a party, but Cyrus' use of the word 'friend' was difficult to ignore. The gathering would be small. Just a couple people, and she had tranquilizers; this wasn't going to be a repeat of the past.

She released a long exhale and nodded. "Okay."

Cyrus let out a whoop of triumph.

Ashleen wished she had something nice to change into. She stared down her reflection in the bathroom mirror and picked at her face. She missed make up. She didn't have a lot of hair to style, but she fussed with it anyway, wondering if she could get a couple of thin braids to stay without hair ties. The hour was almost up before she conceded and went as she was.

"The champion has arrived!" Cyrus announced her entrance with a dramatic flourish, and Ashleen hid her blush with her hands.

"Cyrus, don't!"

Sushila struggled out of a bean bag chair and bounced over to hug her before Ashleen could argue. "Congratulations!"

"Thanks," Ashleen replied in a small voice. "I don't think I ever congratulated you on your knighthood."

Sushila waved a hand dismissively. "Pah. That's nothing. You're a knight captain! And so soon!"

"I know!" Izzy grumbled, "I'm jealous."

Ashleen bit her lip. "I don't think I can take credit."

"What are you talking about?" Dahei retorted. "Own that shit."

"Yeah," Leo agreed. "Tatyana has remained undefeated as long as any of us can remember."

"That's not entirely true," Demetrius countered.

"Shh," Dahei pressed a finger to Demetrius' lips. "You're undermining our efforts."

"So how did you do it?" Prue interjected, disentangling herself from Morpheus long enough to come over.

"I gambled," Ashleen admitted, "Didn't anyone else notice that she wasn't actually strong? At least... not like a tranq is."

The entire room fell silent and stared at her. Ashleen curled inward on herself and back pedaled. "I'm not saying she wasn't good... but."

"No, you're right." It was only the second time Janice had addressed Ashleen, and the latter was glad it wasn't to put a curse on her. "Tranqs get their strength from contact with the blood of Anshathane. It's either inherited genetically, or in rare cases, they come into contact with ichor. Tatyana has neither."

"I had no idea," Izzy said.

"You weren't supposed to," Janice stated matter-of-factly. "Nobody was supposed to know. When she started here, she was a scofflaw. But she was trained in martial arts and preferred not to use weapons. She petitioned the Archwarden to be reassigned as a tranq, and the Archwarden agreed. Since she excelled at using her opponent's strength against them and didn't have the disadvantage of losing her temper, she had an edge in the ranking duels. I respect her cunning."

"And no one noticed?" Izzy asked.

"Her team already knows. I know because I used to be on it, I'm guessing Demetrius knows because he's just been here that long."

Demetrius nodded. "I remember when she was a scofflaw. However, I was not aware that she had not come into contact with ichor. I assumed that was the reason she switched."

"She built a reputation, and those of us who knew respected her too much to besmirch it." Janice scowled pointedly at Ashleen. "It would not be wise to start now."

Ashleen shook her head vehemently. "I wouldn't have even known if Rome hadn't told me."

"Rome?" Cyrus asked, "Who's he?"

"Romulus," Ashleen explained, "The other warden? He and Ivanoff supervise the sim together."

Izzy frowned in confusion, "That sim has only ever been supervised by Ivanoff."

"There is no other warden," Leo said in agreement.

Ashleen shrank in on herself. "I'm not crazy."

"I've sensed him too," Demetrius told them. "I did not know his name until now, but there has been a new warden ever since Ashleen arrived. I thought they came together. He is strong. He is also hiding something."

Prue knit her eyebrows together. "Why couldn't I sense anything?"

"He is masking his presence," Demetrius explained. "It is difficult for me to catch more than a hint of him now and then. But he is there."

"I like where this is heading," Cyrus announced giddily.

"Seems like something we should bring up to Ivanoff," Sushila suggested, her face betraying how much it bothered her.

"Not yet," Izzy countered. "Don't know what this is. Better to sit on it until we do."

Over time the conversations drifted to new topics, and Ashleen sought out a corner seat on the couch farthest from the chaos. She observed her peers casually and put immense effort into not looking like she was avoiding everyone.

Prue and Morpheus had practically melded into one being. Even though they weren't making out, it was blatantly obvious that they wanted to. It made Ashleen sick, and she wished she hadn't come to the party in the first place.

Her silent brooding didn't go unnoticed for long. Despite how much effort she'd put into being inconspicuous, Izzy flopped onto the couch right next to her.

He rested his elbows on his knees and drew close enough that only Ashleen would hear him. "Have you had the dream yet?"

Ashleen jerked her attention away from Morpheus and Prue guiltily. "What dream?"

Izzy made a calming gesture. "Relax, we've all had it."

"I don't know what you're talking about."

He stared at her in silence until she broke.

Ashleen hid her face in her hands. "I don't even like him."

Izzy chuckled. "You're lucky he's dense as a box of rocks, cause you're a horrible liar."

"Wait, what do you mean, you've all had it?"

"Anyone who's heard the whale song has had the dream." He hid a bashful grin. "At least the rest of you have some degree of interest in men. I woke up nauseous more than a few times."

Ashleen's gaze cautiously slid back to Morpheus. "Does he know?"

"Are you joking? Do you wanna tell him?"

"Of course not!" She must have spoken a little too loudly, because Morpheus glanced in her direction and caught her watching him. He averted his gaze immediately and laughed just a little too loudly at something Prue had said. Ashleen told herself she hadn't noticed how he bit his lip when he smiled.

"You're staring," Izzy teased.

"I am not!" Ashleen elbowed him.

Izzy laced his fingers behind his head and leaned back against the couch cushions. "If you say so."

Sometime after Prue and Morpheus had wandered off, Sushila broke out the alcohol and Ashleen had made her escape. She tried to shake off the bitterness that gnawed her insides. She would have liked to retreat to her room, but the couple had probably already thought to take advantage of the empty dorm.

Instead she heaved a sigh and headed towards the gardens. Over the last few days, she'd begun to adapt to being in a high place. That combined with her frustration numbed the fear she normally would have felt toward the apparent height of the perpendicular ring.

When she swung herself out onto the ladder, the orientation of the artificial gravity shifted. She didn't need to finish climbing down, so instead she stood up and stalked through the beds of vegetables.

There was no lighting system since the ring was almost entirely glass, open to the sun from daybreak to dusk. The space was a welcome change when compared to the bland, uniform halls of the rest of the city.

Through the glass, the night sky glittered with stars. Alexandria was outwardly dark, and this far above the clouds there wasn't any light pollution. A nebulous purple gold arm of the Milky Way cut the darkness like a pillar of fire.

Ashleen startled at the sound of someone humming. She glanced to her right. A ways down she could see a silhouette among the slender trunks of some young fruit trees.

A frustrated noise interrupted the humming, then it started over with a slightly different tune. Curiosity drove her towards the voice, and details of the owner's silhouette sharpened, starkly outlined by the celestial glow of the galaxy.

"Morpheus?"

He startled and whirled to face her. Reflected light painted the side of his face in a wash of pastels. "Ashleen? What are you doing here?"

"Avoiding you," Ashleen laughed once, to break the tension. "What's your excuse?"

Morpheus imitated her dry laugh. "Avoiding Prue."

"Why?"

He shrugged and avoided her gaze. "We had an argument. She seems to think she's not enough for me."

"Ah," Ashleen felt a stab of guilt. She'd been the one to bring that up to Prue a while back.

The silence stretched between them, until Morpheus broke it. "If you don't have anywhere to be, you should stick around."

"For what?"

"You'll see." He pulled his hands out of his pockets and rocked up onto his toes in perfect synchronicity with a low rumble that vibrated the floor.

Ashleen's feet unstuck from the ground and she drifted away from it. She flailed, grabbing for something to anchor herself. Her fingers curled around the thin trunk of a nearby tree. She tried to keep her grip loose and gentle, but her heart ticked like a bomb in her chest.

"Relax, it's just like swimming," Morpheus called from somewhere above her. When she looked, he was gracefully tugging himself through the trees toward the back wall. "Come on."

Ashleen swallowed her stomach and forced aside the fear she refused to show him. Ever so slowly, she relaxed her grip on this tree and reached for the next one.

When they'd both reached the wall, Morpheus began to tug himself up with the tips of his fingers, occasionally pushing off with a foot to cross a greater distance. Ashleen squeezed her eyes shut and fought the nausea bubbling beneath her ribcage before following his example.

Her head bumped something and she opened one eye halfway. They'd reached the ceiling. She swore under her breath.

"Wait, are you afraid of heights?" Morpheus' voice drifted from somewhere above and ahead of her.

"So what if I am?" Ashleen struggled to sound fierce despite the quiver in her voice.

When he spoke next he was much closer. "Can I help?"

"If you don't I'll probably either pass out or throw up," Ashleen admitted begrudgingly.

The low thrum of whale song settled in her bones, and she felt the tension ease out of her shoulders. His fingers brushed hers hesitantly, and she peeled her eyes open. He held a hand out towards her, his other steadied him against the ceiling.

For the first time, it didn't feel like his will was usurping her own. The whale song didn't sound like a set of puppet strings. She took his hand, and he pulled her the rest of the way to the ceiling.

The momentum sent them into a gentle spin, and Ashleen's adrenaline fought against Morpheus' song. He flattened a palm against the ceiling and she followed his example. Their spin came to a gentle stop and Morpheus jerked his chin towards something through the glass.

Ashleen tightened her grip on his hand as she worked up the nerve to look at what he wanted to show her. The view before her stole what was left of her breath. Through a gap in the clouds, the lights of a distant city sprawled.

They glittered like an intricate spider web adorned in golden dew. The vantage point Morpheus had found came with a feeling Ashleen couldn't quite explain. Melancholy and profound, it swaddled her in the impression of infinite smallness and an expanded awareness all at once. Her body didn't even matter anymore, the tether that bound her to a corporeal existence had snapped, leaving her floating free in a vast ocean scattered with tiny points of light.

Morpheus called her back when he spoke. She hadn't even noticed him stop singing. "There's something you should know."

"What?"

"My mother was a siren." He took a steadying breath. "I inherited the aura. It influences everyone to some degree or another. Dahei, Izzy, and Demetrius are the only team I've been able to stay with for any length of time. I think it's because they all had strong preexisting bonds. I tend to wreak havoc on less stable team relationships."

The information unsettled her, but not as much as Ashleen would have expected it to. She felt more relief at finally having an explanation for the way he made her feel than she felt fear of his abilities. "Who else knows?"

"The rest of the team, Neele, and the Archwarden."

"Not Prue?"

"I wanted to tell her, but Izzy thought it was a bad idea. Not all huntsmen are friendly to nonhumans."

"Prue would never do anything to hurt you." The words left a bitter taste in her mouth but they were true.

"I know, but I've trusted too easily in the past."

"What do you mean?"

"When I first arrived in Alexandria I didn't have any memories. I was naive, and when Pavane tried to get close to me, I let him."

Ashleen grimaced. "How close?"

The look on Morpheus' face told her everything. "Close. He doesn't know the whole truth, but he's seen enough of me to suspect."

He paused a beat before he continued. "I might've told him everything, but Izzy saw him hit me one day and intervened before then."

Ashleen blew a long breath out through pursed lips. The thought of Pavane hitting Morpheus made her blood boil. She hated the idea of people who would hurt those who trusted them.

"It's strange, my aura doesn't seem to affect you at all," he said, turning his head to scrutinize her.

Ashleen forced out a chuckle. "Oh, I've felt its effects. It's sort of nice, knowing it's not just me."

He ducked his head, but Ashleen could have sworn she'd seen a flicker of disappointment.

"It won't tear the team apart," she assured him.

When he looked at her again, his expression was soft. "I'm glad. Izzy and the others are the closest thing I have to family. I don't want to lose that."

"You won't."

"And you won't tell anyone?"

"On two conditions." The sincerity in his eyes made her heart flutter. "First, why didn't you tell Izzy I hit you?"

Morpheus dropped his gaze thoughtfully, "I guess I empathize with you. I know what it's like, to be able to do real damage without meaning to. Alexandria is a chance to write a new story, no matter what came before. I didn't want to ruin the first page of yours."

Ashleen didn't have the words to reply. More guilt was the last thing she needed tonight, but she wished she could take back all the judgements she'd made of his character up until this point.

"And the second condition?"

She allowed herself a weak laugh. "Don't tell anyone I'm afraid of heights?"

The smile that spread over Morpheus' face stole the breath from her lungs. "I think that can be arranged."

11

Enter the Library

Demetrius felt around for his other shoe. It couldn't have gone far. Ah. There it was. He shoved his foot into it and recoiled as something that shouldn't have been there dug into his toe. Odd. He slipped his hand into the shoe and felt around. The offending object tumbled into his palm and sent a chill up his spine. He dropped his shoe and ran his thumb along the cool surface of a ring.

At first he thought it might be the one Dahei had lost, but he knew every ridge and bump of Dahei's rings by heart. This one was new. It was a smooth band with a comforting weight, but he had no way of knowing what type of metal it could be.

There hadn't been any moment overnight that anyone else could have lost their ring in his room. If it wasn't Dahei's, then it had to be his. Demetrius had given up hope of ever finding a ring years ago. He'd assumed he'd sacrificed his counterweight with the rest of his people.

"Hey," Dahei grumbled, voice rough with sleep. He rolled over and brushed his knuckles along Demetrius' arm.

Demetrius startled, sucking a breath through his teeth, when the normally cool metal on Dahei's finger burned him. That had never happened before. He would have remembered it.

"Sorry," Dahei yawned. "Didn't mean to startle you. What are you doing?"

Demetrius curled his fingers closed around his ring; there would be a better moment for this conversation. A moment when Dahei was fully awake, when he wasn't still recovering from possession and an encounter with Hideo.

Demetrius slipped the ring into his pocket and ruffled Dahei's already spectacular bedhead. "Nothing. Breakfast."

"Ugh. Stop," Dahei batted at him.

Demetrius chuckled, "I need to send a message to my sisters. Do you want some coffee?" A practiced gesture had a handful of butterfly-like wisps tumbling out of his hair.

"Mhmm," Dahei nodded and forced one eye open. "How are your sisters?"

"I had to teach them a gesture to banish spirits that scared them. So far they have not drawn the attention of anything serious," Demetrius explained.

"Lucky. I probably owe my brothers an update too."

"Do you think they would get along?"

"Maybe."

"We could put them in contact with each other," Demetrius suggested.

Dahei rubbed his eyes. "Are you playing matchmaker? Thought that was Izzy's thing."

Demetrius chuckled. "Just a thought."

"Sou desu ne?" he laughed, then turned more serious. "You sure you're okay?"

"Fine." Demetrius' fingers returned to his pocket to dance over the ring.

Dahei's expression softened. "I'm sure they're okay."

"You're probably right."

"Are we getting coffee or not? If you're just going to sit there I'm going back to sleep."

Morpheus rested his chin in his palm and absentmindedly pushed his coffee mug in a circle with the tip of his finger. He'd only managed to get a fitful four hours of sleep the night before. His mind had kept him up running laps around the argument he'd had with Prue and the conversation he'd had with Ashleen.

He hummed a few bars of the melody he'd come up with last night, the perfect lyrics hovering just out of reach. He sighed his aggravation as Prue sank into a chair next to him, her tiny hands cupping the sides of her mug.

One breath of silence. Two breaths. Three. And a half. "Is that a new song?" Prue blurted, unable to stand the quiet any longer.

"Yeah, I guess," Morpheus dipped a fingertip into his coffee. Still too hot.

"It's nice," Prue told him. Morpheus made a non-committal noise. More silence.

Prue coiled a lock of his hair around her finger and let it spring back playfully. The gesture usually amused him, but today guilt twisted in his stomach. He frowned and leaned away from her.

Prue's face fell and she cleared her throat, returning her hand to her mug. "Can we talk?"

When Morpheus took too long to respond, she pushed on. "What happened last night? You didn't come back. You always come back after we argue."

Morpheus opened his mouth like he was going to say something, then thought better of it. Instead he stared into the steam rising from his coffee.

"Come on Morpheus, I'm not stupid. You're shutting me out. Something's up."

"It's nothing. It was late, and I was tired."

"Did something happen with Pavane? Talk to me." With each new sentence, more alarm trickled into Prue's tone.

Morpheus sank down and buried his face in his folded arms. He knew he owed her an explanation, or at least a decent excuse, but he couldn't find the words for either.

"Someone else then?" She rested a hand on him, "It's okay."

"No it isn't," he said, lifting his head to shake it.

"You know I've never resented you for being what you are, or for any of the people who came before me."

Momentary pain flashed across Morpheus' face before he dropped his head into his arms again, "I only ever wanted one."

Prue chewed her lip, a wrinkle marring the space between her eyebrows. "And it's not me, is it?"

Morpheus sat up, "That isn't what I meant."

"I know it isn't," Prue assured him. She spun the ring on her finger thoughtfully. "But it's the truth, and we'll have to face it eventually."

Ashleen crunched on her fifth strip of bacon. She'd picked this table so she could spy on Morpheus from the corner of her eye. She could still feel him holding her hand and she hated how confused it left her.

Uncertainty made her sick. Every step she took closer to the truth, the blurrier it got. It was easier to dislike Morpheus. It was easier to trust her mother. It was easier to believe ichor, and all the monsters it created, weren't real.

She was sinking in a mire of the half-truths and white lies she had to remember. She didn't feel anything for Prue. Or Morpheus. Her mother couldn't know about what she was doing. Morpheus wasn't human, and she couldn't tell anyone. Tatyana wasn't a tranq, and she couldn't tell anyone. How was she going to keep track of who knew what and what she could and couldn't talk about?

Ashleen wished someone would tell her the whole story from start to finish. The more pieces she acquired, the less she understood. Every time she thought she knew what she was doing, the rules changed.

Two weeks ago, sirens weren't even real, and now her ex-girl-friend was dating one. Did this make Morpheus more or less trust-worthy? On the one hand, he'd told her the truth. On the other, he'd pretty much admitted he could control people, and had attempted to use that ability on her on more than one occasion.

The chair across from her squeaked as it was pulled away from the table and Neele sank into it. "Morning!"

Ashleen tore her attention from Morpheus and hoped Neele hadn't noticed her staring. "Morning."

"How are you adjusting?"

"Alright, I guess."

"I heard you made knight captain yesterday. I'd say you're doing better than alright."

"I got lucky. I'm honestly surprised they gave me the title at all."

"If you say so. The Archwarden is quite impressed, she'd like to have a word."

"Now?"

"If you're done staring at Morpheus, yes."

Ashleen cringed. "You saw that?"

Neele smiled. "My dear, subtly is not your strong suit."

Ashleen sighed and followed Neele to the infirmary, where she took the long hall that led to the Archwarden's office.

When she entered, she found Amaris seated in her velvet arm-chair, pouring over stacks of documents on her desk. She looked as if she'd aged five years in the last two weeks. It took her a moment to notice Ashleen's arrival, but when she did, she hurriedly cleared away the files.

"Ashleen! I apologize for my state of disarray, my work has had me a bit preoccupied lately."

"It's okay," Ashleen assured her, crossing the room to take a seat in one of the armchairs positioned across from her.

Amaris pulled a tea tray over from the edge of her desk and poured two cups.

"Neele said you wanted to talk to me?" Ashleen asked, taking the delicate cup that was placed before her.

"Yes, you have progressed faster than I could have hoped for," Amaris said, offering Ashleen a cookie. "If I had any doubt that Connor was your father, I don't anymore."

"The last time we spoke, you said my father was an archknight."

"Dear, your father was the archknight. It has taken me decades to rebuild in his absence."

Ashleen swallowed her anxiety with a sip of tea. Every time someone brought up Connor, it was to praise him. Though she could barely remember her father, the shoes he'd left seemed to keep growing. She wasn't sure she would ever be able to fill them at this point. "I just got lucky."

Amaris waved a hand, "Psh. I've kept this city running for over forty years. There's no such thing. Most tranqs rely on ferocity and adrenaline to win a fight. I have only seen two tranqs over a gladiator rank win a fight without their rage. You, and your father."

Amaris' cat padded over and hopped into Ashleen's lap. "What about Tatyana?"

"Tatyana is a tranq in name only."

Ashleen set down her cookie to scratch the purring tabby's chin. "You could have changed that, if you'd given her ichor. She's far more experienced than I am, why not make her into an archknight?"

Amaris spread her hands on the table, smoothing an invisible tablecloth. "Ichor is dangerous and unpredictable. Most tranqs already have it in their bloodline, which gives them a certain predisposition for it. If I were to give Tatyana ichor, there's a higher chance it would either kill or subsume her."

She poured more tea for herself. "You have already proven you can use your ichor without letting it control you, which means right now, you are the best candidate in the city to don the mantle of Vanquisher."

Ashleen jerked her hand back as the cat nipped her and leapt out of her lap. Apparently it had had enough scritches. "Who are the other archknights?"

"It is up to them whether or not to reveal their identities to you, should you join their ranks. I'm the only one who can create new archknights, but other than that they govern themselves." Amaris smiled. "I know Barrage likes to give new members a probationary period while he decides whether or not to trust them."

"Barrage?"

"The deadeye archknight. The others are known as Façade, Proverb, and Diva. The scofflaw, beckoner, and vesper, respectively. I think you would like Diva. She and you are quite similar."

Ashleen inspected her knuckle for blood. She'd had worse from her own cat, but it still stung. "If I were to accept the rank, what then?"

"Well, you'd have to pass several ordeals before you could officially join the ranks. The archknights share a psychic mesh with each other that allows them to communicate telepathically. In order to connect to that mesh, you will have to pass a test for each member of their own design. The final ordeal is yours alone; in order to pass it, you will have to establish equilibrium with your own ichor. It will not be easy."

"What happens if I fail?"

"If you are subsumed by the ichor at any point, the other archknights will kill you."

She said it so matter-of-factly that Ashleen wondered for a moment if she was serious. "And if I choose not to join?"

"Then you return to your normal duties. But without you, we may never stabilize the tranqs, and your father's mission will go unfinished."

Ashleen weighed her options. She might never fill the void her father had left, but it would be worse not to try at all. She'd never been motivated by power, but if she saved the tranqs, she could also save herself. If she could defeat Anshathane, or at least reach him, there was a chance she could fix everything. She could atone for everyone she'd hurt, and prevent perhaps countless future deaths.

If she had an ability that could potentially turn the tide in a losing battle, did she have a right to keep it to herself? Even if she returned to her normal duties, Ashleen hadn't seen a single huntsman over the age of thirty-five. It wasn't as if she were giving up some cushy office job. It wouldn't be long before she met a monster she couldn't beat anyway.

A memory from her childhood jumped to the forefront of her mind. She'd spent hours designing hero costumes with her mother when Alice had caught her crying about her abilities. Once she'd daydreamed about fighting alongside characters like Wonder Woman or Carol Danvers.

Now, the opportunity to do exactly that was resting at her feet, all she had to do was survive her own super serum. "When do I start?"

"Right now, if you wish." Amaris reached into her desk and passed her the same vial she'd shown Ashleen earlier.

Ashleen rolled it back and forth between her fingers and watched the ichor within defy gravity. Nerves bit at her as she loosened the cap and unleashed the inky substance. It wasted no time slipping over the edge of the vial and onto the back of her hand.

She hissed. It was hotter than she had anticipated and burned like lemon juice in a cut. It spread over her skin and her heart raced as it crept up her arm. It reached her shoulder and showed no signs of slowing.

Ashleen dropped the vial and clawed at the ichor with her opposite hand. Instead of coming off, the oily substance only spread, tracking up both arms and slithering onto her neck. This couldn't be right, there hadn't been that much in the vial.

Even though she'd chosen this, Ashleen could feel panic sinking icy claws into her heart. She glanced down and immediately wished she hadn't. The ichor had already spread over the rest of her body. It seemed to slow as it slipped over the ridge of her jaw, savoring her terror.

Ashleen pressed her lips into a firm line and held her breath to quell a whimper as the ichor began to bubble with anticipation. It enveloped one ear, then the other, and all she could hear was her own heartbeat drumming out a horrified rhythm in her chest. When it reached her nose, she smelled the metallic tang of iron and acrid chemicals. It burned the back of her throat like the water in a chlorinated pool.

She shot a panicked glance at Amaris, pleading for help, or advice, or anything that could reassure her that she wasn't about to die. All she received was a nod of encouragement before she squeezed her eyes shut and the ichor suspended her in emptiness.

Four inky figures melted through the walls. One of them approached the slumped figure in the chair. She continued to twitch, fighting to draw enough air through a thin, opaque film.

"You warned her of the dangers?" he asked, his voice buzzing like a provoked hornet's nest.

"Of course."

"Hmm." One of his eerie yellow eyes drifted off the side of his face and slid through the ichor coating him to the side of his head. "Proverb. What can you see?"

An archknight with a mask of oily raven wings that concealed its entire head and two sets of arms stepped forward to peer at the unconscious tranq. "The oncoming storm will bow before a mind that is wise enough to navigate it," they said cryptically. "But even a wise mind easily wanders without anchors."

"That doesn't sound good," a feminine voice interjected. A willowy archknight with a mane of writhing tentacles watched from her spot anxiously.

"Shall we introduce ourselves?" the smallest archknight called from his perch on the back of Ashleen's chair. He tilted it back and balanced precariously on one leg before letting it crash back to all fours, jostling its occupant.

"Hellion," the first archknight scolded. "'Verb, you're the most experienced. You should go first. Explain the rules."

The four-armed being extended two of their hands toward Ashleen's head. "As you wish."

The floor spat Ashleen out into a vast archival space. She sat up and inspected her arms. The ichor had vanished and she didn't feel anything unusual, beyond that she had no idea where she was.

"Hello?"

"Welcome to the Library," an automated voice replied. Floor to ceiling shelves flickered to life and bands of blue light raced along the spines of digital files. Lighting from below flooded the space with shattered refractions as it shone up through water contained beneath a glass floor. Shadows played along the walls as roving bands of tiny squid fled from the light.

Whoever had designed the space had put a great deal of time into imagining it. It felt just as real as any sim she'd experienced so far, and yet, this wasn't a place that could possibly exist outside of imagination. She ran her fingers along the spines of the glimmering files. How far did the detail stretch, exactly?

She started to tug one free of the shelf when the voice spoke again. "If you have a question, you need only ask."

Ashleen dropped her hand to her side. "Where am I?"

"Location, unknown. Tracking subroutine, offline."

"Typical." Of course it couldn't tell her where she was. This place didn't exist.

"Would you like to ask another question?"

"What is Alexandria?" If this space was inside her head, it would not know anything more than what she knew.

"Alexandria is the final existing seat of 'The Order of the Huntsmen'. It is currently under the leadership of 'Amaris Faustian.' Would you like to know more?"

Intrigued, Ashleen continued. "Yes, tell me about Amaris Faustian."

"Amaris Faustian. Current location, unknown. Birthplace, unknown. Occupation, Archwarden of Alexandria. Designation, scofflaw. Family relations, mother, deceased. Father, unknown. Two children, deceased. No further information available. Do you have another question?"

Whatever it was, the Library wasn't tethered to her existing knowledge. She'd known nothing about Amaris' designation or her family. "Files on Ashleen Gallagher."

"Ashleen Gallagher. Current location, unknown. Birthplace: Dheering, Washington. Occupation, huntsman. Designation, tranq.

Family relations, mother, Alice Gallagher. Father, Connor Gallagher, deceased. Would you like to know more?"

"Files, Connor Gallagher."

"Connor Gallagher has left a recorded message for ID: Ashleen Grace Gallagher. ID, confirmed. Playback message?"

"Yes!"

Several of the glowing files slid up their shelves and spiraled on the ceiling. Their spin accelerated until they emitted a beam of hazy light all the way to the floor. Within the light, a figure glitched into visibility.

Ashleen's heart skipped a beat. In the hologram, Connor Gallagher looked barely older than she was. He was taller, perhaps a bit broader, but not by much. The whole image was tinted blue, but she guessed his hair was the same color as hers, since he had the freckles to match.

"Ashleen," the hologram spoke. "No matter how much I might've wished otherwise, it was inevitable that you'd end up here. I regret nothing more than that I was never there to guide you against the same problems I faced. I can only offer you one piece of advice..." He paused as if ensuring he had her attention. "You can trust the archknights. Earn their confidence, and in return you will earn the truth."

Ashleen opened her mouth to ask a question and yipped instead as the glass beneath her feet shattered, plunging her into the squid-filled water. She fought to swim back to the surface, but her kicking only sucked her down. The light grew dim, then faded out entirely.

Where was the bottom? Surely she should have hit it by now. Even as she processed the thought, glaring light blinded her. Sinking changed to falling, and she gasped for air even as it was ripped from her.

Ashleen landed on a silvery surface, cracks splintering out from the impact points of her hands and knees. She coughed violently. Salty water streamed off of her and stray squid writhed nearby. When she'd finally blinked enough of the sting out of her eyes that she could see what was before her, she reeled backwards.

A starving wolf snarled at her from her reflection in the mirrored floor. It had eerily reflective eyes and gore trailed from its muzzle. Its forelimbs were too long for its body and its shape seemed to warp, odd lumps appearing where they didn't belong before sinking back down.

She stood. Her patchy black fur seemed more liquid than hair. When she touched it, it clung to her claws and left stringy trails as she pulled away. Her outline was blurred by sooty smoke.

To her right the surface of the mirror rippled like water, and a four-armed figure rose out of it. Their body was shrouded in misty scarves and their face and head were hidden by a many-winged crest.

"Proverb," she greeted them, unsure how she knew who they were.

"Vanquisher." Proverb dipped their head respectfully.

Proverb waved a pair of taloned hands and the world around them shattered, spinning into a magnificent fractal of itself with a tinkling of glass. The two of them were standing in empty air. Below them, a labyrinth of skyscrapers sprawled. Above them, the exact same city was mirrored.

Proverb cocked their head, birdlike. "Step carefully, voracious one. A mind is a perilous place to wander."

"You know that's not much help," Ashleen growled, the wolf roughening her voice.

"It will help. If you listen," the beckoner gestured at their surroundings. "If you seek the truth, you will have to master each of us, and then yourself."

Before she could ask more questions, a clock tower struck twelve, and Ashleen fell. Straight up.

12

The Hanged Man

The wind lashed at her fur and stung her eyes. Panic burned her throat as the skyscrapers drew nearer, spires of cement and steel ready to slice her open. Windows shattered as she passed them, shards of glass raining in her wake. She rolled and narrowly missed a jagged antenna atop the tallest building. A second later she collided with its sloping roof.

She scrabbled for purchase and a terrified shriek burst from her chest, but she was falling again before she could catch hold of anything. Her heart played her ribcage like a xylophone. This was the end. She was going to hit the ground and die.

A magnificent marble cathedral rose out of the monotonous grey, its roof adorned with Raven-esque gargoyles. Ashleen crashed through the domed ceiling as if it were mere plaster and slammed into the floor with a bone rattling thud. It took her several minutes to realize she wasn't dead and she cautiously pushed up to her knees. Nothing seemed to be broken, but it still felt like she'd hit a marble floor at terminal velocity. She should be dead.

Gradually, she picked herself up and examined her surroundings. She knew this place. This was the Crypts of Muginn. Her mother had always promised they'd come here when she was older. The vaulted ceilings and elaborate arches took her breath away. The stained glass windows cast the interior in a rainbow of flickering lights. Ashleen drew her eyes to the ceiling. Even the mural there was a perfect copy of the real thing, with the exception of the hole she'd fallen through where Anshathane's head used to be.

She padded between the columns toward the dais at one end of the vast room. A strikingly life-like alabaster rendition of the gods rested there. The androgynous Muginn, veiled in gossamer stone fabric that concealed very little, massive wings outstretched. The near skeletal form of her son, Ikalusca, lay prone before her. Her consort, Anshathane, stood behind her, his hand resolutely on her shoulder as he looked on. Inky water flooded from the wounds in Ikalusca's head and side. The same imitation of ichor dripped in rivulets from Muginn's face as the deity cried over the body of her child.

Anshathane's eyes seemed to bore into Ashleen's soul, asking a silent question she couldn't answer. Something didn't feel right. There was a detail missing. She turned a circle. There weren't any doors. A damp draft caressed her face, and the sound of stone grating on stone made Ashleen's hair stand on end.

Slowly, she turned back to face the statues. Muginn had stopped crying and was now looking right at her. All three deities were pointing at something. For a long moment, Ashleen couldn't tear her eyes off them, terrified that they would move again when she wasn't looking.

When she finally convinced herself they weren't going to kill her the moment she blinked, she glanced in the direction they were pointing.

Nestled on the far wall was a small door too short for her to go through without crouching down. Ashleen's insides twisted. She knew it led into the catacombs, a sacred space meant only for the corpses of Muginn's most loyal apostles. Ashleen wasn't even a beckoner. She had no right to enter those halls.

The tiny door creaked open and swung inward and an impossible blackness seemed to creep out towards her, humming with whispers she couldn't quite hear. Ashleen shuddered and recoiled, but when she tried to step backward, the portal sucked her in. Her feet slipped along the stone. She struggled for a handhold, but found only polished floors. If she survived this, she and Proverb were going to have a talk about how much falling they'd put her through.

Ashleen squealed as she slipped into the catacombs and the doors slammed behind her. The stagnant air reeked of decay and death. Bioluminescent moss glimmered dimly in the darkness. Under normal circumstances she'd be blind, but the eyes of Ashleen's ichor form reflected the moss enough that she could make out the outlines of her surroundings.

The door had vanished behind her, she could only go forward and hope the tunnel led to an exit. As her eyes adjusted to the gloom, she wished they hadn't. Human skulls leered out at her from the walls and she couldn't shake the feeling that something was watching her, just out of sight.

Fragments of bone that had escaped the walls' mosaics crunched under foot and Ashleen cringed. She absolutely shouldn't be here. The Raven would punish her when she resurfaced, if she didn't just claim Ashleen's soul outright.

Something hissed across stone and she whirled, expecting to see some new horror, or perhaps the gargoyles from the roof. The skulls had turned in the walls to watch her.

Ashleen cringed. "Stop that. I'm sorry. I don't want to be here any more than you want me to be here." The skulls slowly shifted to their original positions and she whined a protest at the eeriness of it all.

Goosebumps prickled on Ashleen's arms. People had gotten lost down here. Tourists who snuck in for a peek often turned up months later, bodies desiccated and bent into mutilated shapes, jaws frozen in horrified screams. Only apostles could walk this labyrinth safely, communing with the dead for guidance.

Before her the catacombs branched and split into three directions. One of the gargoyles from the roof sat in the center of the cavern. It seemed to watch her as she drew closer.

"You bring disharmony." The gargoyle's wings unfurled with a tinkling of volcanic glass. "Balance must be restored."

She sank into a defensive stance, "I'm sorry, but it wasn't my choice to come here."

"The choices I speak of are those you haven't yet made. The choices I speak of could kill thousands."

"So I'm to be punished for something that might never happen?" Ashleen protested as the gargoyle began to circle her.

"Balance must be restored," the beast said as it herded her towards the three branches. "Your choice will reveal your path."

Ashleen tore her eyes off the gargoyle to glance at the tunnels. Each had a word etched into the stone above it. The first was "love," the second was "sacrifice," and the third read, "service."

"Only one can break the cycle. Choose wisely."

Ashleen checked on the gargoyle. It had resumed its position in the center of the cavern, so she faced the tunnels. Love beckoned to her with soft, familiar, voices. The skulls in the sacrifice tunnel clacked their teeth at her menacingly. Freakish laughter cackled from somewhere just out of sight, while the shadows leaking out of the service tunnel seemed to writhe, their edges fuzzy.

Ashleen peered at them and squawked in alarm. She shuddered violently. They weren't shadows at all, but rather millions of tiny beetles. They swarmed over what remained of the last tourist to lose their way.

"Love! I choose love."

"A treacherous path indeed," the gargoyle mused. "So easy to lose one's way."

"I won't!" She skirted around the edge of the cavern, keeping as much distance between herself and the beetles as possible, and slipped through the mouth of the kindest tunnel.

"That's what they all say," the gargoyle whispered to the now empty cavern. "What they all say."

Now that she was inside the tunnel, Ashleen felt claustrophobic. Barely any space remained between each shoulder and the walls. She worried that if she breathed in too deeply, she might get stuck, so she kept her breaths shallow.

Every twist set her nerves on edge. The passage squeezed her around impossible corners. One or two panic inducing moments had seen her stuck, one leg crushed against the other until she'd managed to shoulder her way free.

Many branches peeled off of the tightly wound maze, but each only led to a dead end. One had led to a sheer drop. She would have fallen to her death if the sound of something she'd kicked hadn't alerted her to the abrupt change in the floor.

The voices didn't get any louder but the longer she listened, the more it sounded like they could only be calling her. Despite the sweetness of the sounds, the odor of rotting flesh still hung in the air, undisturbed for an unknown count of months or years.

Ashleen squeezed through another panic inducing space and the tunnel widened again. Her stomach flipped. The two paths she'd avoided earlier lay before her. The laughter and clacking skulls in sacrifice, the writhing mass of beetles in service.

Between the two paths sat a pair of gargoyles. They were positioned back to back and stared in opposite directions. As Ashleen approached they remained unmoving. Glassy stone gave their unblinking eyes a lifelike gleam, but neither one betrayed a clue that might direct her choice.

Careful to avoid the pulsing swarm of beetles, Ashleen sank into a cross-legged position before them. The ichor wolf melted into her skin, cued by some subconscious impression that it was no longer needed.

Indecision crippled her ability to move forward. If love had just brought her right back to where she started, she must have made the wrong choice. One of these paths was the right one, but that suggested that she only had one more chance to select it. Neither option seemed particularly pleasant and both seemed to end in death. She forced herself to ignore the way the beetles skittered in and out of the corpse's eye socket.

Ashleen bent her hands into the triangular channeling gesture she'd seen the apostles in her hometown use. She wasn't a beckoner, but neither were they. Their connection to Muginn was still sacrosanct; that had to count for something.

The rustle of feathers drew her attention. When she blinked, both statues had turned to look at her. They crouched like cats about to pounce. The whispers leaking out of the cave behind her had changed. Now they sounded more like music. The sighs were violins. The bellows were pipe organs. Both instruments were commonly played in canticles to Muginn.

When Ashleen refocused on the gargoyles, they'd moved again. They watched her from either shoulder. She had no idea how she hadn't seen them when they were so close to her.

She dipped her head in prayer. "Mother, which path would you have me choose?"

In a movement too fast to trace, both statues cocked their heads to listen.

Hot breath condensed on the back of Ashleen's neck and something distinctly not Raven snarled. "You would pray to a god you are not promised to?"

Ashleen twisted to look. Her ichor rose through her skin and her wolf's jaws slammed shut over her face like a visor. She bared her teeth at the boney, hairless wolf she was now nose to nose with.

It recoiled toward the edge of the room when she pushed herself up to her feet. The starving creature skirted around her and darted down the tunnel to her right, dissolving into the mass of beetles. The two gargoyles had vanished.

Ashleen blinked rapidly. The lack of any daylight made her blind to how many hours had passed, if time was passing at all. Proverb had said she would have to "master" the other archknights.

She'd taken it to mean defeating them in some way. But if that was what they had meant, it seemed odd that she was down here alone. Amaris had described the archknights as a cohesive unit. They had to work together. Maybe 'master' wasn't meant to be understood as defeat. Maybe it was meant to be understood as mastery of a topic, or skill.

She'd been going about this all wrong. It wasn't a test; it was an introduction. An introduction to Proverb. She examined the two tunnels again. One of these paths led to a connection they shared; she just had to pick the right one.

They were a beckoner. True beckoners would be devoted to Muginn. Ashleen was no expert, but she liked to think of herself as devout. She examined the paths before her. When viewed from a religious standpoint, they seemed a little less menacing. The Raven was a deity of death. The sacrificed skulls clacked their teeth ominously, but while Ashleen knew Muginn had been offered sacrifices in the past, the practice was frowned upon now.

She grimaced at the service tunnel and the carpet of beetles tracing swirling patterns over the corpse resting there. As disconcerting as it was, this was a better representation of Muginn's statutes. Muginn sanctified a death that served a purpose. Though many Ravenites dreamed of a heroic death, feeding beetles was still a purpose.

She squeezed her eyes shut and stepped into the skittering mass.

"Well done."

Ashleen's eyelids lit up red with unexpected light. When she adjusted to the change enough to open them, the beetles were gone. Clouds clung to her feet. She was back where she'd begun, a city sprawling far beneath and above her.

Proverb stood nearby. They extended a hand.

She took it and the ichor on their palms thinned until they were touching skin to skin. A flock of ravens crashed past her, their wings stinging her face and their claws catching in her hair. Their cries deafened her. Her surroundings plunged into absolute darkness and her veins itched as if they were moving.

A young boy addressed her. "What will you give me in return?"

She heard herself answer, "Anything, everything."

The boy tsked. "I hope that when we next speak, you will have learned how to bargain properly."

Proverb let go of her hand, and daylight returned with a vengeance. When they spoke, Ashleen heard their voice both inside and outside her head. "Temper your feelings, Barrage will not be as gentle as I have been. A perilous path lies at your feet, forge each bond strong, or you will break."

Ashleen started to ask a question, but Proverb gestured and she dropped through her cloud, spiraling down toward the city below. The tallest skyscraper split and twisted open to swallow her.

Proverb withdrew their hands from Ashleen's unconscious form. "The vanquisher prevails."

"But?" Barrage hadn't moved a centimeter from where he'd been standing for nearly an hour.

"There was something else, only for a second. Something spoke to her that wasn't me."

"Could it have been the ichor?" Diva suggested.

"It could have been. Her's is... strange to me."

"Anshathane is strange to all of us right now." Barrage started towards Ashleen. "Façade, watch the room."

Façade stood from his crouch. "As my liege demands," he saluted with a flourish. He vanished and reappeared crouched on the back of the Archwarden's chair.

"Must you have that specific perch?"

Façade snorted. "Absolutely."

She swatted at him, but he simply leaned out of reach. "Pest," she huffed.

Façade held his hands to his chest in mock hurt. "Why must you wound me so?"

With a defeated sigh she offered him a cookie and returned her attention to Ashleen, alert for any signs that she might be rejecting the transfusion.

Ashleen fell through the darkness for several minutes before she was spat out of a muddy puddle and landed on the sun scorched ground. She lay still, waiting for her racing heart to slow. Why did there have to be so much falling?

When her pulse had regulated, she sat back on her heels and inhaled the parched air. The scent of burning sagebrush singed her nostrils and she coughed. The air tasted chalky. Water seemed like a distant memory after only a few short breaths.

Drought cracked the ground, which seemed to climb gradually upwards in all directions away from her as if she were in the center of a massive crater. The sun beat down on her. Its oppressive heat could have been cut with a knife.

Ashleen turned, searching for a landmark to orientate herself. Cut out of one side of the crater was a triangular portal. It rose above the lip of the depression, its inky edges cut through the sky in a way that gave the impression it was a hole in the world.

Much closer than the mysterious doorway, strange rock formations grew out of the dirt. Haunting snippets of conversation drifted to her on the breeze as she drew up on them.

It only took her a moment to realize the source of the voices came from the stones themselves. Wind whistled through strange holes bored into them to create a haunting symphony of overlapping phrases. She wandered farther in, her steps upsetting locusts hidden in the dry grass.

A child screamed. A man begged for more time. The echoes of gunfire ricocheted about, bouncing from pillar to pillar. A woman pleaded for mercy. Someone's dog barked, then yelped in pain and fell silent.

"So. You've arrived at last."

Crouched atop the pillar nearest to her was an inky figure. He appeared human-shaped, but the ichor form concealing him seethed with constant motion. It broke and shifted in mesmerizing geometric patterns. Ashleen's awe quickly became horror as she focused enough to realize he appeared to be covered in a writhing mass of black bees.

She leaned away from him. He chuckled like a kicked hornet's nest.

"Barrage?" Ashleen said, remembering Proverb's warning.

He opened several sets of perfectly circular yellow eyes and let them slide in unpredictable trails through the mass of bees.

"Stop that. Please," she added belatedly.

The eyes closed, "The truth can be ugly. Are you sure you're worthy of it?"

"What?"

A train whistled in the distance. "I hid a bomb on that train. If you want to save your friend, you don't have time to waste asking stupid questions."

Ashleen whirled around. She didn't see a train. How was she supposed to defuse a bomb on a train she couldn't even find? "That's not fair!"

"Life isn't fair," Barrage countered. He snapped his fingers, and the ground between them fractured like a kaleidoscope. Etchings like crop circles sent the place she stood rushing away from him.

When the space between them finally stopped spreading, Ashleen was in the middle of nowhere. The only visible landmark was the ominous portal on the other side of the crater.

She could hear the train thundering over its tracks now, but she still didn't see anything. Where was it? There was nothing to block her view as far as she could see, besides the lip of the crater.

She took a step forward, one foot crossing the perimeter of the nearest crop circle. With an ear rending blast of its whistle, a train exploded out of the ground, missing her by mere inches as it roared into the sky.

As she watched, it reached the peak of its arch and began to plummet back down. It ricocheted off the ground, rising back into the sky.

"What--" It took Ashleen a second to remember she needed to be on the train as she watched it porpoise across the crater.

"Tick-tock," Barrage's voice hissed from nowhere and everywhere at once.

Ashleen dropped to all fours and gave chase. Even with her greater speed, the train had a lead she couldn't easily close.

He'd said her friend was on the train, but Ashleen wasn't sure who he meant. Did he know her well enough to guess who she cared about? Did it matter? Either way there were innocent people on board who didn't deserve to be blown up.

Motion in one of the windows caught her eye. Prue waved frantically at her. Ashleen's claws dug furrows in the ground and the ichor wolf's lips peeled back from its teeth. He wouldn't dare.

"Vanquisher," her own voice sounded in her head, warped by the growl of some feral creature. Frustration burned in her veins. She put on a burst of speed.

She drew alongside the manic train and struggled to wrap her mind around how she could board it without being crushed. She watched it hit the ground and begin to arch back into the sky. Her only chance was to make a jump for it when it next touched down.

The train reached the top of its curve. Prue was gesturing wildly, trying to tell her something. Ashleen didn't have time to interpret her charades. The train began its descent.

The roar of an explosion mingled with Prue's terrified scream in Ashleen's ears. A shockwave of superheated air knocked her flying. Debris crashed down around her, whistling through the sky as it fell. A large chunk of twisted steel narrowly missed her head, but Ashleen couldn't gather the strength to move.

For what felt like an eternity, she lay there in the dust, staring at the destruction in disbelief. It couldn't end like this. Prue deserved better. She deserved better. The conversations they hadn't had echoed off the inside of Ashleen's skull.

She'd failed to save Prue. Again. No matter how hard she struggled to redeem herself, to become the protector she was supposed to be, she kept failing. She hadn't even had the chance to try this time. No matter how quickly she'd caught up to that train, it would have blown up before she could get clear.

There didn't seem to be a point to this mindless violence. If Barrage expected her to identify with him over this, he was sorely mistaken. The only identifying she would do would be of his remains after she'd dismembered him and scattered him across this godsforsaken crater.

"Vanquisher."

A red haze descended over her vision, and she worked her way to her feet, swaying erratically. The pillars of stone hiding Barrage were visible only a few hundred yards away. Her chest rumbled around a snarl.

The ichor concealing Ashleen's body seethed and boiled, several faces rose from it and sank back in. "He's pushed her over the brink," Proverb warned the room at large.

Diva shifted her weight anxiously. "I hate not knowing what's going on."

The Archwarden produced a stopwatch and started the time. "If she can't get a handle on herself in the next thirty seconds, I fear we may have to take drastic measures."

"You don't mean killing her!" Diva exclaimed.

"Barrage knows what he's doing," Façade said, casually taking the stopwatch from the Archwarden. "Give him a chance."

"Is there anything we can do to help?" Diva asked.

"Not if you want to be aware of her limits," the Archwarden explained.

"Shh," Façade hissed.

Diva began to mutter every prayer she could remember under her breath, her mane twisting around itself nervously.

Ashleen tore across the desert, unphased by the carefully aimed warning shots blowing plumes of dirt into the air. A bullet whipped past so close it parted her fur, but she could barely feel it.

The ichor in her veins sang for vengeance. Barrage stepped out from behind a pillar. He let go of his gun and it dispersed, the bees it had been shaped from returned to his body.

Ashleen roared, the sound rolling up from deep in her stomach.

Barrage's laughter rang out. "Is that it? You're pathetic."

She could already feel his skull cracking under the force of her bite. Oh, she would enjoy this.

His form warped, hornets seething over his skin. They settled in the shape of a huge wolf, not unlike Ashleen's own shape. Barrage closed the distance between them rapidly, Ashleen slid to a stop to avoid colliding with him.

He echoed her roar inches from her face. The sound that tore from his lungs filled the crater, a twisted mix of wild animal, human scream, and the warbling buzz of some kind of insect.

Dozens of eyes opened on the head and shoulders of the wolf and it stared her down. Ashleen's rage remained, but her ichor had gone silent. Her body wouldn't move.

"Did you think you were the only one with Anshan ichor?" Barrage hissed. "Did you think you were the only one who was angry? The only one who wanted vengeance?"

She couldn't even open her mouth to respond.

"Pull yourself together!" His bees began to rearrange back into his human shape. "While you are a part of this team, I am the alpha. You will do as I tell you, when I tell you, without question. Am I understood?"

Ashleen started to argue. Barrage's hand shot out and sank through her ichor to close around her throat.

She choked on smoke, and gunfire rattled in the distance. She could feel herself calling for someone, but the words didn't make sense in her ears. Her hands were sticky with blood, but she didn't know whose. People yelled somewhere close by.

She couldn't tell if they were on her side or not, and her fingers tightened around a gun she didn't know how to use. This wasn't how it was supposed to go. She knew the plan had failed, but she couldn't even remember what the plan was. The entire warzone had devolved into chaos, soldiers ran past, outlines blurred by fire.

Barrage jerked his hand free of her fur. She opened her mouth again, half to argue, half to ask all the questions racing in circles through her mind.

He shrugged. With the roll of his shoulders, the world tilted ninety degrees, and Ashleen tumbled off her feet. The massive triangle of darkness surged up toward her.

"That was reckless," the Archwarden chastised as Barrage stepped back. "She could have killed you. We could have killed her."

"I had to know she could stop," Barrage explained. "I take enough risks without having to deal with a tranq time bomb."

"You mean you didn't stop her?" Proverb asked.

Barrage chuckled. "No. If she had not wanted to stop, she would not have. I do not think she is aware of how much control she truly has."

"That's why I chose her," the Archwarden interjected.

Façade shifted at her shoulder, "I suppose it's my turn, then."

"Hey, go easy on her, okay?" Diva insisted.

"Patience, Diva," Barrage warned.

Façade stepped backward off of the Archwarden's chair and reappeared at Ashleen's side. "I have just the thing."

13

L'appel du Vide

The portal splashed when Ashleen struck its surface. Viscous arms of fluid broke free, only to curl in around her and suck her down. She forgot to panic. She hadn't died yet, and if she was going to in her current situation, it probably wouldn't be in a portal.

As she sank through the darkness, pinpricks of light began to wheel about her. The liquid portal thinned and the speed of her plummet increased. The specks spun in closer and closer until she could touch them. She reached for one, fingers closing around the light.

Her fall lurched to a stop and she shot forward through a tunnel that reached beyond the edge of her vision. Lights and colors streaked past her. Her body stretched as if pulled by opposing forces.

Then it stopped. Darkness consumed all. For a moment she wondered if she'd assumed too quickly that the portals wouldn't kill her. She couldn't feel anything. Was this what limbo was like? Suspended in emptiness, drifting for eternity?

No. A light had just flickered. There it was again. The intervals between flashes grew shorter and shorter. Her eyes began to adjust to the weird lighting. She was in some kind of spaceship. The antigravity wasn't working, so she floated somewhere near the ceiling of an observation deck.

Ashleen felt along the panes of glass, slowly walking herself towards the floor with her hands. She caught hold of one of the railings that bordered the walkways and pulled herself hand over hand to the control console.

The thud of some mechanism within the ship startled her. With it came the hushed noises of a crowd somewhere nearby. Ashleen turned, but the observation deck was empty. At the other end of the main walkway, there was a massive circular hatch. She could only assume the voices were coming from the other side.

She returned her attention to the console. One of these buttons had to be a control for the door. There. Near the top of the panel was a green button. She couldn't recognize any of the symbols labeling things, but in her gut, this one felt like the right choice.

She pressed the button and the deck rumbled beneath her feet. With an unsettling groan, the hatch opened. The artificial gravity activated and Ashleen's feet connected solidly to the ground again.

Neon colors and pulsing music greeted her on the other side. The overhead lighting was dim, a subtle violet that cast impossible shadows. More of the symbols she didn't recognize hung from back lit signs on the walls. The music's heavy bass pumped out a beat that demanded dancing, and yet nobody was.

Throngs of people milled about, but no one seemed to notice her entrance. Everyone was hidden in ichor forms of various shapes and sizes. There were humanoids, quadrupeds, some had massive wings and others, ram-like horns.

All of them had curious patterns in their ichor, little lines and creases that gave them a robotic appearance. In place of eyes, they had glowing purple lights. About half of them were holding what appeared to be fruity cocktails.

Other inky figures stood behind the counters and booths, hawking a variety of unknown items. Ashleen wandered closer, careful to linger on the edges of the crowd so as not to attract the attention she'd avoided so far.

She wasn't sure what was being sold. Various forms of technology and food changed hands in return for currency. If it weren't for the seriousness of the ordeals, Ashleen could have wasted hours wandering the ship, investigating every nook and cranny. This was the most interesting scene she'd encountered so far.

"Like what you see?"

Ashleen whirled toward the source of the voice. Leaning against a table she hadn't noticed before was a small being. He had digitigrade legs like she did, but that was where the similarities ended.

In place of eyes, he had a glowing purple symbol, like the power button on a computer. A single prehensile tentacle extended off the back of his head, reaching almost to his waist. He shared the mechanical lines she'd seen on the others.

"Façade?"

"The one and only." He gestured to her. "Come. Sit."

She did so, and he produced two shot glasses. He filled both with a clear liquid, and pushed one toward her.

She held up her hands. "Oh no, thank you. I don't drink."

"Here you do." He knocked back his shot, his hand and the glass passing through the ichor of his mask as if it didn't exist. "I'm going to ask questions. You're going to answer and then drink. If you've answered honestly, that..." he gestured to her glass, "will be water. If not..."

"How will you know if I'm being honest?"

"It doesn't matter if I know. You'll know."

Ashleen shrugged; she supposed that made sense. Either way this was a welcome change compared to flesh eating beetles and exploding trains.

"What's the biggest mistake you've ever made?" Façade asked.

"Murder," she answered without hesitation, and attempted to knock back the shot with the ease she'd seen him do it. She choked as alcohol burned her throat and her eyes watered.

Façade burst out laughing and slapped his knee. "Wow, you really don't drink, do you?"

"Was it ever water?" she demanded bitterly, watching the glass refill itself.

"Of course, I'm not that mean."

"But I wasn't lying."

"Apparently you were. A little tip, it's easy to know when you lie to other people. To yourself? A bit trickier."

"I don't know the right answer."

"That's fine. I don't need the right answer. We do this until you answer truthfully three times. Next time, maybe give it a little thought."

"That doesn't seem fair. You're not answering any questions."

Façade shrugged. "Ask me whatever you want."

"Well then, what's the biggest mistake you've ever made?"

"Falling in love." He drank, and Ashleen had no idea whether he'd gotten water or alcohol. She could almost feel his smug grin.

She huffed. "Fine."

"Most influential person in your life?"

Ashleen thought. Her first instinct was to say Prue, but Prue had only been influencing her life for a few years. If it wasn't Prue, that only left one person who she'd known longer. "My mother." She hesitantly lifted her glass, sipped, and grimaced. She forced down the rest of the vile liquid.

Façade chuckled. "Do you know yourself at all?"

"What about you then?"

"That's easy. I'm the most influential person in my life." Again, she had no idea whether he'd lied or not. "If you could permanently forget one memory, which one would you pick?"

"I don't know." She took a sip and was met with water. Perplexed, she examined the glass, rolling it between her fingers.

"I don't know either. Didn't know not knowing was a valid answer, did you?"

She shook her head.

"If we had all the answers, we wouldn't be human. You need relationship advice. Who's the first person you go to?"

"Prue." More water.

"Making progress. I'd go to Barrage."

"What?" Of all the archknights she'd spoken to so far, Barrage seemed like the most unstable. "That's a horrible idea!"

"Oh I agree. Doesn't change my answer. How well do you handle failure?"

"Pretty well, I think." Ugh. Not water. Alright, she'd known that was a lie.

Façade tsked. "You were doing so well!"

Ashleen forced herself to empty her glass. Strangely, she hadn't started to feel the effects she would've expected by her third shot.

"What's the biggest lie you've ever told?"

Ashleen liked to believe she was an honest person, but it was more that she was just a bad liar. She'd never woven some elaborate scheme because she would not have had the wherewithal to maintain it. That didn't mean she hadn't lied, over and over again about the simplest things, and more complex ones too. "I'm fine."

"That's a good answer. Personally, mine is 'I don't care'." He raised his shot glass. "Shall we?"

They drank at the same time, and Ashleen's shoulders sagged with relief when she was met with water. As always, it was unclear what had been in Façade's glass.

"It seems we have similar issues. Hand?"

Ashleen offered her palm, bracing herself for what would happen when he took it. The scenes crashed past her like water. Shadows danced as a light swung back and forth. Someone took her hand and pulled her along as they ran down an alley. Someone else's skull gave way under the swing of her bat.

"Here's your cut," someone said, and tossed her a stack of bills.

Someone else punched her and she tasted blood. Then she was running. She had no idea why or where she was going, only that she couldn't stop.

The sensations went dead and she got the impression of someone slamming them into a chest and throwing away the key.

"That's more than enough of that, don't you think?" Façade said from somewhere to her right.

"It can't be good for you to lock everything up like that."

"Mm. Maybe not. But I don't care."

She wondered if he was lying, but his personal thoughts weren't her business. "One more archknight then?"

"Two. You're one of us, aren't you?"

Ashleen groaned, her body and her mind ached. "I just want it to be over."

An apologetic line slanted across the lower half of Façade's face. "Sorry, wish I could tell you the worst was behind you." He reached up and flicked the center of her forehead.

Her body was thrown backwards through the hatch, and glass shattered around her as she exploded through the observation window, spiraling into the frigid void of space.

"How is she?" Diva asked when Façade stepped away from Ashleen.

"Tired," Façade replied. "Wish we could make it easier for her."

She tugged at a tendril of her mane. "What if I mess this up?"

"There isn't time for you to doubt yourself," Barrage quipped.

"Right," Diva tugged her chair over and perched on the edge of it. She took a steadying breath, and gently cupped Ashleen's face in her hands.

Ashleen broke the surface of the water back first, but it did nothing to slow her descent. Clouds of bubbles surged past her, dancing in her hair and tickling her fingers. Her ears popped, and the daylight above her shrank into a smaller and smaller circle.

Ashleen collapsed inward on herself and squeezed her eyes shut. She tried not to think of the horrifying creatures she might find when she reached the bottom, with their lamp-like eyes and needle teeth.

Instead her thoughts helpfully roamed into scenarios of getting lost in a submerged tunnel and never seeing the light of day again. She silently berated herself, a wandering mind would do her no good here.

Her hand brushed against the silty sea floor. She'd reached the bottom. Ashleen opened one eye, and then the other. She'd expected total blackness, but everything was lit by a subtle aqua glow from an unknown source.

She righted herself, grimacing as the sea muck sucked at her feet. There was nothing in the vicinity. No structures, no landmarks, just water, silt, and mystery particulate as far as the eye could see.

There was no light above her to indicate the surface, but she could hear a pod of whales in the distance, clicking out a conversation with each other.

"Diva?" No one answered her. She had no idea what she was supposed to do. If there was a puzzle to complete, or a task to accomplish, there was no sign of it. Perhaps something had gone wrong. Ashleen refused to imagine what that might entail. The whales called in the distance again, and she started towards them.

It felt as if she'd been walking for hours, but nothing had changed. The whales didn't sound any closer, and she wasn't even sure if she was heading in the right direction anymore.

"Hello?" Her voice echoed back to her through the water. "Is anyone out there?"

At this point she almost would have been grateful to see a scary fish if only so she wouldn't be so alone. She'd never been this lonely in her entire life. Anxiety ate at her nerves. If something had gone wrong, maybe she was trapped down here.

"Hello?!" She tried again.

Something responded. Or had it just been her echo? She went dead silent, listening. Nothing.

"Hello?"

She was sure there had been a response this time, but it was too faint for her to make out what was being said. "What?"

Whoever was answering sounded like a child. "Mama?"

Ashleen veered towards the voice. "Who's there?"

"Mom!"

She almost tripped over her feet in her eagerness to find another living being. "Keep talking!"

Her legs burned from all the walking she'd done, but she'd made progress. The child's cries grew in urgency and volume as she drew closer. With each passing minute, it seemed more likely that there were several children, rather than one. Not that Ashleen would complain. She'd take as much company as she could get right now.

The children spoke in several languages, but the word for mother was near universal. Even if she didn't know the word, she could recognize its meaning from the tone and inflection with which it was said.

"Mama!"

Ashleen redoubled her efforts, and something came into view as she reached the top of a steep incline. At first, she wasn't sure what it was, a pale shape in the distance. As she drew closer, she realized she'd stumbled across the carcass of a whale.

Its ribs jutted starkly upwards, and crabs of varying sizes scuttled over it, gleaning a meal from the fatty remnants. In the cavity where the whale's organs would have resided, there was a dark, writhing shape.

Desperation crept into the voices of the children. Ashleen pushed down her trepidation and approached. She drew close enough to wrap her fingers around one of the whale's thick ribs. She couldn't see any children anywhere.

"Hello?"

At the sound of her voice, the inky shape split and scattered. Her surroundings plunged into darkness. The children cried louder. Something grabbed at her leg. Something else tried to hold her hand. Something tugged and prodded at her fur.

Terror crawled under Ashleen's skin, but she couldn't bring herself to lash out. What if she hurt one of the children?

"Mama!"

"Mom!"

"Mum!"

"Mommy!"

"What do you want?" Ashleen demanded, trying not to imagine something looming out of the darkness at her.

"Play with me!" one of the children pleaded. Her voice was followed by a cascade of giggles.

"Aren't you lost? Where's your mother?"

"Talk to me! Listen!"

"I don't wanna play all by myself!"

"What's your name?" Ashleen asked.

"You choose!" More giggling.

She tried again, "How long have you been down here?"

It went quiet, and a chill crept up Ashleen's spine.

"Will you be my friend?"

"Can we be friends?"

"Let's be friends forever and ever and ever!"

"Okay," Ashleen conceded. "Let's be friends. What's your name?"

For a moment, there was no answer. Then the area was lit by a subtle magenta light. A thin woman sat before Ashleen in the vacant ribcage of the whale.

"I would've thought you'd know my name by now." The glow appeared to emanate from bioluminescent markings along her torso, thighs, and in her dancing mane of tentacles.

"Diva."

"That is what they call me."

"Have you always been this lonely?"

"As long as I can remember. What about you?"

"Sort of. It was less lonely for me though and more... lost. I'm not sure I've even considered anywhere home."

"Looks like we have that in common," Diva said, extending a delicate hand towards Ashleen.

The moment their fingertips brushed, someone shoved Ashleen up against a wall.

"Hey, what do you think you're--" He grabbed a handful of her hair and yanked her head back. "Ow!"

Ashleen shoved at him, but there was no strength in her arms. She could feel his breath, warm and damp, against her ear. He pinned her wrists above her head.

"Let go of me!"

"You can struggle all you want, I kind of like it," he leered at her, his free hand slid over her ribs.

Ashleen headbutted him as hard as she could.

"Why you--"

Diva dropped her hand and danced backward several steps. "I'm so sorry! I didn't mean for you to see that."

Ashleen was back in the whale's chest cavity. She shuddered and scrubbed her arms with her hands. It took her a couple moments to calm down enough to realize Diva was shaking.

"Are you okay?"

Diva's voice broke when she answered. "I'm fine. How about you, are you--"

"I'll live."

"I'm really sorry."

Ashleen sighed. "I accept your apology, but I don't really want to discuss this. Can we move on?"

"Of course." She came forward and placed a hand almost too carefully on Ashleen's shoulder. She pushed lightly, and the world tilted as Ashleen let herself fall. She hit the sand and sank peacefully through it.

Diva surfaced and sucked in air like someone who'd been at the bottom of a real sea, not an imaginary one. She leaned back in her seat and ran her fingers through her agitated hair.

Barrage opened an eye to scrutinize her. "Diva. Is there something we need to discuss?"

"What?" It took her a moment to piece together his implications. She shrank, trying to hide in her mane. "Don't tell me everyone felt that?"

"Really wish I hadn't," Façade said with a shudder.

"It's just an old dream," Diva assured them. "I didn't mean to share it like that."

"We do not control what the mesh shows us, only what we do with it," Proverb replied.

"I'll try to keep that in mind, thanks," Diva said.

Barrage heaved a sigh and turned his attention back to Ashleen. "It's up to her to decide what to do now, we've done all we can."

14

The Infinite Waiting Room

Ashleen slammed into a chair with enough force to tip it back into the wall and bounce it off the wall to dump her on the floor. When she recovered enough to get to her feet and examine her surroundings, she found herself in a waiting room.

The first thing she noticed was that her ichor form had vanished. The whitewashed walls and flickering fluorescent lights made her head ache. A single painting of a yellow flower hung on the farthest wall, and the coffee table was blanketed with ancient magazines, their pages curling and torn.

She touched one of the potted plants, and grimaced at the waxy plastic between her fingers. The whole room seemed fake. A secretary sat at a desk across from her, scribbling out notes on a document.

Ashleen padded over the matted carpet toward her. "Excuse me, could you tell me where I am?"

"Straight through the door, Miss. Your doctor is waiting," the secretary told her in an overly sweet tone.

Ashleen straightened. She was certain there hadn't been a door there a second ago, but when she glanced to her left, it stood out starkly against the wall. She squared her shoulders and crossed the room to open it.

It led to a second waiting room nearly identical to the one she'd just exited. A fish tank sat in the corner this time, and the secretary was a redhead instead of a brunette. The door had vanished behind her as if it had never been there.

Ashleen ignored the secretary in favor of searching for clues. She'd been warned that this would be the hardest ordeal, but she'd assumed she knew herself well enough that it wouldn't matter. Nothing about this setting had any familiarity to it.

There were no windows and no doors. Ashleen double checked this time to be sure. Aside from the secretary's hair, the fish tank was the only difference. She drew closer to it. Perhaps it was hiding something.

She looked in through the top of the tank and recoiled immediately. All the fish were dead, floating belly up on the surface of the water. They smelled like they'd been dead for a very long time. The lights flickered ominously and a few of them blew out.

The secretary clicked her pen and stood up. "Straight through that door, Miss. Your doctor is waiting."

A door etched itself into the wall line by line as if someone were drawing it for her. Ashleen eyed it warily, but there didn't appear to be other options. The door spat her out into another waiting room.

The lights continued to flicker. They'd grown even dimmer than the first two waiting rooms. The yellow flower leered at her from its place on the wall, and now a rubber duck was floating in the tank with the dead fish. An intimidating stain stood out against the ratty carpet. The secretary was now blonde. Ashleen cleared her throat.

The secretary stopped scribbling and began to click her pen anxiously. "Miss, please go straight through that door, your doctor––"

Ashleen crossed the room in a few strides and grabbed the desk with one hand, intending to flip it. The desk only scooted against the floor underwhelmingly. Her strength was gone. Instead she settled for pounding her fist on the desktop menacingly. "What's going on? Tell me now."

The secretary whimpered and vanished. Ashleen reached for the files she'd had been working on and flipped open the folder. Her own face stared back at her. The secretary had been aggressively circling one line of text.

"Extremely dangerous. Avoid contact. Subject should be quarantined at all times."

Ashleen's skin prickled. She looked around for a mirror and one drew itself into existence on a nearby wall. She approached with trepidation and inspected her reflection.

She looked normal. In fact, she looked better than normal. Most of the things she disliked about herself were mysteriously absent. Her hair was redder, her eyes bluer. Her shoulders were narrower and all of her curves were more pronounced. She even appeared to have shrunk a few inches.

A door on the other side of the room swung open with a drawn-out creak. A woman stood on the threshold. Her shoulder length black hair was caught up in a low ponytail. She had the same face as the secretaries, but there wasn't any fear on it. Rectangular glasses perched on her nose and she carried a clipboard hugged to the chest of her white lab coat.

"Miss, please come with me. It's time for your appointment."

Ashleen felt herself being drawn forward against her will. "But I didn't schedule an appointment."

"Come along!" said the woman, ignoring her comment and making a sharp gesture. An invisible force sucked Ashleen through the opening. The door slammed shut, submerging her in caliginous shadows. A single flickering bulb fought a losing battle against the dark.

This wasn't a waiting room. An operating table commanded its center. Dirty scalpels and other tools sat in a tray to one side. She swallowed against a spell of nausea.

"Wait here!" The doctor slipped through a door Ashleen hadn't seen a second ago. It disappeared behind her.

"Don't leave me here!" But it was too late; the doctor was already gone. Her breath curled on the air and Ashleen rubbed her arms. Her jacket had vanished and in its place was a thin hospital gown.

The lone fluorescent bulb strobed, and in the flashes Ashleen saw the outline of a door etch itself into the wall. She pushed forward and knocked into several tables, sending them rolling across the floor.

She yanked the door open. A tidal wave of oily ichor surged over her. She didn't have time to scream. The fluid swept her off her feet and she went under as it flooded the room.

Diva surged upward from her chair. "She needs help!"

"Sit down," Barrage commanded.

"How can you all just stand there and let her drown?"

Façade placed a hand on Diva's shoulder and forced her back into the chair. "There's nothing we can do."

"He's right," the Archwarden agreed. "She has to find equilibrium on her own, if she doesn't, she'll be more of a hazard than an asset."

Another wave of panic washed over their minds, this time accompanied by a terrified scream.

Diva broke Façade's grip and surged forward.

The bees on Barrage's skin shuffled restlessly as he barked a warning. "Diva!"

A new door opened and spilled Ashleen into an empty space. She pushed up to her hands and knees, gasping for air and shaking uncontrollably as ichor dripped in viscous rivulets off of her.

"Thanks," she gasped. The ichor stung her skin. She struggled to rub it away with her hands, but it simply smeared around. "Can I have a towel?"

A spitting, burbling sound like drowned laughter echoed from behind her. Ashleen rubbed her eyes. They burned and watered, but she thought she could see the other archknights. "Façade? Diva?"

The only answer was more of that horrible laughter. Something with six limbs––Proverb?––dropped to the ground and scurried rapidly towards her. Ashleen yelped and scrambled backwards, but not fast enough. It grabbed her ankles; its touch burned like acid. Ashleen kicked weakly. Of all the times for her strength to fail, why did it have to be now?

One of the others stumbled into Proverb, and the two merged. They flailed about until they had all become one, a writhing mass of hands, clinging to and scrabbling against Ashleen's skin.

She screamed. The more she fought, the more the handsy glob of ichor pulled her in. A whispered argument of voices echoed in her head.

"Diva!" This was Barrage's hornet's nest tone.

"She has to find equilibrium on her own." That was Amaris.

"Please!" Ashleen called out to them for help.

"There's nothing we can do," Façade seemed to tell her.

"Let her drown?" This was Diva.

"Help!" Ashleen sobbed.

A body emerged from the wriggling mass. It knelt next to her. "Aw, poor little thing."

"What are you?" Ashleen tried to sound intimidating and failed miserably as one of the many hands found her hip and her question ended in an undignified squeak.

"I'm you, silly. You really ought to let me in." The Ashleen globule reached down to pinch her nose. "Too bad you have such a limited view of yourself. Really. Just imagine everything I could do if I had a body like yours."

Proverb wove Barrage and Façade's psyches with their own to create a barricade around Ashleen's mind, blocking Diva's attempts to reach her.

"Stop it!" Diva shouted. "Let me in!"

"Or you'll what?" Barrage snarled. "Sit down."

"It's our mission to save the tranqs. How many have you sentenced to death already? How many have we killed because you wouldn't help them? Aren't you sick of these birdshit double standards?"

"She has a point," Façade agreed.

Proverb faltered. Diva unleashed a reverberating cry that shattered their concentration and burst through the barricade. She tore open the door on the edge of Ashleen's psyche and threw herself into the mindscape.

"What's the point of resisting?" Ashleen's reflection mocked her. "Aren't you sick of these birdshit double standards?"

Ashleen's lungs struggled to filter air she didn't have. The ichor version of herself grinned too wide, exposing blindingly white teeth. "What are you going to do? Suffocate? Let me in."

Her throat contracted and her vision flickered at the edges. Against her will, her lips parted to suck in a breath.

Her ichor self's body rippled, and it heaved itself into her open mouth. Ashleen choked and gagged as ichor flooded her lungs. She let out a disgusted, gurgling scream. The many armed beast holding her down began to writhe again.

A hand dug its fingers into her thigh, and Ashleen swore she could feel her flesh melting under the touch.

"You're only weak if you choose to be!" Diva's voice echoed and burst from the center of the handsy glob as if it were a portal.

Ashleen reached for the hand on her thigh and closed her fingers around its wrist. The connection she'd recently forged with Diva unfurled, and all her pain drowned in their union.

"This is your ideal!" she continued. "This is how it ends if you can't learn to love what you are! Your own ideas of perfection are going to kill you!"

Ashleen closed her eyes. She needn't fear her rage when Diva had her. Somewhere in her heart, she knew that if Diva was holding her leash, it wouldn't snap. She reached for the brutish power she knew she had and felt it brush the tips of her fingers.

She drew it into herself and the blood in her veins heated to a boil as rage seethed in her lungs. She kicked free of the writhing arms, and punched the reflection trying to drown her with all the strength she could muster.

The ichor sprayed across the walls, ceiling, and floor. She watched it hiss and fizz until it went still, then rolled over and coughed until she threw up. When she'd cleared her stomach and lungs of the gooey black substance, she collapsed in the slimy puddle.

The strength she'd mustered left as quickly as it had come. The flickering light finally died and she was alone in the darkness. Ashleen closed her eyes and resigned herself to whatever fate awaited her.

Consciousness came with a wave of aches and pains. Ashleen chased sleep even as it slipped through her fingers. Somewhere nearby, she could hear familiar voices.

"Is that poetry? Damn you've really got it bad, don't you?" Dahei said.

"It's a song, and no I don't," Morpheus answered.

Dahei snorted, "You keep telling yourself that."

"I'm sure Prue will love it," Izzy interjected, but when Ashleen opened her eyes, he was staring at her. They were in the infirmary, and the medical white surroundings had her hair standing on end after what she'd just endured.

She tried to sit up, but Izzy caught her shoulder and pressed her back into the pillows. "You look like hell, you need rest."

"Hey, Neele!" Dahei alerted the head medic to the situation.

Neele descended on her from out of nowhere. "It's good to see you back in the world of the living. You gave us quite a scare."

Ashleen's skin felt hot, like she was running a fever or had a severe sunburn. "What happened?"

"You were found passed out in one of the sim rooms," Izzy told her. "Looks like your sim glitched, you're lucky to be alive."

"What's the damage?"

"It's mostly minor cuts and bruises that will heal on their own. However there's a large second degree burn on your left thigh," Neele summarized.

"A burn?" Ashleen's memories were still foggy, as if she'd just woken from the middle of a dream.

"Yes, in the shape of a handprint. You'll probably have a scar. Do me a favor and don't go into any simulations alone for a while, doctor's orders."

Ashleen grimaced as Diva's warning came back to her. It had saved her life, but clearly it had come at a price. Burns could take forever to heal. "How long have I been out?"

"Two days."

Ashleen balked, "Ugh. How long has it been since I showered? Actually, forget it. I don't want to know."

Neele barked a laugh. "My dear, I don't think anyone is judging."

Ashleen closed her eyes. "I'm judging. I don't wanna think about how I must smell."

"Kind of like bacon. I don't mind it," Dahei quipped.

"Shut up, Dahei," she retorted.

It took her a second to realize Demetrius was already in the room. He'd probably been there the whole time, melting into the shadows between the shelving and Dahei's smaller body. He had a knack for going unnoticed effortlessly. Ashleen was still getting used to it.

He stepped out of the shadows and approached her, a handful of his butterflies tumbled about the room to alight on various surfaces. He extended his hand and his fingers danced over the edge of her cot and onto her arm. He followed it to her hand and squeezed gently. "How are you feeling?"

"Gross. And tired."

Demetrius chuckled. "You need your rest. We should go."

Izzy gestured for the others to follow him. "I agree. Come on. Work won't stop just cause we're down a person."

Guilt bit at Ashleen as she watched them leave. She should be out there with them, not bedridden. The whole point had been to get stronger and become a better tranq, but here she was again, a burden to her friends and family.

The keen of Diva's mind brushing against hers woke Ashleen in the middle of the night. The ichor wolf surged to the surface of her skin reflexively, and Ashleen thanked the gods that there was no one else in the immediate vicinity to see it. With the lights off, her surroundings were eerily reminiscent of the nightmare she'd barely escaped.

Ichor seeped through the floor and Ashleen choked on her bark of alarm. She struggled upright and the burn on her leg protested violently.

The ichor reformed and a thin slip of a woman skipped closer to her. Diva. "It's just me! I'm sorry. I should have warned you."

Diva's tentacles projected her concern, coiling and uncoiling in a motion similar to a person's hands wringing. They cascaded down her back, the longest ones brushing her thighs, which gave her the visage of a Lovecraftian Rapunzel. Her muted magenta bioluminescence lit the room.

Ashleen gathered herself with a slow breath and struggled into a seated position. "Would've been nice."

Diva dipped her head towards the burn. "That's actually why I'm here."

"You don't have to apologize. I'd be dead if you hadn't intervened."

Diva wilted and her glow dimmed. "The others are mad at me."

"Why?"

"We're not supposed to influence the outcome of the ordeals."

Ashleen would have done the same thing if their positions had been switched. Diva seemed to be the newest member of the group, besides herself. It put them on somewhat even footing. She had no doubt that Barrage would target both of them for doing the right thing instead of the logical thing, but that only encouraged her to nurture a strong bond with Diva. Together, maybe they could talk some empathy into him.

"I think I can accelerate the healing," Diva said, tugging at a tendril nervously. "I mean, it's only fair. After what you saw."

Ashleen fought the sick feeling in her stomach at the memory Diva had shared with her. She still didn't feel comfortable talking about it. While she knew logically that it had happened to Diva, the way she'd experienced it made it her own memory now. She could finally understand why Prue hadn't wanted to talk about her experience.

"Vanquisher?" Diva pressed, "It would help you get back on your feet faster."

Reluctantly, Ashleen nodded in agreement. As much as she disliked the parasitic tendencies of vespers, she couldn't stand being dead weight any longer than absolutely necessary.

Diva perked up, a bubbly giddiness to her movements that telegraphed her smile even if she couldn't see it. She skipped closer and cupped her hands over the burn on Ashleen's leg.

She noted the care Diva took to avoid touching her, and a swell of gratitude rose within her chest. Whatever painkillers Neele had given her were definitely working, but her skin still felt like it radiated heat.

Diva hummed a strange lullaby and Ashleen squirmed. "Keep still!" Diva hissed in her head.

"It itches," Ashleen complained, but she did her best to not to move again.

Diva's song continued for several minutes. When it drew to a close, she dropped her hands to her sides and straightened. "It's not fully healed, I did as much as I could, but I want to avoid drawing too much attention. If we do this in stages, I could get you fighting fit in about a week."

It would have to do. As much as Ashleen wished she could walk out of here tomorrow, it wasn't worth the eyebrows it would raise.

In the absence of any reply, Diva tiptoed away, sinking through the floor as she went.

Ashleen grumbled to herself and the ichor sank beneath her skin once more. Keeping this many secrets made her sick. She wished the path towards truth wasn't so dishonest.

It took several days and a fair amount of needling before Neele had allowed Ashleen a trip to the showers. "You are not strong enough. You could infect your burn. More time! More time!" Neele had argued grouchily. Even after Ashleen had managed to convince her, Neele forbade her to go alone, and so Prue had volunteered to accompany her.

Ashleen hissed and bit down on a pained cry as the steam seared her leg. She'd done her best to keep it out of the water, but the heat from the shower was still agonizing.

"Ash? You okay?" Prue asked, her tiny voice echoing off the tile.

"Yeah. Fine," Ashleen answered through the sting of tears. It was the first they'd spoken to each other since Ashleen had suggested to Prue that Morpheus could be toying with her. Even arranging to accompany Ashleen, Prue had spoken to Neele directly.

"You don't sound fine," Prue argued after a long silence.

"It's just the hot water," Ashleen said, scrubbing shampoo into her hair. "I'll manage."

Prue didn't acknowledge her reply. The quiet stretched on for several minutes. "I'm not sure I should stay with him," Prue said finally.

Ashleen paused, hands full of foamy suds. "What are you talking about?"

"Morpheus."

Ashleen snorted and returned to rinsing away bubbles. "I had actually pieced together that much, but thanks."

Prue took a shaky breath. "We had an argument. Well... Two, kind of."

Ashleen didn't have a reply, so she didn't offer one.

"He's... distant. Less affectionate. I don't know what to think."

Ashleen thought of the song he'd apparently been writing for Prue. "Maybe he's just trying to think of how to make it up to you."

"I don't think so. He ignored me all day yesterday."

Ashleen didn't think she was the person to ask, but if Prue wanted her advice, she'd give it. "If you're unhappy, you shouldn't waste time with someone you're not meant to be with forever," She winced. The words sounded harsh, even to her own ears.

"I suppose you're right. But it's difficult, you know? I really do care about him. And I'm... a little scared to be alone."

"I mean, it's entirely up to you." Ashleen finished rinsing and turned off the water. "Pass me the towel?"

Dahei twirled the recorder about his fingers, trying to think of yet another lie to feed his family. He doubted they knew anything about him anymore. They hadn't been aware of how he spent his time for at least seven years. He'd been making up fake clubs to go to since he was fourteen, when he'd begun a life of petty crime and odd jobs in an attempt to bring in more money for the family.

Things had spiraled out of control and he'd borrowed money from the wrong person and fallen into debt with the local yakuza boss. The web of lies he'd spun starting at that point now painted Dahei as a successful college student on a scholarship overseas.

He scanned his disorganized chicken scratch notes now, trying to think of something he could say that didn't contradict anything he'd already told them. What year had he told them he was starting college? Ah, there it was. 2015. Which meant that he should be getting close to an associates degree now. What did he say he was studying?

Computer Science? Something to that effect. Something to do with technology that sounded impressive. Dahei snorted. He didn't know any more about computers than he had when he was fourteen.

He could tell them he'd gotten a new job, but he was pretty sure he'd already told them about that. He couldn't remember what he'd said he was doing. Too risky to discuss that then. Maybe he could say something about finals or midterms. They'd believe that, wouldn't they? Dahei shut his eyes and pinched the bridge of his nose. Lies were exhausting.

His eyes fluttered open. There was a topic he'd been avoiding since the beginning. One he could actually tell the truth about. He flipped the recorder over in his hand and pressed the button.

"It's me. Things are great. Actually, I met someone," he began in Japanese. "I think you'd like him."

Dahei could already hear his younger brothers freaking out over the news. He could almost hear money changing hands. His grandmother had always suspected he was gay. He knew his mother's first question would be, 'When is the wedding?' followed immediately by, 'Is he rich?'

His family wouldn't care that he hadn't ended up with the pretty girl most of them had assumed he would. Even so, Dahei wasn't sure he'd ever be ready to answer all of his mother's questions.

Demetrius leafed through the papers in his lap, reverently feeling along the crumpled edges. The envelope had come in the weekly box of supplies for the dorm, and Morpheus had said it was from his sisters.

Demetrius had already listened to the recording, of course, but he'd have to wait for Dahei to interpret whatever was on the paper. He could hear him dictating a letter to a recorder in his room. Dahei had taught Demetrius the basics of Japanese; he was by no means fluent, but he avoided eavesdropping anyway.

His mind alighted on the ring he was currently hiding in his pocket, and the bloom of heat that Dahei's ring left in its wake. There still hadn't been a good opportunity to speak to him about it.

Demetrius shuffled through the papers again. He supposed that wasn't completely true. He'd been avoiding it. He'd never been shy about his relationship with Dahei before. Careful of course––Dahei could be capricious––but never shy.

He'd never expected to find a ring. According to others he'd spoken to, most people found their rings around the same time they hit puberty. His had passed without any sign of one, and after what had happened to his tribe, he'd assumed he'd never receive one.

He was turning twenty-seven in a few months, and almost everyone he knew had already found their counterweight. The thought that his had been standing at his side for years without him noticing blew his mind.

The door to Dahei's room clicked open and his feet padded across the carpet towards the couch. Demetrius' fingers curled around the ring he'd been hiding as he tried to work up the courage to say something.

"Your sisters replied?" Dahei asked, noticing the creased papers in Demetrius' lap.

Demetrius drew his hand out of his pocket. He'd waited this long, he could wait a few more days. "Yes, the recording said they had drawn pictures, but my wisps don't see that way."

Dahei flopped down unceremoniously beside him. "Give it here."

His knuckles brushed Demetrius' arm to show the location of his hand, and Demetrius' heart missed a beat. Dahei had adapted so well to his blindness that Demetrius doubted he even thought about it anymore. He made it seem so casual, little gestures or certain phrasing that painted a world in Demetrius' mind he'd never seen with his own eyes.

It didn't even matter that Dahei had never managed to confess his feelings word for word. His language was subtler, quieter, but Demetrius could hear it as clear as if he had shouted it.

He placed the paper in Dahei's hand and listened to the rustling as he sorted through them. "There are a lot of butterflies. I think this one's a drawing of you, but..." he trailed off, chuckling.

"What?"

"You sort of look like a peanut, or maybe..." The papers rustled again as Dahei turned them, "A weird beetle?"

Demetrius laughed. "Sounds like they got my good side."

Dahei lightly smacked Demetrius' arm with the papers, but laughed along. "They drew each other too. Eshe is wearing a tutu, like a ballet dancer. And Ife is... A veterinarian, I think. An animal doctor," he explained before Demetrius could ask.

"How can you tell which is which?"

"They wrote their names. Do they know you're blind?"

"Yes, but I ask them to send their art anyway. I like it, it makes me feel closer to them." Dahei caught Demetrius' fingers and gave them a comforting squeeze.

Demetrius ignored how warm Dahei's ring felt as it pressed against his knuckle. There would be a better time; he'd reveal his ring when he could do it with the romance and ceremony that Dahei deserved. Maybe there was someone else in the city who could tell him about Japanese courtship customs.

Izzy retrieved a lighter usually reserved for igniting fuses from his pocket and lit some incense Demetrius had given him. Normally, he wasn't the religious type. He didn't have time to worry about the

afterlife. Since the cemetery he'd seen in Dahei's subconscious however, he hadn't been able to shake a nagging feeling at the back of his
mind.

As sandalwood and sweetgrass wafted about his head, he contem-
plated the slips of parchment he'd gathered. Perhaps he should have
afforded more time to the people he'd lost along the way. Honored
their sacrifices more than he had.

He penned his mother's name, Josephine, on the first scrap in
shaky letters. Hideo's name was marked onto the second piece. He
listed a few more names of people he'd sent to Muginn himself.
They'd been on opposing sides of a war none of them had started,
and he'd cut short the lives of people who'd had families. Mothers,
brothers, spouses and children.

Maybe his father had been right about his raids against the guards
being overzealous. Levi had never been the best at explaining what
he meant in terms Izzy could understand, but he didn't doubt his father's wisdom.

Izzy dragged the last shred of parchment toward him with the tip
of his finger. He tried to write the letters of Alexis' name neatly, but
the tremor in his hand betrayed him. He swore and dropped the pen.
Scowling at the offending appendage as he began to work the cramps
out of it.

He'd tried everything, but he'd never been able to overcome the
trembling. His handwriting had already been barely legible to begin
with and after the explosion that had given him his scars, it had only
grown worse. Sometimes the shakes even interfered with his aim, especially if he was tired.

Izzy's mind wandered back to Alexis. What would she say, if she
could see him now? He raised his eyebrows. Probably something
snarky and pitiless, if he was being honest. She'd always had more
than enough attitude for the both of them.

Sometimes he blocked out the memories of the ravaged campsite and the blood-soaked soil with daydreams of coming home to find her asleep on the couch, the T.V. spilling blue light across the planes of her face.

His shoulder twinged and he winced, reaching up to knead at it. The incense had started to cloud the room. Izzy turned his attention back to the stack of papers on his desk. He picked up the first one and pricked his finger, smearing the ink across the parchment with his offering. He lit the paper with the smoldering incense and held it a few more seconds while the fire caught before dropping it into a nearby bowl to consume itself.

After he'd lit the parchment with Alexis' name and placed it in the bowl, he crossed his arms on the edge of the desk and rested his head atop them. Sometimes she would appear in his dreams, but she never spoke. She simply watched him from a distance with a pain and longing in her eyes that broke his heart.

He'd tried to approach her, but she always fled. He couldn't help but wonder if she avoided him because she blamed him. He knew it was a lie, fabricated by the darker parts of his mind in an attempt to drag him back into the pit of depression he'd spent two years climbing out of. The thoughts lingered all the same.

Izzy wasn't sure he would have made it through to the other side without Dahei pulling half his weight. He might even owe him his life. He couldn't know what would have happened if Dahei hadn't kept him busy, provided him with task after task so he didn't have time to think, let alone wallow in his grief.

Somehow he'd reached the other side. It still hurt to think about Alexis, but he could do it now without wanting to follow her into the abyss. That, in and of itself, was an achievement he could be proud of.

15

Pulling Splinters

Sharing one's mind with four other people was a strange sensation. The idea of them listening in on her private thoughts unsettled Ashleen, but this wasn't like that. The other archknights weren't in her head, per se. Rather, it was more like there were doors just at the edges of her unconscious, and they were on the other side of them.

She knew she could knock on one if she needed to, or if she intended for them to hear a thought, they would. It was like being in a house with family members, but everyone was in their rooms and no one was actively paying her any attention.

Ashleen had grown up in a house that was frequently empty. Her mother tried to be home as often as possible, but she still had to work to provide for them. She was used to nobody being around to hear her, whether she was thinking out loud or butchering the lyrics of her favorite songs.

Now that she had to be more careful with the volume inside her head, she found herself analyzing the others sharing her space. She didn't mind Diva overhearing her, nor did she mind Proverb. Both had, at one time or another, made a clear choice to take her side.

Facade's loyalties seemed to fluctuate. Some days, he was a supportive ally. Others, her struggles seemed to bring him a little too much glee. He reminded her of a court jester, hauling around a bag of biting humor to dig through whenever the opportunity arose.

Barrage seemed more inclined to listen to him than any of the rest of them, however. Ashleen wasn't sure why this was, but she'd made a note of the realization. Perhaps in the future, Facade would be key in swaying Barrage to her side.

The latter was a source of constant conflict. Ashleen disagreed with almost everything he'd said so far. Barrage seemed determined to be a bitter pill. He drew attention to failure and underlined negativity wherever he encountered it. Though Ashleen had never been a glowing optimist herself, she found his constant criticism grating.

When she slipped up with the volume of her thoughts, he and Facade were the most likely to mock them. Proverb and Diva were both known to calmly alert her to her mistake instead.

Sometimes she caught herself tip toeing in her own mind. She hated that, however; Diva would occasionally butt in on a spiral of anxiety, or Proverb would answer a question she hadn't meant to ask so loud. In these moments, Ashleen found herself enjoying the company, as strange as it may be.

Prue made a noise in her throat. Ashleen glanced at her. She'd been silent this whole time, lost in thought as she kept pace with Ashleen back towards the infirmary. She met Ashleen's eyes and then looked pointedly ahead with a small jerk of her chin.

Ashleen followed her gaze and clenched her jaw when she saw Pavane striding toward them from the opposite direction. She fixed her gaze on the dull carpet. Perhaps if she pretended not to notice him, they could pass each other without incident.

She kept him in her periphery, waiting for a sign that would give away his intention. Despite his regal saunter, Pavane looked terrible. Sick. There were dark circles under his eyes, which seemed even more sunken than she remembered.

Prue pressed into Ashleen's space, tucking herself against her side. The gesture startled Ashleen and she shifted her attention from

Pavane to stare at Prue. Prue didn't seem like she was aware of her actions, her own focus glued to the phantom of a man drawing up on them.

Hackles rose on the back of Ashleen's neck as she realized Prue probably couldn't help her reaction to Pavane's predatory aura after what she'd experienced. The ichor responded to her rage, seething beneath Ashleen's skin. She forced it down. She didn't need it for a loser like him.

For a moment it seemed like he wouldn't notice them as he strode down the hall with an unnerving blank stare. Just as he was about to pass them, however, his gaze alighted on Prue and Ashleen caught a glimmer in his dark eyes.

Glee bubbled in her stomach. Ashleen silently pleaded with him to give her an excuse. Pavane didn't stop as they passed each other. He didn't open his mouth to say anything. Ashleen was almost disappointed. Then Pavane lifted a hand and brought it down on Prue's rear with a resounding slap. Prue yelped and skipped forward several steps.

Ashleen whirled and decked him with controlled force. He'd be fine, but his teeth clacked together satisfyingly. Pavane stumbled off balance and landed heavily on his rump. He grimaced and tucked his fingers into his mouth. They came out bloody. He'd bitten his tongue.

"You bitch!"

Ashleen dropped into a crouch next to him. "Wanna say that to my face?"

Pavane narrowed his eyes at her. He pushed himself to his feet and stalked away from them, a shade too clever to take Ashleen's bait.

"Shame. Would've liked to hit him again."

"Ashleen, your leg!" Prue exclaimed.

Ashleen glanced down to see her burn had begun to bleed. Red stained the bandages and seeped down her thigh. She must have pulled something when she'd crouched down. "I didn't even feel it."

"Come on, we have to get back to Neele."

Ashleen groaned. "She's not gonna let me out of her sight after this."

When they arrived at the infirmary, Ashleen sat down on one of the cots. Prue called for Neele. When she didn't get an answer, she wandered about the immediate area, searching for the medic. She returned alone.

"I can't find anyone," Prue explained anxiously.

"Odd. You think they all went to lunch?"

"It doesn't seem likely that Neele wouldn't have left at least one or two medics behind in case of emergency."

Ashleen gingerly tugged at her bandages to see if the bleeding had stopped. "Damn." It hadn't.

"I'll go find help."

"Prue!" But Prue was already gone, the door sliding closed behind her.

A few minutes later, the door hissed open again. Ashleen looked up, expecting to see Neele or one of the other medics. Instead, Izzy was striding towards her.

"I heard you punched Pavane," he said, dropping a tattered messenger bag at the foot of the cot.

"Well somebody ought to stand up to him."

Izzy shrugged and crouched next to the bed. "I'm not disagreeing with you. Let me see..."

He pushed up the hem of the shorts Neele had lent her and plucked at the bandages. He wrinkled his nose. "Looks like you did a number on it. Let's hope it hasn't started to stick to the gauze. I need some scissors." He straightened, casting about the infirmary as if trying to guess where what he needed might be.

"Why are you here, anyway? I thought Prue went for a medic."

"I am a medic. In a pinch. Aha." Izzy tugged open a drawer and returned with a pair of scissors. He knelt again, carefully cutting the gauze away from her leg.

"What do you mean, in a pinch?"

"Well, my father is a medic. He insisted that if I was going to be so fascinated with guns and bombs, I ought to know how to treat the damage they inflicted. Don't worry. Seen my fair share of burns. I know how to handle them." He carefully lifted the bandage away from Ashleen's leg and inspected her injury.

"Aw, this one isn't that bad at all. I don't know what Neele was worried about."

Ashleen hazarded a glance down at her leg and immediately averted her gaze as a wave of squeamishness overtook her. The burn was a mass of angry blisters, and currently covered in a delightful smear of blood and pus. "What do you mean it isn't bad?!"

"Fledgie," Izzy addressed her patiently. "I want you to look me in the face and ask that question again."

Ashleen glanced at him, and then away again as her face heated. She could only imagine what had happened that had left the diagonal scarring. She'd seen the scar that tugged the corner of his mouth down, but this close she also noticed part of his eyebrow was missing and a notch had been taken out of his ear.

Those weren't even the only scars on his face, let alone the rest of his body. She'd seen several poke above his shirt collar from time to time. When he took his jacket off, his right arm and hand were striped with dozens more.

"Point taken."

Izzy returned his attention to her leg. "Trust me, it could be worse. Now, I need something to clean this with." He washed his hands in a nearby sink and strode across the infirmary. He returned with a damp cloth. "This may sting a bit."

He began to dab softly at the mess on her thigh, careful to avoid the worst areas of the burn. It did sting, but only around the smaller blisters. Around the largest mass, she couldn't feel anything at all. Ashleen suspected it was that patch that was the source of all the blood.

"Where do you think Neele went?" she asked, trying to distract herself.

Izzy paused, and set the bloody rag aside. "Don't know. Maybe a team on the other side of the city worked a rough job."

"Prue said it was––ow!" Izzy had produced a salve and was spreading it generously over her burn.

"Sorry."

"Prue said it was unusual for her to leave it unattended like this."

"A little, I hope everyone's alright." Izzy applied another layer. "Do you want another recorder to send to your mother? It's been awhile since the last one, hasn't it?"

"Oh, yeah. Sure. Thanks." Ashleen had been so busy in the past weeks that she hadn't thought of how mad with worry her mother must be. Alice had always been anxious, especially where Ashleen was concerned. Given recent events, Ashleen supposed she was right to be.

"Remind me to get one for you." Izzy sat back on his heels, inspecting his work. "Best to let this air for a bit. It'll do it good, and I don't want it to stick to the gauze."

"Thanks. Do you send messages to anyone?"

"What?"

"You have so many of these recorders, but I haven't heard you talk to anyone."

Izzy stood and crossed to a sink, rinsing the excess salve off his hands and disposing of the dirty rag. "I try to send them to my father sometimes, but we didn't part on good terms. Suppose I mostly keep them around for all of you."

"That's really thoughtful," Ashleen murmured, humbled by Izzy's unconditional kindness.

Izzy shrugged and reached for the satchel he'd left nearby. He retrieved a folded up article of clothing and passed it to her. "I brought you a fresh pair of shorts. I wasn't sure how bad the bleeding was; I figured you might want something that wasn't stained."

They were identical to the ones she was wearing, down to the size. She wondered if Izzy was just a good guesser or if he actually knew what size she wore.

"You can just throw those away." He gestured to the shorts she was wearing. "You'll never get the stain out."

Ashleen knew she probably could get the stain out if she rinsed it now, but her painkillers were starting to wear off. Exhaustion had begun to creep into the edges of her consciousness like cobwebs. She nodded her understanding.

"I should go. And you," Izzy stabbed a finger at her, "need to rest. Do yourself a favor and change out of those before you doze off?"

"Wait, so, how hard did she hit him?" Morpheus leaned forward from where he'd reclined on Prue's bed.

"I don't know. He bit his tongue and landed on his butt though."

"I wish I'd been there to see the look on his face. Though, she'd probably just as soon hit me as him."

Prue scowled, confused. "What do you mean?"

Morpheus pouted. "Where have you been the last few weeks? Ashleen hates my guts."

"I don't think that's true. She's stubborn and opinionated. She needs time to get used to you. That's all."

"What do you mean that's all? She'd been avoiding me since––" He caught himself before he mentioned the garden. "She got here," he amended. "She hates vespers."

"Have you tried being yourself?"

Morpheus snorted. "How am I supposed to be someone I don't remember? Besides. No one really wants that."

"Morpheus..."

He plunged ahead. He didn't have the confidence to withstand one of Prue's lectures right now. He already knew what she would say, and he already knew she was right. "I've tried everything, thank you very much."

"Morpheus."

"I can't get kicked off another team, not over something this stupid. But she doesn't trust me as far as she can throw me, and that distance is... far."

"Morpheus!"

"What?!"

"You know you're in love with her, right?"

"In lo–– What?" he stammered. "That's ridiculous. Since when?"

"Since the beginning, I think." Prue took a shuddering breath and pressed her lips together to hide their trembling. "That's why I'm breaking up with you."

"Prue!" Morpheus stumbled over his words in disbelief. "It's not like––What do you... I don't understand."

"Get out of my room."

"Don't do this. Please don't do this."

"Go."

Morpheus heaved himself to his feet and crossed the room. He hesitated with his hand on the doorknob, his eyes downcast. "I'm sorry."

Prue didn't look at him. Probably because she couldn't look at him. "Just... Go."

Numbly, Morpheus wandered past Cyrus and Sushila and exited Leo's dorm into the hall. Prue's quiet sobs echoed in his ears, muffled by the door moments after he'd closed it. He curled his fingers into fists. He wanted to turn around. Deny everything and comfort her, even though he knew it would be a lie. She was right, and he hated himself for it.

Ashleen slowly became aware of frigid steel biting into her skin where it touched her. Someone had strapped her to a table, fluorescent lighting strobed overhead. Its pulses stabbed her eyes. No. Not here. Anywhere but here. Ashleen fought against the straps binding her wrists and ankles.

"Listenlistenlisten," the ichor buzzed inside of her. "There is still time to let me in. Let me in. Let me in."

Ashleen swallowed against the acidic rage that coated her throat. "I won't."

The voice didn't respond, instead it merely chuckled at her.

She sucked in a deep breath. She'd survived this scenario already. She could do it again. She sought out the strength she knew she had.

She blinked, and she was in the library. She was fairly certain she'd already passed all the ordeals, unless the last few days had just been a break in the nightmare. Ashleen checked herself over and breathed a sigh of relief. She looked like her regular self, which meant that most likely, she still had access to her strength.

"Of course you do," a hollow voice answered her realization. "What reason would I have to disarm you, sister?"

Ashleen spun. "Who's there?"

"Do you not know me? I know much of you."

"Identify yourself."

"I am the Library. And you, you are the Vanquisher."

"I know who I am."

"Are you so certain? You can only know who you were yesterday. Each day we awaken as a different person than we were the day before. Each choice you make today will define your understanding of yourself tomorrow," the Library explained patiently.

"Enough riddles. Why am I here?"

"To find a father, knowing you."

"What's that supposed to mean?"

"It means, whatever you think it means."

With each progressive word, the Library reminded Ashleen more of a giant blue caterpillar, perched pretentiously atop a toadstool. She'd had just about enough of it. "Do you have more information about Connor Gallagher or not?"

"Perhaps I do, perhaps I don't. What is it you want to know?"

She huffed out an annoyed sigh. "Listen here, Absolom––"

"I beg your pardon?"

"I have better ways to spend my time, why don't you get to the point?"

"It is not I who needs to 'get to the point' as you so eloquently put it."

Ashleen had never expected to be this frustrated by a library, of all things. In her youth, the quiet and the books had always been a place of respite and escape. This library, however, was beginning to feel more and more like a trap. "I did get to the point! I told you exactly what I wanted, it's you who refused to answer."

"Or perhaps," the Library went on, as if she hadn't spoken at all, "you simply do not know yourself well enough to ask the real questions."

"I'm leaving," Ashleen announced, and focused on imagining a door into existence. Nothing happened, "Screw you."

"Is that what you want now?" Amusement danced in the Library's words.

"No!" Ashleen felt around at the edges of her mind for the doors she knew were there. Her hand found a knob.

"I wouldn't open that one, if I were you."

"Get out of my head!" Ashleen wrenched the door open and was swallowed by an inky blackness. Panic clawed at her lungs, ragged breaths shredded her throat as she fought against an intangible foe.

"Listenlistenlisten," the ichor hummed both within and about her simultaneously. "Let me in, let me in, let me in."

"Never! I won't be your tool."

"Mine. Mineminemine," The ichor snarled, its tone wolfish.

"Bite me," The words left her before Ashleen had fully thought them through.

The viscous ink formed into the jaws of a wolf, and snapped closed around her throat. Even as the teeth broke her skin, she felt her limbs stretch, the joints dislocated and relocated. Ashleen unleashed a gurgling scream that shifted through the spectrum to a howl as her jaw stretched into a muzzle.

When she opened her eyes, the world had gone red and she was back in her dorm. Her grotesque, lycanthropic form hunched in the center of the room. Her head was heavy. No, not her head. There was something in her mouth. Ashleen unlocked her jaws. A body crumpled to the floor with a sickening series of thuds.

A horrified wail tore free of her chest as she recognized Prue's ravaged form. She'd been ripped open shoulder to hip, internal organs in complete disarray. A crimson pool squished between Ashleen's toes.

The door to Morpheus' room flew open and banged against the wall. He hovered on the threshold, a devastated expression frozen on his features.

Ashleen shouted for him to run, but the only sounds that left her were predatory snarls as the wolf lunged for him. Her jaws closed around him and Ashleen felt his ribs crunch in her mouth. Her chest heaved with the force of her sobs, but she felt the thrill that surged through the wolf as purely as if it were her own.

The hatch creaked open and someone hurried into the dorm behind her. Ashleen turned. Her ears flattened against her head. Before her stood her father, his eyes narrowed with disgust.

"Selfish brat," he hissed. "Fighting against the gifts I gave you. Rejecting the power you were granted." His image flickered, sometimes it was her father. Sometimes, it looked very much like Rome. Between the two was a massive, deformed wolf, easily three times her size even with her ichor form.

"I don't want this!" she cried. "Nobody wants this. They didn't deserve this. Prue didn't deserve this!"

"Retribution!" her father demanded, and her blood sang with the command.

Ashleen shoved it down and a pulsing migraine rose up to take its place. "For what?" Pavane's laughter bounced off the walls. "Stop it!"

"Vengeance!" Rome's command urged her to rip throats from the entire city, gorge herself on their blood.

"I won't!" She fought against the ice picks driving into her temples. Her eyes watered.

"Wrath!" The massive wolf roared, oily ichor drooling from his maw.

His will crashed against the gates of her resistance like a battering ram, and her mind shattered. For what felt like an eternity, there was only rage, blood, and the shrieks of her victims.

"Vanquisher." This was a new voice, one she couldn't quite place. It washed over her like cool water. "Sweetheart." It was only a word, but it brought with it a wave of comfort. Rain on the window. A cup of hot chocolate. Her mother humming. The crackling of a fireplace. Her cat Murphey purring in her lap.

Ashleen forced her eyes open and sat bolt upright. She was back in the infirmary. All the lights were off and no one was with her. She was herself again. She drew her knees up to her chest and began to rock back and forth. She sucked in shaky breaths and swiped tears from her eyes.

"You were dreaming," Diva crooned in her mind. When Ashleen didn't respond, the vesper didn't say anything more, instead soothing Ashleen with her presence and a series of lullabies looped through the shared space of their psyches.

Eventually Ashleen's breathing slowed to a regulated pattern and Diva left her. She snatched her water bottle and tranquilizers off the bedside table. She shook two into her hand and downed them before she could think the choice through.

No doubt Neele would disapprove; the last pill she'd taken hadn't even worn off. It didn't matter. She could still taste Prue's blood in her mouth, still feel Morpheus' ribs cracking between her jaws. She couldn't risk the ichor taking over. Not when Diva wouldn't always be there to save her.

16

The Howling

Ashleen hunkered down behind a tree, listening to gunfire and the twang of bowstrings as the deadeyes slowly picked people off from the canopy. She cursed under her breath. They had an obvious and unfair advantage in this scenario.

When Ivanoff had announced and scheduled an open arena sim, Ashleen had thought it would be fun. An excellent opportunity to test her skills. Unfortunately, the huntsmen were a little more gung-ho about 'every man for himself' than she'd anticipated.

She resented Ivanoff for the heavily forested setting she'd whipped up. The scofflaws and deadeyes had immediately taken to the trees and made easy pickings of anyone less stealthy. Ashleen had hoped for the opportunity to work with and learn from some of the other tranqs, but all of them had run or attacked her on sight.

She ducked around a tree and darted under a rocky outcropping. She peered up through the branches and felt around for a good-sized stone to fold into her palm. While tranqs were better suited to close quarters combat, Ashleen could throw a rock with lethal force if she wanted to.

"Up and to your left, roughly forty-five degrees," Barrage hissed in her mind.

Ashleen looked. She thought she could see a figure crouched on a branch, a deadeye with a compound bow clutched close to their body. Their back was to her. She slowly raised her arm and took aim. The rock flew and struck the deadeye square in the back. He over corrected his balance and careened off the branch.

As he tumbled through a shaft of sunlight and dematerialized, Ashleen recognized Cyrus' gold curls. She clapped a hand over her mouth and prayed he hadn't seen her. If he had, she'd never hear the end of it.

"That is totally unfair, why are you ratting on other deadeyes anyway?" Façade interjected.

"Life isn't fair," Barrage countered.

"You're using ichor around this many people?" Diva chided. "What if somebody sees you?"

"I'd see them first. Besides, I don't need ichor to be aware of my surroundings."

Ashleen felt the roll of Diva's eyes as if they were her own. That was new. Was it just a quirk she shared with Diva or could the other archknights do it too? What else could one communicate through their psychic link?

"Best to have an open face, yet conceal your thoughts," Proverb interjected, and Ashleen realized with embarrassment that she'd been thinking aloud. Again. The line was so easy to cross.

Diva's sympathy reached out to her. She'd had to learn this lesson recently herself. She'd tried to explain the difference to Ashleen, but every mind had an 'accent' as it were. No two felt exactly alike, and so in the long run, she'd have to figure it out through trial and error.

Barrage was the best at it. While all the other archknights had no difficulty closing off their minds from hers, she could always feel them, lingering on the edges of her consciousness. Present, but not hovering.

Barrage on the other hand, sometimes flickered in and out before vanishing entirely, like a bad cell signal. The first time it had happened it had scared Ashleen. She'd thought he had died before Diva reassured her that he would return eventually.

She'd been right, of course, but he'd been gone for almost two entire days. Ashleen was starting to grow suspicious. He was obviously up to something if he felt the need to hide from them so completely. No one was able to tell her where he went, so Ashleen was building up the courage to confront Barrage about it directly.

Her father had told her the archknights knew the truth. The existence of the truth implied the existence of a lie, but she had no idea who was lying to her. She wasn't sure she'd ever be able to earn Barrage's trust. What was worse, she didn't even know what the lie might be about, only that it existed. The knowledge made her second guess everyone she spoke to.

A twig snapped and Ashleen crouched low, pressing farther back under the outcropping. If Barrage could pick her out so easily, no doubt another deadeye at the right angle could as well. She eyed a lichen-covered branch a few feet from her. She might be able to use that to help disguise her eye-catching ginger hair.

A shuffle of steps nearby startled her, and Ashleen froze, hoping whoever it was hadn't spotted her. A pair of feet stumbled into view. Whoever it was had their back to her; they clearly weren't aware of her presence.

She shifted her weight forwards, preparing to tackle the person when Barrage's voice hissed in her mind again: "We have to go."

Ashleen shut her eyes and focused on Barrage's location like Diva had shown her. Her body sank into the floor of the sim room, traveling along the ichor lattice within the city's walls. When she opened her eyes again, she was inside a mantacraft with the other archknights.

She pulled the ichor wolf's jaws closed around her face. The sensation of ichor travel always made her uneasy. When she'd demanded to know how it worked, Diva had tried to explain.

"It's like the sim rooms. Since everything in there is an image projected by ichor, you can change the world around you with enough mental acuity. The ichor is in you now, so the same concept applies in reverse. Focus, and you can change yourself around the world."

She'd made a joke about bad game graphics and clipping through walls, but Diva hadn't understood.

"Rise and shine beautiful!" Barrage buzzed amicably to the ship as he swung himself into the pilot's seat.

Lights flickered to life all around the cabin. "Good evening, Barrage. Where will you be taking me today?" The ship's words were spliced together and her inflection was off. Her sentences were intelligently composed out of hundreds of individually recorded words, rather than preprogrammed phrases.

"Germany," Barrage said, sounding almost chipper.

"Well it's about time. I've only been asking for five years."

"Is this normal?" Ashleen thought to Diva, careful to close off her mind to the other archknights.

"You mean the way he talks to the ship? Yes."

"I've never heard him sound happy before."

"It's only when he speaks to the ship."

"That is weird."

"You're preaching to the choir. It still freaks me out a little."

"Ha. Choir." Ashleen bit her lip to quell a giggle.

"What do you--oh. Ha ha. Very funny."

"What's the mark?" Façade asked aloud as the engine hummed to life.

"Bessie, read us the file." The irritated edge Ashleen had learned to expect from Barrage returned to his voice.

"Wardens have tracked a pack of lycanthropes to northern Germany. Until recently they had been lying low, somewhere in Scandinavia. But they are on the move, and they are targeting temples to Muginn. Casualties have been minor. However, they are targeting larger and larger cities. The wardens believe they may be on their way to the Crypts of Muginn."

"How did this make it all the way up to us? Shouldn't it have been taken care of by a lower ranking team when it was a smaller problem?" Façade asked.

"It was," Bessie answered. "The pack was supposedly exterminated by Leo and his team. It was reported in turn by their deadeye that one of the lycans escaped. The wardens believe that escaped lycan is the leader of this pack."

"Typical," Barrage scoffed. "Never count on a novice to do an expert's job."

Ashleen bit down on the indignation that burned in her stomach on Cyrus' behalf. There was no point arguing with Barrage. She'd tried a couple times already, and he always found a way to make her feel like an idiot.

Diva leaned in and let her shoulder bump Ashleen's. The gesture was meant to be comforting. She listened a bit closer to Ashleen's psyche than the other archknights, toeing the line between polite and hovering.

Ashleen suspected that she may have listened in on her nightmares, and appointed herself to monitor Ashleen's mood swings. She subtly returned the bump, reassuring Diva that she had things under control.

Bessie's hull sang as it slipped through the ichor alloy of Alexandria's hangar, and Ashleen's body went weightless. In spite of their lack of seatbelts, no one went flying about the cabin. The ichor of their suits had secured itself via electromagnetic interaction with ichor inside Bessie's metal plating. Ashleen could move if she so chose, but doing so required immense effort, and she found it was much less tiring not to.

Bessie righted herself and flipped an agile turn to head southward. "I estimate arrival within forty-three minutes."

"So tell me about the pack leader," Ashleen said aloud. "If he was the only survivor, and there's no record of him turning civilians, where did he find the framework for his new pack?"

"There is no record of casualties," Bessie confirmed. "Yet witness accounts suggest there were at least five lycans in the area. The wardens theorize the straggler encountered a farm and turned the family and workers. Remote location would delay the public's notice, and if he turned all of them, there would be no one left to report it within the estate."

"That's horrible."

"I've seen worse," Barrage stated.

Ashleen resisted the urge to rip his head off. Just because he'd seen it before didn't make it any less sad. "Do we have a plan of attack?" She asked, trying to distract herself by mapping out the situation in her mind.

"Don't," Barrage barked a laugh.

She was going to kill him.

"Only a fool tests the water with both feet," Proverb added.

She was going to kill both of them. "I just want to know what the plan is so I don't have to test the water with both feet," she said through gritted teeth.

"Lycans are at their most dangerous in close quarters," Façade began. "Proverb and Barrage will probably do most of the work. Diva can mimic their cries, so it's likely she will be creating confusion in their ranks. That will make her a target for the alpha. It will be up to the two of us to make sure she is defended at all times."

"Thank you."

"Don't thank me yet. In the long run, you should take the brunt of the counterattack. Your ichor is native to Anshathane. You're effectively immune to lycanthropy, because you're already infected. If you get bit, it's just a bite. If I get bit, we have a problem."

Ashleen didn't like the idea of being thrown onto the front lines in her first archknight-level encounter, but she understood his reasoning. "Will do."

The rest of the flight passed in relative silence. When they touched down in Germany, Ashleen took a moment to shake the numbness out of her limbs.

"We're approximately a mile from the nearest settlement. That said, under no circumstances are you to allow a single lycan past you. We are drawing a line in the sand. No matter what you see out there, you kill anything that approaches that line on sight. Understood?" Barrage ordered.

Nobody spoke, but a wave of affirmation rode the psychic link.

Bessie's door opened, and the archknights disembarked in silence, all of them moving into position without direction. Ashleen didn't hear anything more through the link, but inferred from her discussion with Façade that she was to hang close to him and Diva.

Façade led them across an open field, silently arranging them in a way that covered the most ground possible without stationing them too far apart. A little way away from them was a sparse copse of trees that provided just enough cover to unnerve Ashleen.

The entire area was extremely open; in fact Ashleen could see the lights of the distant city on the horizon behind her. There was no possible way for anything to sneak up on them, so she couldn't explain the tingling feeling that they were being watched.

She crouched low to the ground and peered into the spaces between the trees. The shadows seemed to writhe beneath them, but she couldn't tell if something was really there or if she was manufacturing a presence with her anxiety.

"Did you see that?" she asked Diva, careful to ensure she didn't blurt her thoughts to the rest of the team.

"No. But you and Barrage have better night vision than the rest of us."

That did nothing to set her nerves at ease. Ashleen shifted her attention back to the copse just as the treeline erupted. Almost simultaneously, the peaceful night shattered in a hail of gunfire and the roaring flames of more hellhounds than Ashleen could count.

Twenty feet to her left, Diva's Lovecraftian hair wriggled to life and the howls of at least five different wolves ricocheted out from her. The line of slavering lycans broke, splitting off into confused groups.

Façade's voice interrupted her thoughts. "Stay here. I'm running clean up."

"Wait! Façade--" Ashleen replied out loud, forgetting he wouldn't be able to hear her between distance and din.

"Do not leave Diva unguarded," Barrage snapped.

"Understood," Ashleen said, holding her ground.

For a few seconds that stretched into minutes, Diva's diversion went unchallenged. Then a united howl rose up and brought order out of the chaos.

Ashleen edged closer to her. She knew they were supposed to be holding a line, but it made her uneasy to leave Diva so exposed.

Two wolves broke out of the mire and started towards them, but before Ashleen could so much as raise her hackles, Barrage had killed them with two clean head shots. He repeated this with five more lycans, their bodies collapsing in pools of ichor a way off from where they were any threat to Diva or Ashleen.

One trio was cleanly dispatched by Façade in passing, and it began to appear that Ashleen would not have to do anything at all. The tension started to leach out of her shoulders.

A low snarl to her right brought her to all fours, the ichor wolf's muzzle peeling back from its teeth to answer the sound. A few short paces from her was a lycan that easily matched her size, dwarfing all the wolves she'd seen so far.

"I have eyes on the alpha," Ashleen alerted everyone.

The ichor roiling about her demanded the alpha's blood. Instead, Ashleen forced herself back a few paces towards Diva. A new song entered Diva's chorus, and the voices within the ichor quieted.

Ashleen dropped back another step. The alpha charged her, and her heart kicked against her ribcage like a frightened rabbit. Her blood rushed in her ears, and before she could think it through, Ashleen loosened her grip on the reins.

Her body moved of its own volition, but the red haze she'd come to expect didn't descend. She met the alpha mid stride, throwing her weight into him and pushing him back. He stumbled and rounded on her, and his teeth sank into her shoulder.

Ashleen flinched, but the pain never came. Her taloned hand slammed into the alpha's throat and he fell back, coughing. Confidence restored, she planted her feet and roared at him. He raised a clawed forelimb to return her strike.

She startled at a light patter of footsteps up her back. Before she could react to them, Façade leaped off her shoulder. He twisted in midair. His ichor blade flashed like obsidian as it sliced the alpha's hand from his arm.

Façade vanished and reappeared on the alpha's back. He drove his sword between the lycan's shoulder blades and paused just long enough to draw a new one from the symbol on his visor before he vanished again.

Ashleen wanted to stare, but the ichor had other ideas. While the alpha howled in pain, she slammed into him and rolled him onto his back. Before she could catch herself, her jaws closed around his throat and she bit down. With a sickening squish, the alpha twitched and went still.

"Sorry to rain on your parade," Barrage interjected psychically, with a tone that indicated he was quite the opposite. "That wasn't the alpha."

Before Ashleen could ask what he meant, there came a howl like a gust of wind across the plain. The remaining lycans, their numbers greatly reduced between Barrage and Proverb's efforts, began to spiral inward.

The large wolf between Ashleen's feet quivered and then popped. Its form splattered her with stray droplets as the remaining liquid began to drain inwards with the spiral of lycans.

"Gross!" she exclaimed.

"It would seem there was only ever one lycan."

A single, massive, beast rose from the center of the spiral. It shrieked at them, its cries piercing Ashleen's ears like a needle. To her astonishment, she could understand them.

"Wait. Can you hear that?"

"The unholy caterwauling? Pretty sure they can hear that all the way in town," Façade assessed.

"You understand it, don't you?" Ashleen addressed Diva directly.

"What? Of course not. I just mimic the sounds I hear. I don't know what they mean."

"It's Anshan ichor. Like calls to like. Don't listen," Barrage explained.

"But he's asking for help!"

"That's a ploy. Did I not make myself clear? Kill anything that approaches the line in the sand, no exceptions."

"What if he's lost control? Maybe he doesn't want to hurt anyone." On the one hand, Ashleen knew they had to stop the lycan. On the other, she could see herself in the beast before her. There had to be a nonviolent solution.

A soothing hum filled her ears and blocked out the cries. "Maybe this will help," Diva offered sympathetically.

Ashleen wanted to quip that just because she couldn't hear them anymore didn't mean they had stopped. But Diva's heart was in the right place, and she couldn't bring herself to snap. "Thank you for trying."

A quiet presence seeped into the psychic link. Proverb had a plan and requested with gentle urgency that they hold their positions. Barrage confirmed the request and for a time they waited while the massive ichor alpha continued to form.

Ashleen scanned the battlefield for her teammates. A significant distance away she thought she could see a lone upright figure against the trees, but she was too far to be sure. Just as she was about to ask what they were doing, a dog sized object hurtled over her head.

She yelped and ducked belatedly as it was followed by another, and then three more. As she focused on them, she realized they were gargoyles. The same ones that she'd encountered during Proverb's test.

Their black stone feathers glinted in the moonlight as they dove in and around the gigantic lycan's head, squalling and screeching. He snapped at them like a dog trying to bite flies out of the air and then he stilled at one flitted past his eye and perched itself on his muzzle.

"Are those––" Ashleen began.

"The honest to Muginn gargoyles off the Crypt's parapets? Yes I believe they are," Façade sounded almost as surprised as she was.

A glimmer of pride rippled through the psychic link from Proverb.

"Excellent thinking, Verb," Barrage said, congratulating them.

Ashleen couldn't hear the lycan's cries anymore due to Diva's song, but she could read his body language as easily as any dog's. His ears were pinned to his head, which was lowered level to his shoulders. His body hunched inward and his pitiful excuse for a tail was tucked between his legs as if the gargoyle were chastising him.

"Does he... recognize it?" Diva inquired.

Affirmation washed out from Proverb.

"There has to be something human still in there!" Ashleen insisted. "How do we save him?"

"We can't." For once, Barrage's tone carried a note of the appropriate remorse. "Let's move, while he's distracted."

Ashleen tried to protest, but the rest of the archknights had begun to circle inward. Diva began a rendition of a popular Ravenite hymn Ashleen recognized. The lycan's head drooped lower, and she felt like someone had stabbed her in the gut.

"Façade, bullets are too small for this one. It's up to you," Barrage hissed.

"Understood. Vanquisher, care to lend a hand?"

"What?" Ashleen asked in a daze.

"Throw me."

"Oh!" Ashleen scrabbled for a solution, something that could avoid all this bloodshed and still save everyone.

"Vanquisher," Barrage growled with warning.

Nausea twisted in Ashleen's stomach. Short of sitting on her hands and waiting for the lycan to eat half her team, she couldn't see an alternative. She reached for Façade. His fingers closed around her wrists and she locked her larger hands around his. He gave her a terse nod.

Ashleen sighed and spun, her momentum and stature pulling his comparatively diminutive form through the air with ease. Rapidly estimating his trajectory, she let go of him at the last second. Keyed into her psychic signals, Façade let go simultaneously and soared through the air on course towards the alpha.

As he flew he began to draw a full length spear hand over hand from the emblem on his visor. He blinked in and out of sight as he drew closer, correcting his course a few feet at a time. Just before he collided with the beast, he reappeared a few feet higher and to the right. He plunged the spear cleanly in through the lycan's eye.

The wolf's howl tore through Diva's song, and Ashleen clapped her hands over her ears as his cries for help cut into her again. Tears pricked at her eyes but she forced herself to watch as his colossal form lost its shape.

Façade rode the wave as the alpha became a cascading waterfall of oily fluid, occasionally blinking back and forth to more favorable positions until he washed gracefully out onto the field.

Barrage produced a device and tossed it into the center of the pool. It seemed only to take a few seconds to do its job, as he immediately strode into the swampy mess to retrieve it. The rest of the archknights began to make their way towards the center as well, so Ashleen followed their example.

Diva's obvious distaste at picking her way through the ankle-deep muck was the only disruption as they gathered around Barrage. In his hand was what appeared to be a glass canister, not much bigger than a spice bottle.

"What's that?" Ashleen asked.

"That," he held it up for her to see, "is all the ichor present in this area, excluding what's in our veins." About a tablespoon of gravity defying liquid floated freely within the tube.

"What about all––" Ashleen looked down at her feet only to discover what had appeared to be ichor a moment ago was now simply mud. "Huh."

"You'd have to get somebody else to explain the science to you, but ichor will fully homogenize with just about anything. You could say it's a very friendly substance."

"Or aggressive," Diva suggested. "It's also highly acidic and will consume anything that can't maintain a balance with it."

"Speaking of which," several eyes opened on Barrage's head and shoulders, "are there any remains?"

"Over here," Façade said, drawing their attention.

Ashleen's stomach crawled into her chest cavity. At Façade's feet was a boy who couldn't be more than fifteen. "He's just a child."

"Misfortune never distinguishes between the young and the old, meek or bold." Proverb put one of their hands on Ashleen's shoulder.

"Look," said Barrage as he crouched and prodded at the child's arm with his fingers. The skin on the inside of his elbow was mottled yellow and purple with old bruising, "Signs of injections. And here."

Ashleen swallowed a swell of nausea and averted her gaze as Barrage dug into an infected cut behind one of the boy's ears. He held out a tiny, bloody, microchip for them to see. "This wasn't an accident. This was done to him."

Ashleen recoiled in horror. "Who would do this?"

"No one with even a shred of humanity left," Diva spat venomously.

"We should go. I'm sure you all have things to do," Barrage straightened.

"That's it? We can't just leave him here!"

"We won't," Diva assured her. "Proverb will tend to the necessary rites and the blood tithe. It's best we leave them to it."

Ashleen allowed herself to be gently herded back to the ship between Façade and Diva. Even Bessie remained silent for the duration of their return to Alexandria. When they had docked and the rest of the team had gone their separate ways, Ashleen intercepted Diva.

"Does it ever get any easier?" she asked, the words catching in her throat.

"No. At least it hasn't for me yet. But I've only been on the team for six months."

Ashleen managed a weak laugh. "Is there any chance, even a small one, that that could happen to any of us?" She'd spent the last forty-five minutes trying to push the boy's cries and the horrifyingly real memories of crushing something between her jaws from her mind.

Diva didn't answer immediately, and Ashleen's heart sank.

"I won't lie to you," she said finally. "There's always a chance. If we aren't strong enough to hold the ichor apart from ourselves, that is our future. That is why everyone was so mad at me for helping you."

"Because now no one can be sure if I am strong enough on my own."

Diva nodded. "I'm sure you'll be fine though. You handled yourself far better than I did on my first day."

"Oh yeah?" Ashleen forced optimism into her voice, but Diva's recounting of her tale was lost in the drone of blood in her ears and her ichor's echoing laughter.

17

Barrage's Bargain

"Ashleen!" Izzy barked at her.

"I'll be fine," she said, sauntering past Dahei into the dark maw of the cave.

Izzy swore. "Morpheus!"

"I've got her, I've got her."

The misty sensation of Morpheus' warding hymn settled against Ashleen's skin. A vampire surged from the shadows. She backhanded it into the wall of the cave. When a second lunged for her, she caught it by the throat and hurled it at the ground with enough force that she heard its skull crunch.

Ashleen stepped back as the vampire she'd slammed into the wall recovered and made a pass at her. As his momentum carried him forward, she kicked one of his feet from under him. He didn't get the chance to recover a second time.

She grabbed a fistful of his shirt and forced him to continue his fall, right onto the stalagmite that rose up from the ground behind him. Dahei cut the vampire's gurgling short with a quick decapitation.

Ashleen ignored his arrival and meandered further into the cave. "Come on you Ikaluscan scum. I know there are more of you."

A swarm of bats answered her taunt. They surged past her toward the mouth of the cave. She let them. Dahei ducked into the breach provided by her larger frame. "Incoming!"

Izzy yanked the pin free of a modified grenade and tossed it just as the first bats exploded out of the cave. The grenade burst in a spray of salty mist. The bats caught in the cloud fell to the ground, dead.

"She's been more ornery than usual, right? It's not just me?" Izzy asked.

Morpheus couldn't stop singing to answer. He offered a nonchalant shrug.

"I suspect there are a great many things she is trying to hide from," Demetrius offered, throwing a gesture. A pair of hellhounds rose out of the ground and bounded about, snapping at the bats that had evaded Izzy's grenade.

Morpheus sucked in a breath between verses. He'd also noticed Ashleen's tendency to stroll into the fray as if she were invulnerable. She seemed not to care how much strain it put on him, and he thought she was almost pleased with the news of his and Prue's recent breakup.

Unfortunately, they'd been at each other's throats for weeks. She'd grown exponentially more apathetic, and her scathing commentary cut deep. If it had only been that, he might not have minded so much, but as a vesper, the loss of Prue had put him in a difficult situation.

He didn't have the latent energy anymore to keep using his abilities at their full potential, and Ashleen's 'devil may care' attitude towards missions had him dipping into the resources he used just to sustain himself.

Ashleen finished wringing an unlucky vampire's neck and glanced up as Barrage's voice buzzed through her mind. "We have a situation. Meet as soon as possible."

She acknowledged the command and followed up with a comment that she had her hands full, but would be there as soon as she could get away. She moved ahead to scout the rest of the cave.

The hunt was for five vampires. She'd killed two, Dahei had decapitated the one she'd impaled, and two had escaped past her to be cornered by Izzy and Demetrius. That should be all of them, but it wouldn't do to let any lurkers escape.

Ashleen checked over her shoulder for Dahei. He was a few yards behind her. She faced forward again and blinked a third eyelid film of ichor over her eyes. Now able to see in the relative blackness of the cave, she forged ahead rapidly.

"Hey!" Dahei shouted after her. He cursed as she melted into the shadows.

"What happened?" Izzy's voice echoed from somewhere outside.

"Ashleen didn't wait for me. I lost her."

Izzy tilted his head towards Demetrius. "Go in after them, won't you? Your wisps have a better chance of finding her than any of us do."

"Indeed," Demetrius gestured and the two hellhounds fell in to flank him. He let his fingertips trail along the walls as he followed Dahei's breathing deeper into the cave.

Dahei relaxed as the dim orange glow from the hellhounds eased the darkness. The path ahead of him forked. "Lend me a little more light?"

Demetrius flicked a finger and the hounds began to pant, their tongues lolling out as the flames in their chests burned hotter. Dahei searched the dust on the ground, struggling to spot a stray boot print or scattered pebbles that might indicate the path Ashleen had taken.

"Looking for me?" A voice shocked Dahei out of his concentration, and Ashleen loomed out of the darkness above him.

"Feathered mother! Don't scare me like that!"

Ashleen waved a hand dismissively. "I was checking for stragglers. They're all dead. We can go." She pushed past them and headed for the exit.

"Hey, I wasn't done talking to you! You can't just run off like that."

Ashleen didn't stop, "Just did. About to do it again if you don't keep up."

Dahei sighed through his teeth and started after her. "Come on."

As the mantacraft began the docking process back in Alexandria, Morpheus tried to broach the topic of Ashleen's attitude shift with her. "You know, it's difficult for me to keep up with you. I'm a bit drained lately."

"If you don't want to ward me, don't," Ashleen cast over her shoulder as she strode down the ramp and across the hangar bay. Morpheus flipped a three-toed raven gesture at her back.

"So," Izzy said, steepling his fingers. "Morpheus. Have you noticed anything off about Ashleen?"

"You mean besides the fact that she's being an absolute––" He grit his teeth and gestured emphatically, "Whatever that was? Why are you asking me?"

The amusement was evident in Izzy's tone. "Your sudden devotion to celibacy speaks volumes."

Morpheus rubbed his temples against a rapidly encroaching migraine. "Suck an egg," he sighed. "She's filled her prescription for tranquilizers twice this week."

The amusement vanished from Izzy's voice. "And you were going to tell me this when, exactly?"

Ashleen scowled as she stomped down the hallway. She'd put off eating all day and it had been her intention to grab something after her return from the hunt. Unfortunately, she'd already left Barrage's summons unanswered long enough.

She was undoubtedly in for an earful, and there was no time for food. She raised her head to do a quick sweep of her surroundings before she called her ichor wolf to the surface and melted into the floor.

"Oh, please take your time," Barrage stated sarcastically as she rose up within his mantacraft.

Ashleen didn't respond except to duck her head in a weak attempt at appearing apologetic. He seemed to sense her insincerity and his bees pulsed in menacing patterns. "Where were you?"

"You're one to talk," Ashleen snapped. "You've been on and off the grid all week."

Barrage opened an eye just to narrow it at her, but he didn't press the issue.

"Do we have any evidence on who's been experimenting with ichor?" Diva interjected.

"Yes, actually," Barrage answered. "I managed to find a line on a homunculus who's willing to talk."

Façade recoiled. "You couldn't find anything less disturbing? Who's its deity?"

"Ikalusca."

He shuddered. "I swear to the Raven, if there's a repeat of last time, I'll kill you."

"Wait, what?" Ashleen blurted.

Barrage chuckled. "I haven't laughed that hard in years."

"Yes, I remember," Façade quipped irritably.

"Do you remember this?" Ashleen asked Diva non-verbally.

She felt Diva shake her head. "It was before my time. Don't bother, they're never going to tell you."

"That was very funny," Bessie commented.

"You weren't even there!"

"No. But Barrage told me all about it."

Façade dropped his head into his hands. "Wonderful. The ship knows. I'm never going to live it down."

Their flight this time was almost twice as long as usual, but Ashleen didn't mind that much. If she couldn't eat, at least she could sleep. She tried to grab some shuteye wherever she had the opportunity these days.

Now that her leg had healed, it was full steam ahead with Izzy's team. On top of that, the archknights did nearly all of their missions after dark, which meant she was losing between two and three nights of rest every week.

This was only exacerbated by how difficult the double dose of tranquilizers made it to wake up every morning. She told herself the lethargy was worth it. Ashleen hadn't had another nightmare since, and the ichor wolf was quiet. It obeyed her whims with the enthusiasm of a sulky preteen, but it no longer forced its will on her.

When Bessie landed, Barrage drew their attention. "I was unable to confirm this, but it is likely we are dealing with one of the sidhe. Watch your back and let me do the talking. Whatever you do, do not defame the gods in its presence."

The other archknights acknowledged his commands, but Ashleen knew they were mostly for her benefit. They disembarked from Bessie into a swamp. The air hung humid and stagnant with the scent of decaying plant matter, and the soft ground sucked at Ashleen's feet.

"Gross." she protested. Diva's agreement echoed in her mind.

Barrage shushed them and led the way further in, indicating the safe path. "Step where I step, ignore the lights."

Ashleen kept her head down obediently. As much as she liked to rebel against him, she knew better than to mess around in proximity with the sidhe. Second only to the gods, the sidhe were said to be the original soldiers that fought in the first conflict. Very few of them remained, but those who did had lost none of their potency.

The swamp grew denser around them, tree trunks and vines crowding in as if to block them out. Ashleen had the distinct impression of being swallowed. A flicker caught the corner of her eye, and she reminded herself not to look directly at it.

The deeper they went, the quieter it got, until the silence was almost as oppressive as the humidity. Just as the claustrophobia began to set in, the treeline broke and they emerged into a small clearing. At the center, in the only shaft of sunlight Ashleen had seen in quite some time, sat a terrifyingly beautiful creature.

In form, it looked quite similar to Diva, all willowy limbs and delicate bones. It even had the same mane of writhing tentacles. "Oh, Barrage. I don't recall agreeing to..." she scanned the archknights, "others."

"We didn't agree on anything except an exchange for information," Barrage countered.

"You have what I requested then?"

"I do," Barrage said, producing a vessel that looked just like the one Ashleen had seen him use after their fight with the lycan.

The sidhe purred. "Ah, Anshan ichor." Its lidless eyes passed over Ashleen's wolfish form. "So hard to come by these days."

"And our bargain?"

The sidhe chuckled. "I'm honestly surprised you had to come all the way to me. He's been right under your noses this entire time."

An alien presence pushed against Ashleen's mind. She yelped as white-hot pain lanced through her temples. Away to her right, Proverb echoed her cry.

"These two," the sidhe continued, "are quite familiar with him. You humans. So shortsighted."

"A direct answer. Or I keep the ichor."

"He goes by Romulus these days," the sidhe hissed, its eyes lingering on Ashleen. "This one calls him Rome. That one," she glanced at Proverb, "knew he wasn't human. Now, the ichor."

Barrage tossed the vessel to the sidhe; even as it left his fingertips, his voice echoed through the psychic link, "Be ready for a fight."

The sidhe crushed the vessel in her hands and inhaled its contents. Her tentacled hair coiled in delight.

"I don't suppose," Barrage commented amicably, "you happened to be in a mood to let us leave peacefully?"

"When you brought me such a delectable selection of ichor strains?" the sidhe crooned. "How could I resist?"

"I had a feeling you might say that," Barrage brought his hands together and as he pulled them apart, an impressive rifle formed between his palms. He turned it on the sidhe and shot her between the eyes without hesitation.

She laughed. "You'll have to do better than that."

"I know. That's why I brought them."

Ashleen bared her teeth in a slavering snarl and launched herself at the sidhe. The sidhe flickered out of sight, just like Façade, and reappeared a few yards out of reach. Her mouth opened far too wide, displaying needle-like teeth as she unleashed a piercing shriek.

Diva countered with her own wail and matched the sidhe's pitch precisely. Ashleen's ears rang.

Façade was keeping pace with the sidhe and matched her blinks through the clearing. However, he was unable to land any strikes on her as she bobbed and wove about his blades. Ashleen reached for his psyche, and felt him welcome her in. She couldn't teleport, but if she knew where they were going to reappear, she could be there. Façade fed her the information as quickly as he could process it and she whirled to spring into the air.

Just as she began her descent, Façade and the sidhe popped into existence below her. Ashleen shifted a hair to the right and Façade faked a strike at the sidhe that left her wide open. The ichor wolf's claws sank into the sidhe's shoulders and Ashleen dragged them down her back. She bit down on the nape of the sidhe's neck and twisted, hurling her across the clearing. Any lesser being would have been killed, but the sidhe seemed merely annoyed. She recovered and rolled away from Façade's finishing blow as he appeared beside her.

"Keep her busy," Barrage commanded. "Verb and I need a few minutes."

Out of the corner of her eye, Ashleen could see the two of them. Proverb was engaged in a flurry of movement that involved all four hands and their feet. Barrage was absorbed in shaping something big out of his ichor, bees dancing across the surface of his skin busily.

Façade and the sidhe vanished. Ashleen crossed the clearing in two bounds. Even as he reappeared, Façade ducked the tackle Ashleen had planned for the sidhe.

The sidhe slipped around her and Ashleen's pulse tapped out a warning in her ears. "Diva!"

Ashleen turned to pursue the sidhe and startled as the creature bounced off an invisible barrier.

The air around Diva began to shimmer. The sidhe ducked, and Façade tumbled over the top of Diva's dome.

"Vanquisher, get Façade," Diva demanded.

Ashleen was already moving as she felt the thought form in Diva's mind. She ignored the sidhe and slid over the top of the dome after Façade. When she collided with him, his ichor merged with hers and folded the two into the form of an even bigger armor-plated lycan.

A split second later, Diva's barrier exploded outward with a deafening shriek. The force of the explosion sent the two of them flying, and Ashleen felt her ichor struggle to retain its shape against the force of the sonic wave as it rolled over her.

She glanced over her shoulder. The sidhe was coughing up blood, but hadn't moved. Somehow it was still standing. Diva had unleashed a short range burst of concussive force equal to that of a small bomb. If Façade hadn't been sharing ichor with her, they both would have suffered internal damage.

"Lemme out," Façade protested and struggled free of the ichor wolf, tumbling onto the ground. The ichor reformed around her, the damage Diva had done rapidly repairing itself.

Ashleen left him there and charged past Diva to slam into the sidhe. The pair collapsed in a tangle of limbs, the sidhe too strained now to outmaneuver them. Unfortunately, despite being winded and seeping more blood than any natural being ought to be able to lose while retaining consciousness, the sidhe was still a capable opponent.

She headbutted Ashleen in the face, which had little effect as the ichor protected her. Ashleen wasn't as protected, however, from the follow up kick which sent her flying across the clearing.

"Vanquisher, get your furry ass over here!" Façade snapped.

Ashleen righted herself and turned to see him struggling against the sidhe's onslaught as she bore down on him. He'd put himself between her and a clearly trembling Diva.

Ashleen willed herself forward and grabbed a handful of the sidhe's tentacled mane. She twisted the tendrils around her hand and yanked her head back.

The sidhe unleashed an enraged scream and Ashleen fell back as the tentacles attempted to coil around her neck. The sidhe redoubled her attack on Façade.

Ashleen gathered herself and realized with a start that she couldn't feel Diva psychically anymore. When she searched for her, she spotted her exactly where she'd been left. Diva sank to her knees in the soggy moss, her chest heaving with the force of her breaths.

"I'm fine, just a little over-extended," she answered Ashleen's wave of concern.

Ashleen turned her attention to punching the sidhe in the side of the head and she realized she couldn't remember when Diva's hymn had settled over her, only that it had. Ashleen couldn't tell one hymn from another, but it seemed like Diva was warding all of them individually. She'd also probably been enhancing Façade's speed, all on top of her screaming match with the sidhe and the wall of concussive sound she'd created with her dome.

"Focus!" Barrage barked at Ashleen. A moment too late.

The sidhe's heel struck Façade's temple and he went careening out of range. He didn't get up. Ashleen grabbed for the sidhe, but to no avail. The clumsy reaction left her open to strike and the sidhe went for her throat. Her grip was so strong that even through the ichor Ashleen could feel the blood and oxygen supply to her brain slowly being restricted.

The sidhe froze. Her eyes displayed fear for the first time. Ashleen gasped for breath and struggled to escape. In her peripheral vision, she saw Proverb approach.

Their arms were locked in an elaborate gesture, woven and intertwined within each other. With a subtle twitch of one finger, the sidhe's grip loosened and Ashleen dropped to her knees, coughing.

"Are you alright?"

She couldn't get enough air to answer, so she simply nodded.

Barrage brushed past her on the other side. He had a massive firearm propped on one shoulder. "Get out of the way."

If she hadn't been so busy trying to catch her breath, Ashleen might've had a quip for him. Instead, she struggled to her feet and begrudgingly started to back away.

"Take Diva with you."

Ashleen took Diva's outstretched hand and helped her to her feet. Together they made their way over towards Façade, who was working his way upright.

"I'm gonna feel that in the morning," he grumbled.

"Come on," Ashleen told him. "I get the feeling we're not needed anymore."

Façade shook his head as if to clear it and glanced in Barrage's direction. "Damn, he hasn't used that in a while."

"What?" Ashleen and Diva asked in unison.

"The sidhe is gonna feel way worse than I am. Come on, let's go." Façade led the way back to Bessie.

When they were halfway there by Ashleen's estimate, the silence was disrupted by a blast that sounded as if it had come straight out of a sci-fi movie. Façade chuckled gleefully. "Too bad she isn't dead."

"Do you think he'll take her ichor?" Diva asked.

"No. He made a deal. Besides, haven't you been paying attention? Someone inside Alexandria has been experimenting with it. The more we keep out of their hands, the better."

When Bessie had docked and the others had disembarked, Diva caught her attention.

"Vanquisher, can I talk to you for a moment?"

Ashleen was starving and half-dead with exhaustion, but she couldn't say no to Diva. "Sure."

"About earlier," she began haltingly. "When I over-extended my-self?"

"I'm not judging, it happens to everyone."

"Yes, but..." she trailed off, suddenly shy. "Vespers thrive on inti-macy. I messed up today, and we were lucky. I'm worried my lack of resources could endanger the team."

An uncomfortable silence stretched between them for nearly a minute while Ashleen tried not to imagine what Diva could want from her in the context of the situation.

"Look if I'm overstepping my bounds you can hit me, but I have to ask."

"What?" Ashleen wished she could walk away from this conver-sation without feeling guilty about it later.

Diva took a breath and gathered her thoughts. "I can pull on the psychic connection we share to sustain myself. I know we don't know each other that well, but if I had better options I wouldn't ask."

Ashleen hesitated. She supposed it wasn't asking for much, all things considered, but she'd always been on the more conservative side when it came to relationships. What Diva wanted was a bond that felt sacred to Ashleen. She wasn't sure she could offer it up like it was food for some kind of elegant parasite, even if she wanted to.

"Don't think of it as feeding," Diva interjected, and Ashleen cringed, realizing that she'd thought aloud again.

"I'm sorry, I didn't mean--"

Diva waved a hand dismissively. "I know what you meant. Some of us are not as considerate with our abilities. There are vespers that get a thrill out of taking energy by force, even though it's against Ikalusca's statutes. If they studied the lore, they'd know such prac-tices will eventually strip them of their abilities."

"They will?" She hadn't heard of that before.

"Of course. Ikalusca is no less a god than Anshathane or Muginn, and both of them retaliate against those who misuse the power granted to them. Are you religious?"

"Yes, but I was brought up Ravenite." Ashleen feigned ignorance, careful to gloss over any more hints of her distaste for the kraken deity.

"I'm not surprised. A lot of people shy away from Ikalusca, they don't understand his teachings."

Ashleen let her intrigue brush against Diva's mind. Regardless of her feelings, she'd always been curious. It would be interesting to hear a perspective on Ikalusca that wasn't in opposition to him.

"What do you think Ikalusca is the god of?"

She wasn't sure how to answer. She'd always assumed he was a 'red light district' sort of deity. The priests in her hometown had always painted him as a god of secrets and subterfuge, among other, less church-friendly things.

Diva chuckled; she'd been listening in. "That's what most people think. But they're wrong. If Muginn is the god of death, and Anshathane is the god of life, what does that make Ikalusca?"

"I don't know." There didn't seem to be a third option.

"Let me try again. If Anshathane is the waxing moon, and Muginn is the waning moon, what's in between?"

"The full moon. Or the new moon."

"Now you're getting it. Ikalusca is the deity of new beginnings and change. Of rebirth, and unrealized potential. He reigns over transitions, revelation, and revolution. People seeking to turn over a new leaf would be better off burning his incense than any other deity's."

Ashleen's discomfort began to melt away. Her interest in the topic supplanted her exhaustion. "Okay, but what does that have to do with how the vespers are?"

Diva took a moment to think. "It's difficult to explain. He's a deity of entropy, and I think that's where a lot of people get confused. They assume that Muginn's affinity towards balance and Ikalusca's affinity for chaos are opposites. That because balance is 'good' that means chaos is 'bad'. And they forget that Muginn is the god of death because of everything they did to save their son from it."

She paused to make sure Ashleen was following. "Vespers, and others who adhere to Ikalusca's statutes, endeavor to stir things up. We're officially labelled disturbers of the peace, and that's what gets people so bent out of shape. But we aren't meant to just cause chaos willy nilly, only where it's needed. They forget that peace and stagnation can look a lot alike, but one of them is, by definition, a detriment to humanity and society."

"White rabbits and red herrings..." Ashleen mused.

"I'm sorry?"

"It's a story, well, one of them is. The other is a literary device. There's a book about a little girl that follows a white rabbit into a world where everything is backwards, and a red herring is a specific kind of diversion meant to throw someone off a scent."

Diva inclined her head. "That seems like an accurate assessment."

Ashleen sat down in one of the unused seats. "So why the emotional manipulation?"

"That's easy. People don't act unless they have strong feelings about something. Vespers are uniquely positioned to be either the thing people care deeply about, or the thing that tests their devotion to something else."

"Like Helen of Troy."

"She's a very famous vesper, yes."

"You're serious?" Ashleen stared at her in disbelief and ran through a list of other historical figures known to have played similar roles. "How many empires have you destroyed with seduction?"

Diva shrugged. "If Muginn and Anshathane had meant for those people to be together, do you think Ikalusca would have been able to sway them so easily? You claim my god toys with people's emotions, but yours is the mastermind behind covenant bands. I fail to see the difference."

Ashleen hadn't thought of it that way before.

"So what do you think?"

She'd almost forgotten about Diva's initial question. "Oh. Um." It still made her uncomfortable, and she wracked her brain for a justified reason to say no.

"Look," Diva forged ahead. "I won't pretend to know what the gods have planned for us but I promise I'd never intentionally manipulate your feelings. I would only use this as a last resort, and never without your permission."

Ashleen drew a deep breath. What she needed was more time to think, but if there was an emergency and lives hung in the balance, it didn't seem right to risk them over modesty. "You swear?"

Diva lurched into Ashleen's space. "Yes!"

Ashleen tried to lean away but her back hit the wall. "Can you try to give me some time? I mean, if people will die if you don't, then I can't say no in good conscience. But..."

Diva leaned back out of her space. "I don't mean to ask so much––"

"You're not," she interrupted her. "You just want to help people. I understand that much. But I'm not like you. That area of my life... it's supposed to stay separate from everything else."

"It's not happening like you thought it would, is it?"

Diva's shift in tone caught Ashleen off guard. "What do you mean?"

"Do you know what it's like to be a vesper without a counterweight? All my life, I've only wanted one person I've never been able to find. But as a vesper? As an archknight? I don't have a choice. I have to take what I can get even if I'd rather wait for the person I'm destined to be with."

Ashleen's breath caught in her throat. She didn't imagine she would fare well at all if she were in a similar position. "I'm sorry, I had no idea."

"You couldn't have known. I'll give you all the time you need."

"I ship it," Bessie said, choosing that moment to alert them that Barrage hadn't powered her down.

Ashleen choked on a laugh, a gruff barking noise that shook her frame.

Diva turned, frowning at the ship's dashboard. "What? What does that mean?"

Ashleen couldn't stop laughing long enough to answer her.

"I don't get it, what's so funny?" Diva stared down at Ashleen, perplexed.

"It's an internet thing," she managed finally, and stood. "Come on, let's go. Good night, Bessie."

"Good night, Barrage," Bessie answered, powering down.

"It's sort of odd how she only ever uses Barrage's name when she responds to commands," Ashleen pointed out. "Do you ever feel like he's got some sort of kinky thing with the A.I.?"

"Sometimes I wonder," Diva admitted.

"Anyways, I should go. My team's deadeye has been watching me like a hawk recently."

"Alright, I'll see you next time."

"See you," Ashleen slipped through the floor and disappeared.

She sat in the empty sim room for a while after the wolf had sunk back into her skin. There were several smaller, less popular rooms that most people avoided. They were the perfect place to rise through the floor and shift from Vanquisher back to Ashleen without an audience.

She pondered what they'd learned from the sidhe. Ashleen understood that most of the high-level technology within Alexandria, including the sim rooms and anti-gravity, were powered by ichor.

She'd never questioned where it was coming from. Why should she? Most people didn't worry about where the water in their pipes, or the electricity in their cables came from unless it wasn't working properly.

That was before she'd seen what had been done to that boy. Most lycans were victims of misfortune, wrong places, wrong times, and regrettable encounters. Experimentation and torture couldn't be considered accidents.

The sidhe had mentioned Rome, but Ashleen had a hard time imagining him as the mastermind. He didn't seem to have a motive, and he'd never expressed any interest in ichor to her.

Barrage was more the schemer type; if he hadn't been working in direct opposition to this, he would have been the first person Ashleen suspected. After the conversation she'd had in Leo's dorm several weeks before, she'd assumed she was the only one who could see Rome.

Assuming Barrage was aware of him, she couldn't understand why he would keep it a secret. If Rome really was up to something, it didn't make sense to sit around and wait for him to get away. They should be confronting him right now.

Ashleen sighed and reached for the shirt she'd stashed in this sim room a few days ago. She'd learned recently it was nice to have a spare, as an unfortunate side effect of her tranquilizers appeared to be excessive sweating.

After work as Vanquisher, she was always drenched. She wasn't sure why, and she couldn't exactly ask anyone without alerting them to what she'd been doing. It was gross, but hardly life threatening, so she'd elected to ignore it.

The sidhe hadn't landed that many hits on her, but Ashleen's body still ached. She checked the burn on her leg. It was a livid red, but the skin wasn't broken anymore, and she didn't feel much pain. The outline of her scars had settled. The worst of the damage was from where the heel of Diva's palm had landed, but there were raised bumps for the tip of each finger too.

Ashleen doubted Diva meant to hurt her, but the scars were one more glaring warning of the dangers of ichor. A teaspoon had been enough to make her imagined nightmares real enough to leave permanent scars. She didn't want to imagine what might happen if the ichor in the walls decided it didn't want to be a city anymore.

She tugged her shirt over her head and her mind wandered to Morpheus. He was half-siren. He'd been born with a diluted variation of ichor in his veins. From that perspective, as a tranq, she probably had an iteration of the same thing. They couldn't be the only ones. If someone wanted to toy around in ichor, Alexandria was rich with it in more ways than one.

One of the medics could easily draw blood from any of the wardens or huntsmen under the guise of testing. She didn't think Rome was a medic. She'd never seen him anywhere near the infirmary.

Ashleen knew the other archknights would probably rip her to shreds for this, but she was tired of sitting on her thumbs waiting for other people to tell her things. She'd confront Rome herself and discover the truth.

She gathered up her dirty clothes and threw open the sim room hatch. Rome was waiting right at the foot of the ladder. She squeaked, and pressed a hand against the erratic pounding of her heart.

"You scared me. Actually, I was about to come find you."

Rome's face was unreadable. His discerning stormy eyes traced her movements attentively. "Are you ready to listen to me yet?"

"I think--wait, what did you say?" Her blood ran cold.

"Don't you think it's rude to ignore your patron for so long?" Rome laughed once in a way that sounded akin to a dog's bark. "I went to all this trouble to be here in person. To get one of my children to listen to me, and look at you all. Doping yourself up on drugs to block out my calls. It's absurd."

Ashleen tried to come up with a plausible explanation for what was happening. "You're joking, right?"

Rome just stared at her. "Muginn was always better with humor."

"You're not joking." Ashleen was torn between trying to run from him and a bout of nervous laughter. "Prove it."

Rome, or Anshathane, laughed again. "That's not how it works."

Ashleen rolled her eyes before she could stop herself. "Of course it is. Gods create us, guide our actions, perform miracles..." She trailed off, grasping for other things she'd read about the gods doing.

"I'm afraid you've been horribly misled. Gods don't create humans. Humans create gods."

"Then how do you explain," she gestured broadly, nerves starting to get the better of her. "all of this? Ichor? Monsters? The world?"

"I don't." Anshathane leveled a cool stare at her.

The more she thought about it, the more Rome being a god made sense. "Then how am I supposed to know what the truth is?"

"There isn't one. Truth is a lie created by those who seek control."

"That doesn't make any sense!" She could feel panic beginning to coat her insides.

"Does it not?" Anshathane grinned wolfishly at her. "Truth is a lie because it implies that there is only one path. One right way to do things. One perfect pattern to base one's life off of. Therein lies the deception. There was never a single truth. Everyone has their own. You should be focused on yours."

He turned on his heel and padded off down the hall. Ashleen slid down the ladder to chase after him, but he was gone. She couldn't decide whether his disappearance relieved her or not. She'd always taken his knack for vanishing to be natural stealthiness, but now she could see what had been right in front of her the entire time.

She growled to herself. She wanted a straight answer. She was sick and tired of all these tangled webs and backwards explanations.

Ashleen's wolf bubbled up over her skin, and Diva rose through the floor. "Vanquisher, what's wrong?"

"What are we actually doing here? Is saving people our true purpose or is it just a side effect of the main directive?" She snarled.

"Main directive?"

"We're told to hunt down and kill anything with ichor in its blood. We're told to gather that ichor and bring it back here."

"For safekeeping. Ichor is dangerous to humans." Diva reasoned.

"And yet, everything in this city runs on it. We run on it. Are we actually doing this solely to benefit humanity or are we just helping someone else corner the market?"

"It took the two of you long enough to reach that conclusion. I thought I would shrivel up and die while you both played at altruism," Barrage drawled as he rose up through the floor and blinked a headful of eyes at them. Façade and Proverb followed close behind him.

"How long have you known?" Ashleen demanded of them.

"About the Archwarden? Four years. Anshathane? Roughly forty-five minutes," Barrage answered.

Ashleen's heart tripped over itself. "What do you mean, the Archwarden? What are you——" She was interrupted by Anshathane's reappearance.

A few of Barrage's eyes reorganized themselves to observe him. "Do you want to tell her or shall I?"

Anshathane gestured an invitation. "By all means."

Barrage returned his attention to Ashleen. "Why do you think that tranqs rage?"

She glanced back and forth between them. "Amaris told me that Anshathane had driven them to destroy the city. My father died in that attack."

"Connor Gallagher led the attack. Did she tell you why it happened?"

"I—— I can't remember." Ashleen dropped her gaze to her hands, uncertainty squeezing her in its grip.

"She slaughtered every last one of my clerics," Anshathane snarled.

Ashleen braced herself for retaliation. "Couldn't Muginn just... bring them back?"

"He did." At the mention of his mate, Anshathane seemed to relax. "He gave me your father. And you. That it took nearly forty years to get you both to listen to me is not his fault."

Ashleen couldn't breathe. Blood rushed in her ears; none of this made any sense. She'd gone from a nameless introvert in a small town to living in floating cities, killing vampires, and having conversations with gods.

A hand on her shoulder shook her back to her senses. "I'll explain more later," Barrage told her. "Somewhere where the walls aren't listening to us. If you have any affairs to address, you have the next twenty-four hours to do so."

Mother of Serpents

"Archwarden." Neele pressed one hand against the corner of the massive mahogany desk, demanding the elder woman's attention. "We have a problem."

The Archwarden tilted a vial of ichor back and forth. "I admit, I didn't expect him to wait so long. I wonder if he recognizes the true value of the Vanquisher, or if he's just playing keep away because he knows I was interested?"

"How much of the plan do you think he's managed to piece together?"

"Barrage is cunning, but inexperienced. I suspect he stalled for time to allow his partner to build up their little secret army. If he knew the extent of my reach, he wouldn't bother running."

The Archwarden crushed the vial in her hand, unfazed by the glass as it sliced open her palm, and watched as the ichor crept into her bloodstream. "The longer he believes he's caught me in a checkmate, the more time I have to tighten the noose."

"Should we just let him go, then?" Neele asked, careful to keep her expression nonchalant.

The Archwarden's gaze slid over her. "No, if we let him go so easily, he will suspect something. Mobilize the counter measures."

Neele hesitated. "The vesper has lost equilibrium with his ichor. It might be wiser to keep him off the field."

"There's nothing we can do to stop his evolution now. If it will absolve you of your bleeding heart, offer Ikalusca a tithe and hope he is in a giving mood."

Neele pressed her lips into a thin line. She'd argued against the creation archknights since she'd learned of them for exactly this reason. If a being as powerful as an archknight went nuclear, a lot of people could get hurt. She'd just have to hope that he could maintain his feeble grip on stability long enough to satisfy the Archwarden.

"What about the deadeye? That team doesn't have one."

"You'll go with them. I'm appointing you their leader."

"Me? But I'm not..." She trailed off as the Archwarden stared at her analytically.

Neele's eyes dropped to the hand she still had pressed to the Archwarden's desk.

"Oh dear, you didn't think I'd forgotten about your little gift, did you?"

"It's not a gift," Neele corrected tersely.

The Archwarden stretched across her desk to press a knuckle under Neele's chin. "People like you are extremely rare these days. You should be proud."

Neele swallowed her nausea. "Yes, ma'am."

Ashleen had been a mess of frayed nerves all day, and hadn't been able to focus on anything. She barely managed to choke down half her dinner as she watched the sky go salmon through the glass ceiling.

She didn't have any talismans or charms for luck, beyond the ring adorning her pinkie. She fiddled with it now, rolling its bands over and over each other. Part of her wanted to tell Izzy. Or Demetrius. Even Dahei or Morpheus, if they would listen. But she couldn't risk painting a target on their backs.

She wished she could run. Bury all her problems somewhere that no one could ever dig them up again. She wanted to go back to the person she'd been a year ago, when monsters weren't real; when her biggest concern was what she would do when Prue went off to college.

The sky dipped from pink into lavender. It was time. Ashleen took her plate to the bus tub and bit down on her resolve. She made her way to her empty sim room and shut the door behind her. Her ichor wolf bubbled to the surface and she dropped through the floor. For a moment, she hoped she would keep falling.

Unfortunately, when she opened her eyes, she was aboard Bessie. The others had already gathered, and a solemn atmosphere choked the space. Ashleen didn't have the heart to disrupt it, even though questions kept running laps in her mind.

"Rise and shine, Bessie." Barrage wasn't cheerful when he greeted his ship this time, and goosebumps crawled along Ashleen's skin.

"Where to?"

"The rendezvous."

"Is it time already?" Bessie asked morosely. Great. The dismal aura had infected the ship too.

"It is."

Ashleen brushed against Diva's mind. "Where are we going?"

"I don't know."

"I couldn't trust either of you," Barrage stated bluntly, as if he'd heard their exchange. Bessie dropped out of the docking bay and swung them into the perfect flip, accelerating as they headed South.

Ashleen bristled. "You've been insisting we put blind faith in you the whole time, yet you couldn't afford us the same courtesy?"

"There was no way to know which side you were playing for," Façade explained.

"Which side?" Diva interjected. "We passed the trials didn't we? We're all linked to each other."

"We don't have time for this," Barrage hissed.

"I vouched for you," Proverb admitted.

"Thank you Verb," Ashleen replied pointedly.

"It's true that you're both very emotional," Façade added. "I highly doubt you would be able to mask your own guilt."

Ashleen couldn't decide whether or not she ought to be offended by that observation.

"Feelings can be faked. They could still be traitors," Barrage quipped.

Diva beat Ashleen to the retort. "Excuse you?"

"I hate to interrupt, but another mantacraft has locked on to us," Bessie alerted them.

Barrage spat out an aggravated curse, "Bessie. Evasive action as you see fit. Façade. She could use a copilot." He stood from his seat and materialized a sniper rifle. "Proverb. Can you give us an escort?"

Proverb inclined their head and began to weave intricate gesture work with one pair of arms. Façade deactivated the magnetic charge holding him in place and made his way toward the head of the ship. His impeccable balance allowed him to remain unfazed as Bessie pitched and heaved.

Barrage tipped backward towards the floor. Ashleen flinched, but instead of impacting a solid surface, he sank through it as if it were water.

Bessie rolled right, and one of Proverb's gargoyles appeared through the windshield as it passed them, exploding in a hail of granite that rattled against the ship's hull.

"What was that?" Façade asked. "Mantacraft don't have firepower, do they?"

"No," Barrage answered, his irritation making the word pierce Ashleen's mind like a shard of glass. He rose back up through the floor, "None of my ammunition is touching them. I was afraid of this. Our pursuers are no average huntsmen."

"We have a plan, right?" All traces of indignance had left Diva's tone, and Ashleen envied her ability to trust Barrage so easily.

He didn't answer Diva's question, which told Ashleen things she wished it didn't.

The minutes dragged on. After nearly an hour of Bessie's dipping and weaving, Ashleen was starting to feel sick. She didn't know where they were or where they were going, and Barrage's silence only continued to eat at her patience.

Proverb had long since given up on maintaining their escort. They claimed the opposing beckoner was so precise in their counter gestures that their attempts to wrest control from Proverb resulted in all their gargoyles shattering like the first.

A strange sound rippled the air around them.

"This should be impossible," Diva muttered, her delicate tendrils twisted about each other anxiously. "This level of power would only be available to a vesper the same caliber as me. And I can't use it right now, in the state I'm in."

"Assume there is another vesper at our level," Barrage said. "What are they trying to do?"

"If I had to guess? Trying to find a resonance that will tear apart the ship."

All at once it hit home that Bessie had stopped talking. She'd re-purposed her energy to keep them airborne, shifting the resonant frequency of her ichor up and down the scale so the vesper couldn't hit it.

Sure, the ship could talk. It had even joked on occasion. But Ashleen didn't understand how she was able to manipulate ichor intelligently, as if she were one of the archknights herself. Perhaps Barrage had discovered a way to program her for the behavior.

"We're nearly there," Barrage pressed a hand to Bessie's dash, like someone resting their hand on the shoulder of a friend in need of comfort. "Just a little farther."

The unknown vesper's pitch skittered within a few notes of Bessie's range, and the craft rattled around them. Ashleen's stomach dropped to her feet. Several warning lights burst to life.

Barrage flinched. "Bessie."

"I can't take much more of this," Bessie replied. "Shifting resonance is affecting the integrity of my hull."

Ashleen wasn't sure if Bessie actually sounded tired or if that was simply her imagination projecting itself on the mantacraft.

"I know," replied Barrage, setting his other hand against the dash.

Another wave of sound washed over them. "Hull integrity at ten percent."

Barrage closed the last eye he'd been keeping open. "Brace yourselves."

"Good night, Barrage." The mantacraft initiated its shutdown command of its own accord.

For a long pause, Barrage didn't answer.

"Five percent. Three percent. Two percent."

"Good night, Bessie."

She vibrated apart around the archknights, scattering them through the sky as the electromagnetism that held them in place flickered out. The air filled with an echoing scream. Ashleen wasn't sure whether it came from her or the enemy vesper.

Debris and archknights rained down, sooty metal and dark ichor marring the white sand. Ashleen impacted the beach like a meteorite and a plume of dust fountained up about her.

The ichor wolf bore the brunt of it. She'd been left breathless, but out of fear rather than the landing. As far as she could tell, she was otherwise unharmed.

A different sort of pain settled in her chest, followed by a lump in her throat. Grief crashed over her mind and Ashleen was left drowning in feelings that weren't hers. Even as she struggled against the current, the flow weakened, and her senses cleared.

She fought to reclaim her breath, and pressed out with her mind, feeling for the doors of the rest of her teammates. She traced the grief to Barrage. As she watched, it seeped back under his door and its influence over her faded as he pushed it down to deal with the situation at hand.

Unwilling to disturb him during his moment of weakness, she turned her attention to the others. She could sense all of them, and they all pressed back against her as they ran their own checks. All of them except Diva.

She nudged Diva's mind again. No response.

"Vanquisher, Diva is your responsibility. Track her down and sit tight. Proverb, Façade, scout the perimeter. Do not engage. I'll cover you all from here." Barrage had gathered himself enough to return to barking orders.

If Ashleen had disagreed with them, she might've been annoyed by how quickly he recovered from whatever had just happened. She clambered out of the crater her impact had created and kept low. At least as low as a hulking wolf beast could keep.

"This situation isn't ideal. Whatever is in that mantacraft has been dosed with higher quantities of ichor than any of us. Prepare to be outmatched, and stick to guerrilla tactics. Backup is inbound with our ticket out of here, but until then we're on our own." Barrage addressed Ashleen directly, "Vanquisher, I don't want to see any pointless heroics from you or Diva. If something comes at you, kill it. I don't care who it is."

"What's that supposed to mean?" Ashleen picked her way through the rubble, her eyes rapidly darting across the landscape for any sign of Diva.

"It doesn't matter what it means. Just follow orders."

Ashleen heaved a scrap of curled, smoking metal out of her way. The ichor wolf protected her easily from heat and sharp edges, but it wasn't helping her pinpoint Diva's location. It was as if the vesper was everywhere, spread across the beach like soft cheese on a cracker.

Ashleen's stomach knotted as she realized that was a definite possibility. Diva's ichor wasn't geared to soak damage like hers was. But she could still sense Diva's mind, fluttering weakly against her psyche like an injured bird.

She growled in frustration, loping across the beach toward another piece of debris. Her breath caught in her throat. There was a body next to this one. It had to be Diva. No one else had been in the craft with them. A spray of inky black saturated the ivory sand around her.

"Diva!" Ashleen crossed the space between them in two steps and came to a dead stop, her feet frozen to the ground. Diva had skin like a porcelain doll, and a mess of red curls sticky with the remnants of her ichor form. Or his.

There was only one person Ashleen had ever encountered with hair that color. It made a mockery of every protagonist from every teen romance novel Ashleen had ever read.

With considerable effort, Ashleen unstuck her feet from the ground and finished her approach, crouching at Diva's side. The vesper wasn't making any noise; in fact he appeared quite unconscious.

Yet he pulled at Ashleen with all the power of the siren he was, just like he always had, in the same way she so hated.

In spite of how uncomfortable his aura made her, she couldn't just leave him there, especially not if he really was injured. She wrapped a hand tentatively around his wrist, fighting the swell of revulsion that rose within her as his aura wormed into hers and began to drain her energy. Diva had told her not to think of it as feeding, but it didn't help that it felt like this.

The ichor pooled across the beach steadily began to trickle back over Diva's form, reshaping into the mane of tentacles and willowy limbs she'd become accustomed to. Ashleen nipped her lip and quickly swept her gaze over Diva's ichor form. She was visibly feminine. Ashleen had definitely not filled in any blanks with wishful thinking.

Diva whimpered deliriously and shifted. He, she? Ashleen would have to ask later, when it was less awkward.

"Vanquisher," Diva stretched, cat-like, their tone equal parts sweet innocence and flirtatious.

"Morpheus." The word had come out an octave higher than she'd meant it to, and Ashleen coughed to clear her throat.

Diva collapsed in on themselves. "So you figured it out."

Ashleen tore a page from Barrage's book and shoved her confusion aside. "You're not getting out of this talk, but we have bigger problems right now. Get up."

Diva nodded and allowed themselves to be pulled upright. Their mass of tentacles cascaded forwards over their shoulders as they struggled to find their footing. Damn they were unfairly attractive. Ashleen rolled her eyes skyward and spat out a number of choice swear words under her breath.

A shadow blotted out the stars as it cleared the cliffs, announcing the arrival of their pursuers. She yanked Diva against her chest, tugging them under the shelter provided by some of Bessie's debris.

Diva hissed against Ashleen's shoulder. "Hey! Be gentle."

"I'm sorry, I didn't ask if you were okay."

"I'll be fine, if you don't break me first," Diva said, shoving at Ashleen.

Ashleen opted to ignore them in favor of watching the mantacraft circle in for a landing. As it was finishing its descent, four shapes melted through the hull and dropped to the ground. They pushed out a short way and set up a perimeter.

The mantacraft opened and a ramp descended. There at the top of it, stood Neele. Ashleen's heart froze in her chest and she sank further down into her hiding place.

Diva's psyche echoed her alarm. "Wait a minute, that can't be right. She wouldn't--"

Ashleen's ichor boiled against her skin and the wolf surged against the tranquilized coma she'd been keeping it in. How dare she. Ashleen thought of all the times Neele had hovered over her with a concerned expression. All the times Neele had patched people up in a charade of tenderness. She couldn't decide whether to throw up or rip Neele's throat out with her teeth.

"Pull yourselves together," Barrage chastised them. "We're not out of this yet."

Ashleen closed her eyes. He was right. Why did he always have to be right? She tore her gaze off Neele and inspected the others. There was a beckoner with a third set of arms, a scofflaw in ebony armor reminiscent of a medieval era knight and the tranq was a wolf, like her, but far scrawnier.

It was the vesper that held her attention. It was horrifying; every inch of it pulsated with tentacles. Occasionally, one would slip, revealing far too many mouths full of needle-like teeth.

"What the fuck is that?" she hissed psychically to the others. She didn't have to explain which one she meant. They could all see it.

"The highest threat," Barrage answered.

"Is that a chrysalis?" Façade interjected, Ashleen's abject horror echoed in his tone.

"No, but it's close. If you have a patron god, pray to them now."

Neele gestured and the vesper's full body surged upward from the ground as its mouths unleashed a bubble of sound that rippled the sand like water.

Ashleen instinctively folded the wolf's ears back into its head, but a second too late. The warbling combination of wail and bellow rattled her bones. It bounced off the inside of her skull, phasing through a spectrum of screams. She heard her mother, then Morpheus, then Prue before the sound settled on the simple cry of an infant.

The ichor wolf clawed at her from the inside desperately. "Protect," it insisted. "Protectprotectprotect."

Ashleen sank to her knees in the sand, metal crumpled in one of her hands. Bones creaked in the other. She was dimly aware of Diva struggling against her.

"Stop it! You're hurting me!"

The words didn't make sense in Ashleen's head. An image of someone who could only be Ikalusca filled her mind's eye. His head was split open, viscous ichor staining the water black and dyeing the ground. The rage of a grieving parent coated her throat in a lupine snarl, and rough sobs of a raven echoed with the crash of the waves.

"Something's wrong with Vanquisher! I can't get through to her!" Morpheus had stopped struggling, gritting his teeth in pain as broken bones grated against each other in Vanquisher's grip.

"Barrage is not responding either," Proverb supplied.

"I've got him," Façade assured them. "You try a different angle on Vanquisher."

"What angle? How do you have Barrage?"

"I've met his counterweight. I can project her into his head."

"Vanquisher doesn't have a counterweight," Morpheus protested, involuntarily yelping aloud as Ashleen's grip tightened.

"Figure it out."

Morpheus struggled to think against the pain in his arm. The night before, Barrage had confirmed his suspicion that Vanquisher was Ashleen. He doubted he'd be able to get through to her as himself, but there was one person he'd seen Ashleen trust without reservation. As it happened, he was just as intimately familiar with said person as Ashleen herself was.

Morpheus sucked in a breath, both in an attempt to control the pain in his wrist and to resign himself to the onslaught of Ashleen's fury when she realized what he'd done. When he next pressed against Ashleen's psyche, he did so disguised as an illusion of Prue. The door swung inward.

The image before Ashleen fragmented, and she was in a blank space. Before her, Prue was sitting cross-legged. Her heart ached. Prue was still in Alexandria. Ashleen had neither the option nor the time to save her.

"Ash."

She could feel Prue's fingers in her hair, smell the pear shampoo she always used. She could taste the lip balm Prue liked to wear.

Tears welled up in Prue's eyes. "You're hurting me."

Ashleen didn't hesitate, cradling Prue against her chest and pressing her face against Prue's starlight hair. Reality restructured itself around her. She was back on the beach. Instead of Prue, she found herself curled around Diva, the wolf's muzzle buried in their mane.

For a moment, Ashleen was almost okay with it. Until she remembered who Diva really was. She pushed them away as politely as she could manage. Diva had their arm clutched to their chest, the fingers of their free hand curled gingerly around their wrist.

Guilt stabbed at Ashleen. She'd had a hold of Diva when the cry had hit her, hadn't she? She'd probably broken their wrist.

Ashleen didn't have time to fret or mutter an apology as the debris that had been sheltering them was ripped away, hurled somewhere over the cliff back the way they'd come. Looming over them, slavering jaws parted in a snarl, was the tranq.

The tranq's taloned hand coiled about Ashleen's throat and tossed her aside with disinterest, its focus fixed on Diva. Ashleen rolled to her feet and sprang to their defense.

Regardless of how she might feel about Morpheus, regardless of what they had just done, she wasn't about to stand there and watch them die. They still needed to talk. And she still needed to punch them for impersonating Prue.

Ashleen landed on the tranq's back, her ichor wolf sinking its teeth into the ruff of fur on her opponent's neck. The tranq reared backward and smashed her into the sand, crushing the breath from her lungs. It righted itself, one forelimb pressing down against her throat as it cackled a horrible, hacking laugh.

"Not so weak now, am I, you fatherless mongrel? I will savor this." The tranq's wolf face peeled backward.

Staring down at her from within the nearly hairless skeletal wolf, was Tatyana. Ashleen kicked out with her back feet. Tatyana's ichor parted under her claws, but it sealed up almost immediately.

Tatyana was a true tranq now. Ashleen wouldn't be able to beat her with sheer strength, and she'd never been trained in martial arts. Panic stabbed at her. She'd barely stood a chance against Tatyana with no enhancement whatsoever. What was she supposed to do now?

A gunshot split the quiet and a bullet tore through the skin on Tatyana's eyebrow and nose. Barrage swore. "Damn arm."

Tatyana recoiled, howling as the wolf's mouth slammed shut over her face and she searched the beach for her new assailant.

"Nice shot."

"That was a terrible shot," Barrage hissed. "I was aiming for her eye."

Ashleen skirted around the momentarily distracted Tatyana to find Diva. They had managed to put some distance between themselves and the enemy tranq, now huddled in the shadow of a new chunk of debris.

"In light of recent events, I'm not sure I have the energy to be of much help," They supplied as Ashleen turned to stand guard.

In the distance, the clang of swords could be heard as Façade clashed with the enemy scofflaw. Barrage fired off another shot, but Ashleen had no idea who his target was.

It didn't matter, because Tatyana was on the attack again. Ashleen raised her wolf's hackles and snarled a warning. Tatyana went for a grapple. Ashleen ducked and threw a well-placed swipe that made her stumble.

That wasn't right. That strike shouldn't have landed. Even if Tatyana had allowed it to, she would have countered it in some way, pinned Ashleen's arm, something.

Tatyana had gained strength. She'd gained speed and aggression. But she'd lost the clear mind that had been her advantage for so many years. The fighting style Tatyana was used to required focus and a quick wit, two things that were now dulled by the ichor clamoring in her veins.

Ashleen didn't know why she hadn't seen it before. Tatyana was ungainly, perpetually off balance. She kept shaking her head as if to clear it. It was almost sad to see her like this. Almost.

Tatyana made a grab for Ashleen and left herself wide open.

"Welcome to my world," Ashleen growled, ducking the miscalculated grapple. "It's not all it's cracked up to be." She drove the top of her head into Tatyana's solar plexus.

Tatyana's upper body folded around her as the air left her lungs and she fell back, hacking up slimy ichor.

Before she could recover, Ashleen followed the momentum of her strike and stepped into Tatyana's space. She threw an arm around the sickly wolf's neck and leaned back, using Tatyana's own weight to crush her windpipe. The move was a loose recreation of the hold Ashleen had used to beat her before, and part of her hoped the similarity wasn't lost on Tatyana.

She struggled, clawing at Ashleen's arm. Her fingers dug in and she nearly succeeded in prying herself free of Ashleen's grip.

Ashleen yanked on the first arm she could reach with her free hand, hard. The pop it made as it dislocated was extremely satisfying. Poetic justice. She squeezed harder against Tatyana's throat, but the smaller woman's struggles were already waning.

Just before she passed out, the wolf peeled away from Tatyana's face, and she whispered something with what little breath she could muster. "I'm sorry... she––she tricked me into drinking it."

Tatyana went limp in Ashleen's grasp and Ashleen held on for a few more moments before she lowered her carefully to the ground.

Diva slunk around Ashleen, their chest rumbling with whale song that reminded her of the day she'd lost control during sim training.

"Couldn't you have done that earlier?"

"It wouldn't have worked until now. Besides, I get the feeling I should be reserving what energy I do have for that." They raised their head to the writhing mass of tentacles that seemed to be waiting for orders.

"The scofflaw is Janice," Façade reported.

"The tranq was Tatyana," Ashleen added.

"Safe to assume these are the knight captains, then," Barrage surmised.

"Which means that's—" Diva started, staring at the pile of tentacles.

"Pavane," Ashleen finished. "You know, I don't think it's that much of a change."

Diva choked on a laugh.

Ashleen struggled to remember who the beckoner knight captain was. She'd met her once, she could almost remember her name.

"Winona," Proverb supplied, with a sadness so heavy Ashleen was worried she might be about to drown in it.

That left the deadeye. Ashleen's heart tripped and went sprawling in her chest. Izzy. Izzy was the deadeye knight captain. She spun, searching the shadows for a sixth figure. She'd only seen four, and Neele. Where was he? Had Barrage already killed him?

"Flattering, but I'm right here," Barrage's voice hissed in her mind.

Ashleen had no idea where he meant by 'here', but it didn't matter. He was fine. "I'm looking for—"

"Have you actually looked at any of the debris, or were you and Diva too busy dancing around each other again?"

Slowly, Ashleen turned to face the debris Diva had been sheltering under a moment earlier. It was a fragment of Bessie's wing. Painted on it was the head of an ember orange wolf, wreathed in flame. Ashleen stilled. She'd never paid attention to the outside of Bessie; all this time she'd just phased directly in and out of the ship.

"Izzy?" Ashleen's mind bent trying to attach ruthless, calculating Barrage to grinning, gentle Izzy.

"Everyone has facets they like to keep buried, Ashleen."

"If you're Izzy and Diva is Morpheus--"

"Yes, yes, we're all here. Focus on the task at hand!" Barrage's biting impatience gave Ashleen no time to process.

Soft, malicious whispers skittered at her ears. At first, Ashleen assumed it was her ichor, attempting to twist her in a moment of weakness. A second later, she realized Neele had gestured, and the noise she was hearing came from outside herself. Pavane's cries burrowed their way through her ichor like unwanted bugs. Diva squirmed uncomfortably.

The whispers steadily rose in volume, but Ashleen couldn't tell what was being said. It sounded like English, or close to English, but each time a certain syllable seemed familiar, its meaning evaded her. She found herself straining to hear, to understand. If she didn't know what was being said, it would drive her mad.

"Diva!" Barrage barked. "Delirium cries!"

Diva acknowledged the warning mentally and began to draw themselves up to their full height as they pulled in a breath to sing. Movement drew Ashleen's eye. Neele had vanished from her place on the mantacraft.

Ashleen turned to warn Diva and came face to face with the very person she'd been afraid of. A deep hood hid most of Neele's face. Her ichor took a more vaporous form, seeming smoky rather than liquid like Ashleen was accustomed to. It swirled around her, granting her the wraith-like visage of something more dead than alive.

"How could you--" Ashleen started.

She was interrupted when Neele's hand shot forward like a snake. She pressed the tips of two fingers to Ashleen's throat, as if taking her pulse. Agony swept through her as her blood ignited, acidic in her veins.

Ashleen screamed. The sound burned as it left her, her cry vibrating as if it were boiling. The ichor on her skin began to bubble and fizz, losing its lupine shape. She crumpled, sucking in breaths of cool air as Neele's touch left her. She hit the ground and drew her knees up to her chest. Before she could gather enough space in her mind to warn her team, Neele rounded on Diva.

Diva's hands came up defensively, and they chirped a tune that Ashleen recognized as one of their barrier hymns. The shield was useless against Neele, who reached through to deliver the same treatment unhindered.

Ashleen was helpless to do anything but watch as Diva unleashed the same warped scream she'd made seconds earlier. Neele raised her chin, her head swiveling like a hawk seeking prey and hissed, sidestepping in the nick of time to avoid being trampled by a shrieking dullahan.

Her dodge led her directly into the path of Barrage's bullet. Neele didn't make a sound, though Ashleen watched it pass through her. The dullahan turned to make another charge and Neele took off in the opposite direction, her form dispersing into black smoke on the third step.

Ashleen twisted to face Diva. For the second time that night, their ichor was sprayed across the sand. A quick glance down revealed hers was in the same state, though it had already begun to creep back towards her.

"What was--"

"I don't know," said Barrage, clearly unsettled.

Ashleen tried to get up, but her limbs trembled with aftershocks. Every time she put weight on them, they buckled beneath her. She spat out a mouthful of sand and rolled onto her back, hoping they weren't in immediate danger.

Diva drew in a shaky breath that triggered a violent coughing fit. Ashleen flinched. The whispers were much louder without her ichor. She could feel them pressing in around her mind with a terrifying urgency. The itch of curiosity stung like a spider bite, or poison oak. It was essential she found meaning in them, or it would never stop.

"Diva!" Barrage barked.

"Lay off!" Ashleen snapped. "Neither of us can even stand."

As if to prove her wrong, Diva lifted their head and their impressive mass of tentacles floated into the air about them.

As Diva struggled to stand, Ashleen could see them shaking. They had to be in at least as much pain as she was, but they'd gotten to their feet much faster. Ashleen tried to follow their example. She worked herself into a sitting position, but she couldn't straighten her legs without the burning spasms starting up again.

Diva filled the air with an unearthly melody. Somehow, they sang with the voices of an entire choir. Ashleen had heard Diva use two or three voices at once, but this was on a different scale entirely.

The song blocked out Pavane's whispers. The gnawing anxiety that had been crawling inside her was replaced as warm nostalgia crested in its stead. Sunlight on her face. The comfort of her mother's arms. The taste of limeade in the summer. Watermelon for dinner. Rolling in the mud with her dogs.

Gradually, Ashleen's strength returned. She uncurled her legs and struggled to her feet. The sudden absence of pain left her almost boneless.

"I can't keep this up for long," Diva warned, the psychic representation of her voice shaky with a combination of pain and exhaustion.

"Our backup should be here any minute," Barrage assured them. "Verb. You remember what we discussed?"

"I do."

"For what it's worth, I'm sorry for asking this of you."

"I would have offered whether you asked or not."

Regardless of whether or not it was Izzy under all that ichor, hearing Barrage apologize made Ashleen feel sick to her stomach.

"Wait, what did you ask?" Panic edged Façade's voice. "Barrage, what did you ask!?"

Barrage ignored him. "Fall back. We make our stand at the water's edge."

Façade's anxiety echoed across the psychic link, but he obeyed Barrage's orders without question. Ashleen's feet moved on their own accord, placing herself between Diva and the enemy as both of them backed towards the sea.

Thunder rolled in the distance and movement caught the corner of Ashleen's eye. Something was breaking the surface of the water. If Ashleen had to guess, she'd say it was a craft of some kind. She couldn't turn her head to look.

Tatyana was stirring. Janice approached and crouched to whisper something to her. Neele had reappeared near the abstract shape that was Pavane, and Winona was locked in an all-out war with Proverb.

Proverb's dullahan was still up, gleefully hacking at Winona's hellhounds. Massive, dog-sized ravens dove at the fray from above. Cait sith, similarly sized sidhe that took the form of cats, circled around the battle, tearing at its edges. Ashleen wasn't sure whose side they were on.

Façade was fidgety, unable to stand still as he bobbed to and fro debating whether he ought to stay and help her, or return to Proverb's side.

"You've got this right?" he asked, gesturing at Janice and the now upright Tatyana.

"I most certainly do not have this."

Façade swore, but drew twin swords and remained at her side as Janice and Tatyana closed in.

Ashleen could tell from the gunfire that Barrage was backing up Proverb, but clearly this served as no consolation to Façade, whose ichor was now fluctuating with a near tranq-like agitation.

He rushed Janice, and she parried his reckless attack as if she were swatting a fly. Ashleen hung back, waiting for Tatyana to come to her. Her nerves sang with Façade's contagious anxiety, but if she moved even a foot from this spot, she'd leave Diva vulnerable to attack.

"The water's too shallow for him to come any closer. We'll have to swim," Barrage explained. "Façade, you should go first. Then Vanquisher can follow with Diva. I'll cover your escape and catch up."

"What about Proverb?" Façade demanded.

"I am staying," Proverb replied.

"Birdshit. You are not."

Proverb's tone was apologetic. "This was always the plan. I am the only one who can manage the numbers to ensure your escape."

"We can win this! Then we don't need to escape."

"Don't do this Façade. Vanquisher brings enough obstinance to the party all by herself," Barrage interjected.

Ashleen made a disgruntled noise.

"Learn to recognize a checkmate when you see one," Barrage went on. "Diva's about to collapse. When that happens, and the delirium cries hit again, we lose. Proverb can buy us time with the wild hunt, but they can't be summoned until we're clear, as they will attack indiscriminately."

Proverb continued to weave a dance with their gestures, fully involved in whatever ritual they were currently engaged in. "I will not say goodbye. This is only for a little while."

"You can't promise me that!" Façade ducked Janice's swing. It missed by only a hair. Ashleen started to take a step forward. Façade wasn't paying enough attention; if this kept up for much longer, he was going to lose his head.

"Stay where you are," Barrage barked the order as he vaulted over and slid down a piece of debris.

He fired off a shot at Janice's back and she cried out in pain, but remained standing as he worked his way around to Ashleen's other side. Eyes danced around his form as he continued to fire off shots in all directions.

He jerked his chin at her. "Take Diva and go. We'll catch up."

Ashleen was in no shape to argue. Whatever Neele had done to her had taken its toll. If she stayed on this beach much longer, she'd never leave it. She nodded once and turned towards Diva, she might not approve of his methods as Barrage, but she trusted Izzy.

Diva was already hip-deep into the ocean. Ashleen waded out to meet her. "If I do the swimming, can you keep singing? Façade's going to drag this out."

Diva nodded, but Ashleen could sense the bone deep exhaustion threatening to drown them. She shoved aside her unease and pulled Diva back against her chest as they continued to wade into the ocean.

The dullahan broke away from the battle and tore through the sand, cackling gleefully as it engaged Tatyana and Janice, a pair of hellish hunting dogs by its side.

"We don't have time for this, Façade," Barrage hissed. "We have to go."

"I won't! I just got over Hideo, you can't ask me to do it a second time!"

"I'm sorry."

"It's your plan, why don't you stay behind?"

Barrage didn't answer.

"Façade. Go!" Proverb ordered.

"But––"

"Go. I'll see you again soon."

"Where? In the afterlife? You get over here right now and you come with me."

"Dahei," Barrage's tone was soft. He pulled at Façade's arm. "Come on."

Façade shrugged him off and raised his swords again. "I'd die here on this godsforsaken beach a hundred times over before I left him once."

"Please," they asked in unison.

Façade glanced over his shoulder at Barrage, ichor drawing back from his face so he could make clear eye contact. "Izzy, you know I can't do this. If you could have been with Alexis when she needed you, can you honestly tell me you would have left her behind?"

Barrage didn't have an answer. He'd known separating the two of them would be difficult; he'd hoped it wouldn't come to this.

A second pair of hellhounds rose out of the sand. They bared their teeth, snapping at Façade and corralling him up against the waves. "Leave. Before I make you leave." Proverb's words were a frigid blade between Façade's ribs. "I cannot protect you from the hunt when they arrive, and I refuse to send you to the same oblivion I sent my ancestors."

Façade set his jaw and raised his swords. "So be it."

Barrage slammed the butt of his rifle into the side of Façade's exposed head. "I'm sorry. It's for your own good."

19

Resurrection

The craft Ashleen had seen earlier turned out to be a submarine. She was vaguely aware of what was happening back on the beach, but she'd been shrugging off Façade's distress in favor of keeping herself afloat and making sure Diva's head stayed above water.

Theoretically the ichor should have been able to protect them from the sea; perhaps a more experienced archknight could even manipulate it to breathe underwater for a short time. Unfortunately, Ashleen was neither experienced enough, nor had the energy, to try and wrap her head around how she might accomplish it.

She twisted, trying to see over her shoulder. She couldn't tell if they were close, or if they'd drifted afield of the craft. Diva was barely conscious at this point. She could no longer maintain a counter to the delirium cries, but fortunately it appeared they were far enough away now that it didn't matter.

The rhythmic splash of someone treading water caught Ashleen's attention but she couldn't turn her head to look. Someone she couldn't see in the falling darkness tried to take Diva from her. Ashleen resisted as best she could while still keeping herself and Diva afloat, weakly splashing salty water in hopes of getting it in their assailant's eyes.

"You can barely stay afloat anymore. Let me help."

She recognized the voice and her subconscious screamed that it was important she remember who it belonged to, but Ashleen's exhausted mind could barely recall her own name.

She couldn't deny the truth in his words. If she had to keep this up much longer, both she and Diva would drown. When the man reached for Diva again, Ashleen didn't stop him. She followed as he led the way toward the craft she'd glimpsed from the shore.

"There's a ladder a few feet to your right. You go up first so you can take your friend from me. I need to go back for the others."

Ashleen slid her hands along the hull of the craft until they found rungs and heaved herself out of the water. Her arms protested as she broke the surface and the burden of gravity crashed back into her. She dragged herself hand over hand to the top of the submarine and turned to retrieve Diva.

Apparently they were still conscious, at least just enough to reach for Ashleen as she leaned back down for them. Even as exhausted as they were, Diva was feather-light in her grasp, and they easily ascended the ladder with Ashleen's help.

She still couldn't identify their rescuer in the dim light of the moon, but she could tell he had broad shoulders and a beard.

"Get inside, you'll catch your death if you stand there soaking wet, especially in this wind. Tau will help you find towels and dry clothes if you need them. I'll be back shortly." He pushed off the craft and disappeared back into the glistening waves.

Diva sagged against Ashleen as if about to collapse under their own weight.

"Come on, let's get you inside." She led Diva towards the hatch and started down the ladder first so she could catch Diva if they fell, which they nearly did. No less than four times.

Ashleen guided Diva over to a nearby bench and the vesper slipped from consciousness as soon as they were off their feet. Their aura surged against Ashleen's, pulling at her energy vampirically. Ashleen quelled her squeamishness long enough to wedge Diva securely into the corner, then took several steps back.

The undeniable hunger she'd felt rolling off of Diva terrified her. All the same, she couldn't deny the gratitude she felt that they'd held it back for so long. Perhaps they'd done so out of guilt for using Prue's image to manipulate her.

Ashleen didn't have time to dwell on that right now. Though the ichor had kept her mostly dry, it hadn't kept all the water out and a change of clothes sounded extremely appealing.

"Tau?" She called down the body of the craft.

She was answered by a strange trilling meow, and a cat easily as tall as an average dog loped toward her. As it drew closer, Ashleen recognized the russet fur and tufted ears of a caracal.

She frowned. The creature seemed nothing more than a regular animal. That said, it did bear a striking resemblance to the cait sith she'd seen back on the beach, which meant if she disrespected it, she probably did so at her own peril.

"Are you Tau?"

The caracal flicked its short tail upward as if in affirmation and chirruped at her.

"I was told you could show me where to find towels?"

Tau trotted past her and nuzzled a cabinet at the back of the room. When Ashleen opened it, she found several stacks of towels, dry t-shirts, and sweatpants.

The caracal chirped at her again and padded off back the way it had come, granting her a measure of privacy to change if she so wished.

Ashleen toweled off her hair as she investigated her surroundings. The craft was small; it didn't appear to have anywhere to go beyond the body she currently stood in and the room Tau had just escaped to, which was likely the cockpit.

That meant she'd have to change here. She glanced at Diva as she drew the towel away from her head. Still unconscious. Ashleen only wasted a few moments weighing her continued discomfort against the extremely unlikely scenario in which Diva woke up. She absently bit her lip and turned her back on them to shed her damp clothing.

When she'd finished, she glanced over her shoulder. Diva was still unconscious. The last of their ichor had receded beneath their skin, leaving behind a pallid Morpheus. They looked even more fragile now, their drenched T-shirt clinging to their body and the red of their hair standing out starkly against their near-translucent skin.

With a start, Ashleen realized Morpheus' lips were blue. Their clothes were much damper than hers had been, perhaps a side effect of their exhaustion. If their ichor had lost its integrity at a faster rate there was no telling how far their core temperature had already dropped.

She shoved her fear of Morpheus' abilities aside and pressed the backs of her fingers against their face. Their skin was icy. Ashleen swore. She'd never seen it in person, but she'd read enough about hypothermia to recognize it here.

She couldn't leave them in their wet clothes. Even as she realized it, the thought made her pause. Ashleen pressed her lips into a thin line and swallowed her modesty. Morpheus was already unconscious. If she couldn't bring their temperature back up, there wasn't a guarantee they'd ever awaken.

Ashleen pulled Morpheus' shirt over their head. Frustration bit at her when the soaked fabric resisted removal. The drenched garment met the ground with a wet smack, and Ashleen quickly wrapped a fluffy towel about Morpheus' narrow shoulders.

The pants would have to stay. Izzy could deal with them when he was aboard. There were some lines Ashleen simply refused to cross. Instead she pulled Morpheus against her chest and let their head rest in the crook of her neck.

She murmured a short prayer to Anshathane, thanking him that she'd always run a bit on the warm side. Right now, the extra degree or two might be the only thing that pulled Morpheus from the brink of the abyss.

A series of thuds against the side of the craft announced the arrival of the rest of the party. The hatch opened and Izzy slid down the ladder, ichor receding completely as he impacted the ground.

"Finally," Ashleen addressed him. "You need to get Morpheus out of these pants. They're soaking wet."

Izzy glanced at her, unphased. "You know the quick solution would just be to get over yourself and kiss him." His tone expressed an aggravation Ashleen sensed wasn't her fault.

"I'm not kissing them. You kiss them."

The corner of Izzy's mouth twitched. "It wouldn't have the same effect if it was me. Morpheus and I don't have any chemistry." He took a step towards her and held out his arms. "Alright, give him here. And get me some dry pants."

Ashleen tried not to look too relieved when she passed Morpheus off to Izzy. She was turning back around to hand a pair of sweatpants to him when their rescuer picked his way carefully down the ladder. Dahei was unconscious, slung over his shoulder like a sack of potatoes.

"What happened?" Ashleen asked, keeping her back strategically toward Izzy and Morpheus.

"He wouldn't leave Demetrius. I did what I had to," Izzy answered.

Ashleen had only been half paying attention to the events on the beach after she'd left it, but she was aware that Demetrius had stayed behind, and why.

"He's gonna kill me when he wakes up," Izzy added. "You can turn around now."

The man who was apparently their backup gently laid Dahei down on the bench opposite Morpheus. "Tau, hit the autopilot," He called over his shoulder.

An affirmative chirp was heard from the direction of the cockpit, and the craft hummed to life around them.

"Thank you, Connor," Izzy addressed him. "I know we're a bit ahead of schedule, but there was some divine intervention."

A chill crept up Ashleen's spine and she turned to inspect the man more closely. His back was still to them as he toweled off his hair.

Her tongue felt too large for her mouth. "Your last name wouldn't happen to be Gallagher, would it?"

Connor straightened, and in the submarine's dim lighting, Ashleen's own sky-blue eyes greeted her. "How's your mother?"

Ashleen's voice broke and she ducked her head. "Fine, I guess?"

She remembered in stark detail every time her mother had looked at her with strange sadness in her eyes. Every time Alice would gently cup her face and say things like, "You look so much like your father."

Ashleen had always just smiled and dismissed the gesture, uncertain of what one was supposed to say in such situations. She still didn't know what she ought to have said, but it was clear that Alice hadn't just been speaking from sentimentality.

He'd aged considerably since the time he'd recorded the hologram in the Library, but there was no doubt that he was the same person she'd grown up seeing pictures of. While the images captured his ginger hair and freckles just fine, they did no justice to the sheer size of him. Ashleen had never met someone who made her feel this small before.

She wished she knew the right thing to say, or had anything to say at all. "I--" she started, then fell silent again.

Connor offered her a small smile. "You don't have to say anything yet."

Ashleen chewed her lip in silent gratitude. If she ever had time to come to terms with everything that had piled up over the last month or so, this would be at the top of the list. She told herself she was just keeping busy when she retreated to fuss over Morpheus, she wasn't ready to admit that his presence was comforting. Not so recently after his break up with Prue.

"What did you mean, divine intervention?" Connor was saying to Izzy as Ashleen took one of Morpheus' hands and let their aura burn off the anxiety muddling hers.

"Ashleen caught Anshathane's attention. We weren't going to be able to hide that for long, and I didn't want to risk the Archwarden using her as bait."

"You have my thanks."

Ashleen tried not to feel the glance her father cast at her and tightened her grip on Morpheus. His aura felt different now, meditative instead of vampiric. She wasn't sure if that was due to his mental state or hers.

"What did he say to you?"

"Ashleen?" Izzy prompted.

Ashleen forced herself not to squeeze Morpheus' hand any harder. "He...ah... said something about how all his children were drugging themselves to block out his calls."

Connor straightened. "Just when I thought the tranquilizers couldn't get any worse. You're on them, aren't you? She would have made you take them."

"All tranqs have to take them."

Connor crossed the space toward her in one step and thrust out his hand. Ashleen shrank back against Morpheus.

"Give me your backup supply."

"Are you joking? If I go off them, I'll kill everyone in this cabin."

Ashleen watched Connor make a conscious effort to shed some of the aggression from his posture. "If you don't go off them, they'll kill you."

"What do you mean?"

"How many are you taking these days?" Izzy interjected.

Danger bristled through Connor's stance, and Ashleen shrank even further from him. "How long have you been overdosing?"

"One pill wasn't keeping the ichor quiet anymore. I had help during the ordeals, I didn't know if I'd be able to control it on my own if I didn't overdose."

Ashleen recognized her own expression in the confused crease between her father's brows. "What do you mean, you had help?"

Izzy sighed. "Diva, Morpheus, broke ranks when she went under in the final stage. It's unclear whether she could have pulled herself out on her own or not."

"She's my daughter. She could have."

"You can't know that," Ashleen snapped, hackles rising. "You don't even know me."

Guilt prickled as she watched hurt flicker across her father's face.

"I didn't have a choice," he murmured, more to himself than any of them. He held a tired hand out toward her. "Give me the tranquilizers. Please."

Ashleen glanced at Izzy. He inclined his head. Reluctantly, she retrieved her wet jeans from the floor and fished the bottle out of her pocket. Connor seemed relieved when the pills rested in his hand.

"I really wish you hadn't overdosed. Coming off them is going to be that much more difficult for you now. How long until your last dose starts to wear off, do you know?"

Ashleen scrutinized a patch of floor. "Not really, I take two every four hours so it never starts to wear off."

Connor swore and pinched the bridge of his nose. "Have you ever missed a dose before?"

Ashleen nodded. It was part of what had driven her to overdose in the first place.

"Coming down's going to be ten times worse," Connor said, pocketing her tranquilizers. "We have bunkers built to contain our lycan allies. You'll have to stay in one until it's all out of your system."

As much as she didn't fancy the idea of being locked up like some sort of wild animal, Ashleen was relieved that others wouldn't be in danger because of her. "Where are we going?"

Connor smiled, a hint of pride accenting his features. "You didn't think Alexandria was the only lost city that still existed, did you?"

He gestured for her to follow him and started toward the cockpit. Ashleen hesitated a moment to check the temperature of Morpheus' skin. It had warmed up considerably and enough color had returned to their lips that she wasn't too worried to leave them alone for just a second.

She ducked around Connor into the tiny space. Tau, who had curled up in the pilot's seat, purred a greeting at her. Initially, she couldn't see anything through the viewport except darkness and dust caught in the craft's headlights.

Gradually, the outline of something began to emerge in the distance. Something big. As they drew closer, Ashleen could see lights. What appeared to be a domed city rose out of the sand. A coral reef had grown up around it and countless shipwrecks littered the outskirts. She even counted several planes among the wreckage.

"What did you think was at the bottom of the Bermuda Triangle?" Connor asked. "Welcome to Atlantis."

The beach had gone quiet around him. The rolling thunder had stopped and when he moved, raindrops broke against his skin, but he couldn't hear them hitting the ground. Time had ceased to flow. A rustle of wings interrupted the silence. The sand rippled like water. He could feel it lapping against his ankles.

"Ulterior motives do not become you, Demetrius."

The voice came from everywhere, and nowhere. Demetrius didn't need his eyes to recognize Muginn's presence. "I did what I had to. Izzy would understand."

"Did your friends know you were drawing upon their strength for a greater summoning?"

"No. However, was it not you who placed them in my path?" He expanded his consciousness, sensing the souls of the others he'd been left to 'take care of'. Muginn hadn't taken them. Yet.

The god cackled. "I see you've lost none of your arrogance. If you've brought me here to beg for the restoration of your ancestral spirits, I hope you've planned to supply adequate tribute."

"I've requested your presence with an offer."

The Raven's voice shifted from Demetrius' left to his right, their massive spiritual presence bearing down against his own. A reminder of his place. "Cheeky. What could a mortal offer a god? What proposition is worth eight thousand souls?"

"Eight thousand more souls. One by one, a soul for a soul." Demetrius resisted the urge to gasp for breath. Muginn liked bargains. They'd hear his offer, but only so long as Demetrius remained worthy of respect. Muginn had little patience for those who grovelled or displayed fear in the face of death.

A dark chuckle bounced around him. "Tsk, tsk, tsk, Demetrius. Are you offering to kill for me?" Muginn's tone took a dip into mockery. "Cause we all know how well deals like that turn out."

"The opposite, actually."

"Oh?" Muginn pressed their body against his with interest. They'd chosen a small form and Demetrius had to resist imagining Dahei.

"Eight thousand children, raised in adherence to your teachings. I will rebuild my people, your most devout disciples, from the ground up." He kept his features blank. Muginn was trying to get a rise out of him. Break his focus. Test his conviction.

Muginn's breath ghosted across his ear. "The devotion of the Ravenkin has never been in question. But, child, are you certain you are suited to lead?"

Demetrius' breath caught. He wasn't suited. Among his people he would have been lucky to be selected as one of the matriarch's apprentices. The men were never supposed to be this powerful.

"No. Not lead. My sisters will bear that mantle. I serve only as a vessel for your teachings. When my sisters' daughters carry the eight thousandth child beyond their rites to receive your blessing, you will restore the souls of my ancestors, and their connection to the people I raise onto your wings."

Muginn was silent for a time, weighing his response. "How do you intend to make good on these promises? As powerful as you may be, you are still only mortal. So fragile you are. I could choose any breath I liked to call you back to me."

"Excuse my boldness, but that would bore you, would it not?"

Another chuckle. "And if you fail? If your legacy collapses before it reaches fruition?"

"It will not," Demetrius bit down on his lip. "But if it is collateral you seek, I offer my name. If I am to fail, let my identity be lost to history. Let my soul be yours to do with what you please."

"Not good enough," Muginn hissed, their body abruptly vanishing from his with a rustle of feathers. "There is a storm coming. To turn its tide in my favor, I will require help. There is a young man, Lyric Isolder. Deliver him into my service, and I will agree to your bargain."

Demetrius hesitated. He had not planned on offering anyone but himself. Gods were fickle creatures, prone to toying with the lives of mortals. It didn't feel right that someone else might pay the price for a mistake that was his alone.

"What of it, Ravenkin? Too much for you to stomach?"

"No," Demetrius blurted. After all, he didn't know this man. Perhaps this Lyric deserved the interest of the gods. One stranger's life didn't seem like much, weighed against an entire culture. "I accept these conditions."

"Excellent. Demetrius, son of Kamau, grandson of Ninanzu, we have an accord. When you wake, you will shed your blood and bind yourself to your sacred oaths."

Demetrius' awareness of his surroundings slowly shifted. The sand had stilled, thunder rolled across the sky, and raindrops kissed his face. He'd been standing, and now he was lying in the damp sand.

He sat up, carefully extending his senses to the knight captains. They were still unconscious, and likely would be for a day or two after all the energy he'd drawn from them to manifest Muginn. Neele seemed to have escaped, not that it particularly mattered to him now.

Demetrius pushed aside the nagging guilt of lying to his team, particularly to Dahei. He'd told them he was calling the wild hunt. Instead, he'd been steadily draining the energy of everyone within range as he completed the summoning. They'd cut it close. A few more minutes, and his team would have been just as unconscious as the rest of the knight captains.

He felt through his pockets for an obsidian blade. It brushed against his fingertips and he drew it from the leather sheath he'd stored it in.

The concept of blood tithes was something he'd been desensitized to long ago, as his people had often been covered in scars from their tithes to the Raven. It was said that the larger the scar, the stronger the tithe, or vow taken alongside it.

Demetrius pressed the soles of his feet together and considered where best to break his skin for his promise to bring Lyric into the fold. He'd been raised with a knife in his hands, so Demetrius knew where he could safely tithe, where he couldn't, and how to do so gently, with the least pain.

He decided on the backs of his arms and made the tithe. The cuts were clean and he allowed them to bleed temporarily into the salty sea foam before he pulled off the white t-shirt he'd worn under his jacket and cut it into pieces to bind the wounds.

He paused to admire his work with the tips of his fingers, feeling along the coils of fabric. He'd need to find more to replace the makeshift bandages soon, but for now, this would do.

He shifted onto his knees, then rocked up to standing. The waves lapped quietly at the shore with far more peace than he felt. Demetrius would have given almost anything in that moment to be at Dahei's side.

His guilt over having not taken the time to tell him about their rings stabbed at him. It would take months, perhaps years, to rebuild the trust he'd shaken with the choices he'd made today. Unfortunately, he'd have to deal with that later. He had work to do, and it would take him a long time to reach his sisters.

20

Finding Faith

As they waited for the pressure to regulate between the ship's interior and the docking bay they'd settled in, Morpheus began to stir. Ashleen almost wished they wouldn't wake. She wasn't ready to deal with all the things they still had to talk about.

The sudden reappearance of her father had left her at a loss for words and the shocking truth of the tranquilizers had her on edge. None of this was helped by the inevitability of her last dose wearing off at an unpredictable time.

Ashleen's vision blurred and panic prickled up her spine. It was already happening. She wouldn't even have time to get into a bunker if what her father had said had any truth to it.

"Ashleen?" Morpheus' voice reached her as if from the other end of a long tunnel, "Are you okay?"

She blinked her eyes and her cheeks were met with an unexpected dampness. Oh. She hurriedly scrubbed at her face and swallowed the lump in her throat. Not rampaging yet, it seemed.

"I'm fine."

"There will be medics waiting outside," Connor announced. "Anyone injured should go with them." He retrieved Dahei, who was still out cold, and set about opening the hatch.

Ashleen tried not to think of Neele when she saw the two medics begin to fuss over Dahei and Morpheus. The task was easier said than done. Ashleen wasn't sure how much more truth she could take. She'd spent the larger part of her life demanding it, but now that she had it, she was beginning to wish she didn't.

The larger of the two medics took Dahei from Connor, and the other herded Morpheus away. Ashleen tried in vain to ignore the concerned glances they kept throwing back her direction. Now she was alone with Connor and Izzy, half of the apparent masterminds of her ignorance.

Tau chirped at her as if he could sense she was forgetting his presence, and she scratched him behind one ear without thinking. He seemed not to mind.

"We have much to discuss," Connor began. "But before that, there's someone who'd very much like to see you, Izzy."

Izzy shot him a quizzical glance.

"What about me?" Ashleen interjected, "The longer I'm unconfined, the bigger risk I am."

Connor glanced her up and down. "You have a few hours before you're any threat. It looked like your friend had something he wanted to say."

Ashleen glanced at the door she'd seen the medics disappear through.

"Follow that hall to its end and hang a left. The infirmary is impossible to miss."

Ashleen had mixed feelings about seeking out Morpheus, but she uttered a soft "thank you" to her father and jogged after the medics anyway.

Izzy stifled a laugh as he watched Ashleen go. "You said there was someone who wanted to meet me?"

"Yes, but I should report in. The Order does not like to be kept waiting. Tau will take you where you need to go," Connor said, before going off down the same hall Ashleen had disappeared into.

Tau chirruped at him and flicked his tail before trotting off down a second, wider hall.

They emerged into a vast domed space. Through the glass of the ceiling, Izzy could see the reef that had grown up around Atlantis, and the multitudes of brightly colored fish. How they survived at this depth was a mystery to him, as they were too far down for sunlight to penetrate. There must be an energy source feeding them somehow.

Izzy's immediate surroundings were crowded with a variety of people. He recognized very few humans among them. The majority of the city's inhabitants appeared to be aquatic species. Selkies, sirens, and the like, with a smattering of other races. All of them were coexisting peacefully, and the sight warmed his heart.

A few refugees were eating an unappetizing green paste out of beat-up dishware. He guessed it was seaweed-based. They probably struggled to feed and supply this many people, especially while attempting to keep their existence a secret from the surface world.

Movement flickered in the corner of Izzy's eye. Tau had loped forward a few paces and caught a small girl by the back of her shirt. The girl––she couldn't be more than three or four–– struggled against the caracal. Tau growled through his mouthful of her shirt.

"Tau!" the girl protested. "Lemme go! Mama knows I'm here!"

Tau reluctantly released her and chirped a warning.

"You're not my dad!"

Izzy watched the proceedings with mild interest. It seemed like she could understand Tau's noises as if they were speech. Fascinating.

Tau turned his lamp-like eyes on Izzy and purred something to the child. The girl seemed to notice Izzy for the first time and stared at him wide eyed.

She had a head full of blonde curls and brown eyes overflowing with curiosity. Izzy shifted his gaze to the nearby refugees, seeking out her mother. Tau was right; a child this young shouldn't be unattended. No one in the immediate vicinity bore any resemblance to her, or seemed to be paying her any attention whatsoever.

When he turned his attention back to the girl, she spun on her heel and took off toward a nearby hall. Tau followed after her calmly, and Izzy followed after Tau.

Every few steps, the girl would stop and turn to check that they were still following before she took off again as fast as her tiny legs could carry her. She finally paused by an open door and darted inside.

Izzy stopped in the doorway and watched as the little girl trundled the rest of the way up to a short Latina doing laundry in a basin on the counter. She had her back to him, but that did nothing to disguise the curves he knew so well, or the dark curls she wore in a short but unkempt halo about her head.

His eyes followed the motion of one of her arms and ichor surged just below the surface of his skin. Tau growled at him, fur going up all down his spine and the woman turned at the noise.

"Tau, stay," she ordered.

Izzy brought the gun he'd materialized up and trained it on the woman's heart. "What are you? Doppelganger? Shapeshifter? Sidhe?" He'd never come across a creature that could mimic a human appearance quite this accurately, but the woman before him was dead. There was no other explanation.

"I'm human. Well, lycan now——"

"I don't have time for your games," Barrage's wasp-like buzz slipped into Izzy's voice, and the little girl he'd followed shrank back.

Tau crouched low and slunk across the room to herd her out of harm's way.

"Izzy, it's me. It's really me." She raised her hands placatingly and took a step towards him.

"Move again and I'll kill you. Alexis is dead. You may have taken her face, but you couldn't recreate her ring, could you? That's why you're not wearing it."

"Faith, sweetie, show him your necklace."

The little girl, Faith, lifted her chin and reached into her shirt to retrieve her necklace. Izzy warily shifted his attention from the imposter in front of him to the girl beside him. Dangling from the tarnished chain was Alexis' ring. A pristine dandelion seed sat preserved within the green amber stone he'd worn until he met her.

He lowered his gun uncertainly. It was too precise to be a replica; he could even see the scratches left in the soft metal by the times he'd scraped it engineering bombs. "Alexis?"

She dropped her hands to her sides. "Isidore, you're such a pain in my ass. Put that gun away before you frighten our daughter."

Faith giggled. "She said a bad word."

Tau narrowed his eyes at them shrewdly, then chirped something at Faith and began to herd her from the room.

Alexis didn't wait to be certain Faith was gone before she threw herself towards Izzy. The gun he'd summoned melted back into his hands as he opened his arms. She twisted her fingers in his shirt collar and yanked him down to kiss her.

The dull emptiness he'd felt in his chest for the last four years vanished so completely it left him dazed. He'd accepted that she was gone, he'd grieved her loss and picked up the pieces long ago. He'd also resigned himself to his solitude in her absence. There could be no replacement for Alexis Rivera.

If he had any lingering doubts about her identity, they were burned away in the intensity of her lips against his and the way her fingers trapped themselves in his hair. He couldn't breathe, but he didn't care.

She pressed closer and her teeth inadvertently caught on his lip. Izzy grumbled a protest and pulled away to laugh. "You haven't changed a bit."

"On the contrary, I change pretty frequently, almost once a month." She offered him a rueful look. "But I'm sorry. I'm still waiting for you to disappear."

"Disappear? Alexis, I thought you were dead. At least you've known this whole time that I was alive." The memory of the ravaged campsite stabbed its way to the forefront of Izzy's mind. "There was so much blood. I was sure they'd killed you."

"Are you sure some of it wasn't yours?" She ran her thumb along the scar tugging at the corner of his mouth. "Where'd you get all these scars?"

"I'll tell you later," Izzy whispered. He traced the arch of her dark eyebrow and leaned down to press his forehead against hers. "So, we have a daughter? When did that happen?"

Alexis shoved away from him, laughing. "Fuck you! 'When did that happen' he says. You're such a pigeon."

"I know," he laughed. "What's her name?"

"Faith Anastasia Lazarov."

"You named her Anastasia? Why?! You know I hate my middle name!"

"I like Anastasios, I think it's hot." Alexis struggled not to laugh outright.

"Now you're just making fun of me."

She pressed a kiss to the corner of his mouth. "Maybe a little."

Izzy couldn't tell what time it was within the small room he was currently sharing with Alexis. There was a faint blue glow from the skylight above them, and he could see fish lazily drifting about the reef as they sought their next meal.

It couldn't possibly be sunlight at this depth, so he theorized its source was a nearby dome. It was a wonder how anyone kept a schedule down here. He hadn't seen any clocks on the way in, so he was curious if there were bells that alerted the refugees when to eat, or sleep. He hadn't heard any, but then he'd been somewhat preoccupied.

Tau hadn't returned with Faith yet, and Izzy had been nervous until Alexis had explained that Tau regularly babysat Faith for her. The caracal was clearly intelligent, and Faith could communicate with him. If Alexis was willing to trust him, Izzy supposed he could as well.

Izzy had seen Demetrius summon cats about the same size as Tau, but they were more commonly black, and had a feral look in their eyes.

At the reminder of Demetrius, guilt took root in his stomach and began to eat at him. He certainly hadn't expected to find Alexis here, he had no idea she was even still alive. But the longer he listened to her breathe, the more it felt like he'd made some kind of trade.

As grateful as he was for Alexis' safety, he wouldn't have traded Dahei's happiness for his own in a million years. He'd been friends with Dahei nearly as long as they'd both been in Alexandria. He'd watched Dahei put himself back together after Hideo's death over the course of six years.

Izzy couldn't bear to watch all that progress come crashing down. If he'd had any other choice, he would have made it. There was no way they would have gotten off the beach without Demetrius' help. He'd been planning this since Alexis' apparent death four years ago and he'd known from the very beginning that he needed a beckoner strong enough to call upon the wild hunt.

Demetrius had entered the picture with a timing that was most opportune. In fact, it had been Dahei that found him. Izzy doubted any of them had expected things to progress like they had. He closed his eyes and offered a silent prayer to Muginn for Demetrius' swift and safe return.

Alexis murmured something in her sleep and nestled closer into him. Izzy wrapped an arm around her. Perhaps tomorrow he could offer the Raven a tithe. For now he would enjoy the blessings he'd been granted.

Ashleen pulled up just short of the entrance to the infirmary. Connor was right, she couldn't miss it. Now that she'd arrived, she wasn't sure she was ready to talk to Morpheus. She couldn't even explain why she was here to herself.

Her entire world was coming down around her ears. She wasn't sure why Morpheus' was the hand she wanted to hold. Perhaps it was because Izzy had admitted to keeping both of them in the dark. Morpheus had never lied to her. That had to be all it was. She drew in a steadying breath and turned the corner into the room.

Dahei and Morpheus were in adjacent beds. Nurses bustled to and fro. Ashleen fought the urge to think about Neele again, one more on the ever-growing list of people who'd lied to her. To them all.

Dahei was still passed out. The nurses had pressed some ice to his head, but seemed otherwise unconcerned with his condition. They were more focused on fussing over Morpheus' arm. Ashleen almost turned on her heel and walked out right then. She'd already forgotten that she'd broken it.

"Ashleen!" Too late now, she'd been spotted.

She swallowed in an attempt to force down the knot of anxiety in her chest. Morpheus beckoned her forward with their good hand and she reluctantly obeyed.

"I'm um, sorry about your wrist."

Morpheus glanced down at the splint one of the medics was adjusting. "This? Don't be. Nobody just resists delirium cries. Pavane targeted you and Izzy. We should count ourselves lucky that the only casualty was my wrist."

Ashleen nodded, digging her teeth into her lip. "Can I ask you something?"

"Is it about pronouns?"

"How did you know?"

"It's the first question they all asked when they saw Diva. I like male pronouns, but I'm not sure why everyone seems so preoccupied with them. It doesn't really matter. I'm just me. Demetrius says the ichor's presenting gender has something to do with my worldview, or how I interact with my surroundings, but I still don't know what that means."

"He's probably talking about social constructs."

"What are those?"

She laughed out loud. "Are you sure you're from Earth?"

Morpheus grinned. "You're not the first to ask. Sometimes I wonder myself."

The silence that stretched between them wasn't unpleasant. Ashleen allowed the bone-deep exhaustion she'd been fighting to drag her down and sat on the bed beside him.

"While we're asking each other things," Morpheus began. "I'm not sure how long I was out but I think I missed a few details."

Ashleen pursed her lips. "Only a few."

"You seem distressed."

"Well, I just found out my dad's still alive. Apparently he's been down here this whole time. And apparently the tranquilizers are bad, they're going to kill me if I keep taking them. This is all on top of the fact that you're Diva, and Izzy's been lying to us from the beginning, and both Neele and Amaris are traitors."

Ashleen hesitated long enough for him to stop her rant if he wanted to. When he didn't, she plunged ahead. "I left Prue back in Alexandria with them. Now that I've escaped what's to stop them from targeting her? Or my mother? Apparently the honest to Muginn gods have been trying to get my attention for who knows how long, and what about Demetrius? We left him all alone on that beach."

At the mention of Demetrius, Dahei surged to wakefulness like a drowning man breaking the surface of a lake. "Where's Izzy?! I'm gonna kill him!"

He threw the covers off of himself and his feet hit the floor before Ashleen could react. Just as she was shifting her weight to stand, Dahei stumbled over his feet and began a slow descent towards the floor.

The larger of the two medics caught him before he could hit his head again, but Dahei was unconscious anyway. The medic carried him back to bed.

"Sorry."

Ashleen turned to ask Morpheus what he was sorry for, but the question answered itself as he lifted his hand off her knee. She'd been so distracted by Dahei and her own distress she'd barely even heard Morpheus' whale song.

"I didn't have time to ask permission," Morpheus explained. "He's going to be a danger to himself and others until he calms down. Particularly himself."

"Nice save, not sure I could have caught up with him in this state."

"Listen, about my relationship with Prue––"

"Oh, leave it," Ashleen said, tossing a hand dismissively. "I broke your wrist so I think we're even. Besides, I think you've apologized to me more than anyone I've ever known."

Morpheus opened his mouth to reply, but a quiet knock on the doorframe interrupted him.

Connor hovered on the threshold, an apologetic look etched into his features. "Ashleen?"

"I thought I had a while," she said, trying to keep resentment out of her voice with minimal success.

Connor averted his gaze. "Most likely, you do. But it appears I won't be able to keep an eye on you as I'd hoped. It's safer for everyone if you go now."

Ashleen balled her hands into fists to hide their shaking. She wasn't sure she could just sit and wait while the ichor wolf tore free of the coma she'd been keeping it in. The idea of it overtaking her was just as potently horrifying as it had always been.

Morpheus squeezed her hand. She hadn't seen him reach for it. She turned her face to hide the tears she could feel burning at the back of her eyes.

"I'll come see you. When the medics let me go," he offered.

She spoke around the lump in her throat. "I'd actually rather you didn't."

She'd felt the ichor wolf eat Morpheus. She wasn't sure she could tolerate the thought of him even being in her proximity without a tight grip on its leash. At the same time, the idea of wrestling with it alone wasn't ideal.

She returned his careful squeeze of her hand and stood to follow her father to the bunkers, resignation weighing down every step.

The heavy concrete door scraped against the ground as Ashleen's father heaved it into place. A series of metallic clangs preceded the thunk of the bolt locking her in. This was it. There were no distractions left for her to preoccupy herself with. For however long it took to purge all the tranquilizers from her system, it would just be her and the thoughts she'd fought to silence.

She could already feel the fire of her rage beginning to singe the edges of her consciousness. To reassure herself, she checked the integrity of the bunker one last time. When she'd entered, she'd seen that the concrete walls were at least a foot thick. She'd tested the door as she passed, the reinforced steel was so heavy she struggled to move it.

There were no windows and aside from the door, the only opening was a narrow vent near the ceiling to ensure she didn't suffocate. The grating on it looked sturdy, but even if she did manage to tear it off, she doubted she could fit her arm in past her elbow.

In lieu of a cot, which she might deconstruct to pry open the door, there was a foam mat and a pile of blankets in the corner. A tiny alcove hid a utilitarian bathroom. Everything inside was bolted down and made of the same heavy steel as the door. Ashleen noted several scuffs and dents left by previous occupants and hoped that the space would still be intact when she was stable again.

All in all, it wasn't that different from the cell Ashleen had occupied not so long ago.

"So here we are," she said to no one in particular, "full circle."

She didn't know how long the wolf would keep her under after the drugs wore off, and she wasn't sure who she'd be on the other side of it all. Despite everything she'd been through and the ordeal she was about to face, Ashleen couldn't help but be optimistic about the future.

She'd learned and grown so much in the last month that it seemed irrational to worry whether or not she'd make it through this. Her relationships with the two most important people in her life, her mother and Prue, had been tested. But they hadn't broken. She'd expanded her family in Alexandria. Not just through Izzy's team, but Leo's as well.

A number of her friends were still in the Archwarden's clutches. She had to pass one more test before she could rally and help them, and so she would. On the way to the bunker, she'd been daunted by what lay before her, but now that she was here, she felt at peace. There was nowhere to go now but through, and she was stronger than this. Her friends knew it, her father knew it, and most important of all, she knew it.

When the walls around her appeared to bubble and melt, she simply sat down on the pile of bedding and raised her eyebrows, unimpressed. "Is that the best you've got?"

The dark shape of her ichor self hovered in her peripheral vision. "I'm just getting started," it growled menacingly in her ear.

"Good. Bring it on. I'm not afraid of you. I'm sick of being afraid of myself."

The wolf circled around to stand before her, a reflection of her own form as Vanquisher. It spoke with her voice. "There's no one to save you now. It's just you and me in here."

Ashleen smiled confidently up at the hulking lycan, unphased. "And soon, it will be just me."

Vanquisher bared its teeth and crouched in anticipation. "We will see, little wolf. We will see."

Thank you so much for accompanying me on this journey! I look forward to seeing you again in future installments and I hope you enjoyed Five of Knights. If you'd like to help me continue to elaborate on the world of Alexandria, please leave a review! As a self-published author, reviews are essential to boosting my signal and attracting more readers. If you have a few minutes to write down how this story made you feel, I would be eternally grateful!

Alexandria: This self sustained floating city is the last known base of The Order of Huntsmen. It's activities are overseen by the Archwarden. It remains cloaked and airborne via advanced ichor tech.

Anshan:

Anshathane: The wolf deity of life, war, hunting, and order. Usually disinterested in humans unless provoked. Respected by many but truly worshipped by only a few due to a lack of religious leaders.

Anshathane, Clerics of: Religious leaders devoted to Anshathane. Mysteriously disappeared around forty years ago.

Archknight: One of five top ranked huntsmen, modified with a small amount of ichor. Homunculus level being.

Archwarden: Military leader of a huntsman base, referring to a jailer of ichor afflicted beings. Only remaining holder of this title is the current head of Alexandria.

Australian Prison Colonies: A massive network of colonies originally established by the British. Their original function has long since been forgotten. No one country has an official claim to them, yet security mysteriously remains.

Beckoner: A class of huntsmen known for their ability to summon and control the servants of Muginn or wayward souls through intricate gesture-work and dance.

Birdshit: An exclamation of disbelief or exasperation. The equivalent of bullshit.

Cait Sith: Cat-like servants of Muginn derived from Celtic folklore. They are most frequently seen as dog sized black cats, but can appear in other colors and sizes. Cait Sith and Hellhounds are tasked with hunting the souls that resist Muginn's call.

Centurion: Second to last ranked huntsmen, a novice with potential.

Counterweight: A person's soulmate as indicated by the covenant bands granted by Muginn. It is believed that a person's counterweight is the perfect compliment to them. A counterweight couple is the ideal power couple who perfectly balances each other's flaws and attributes.

Covenant Band: A ring most people find when they hit puberty that warms up when placed in the hand of the finder's counterweight. If misplaced, these rings return to either their finder or counterweight. Though it is more popular for couples to be buried with their rings, some parents pass their rings on to their children, as they believe the rings will bring their children luck and protection. A ring held by the finder's genetic descendant will not return to its previous holder.

Chrysalis: A being that has consumed so much ichor it has lost control over itself.

Deadeye: A class of huntsmen known for an affinity for marksmanship and demolitions.

Delirium Cries: An ability used by high ranked vespers which allows them to warp the minds of those who listen. Prolonged exposure can result in permanent psychological damage.

Dullahan: Derived from Irish folklore and also known as a headless horseman, these servants of Muginn can only be summoned and controlled by advanced beckoners. They're sent to reap the souls of those who have broken pacts with Muginn.

Feathered Mother: An exclamation of shock or surprise.

First Conflict: Also known as the Great Conflict, this event refers to the new gods' war and subsequent routing of humanity's original gods.

Fledgie: Slang, a shortened version of the term 'fledgling'.

Fledgling: Refers to a person who is inexperienced or new.

Gargoyles: Stony servants of Muginn said to carry lesser souls to the afterlife and protect the faithful.

Geist: A soul that has resisted Muginn's call or somehow encountered difficulties on the path to reincarnation. Generally a very minimal threat, easily handled by even low ranked huntsmen if it has not already been captured by a cait sith or hellhound.

Gladiator: A mid-ranked huntsman. These are the average rank in Alexandria.

Goosehat: Someone who is rude or insensitive. The equivalent of a jerk or an ass.

Hazard Rank: A rank temporarily granted to huntsmen who survive lethal blows or are severely injured at the hands of another huntsman during duels. This rank is meant to give them time to recover without worrying about their point value dropping.

Hellhound: The cait sith's canine counterpart, these black dogs are sent to collect evasive souls or to protect Muginn's favored apostles in times of need.

Homunculus: A being that has consumed minimal amounts of ichor and retains the ability to bend it to their will, the archknights are an example.

Huntsmen: Exceptional humans tasked with the collection and containment of ichor. Huntsmen are generally tasked with defending humankind from the effects of ichor, or beings under the control of ichor.

Huntsmen, The Order of: A council that once existed to organize and direct the huntsmen from several base cities around the world.

Ichor: Blood of the new gods. Originally shed during the First Conflict, ichor has strange effects on just about anything it comes into contact with. Used in small amounts, it can greatly enhance the power of an individual or structure. The substance is psycho-reactive and has a will of its own. Given the chance it will overtake its host and seek out more of itself.

Ichor Alloy: A metal infused with ichor. The mantacraft and Alexandria are built almost entirely from ichor alloy.

Ichor Lattice: The ichor as it exists within the walls of Alexandria. Homunculus level beings are able to travel through this lattice without being seen.

Ichor Strain: The strain of an ichor refers to its source deity. Anshan and Ikaluscan are strains of ichor which came from Anshathane and Ikalusca, respectively.

Ichor Tech: Technology enhanced with ichor. Alexandria's anti-gravity, cloaking, and sim rooms are examples of ichor tech.

Ifrit: Fiery, many armed servants of Muginn derived from Islamic mythology. Ifrit are thought to be the souls beckoners sent out by Muginn to punish people who have displeased him.

Ikalusca: The kraken deity of rebirth, secrets, and entropy. Known for instigating revolution and disturbing the peace, he is often looked upon with disdain. His truly loyal followers are few and far between.

Ikaluscan Adherent: Religious leaders devoted to Ikalusca. Few in number and experts at staying under the radar, due to the stigma surrounding their god.

Knight: The highest rank attainable by more than one huntsmen. Knights are truly exceptional in their class.

Knight-Captain: Only one for each class, these are the reigning champions in the sim rooms. No one has been able to defeat them in a one on one duel.

Library, The: A mysterious place existing in a space unreachable by conventional means. The Library is known to be accessible to the archknights, and is capable of containing messages for them as well as a wealth of information they can utilize as needed.

Loon: A crazy person.

Lycan: Refers to any being afflicted with Anshathane's ichor, most commonly referring to werebeasts, but also inclusive of tranqs and several other forms of shapechanger.

Mantacraft: Stingray shaped aircraft used by huntsmen in Alexandria.

Mother Raven: A blanket exclamation, suitable for a number of scenarios.

Muginn: The raven deity of death, prophecy, and balance. By far the most popular deity, Muginn is androgynous. Their pronouns often differ from person to person based on how that person perceives them. Muginn is known for their willingness to bargain and their interest in human affairs.

Muginn, Apostles of: Religious leaders devoted to Muginn. They are most commonly found in the religious capitals of the world, but occasionally travel to spread the Raven's teachings. Of all the religious leaders, these are the most involved with the public and are often sought out for their blessings or exorcisms.

Muginn, Canticles to: Religious hymns sung by Muginn's worshippers.

Muginn, Crypts of: Destination of hundreds of pilgrimages a year, the Crypts are thought to be Muginn's seat of power on earth. The cathedral itself is an architectural masterpiece, but the real power rests in the sprawling catacombs beneath it where Muginn's most loyal are entombed. The catacombs are only supposed to be accessed by ordained apostles, but dozens of daredevil tourists go missing each year when they sneak in.

Nightmares: Flaming horses derived from Germanic and Slavic folklore. They serve Muginn and are known both for carrying souls to the other side and bringing messages to prophets.

Ordeals: Tests completed by new archknights in order to connect with their team and find equilibrium with the ichor in their veins.

Pigeon: Someone who is stupid or oblivious. An idiot. Less common usages refer to someone who is basic, or a pest.

Psychic Mesh: Refers to the interwoven psyches of the archknights.

Ravencursed: Damned.

Raven Eat Your Eyes: An exclamation of distaste, irritation, or even hatred towards someone. The equivalent of 'go to hell'.

Ravenite: A follower or followers of Muginn.

Ravenkin: A people who believe they can trace their lineage to Muginn's original followers. Demetrius' people.

Raven's Teeth: An exclamation of disbelief or in reference to something that can't possibly be real or true.

Raven Swallow Me: An expression of embarrassment or dismay.

Scofflaw: A class of huntsmen known for their use of bladed weapons.

Scrapper: The lowest ranking huntsmen. Scrappers contribute little to Alexandria, and if they cannot bring up their rank, they are excommunicated from the city.

Scripts: Religious scripture.

Shadow People: Groups of wayward souls that have been tainted by ichor. They build hives in unoccupied ruins or ghost towns and flock around a queen. They are capable of possession and are highly dangerous if not approached with the proper caution.

Sidhe: Sidhe are very powerful beings said to have fought in the First Conflict. They generally keep to themselves and are not to be trifled with.

Sim: Short for simulation. Huntsmen are able to use them to practice their abilities in a relatively safe environment. However, because they are fueled by ichor, there is always a measure of risk.

Sim Room: Simulation rooms. These spherical rooms serve as a host location for simulations.

Spirit Guide: A manifestation of one's spiritual self. Only the most advanced beckoners are able to manipulate theirs.

Suck An Egg: An expression of annoyance. Often used to tell off someone who is irritating.

Three-Toed Raven: An insulting gesture, the equivalent of flipping someone off.

Tithe: Blood offered to the gods in hopes of garnering their favor.

Tranq: A class of huntsmen known for their superhuman strength and berserker-like rages. Named for the pills they have to take to maintain a cool head.

Tranquilizers: Pills taken by tranqs to stave off their rages.

Vampire: Low ranked servants of Ikalusca known for their blood sucking tendencies. Rumored to be born when his human followers spiral so far into their depravity that they lose their humanity.

Vesper: A class of huntsmen known for their haunting voices and use of hymns to influence or protect others. They are perhaps most notorious for their need to fuel their abilities through physical intimacy.

Wardens: Wardens are specifically tasked with overseeing, training, and providing for the huntsmen. They are also occasionally tasked with city maintenance.

Wisps: A type of low ranking sidhe that appear as butterflies to the untrained eye. Demetrius can sense the positions of wisps he summons and uses this to navigate areas he is unfamiliar with.

This story would not have been possible without the hours worth of music I listened to while writing it. In acknowledgment of their contribution to my creative process, the top songs for each character, group, and couple are listed below.

Characters

The Archwarden
Bloody City by Sam Tinnesz
Dark Conscience (Instrumental) by Tommee Profitt
Blood / / Water by grandson
Everybody Knows by Sigrid
Vengeance by Zack Hemsey

Ashleen
bodyache by Purity Ring
Action Reaction by Rupert Gregson-Williams
I Feel Like I'm Drowning by Two Feet
Harder Better Faster Stronger by Willa Amai
Our Demons (feat. Aja Volkman) by The Glitch Mob

Dahei
STFD by TeZATalks
Undeniable by Seckond Chaynce
COUP D'ETAT by G-DRAGON, Diplo, and Baauer
High Enough by K.Flay
Play With Fire (feat. Yacht Money) by Sam Tinnesz

Demetrius
The Humbling River by Puscifer

The Power of Balance (An Avatar Orchestration) by Rush Garcia

The Sound of Silence by Disturbed

He Lives in You by Matt Bloyd

Where Do We Draw the Line by Poets of the Fall

Izzy

Crossfire by Stephen

Insomnia by 2WEI

House of the Rising Sun by The Animals

Knights of Cydonia by Muse

Friction by Imagine Dragons

Morpheus

Hypnotic - Vanic Remix by Zella Day

Act Three: Looming by Crywolf

Afterlife by XYLØ

Sweet Dreams (Are Made of This) by Eurythmics

Bad At Love by Halsey

Pavane

An Unhealthy Obsession by The Blake Robinson Synthetic Orchestra

I Walk The Line by Halsey

Uncomfortable by Halestorm

Prue

Casa De Luz (Lights in Highland) by Eliza

Diamonds by Midnite String Quartet

Island by SVRCINA

Couples

Alexis and Izzy

Saturn by Sleeping At Last

Resistance by Muse

Astronomical by SVRCINA

Tip Of My Tongue by The Civil Wars
This Ship Is Going Down by Tommee Profitt and Xeah
Ashleen and Morpheus
Ace of Hearts by Zella Day
Wicked Game by Ursine Vulpine and Annaca
Wonderwall by Ex Makina
Flares by The Script
So Cold by Ben Cocks and Nikisha Peyes-Pile
Please Don't Say You Love Me (Piano Version) by Gabrielle Aplin
Unsteady - Erich Lee Gravity Remix by X Ambassadors
Dahei and Demetrius
You Found Me by The Fray
Another Love by Tom Odell
Rescue My Heart by Liz Longley
Hymnal by In The Valley Below
Echo by Jason Walker
Dahei and Hideo
Sleeping With a Ghost (feat. Cappa) by Tommee Profitt
Pavane and Morpheus
J'te déteste by Shy'm
Prue and Ashleen
Six Feet Under by Billie Eilish
Prue and Morpheus
Play Me Like a Violin by Stephen

Archknights
Soldier by Fleurie
Mars by Sleeping At Last
Game of Survival by Ruelle
Lux Aeterna by Clint Mansell and Kronos Quartet
Heroes (Generdyn Remix) by Zayde Wølf
Claim Your Weapons (feat. Atrel) by Christian Reindl

Uprising by Damned Anthem
Until We Go Down by Ruelle
Liberators by Epic Score
Far From Home (The Raven) Sam Tinnesz

Gods
Anshathane
The Devil & The Huntsman by Sam Lee and Daniel Pemberton
Become the Beast by Karliene
Arthur's Final Battle by Rob Lane
Ikalusca
Revelation by Daniel Pemberton
Sacrifice by Sharon Lyons
Just Like Sleep by Passarella Death Squad
Muginn
The Politics & The Life by Daniel Pemberton and Gareth Williams
Ivar's Revenge by Danheim
Alfadhirhaiti by Heilung

Honorable Mentions

The entire Album of Frightmare by Xtortion Audio was listened to for any and all scenes with Ichor or involving a high creep factor in general.

In the End by Tommee Profitt, Jung Youth, and Fleurie was essential to the writing of the cemetery scene in chapter nine.

About the Author

Kieran is an FtM transgender wiccan with a passion for mythology and lore from a variety of cultures. He has a deep love of questions without answers and 'almost' truths. His favorite way to combat writer's block is with a deck of tarot cards and some herbal tea.

When he's not writing, Kieran can frequently be found gaming, drawing, or pacing in frantic circles muttering about his latest plot twist under his breath.

He frequently fantasizes about owning at least one snake and too many cats, owns more sparkly rocks than he has shelf space, and has so many black T-shirts that it takes him ten minutes to find the one he's looking for.